PIMP MY AIRSHIP

A NAPTOWN BY AIRSHIP NOVEL

MAURICE BROADDUS

ISBN (TPB) 978-1-937009-76-2

Apex Book Company
PO Box 24323
Lexington, KY 40524

Review and media inquiries can be sent to jason@apexbookcompany.com.

Available in trade paperback and DRM-free eBook formats.

For J.J.
(Always Woke)

ONE

A CHANGE IS GONNA COME

Vox Dei Data Files: If decent citizens wish to go slumming for their entertainment, the Two-Johns Theater caters to mostly laborers and local residents. Originally opened as the Little Doo in 1909, by two owners both named John, the Two-Johns Theater officially launched in 1911. Easily among the most clever of the colored performers featured there, Miss L. Tish Lee made her initial appearance at the theater. The theater hosts a variety of entertainers to this day.

SLEEPY WAS A DREAMER. He closed his eyes and imagined wide-open spaces, the feel of grass beneath his feet, and a small place to call his home. He dreamed of a short walk to an ocean beach, not that he'd ever even left the city, but he'd seen pictures and guessed at the smell of salt air, which would fill his nostrils. A cool drink in one hand, he'd watch pretty women stroll by in all manner of *bikinis* (he'd heard tell of the immodest fashions of Albion, especially along the French Riviera). Most of all, he dreamed of the sun. A bright, incandescent ball he couldn't quite focus on, set against the clearest of blue skies, in whose warm light he'd soak in every bit.

Too bad he had to open his eyes.

A sharp jerk of the train sent bodies pressing in on him from all sides. The train rattled and clanged, the tough grind of gears jostling the cabin of bodies as it rumbled along the tracks. The cabin space had been designed for maximum occupancy, not comfort. Folks still had to get to work. A protrusion of elbows encroached on either side of the slight berth Sleepy managed to call his own. Despite this, he counted himself lucky to find a seat on the underground railway. The only reason there were any benches in it at all was due to a lawsuit after a pregnant mother was trampled to death when she doubled over in labor pain. The lawsuit was dismissed, after all, she was still only a dweller, but the Parliament pressured the train manufacturer to add a row of seats to the cabins as a gesture of good will and common decency.

"One seat per passenger." A white man stared down his wire-rimmed, round spectacles at him. His rumpled business suit and crushed bowler marked him as little better than a dweller, but his eyes scored Sleepy with the expectation of deference. The man eyed the spot on the bench and clearly assumed Sleepy would give up his spot, or at least accommodate him. This was the usual dance of polite society.

"Excuse me?"

Sleepy rolled his eyes slowly to him, not in the mood to put up with anyone's foolishness.

"The law says one seat per passenger."

"Do you mean to suggest that I'm ... a lawbreaker?" Sleepy smiled a crocodile grin, cold and predatory. Shifting his wide girth, he spread his massive legs just a little further.

"I mean to suggest ..." the man continued with the measured pause of consideration.

"Choose your next words carefully, like your life depends on it. I don't want there to be any misunderstanding." Sleepy didn't let his smile falter. In fact, he parted his lips wider, presenting rows of bright, pianoforte key-white teeth. They were his pride, tended to each night with exacting care. Unlike the orthodontic nightmare that seemed to be the height of fashion in capital Albion. No hint of a glower nor of menace presented itself. Except, maybe, in his eyes.

"I merely suggest that a portly gentleman such as yourself ..." The man's composure began to falter.

"Portly." With his forefinger, Sleepy nudged his thick, black-rimmed glasses higher along his nose.

"... may need to bear additional consideration ..."

"Consideration." Without breaking his gaze, Sleepy popped the knuckles of each hand, then bridged his fingers in front of him.

"... when it comes to his fellow passengers."

"A ... *portly* ... gentleman, such as myself, may indeed require his own measure of *consideration* after a day's work managing your waste. Allow me to suggest that you kindly shut the fuck up and enjoy your ride."

Shocked by the affront, the gentleman broke his glare long enough to give Sleepy a fuller inspection. Stepping aside, he allowed him more space. The crowd around Sleepy stared with a mix of disdain and pity, undergirded by the presumption that he had been abandoned as a ward of the state from birth and was just another pickaninny fulfilling his destiny. That he grew up with flash mobs of urchins on the streets, pickpocketing the hapless innocent citizens of the overcity, only to graduate to organized gangs before being shipped off to the criminal finishing school, the Allisonville Correctional Facility, a place colloquially known as The Ave. He'd probably be more offended if society didn't seem so hellbent on ensuring that all of his class shared similar stories.

The reality was that most days he might have given his seat up to the man simply to maintain the peace of things. Sleepy valued quiet and order, content to drift through life without confrontation or undue attention. He'd left his unipod at sixteen and was lucky enough to immediately find work at the White River lift station, though as a sewage scraper.

The city experimented with privatizing some of the public works. Commonwealth Waterworks was one of the better ones. The company was steady pay and Commonwealth provided a measure of benefits to their employees. Being a steam engineer, he processed water for the heart of the Indianapolis undercity, the area the residents had nicknamed Freetown Village. Twelve hours of shoveling coal and tending to the machine works. A maze of tunnels and pipes formed the ironworks of the plant processing engine. Fans funneled gas out. Torrents of waste, gravity filtered and captured in basins, left the gray water directed to the steamworks. The mildew veneer of the constant sheen of sweat. A heavy, dull scent of hot, moist funk clung to the air like lavishly applied perfume to a prostitute. He reeked of industrial lubricant, coal, and sweat, all congealing into the sweet tang of fermented grime. With its white stone walls and ornate columns, it was like a temple of waste. And he was its minister.

His uncle worked there before him and continually reminded Sleepy that fortune favored him not only to have a job but to be brought into the plant at so young an age. If his providence bore out, he could retire from the plant. His life was set. Sleepy never—well, rarely—complained. Though he'd worked there only a few years, the many similarly empty, sweat-filled days ahead of him made him wonder if there was more to life than shuffling through a sunup-to-sundown workday six days a week. Earning just enough credits to scrape by, teetering on the edge of financial ruin should he ever miss a paycheck. Needing to fill the settling ennui between work shifts simply because the expanses of idle nothing left plenty of time to remind him of his utter worthlessness to the greater scheme of things.

This was exactly why he couldn't wait to get high.

The gleaming thundering worm rumbled along the raised rail, winding through the intestines of the undercity. Exposed pipes lined the top of the car. Steam coursed through them like blood through constricted capillaries. The heat produced by them added to the swelling temperatures and casual discomfort. Most people chafed within the scratchy material of their clothes, which neared the texture of burlap, given the heat. The air grew heavy with re-breathed effluvia. Sleepy ignored the forest of buttocks crammed into his eyeline. Snatches of the city could be spied from their vantage point as they ringed the city along sub-system 465. The airship docking station. The Indianapolis Aeromotor Speedway, home to the largest airship race, and fastest racing autocarriages, in the world. The heart of downtown, a glistening dream in the distance. The spires of the Indianapolis overcity loomed. Their waning shadows in the sunset plunged the undercity into deeper darkness. The bustle and jolting of the train faded into comforting white noise.

"Don't mind him, brother." One of the eye level asses turned to the side. "Despite the fact that he finds himself riding the same train as us, he believes he's entitled to more. Too many of us never speak to the truth of the matter. Too many of us have forgotten who we are."

"Uh huh."

Sleepy watched the first gentleman inch away from the two of them, scooting out of earshot to pretend that they weren't talking about him.

Turning to the window to study the shadows of the undercity, rather than have a conversation with the profile of someone's trousers, Sleepy focused on his checklist for the night. He performed tonight, and nothing was going to spoil it. "No worries, man. We good."

Encouraged, the set of trousers angled toward him. "I'm only saying that a hardworking man like yourself deserves a moment of respite."

"All I need is a glass of a little sipping something, a smoke, and a pork chop. Life don't need to be no harder than you make it."

"Pork leads to trichinosis of the mind."

"No pork leads to ..." Sleepy ran out of clever retorts once he raised his eyes to meet the man, rather than talk to his crotch. The man's red-tinted hair sprouted into a series of twists, like gnarled fingers protruding from his skull. A beard and mustache framed his mouth. His stylized sunglasses rotated like the blades of a hand fan unfurling, shading studious eyes, reducing his face to glowering slits of eyes that tracked everything with a mix of anger and suspicion. His nose, broad and flared, seemed to snort air rather than inhale it. His thick, white cravat tucked into his burgundy vest. One hand looped through the leather handhold of the train, the other clutched a cane. He shifted his weight, failing to mask a slight limp. Sleepy waved the man off with a sharp flick of his wrist. He didn't have time to waste on all these folks attempting to crowd into his zone.

"You getting ready for something?" the man continued.

"A little something," Sleepy said. "Down at Two-Johns."

"You on tonight?" The man's voice raised with knowing excitement, the way a fan of his might.

At the possibility that the man might indeed be a fan, Sleepy issued him a measure of grace. "Someone's got to hold the mic down."

"All right, brother. I'm in."

I don't recall inviting you along, Sleepy thought. Then again, no need to be rude to a potential audience member since all performers split a percentage of the gate.

The train ground to a halt. Sleepy huffed, pulling himself out of his seat to get off at his stop. The man tipped his hat and parted way for Sleepy.

The train deposited Sleepy at the way station closest to his home at the 38th Street juncture. Two government-issued steammen attended the unloading platform. Their design inelegant, to be charitable, little more than lumbering metal boxes. Twin fans mounted on one of their backs, their air channeled through their body cavity and out the hose attachment on their arms to blow trash into the runoff bin for the other one to collect. The station was less crowded than usual. Sleepy pushed through the sparse queue of milling passengers.

The Eagle Town Homes nestled along the 38th Street corridor. A series of one room, two-story apartments, with a bedroom over a bathroom/kitchenette, they looked like upturned shotgun houses. The rows of townhomes occupied little space. The four-feet space from the sidewalk to the front stoop served as the yard. With the rows lined back-to-back, the city could cram nearly one hundred residences into a city block. Sleepy's neighborhood regulars already huddled about, someone bound to drink too much or get offended at some imagined slight to justify getting into a fight simply to break up the monotony of their day.

Sleepy kicked off his shoes once he crossed his door's threshold.

Gaslit lamps lit up the small, gray box of a room. He opened a window to deal with the heat of his lights. With a somnambulant stagger, he stepped around the electro-transmitter equipment, which took up much of the room. A glass-fronted cabinet with spires to boost a signal, custom-built speakers, twin phonograms. With his portable broadcast unit, he had grand designs to broadcast his poems backed by music tracks. He even saved credits with the dream to one day fashion a studio in which to play and record his music.

Streaked with steam-driven coal mixed with oil, he peeled off his outerwear before he wandered into his bathroom. The same mixture coated him from head-to-toe, finding its way into places he didn't want to think about. The water shuddered through the pipes before pouring down on him in a lukewarm piddle. Hands pressed against the stall wall like he assumed a position to be frisked by the water spray, he suspected that if he spent the next week under its tepid stream, he wouldn't be able to fully remove the stain of his labor.

After twenty minutes, Sleepy wrapped a towel around his waist and staggered out of the bathroom. He paused in front of his floor length mirror, clutched the folds of his belly, and jiggled it. He never excused his shape with word games about how greater girth made for a greater man. He simply was who he was, and he was content with that.

Sleepy opened the armoire and selected his most elegant formal wear. Throwing on his black-stripe coulter shirt over his undergarments, he primped in the mirror. With the solemnity of donning armor, he fixed his black Y-back braces to his pinstriped pants and buttoned his red vest. With each new piece of clothing, he transformed from city worker to stage performer. Sleepy fussed with his silk cravat, adjusting it several times because it didn't quite look right to his exacting eye. Now was one of those moments he missed his brother. He'd always fastened his ties for him.

By the time he slipped on his formal tailcoat, gray gloves, and gray-felt top hat, Sleepy had transformed into a new man.

VOX DEI *DATA FILES: "Indianapolis—the hope of Albion."*
Though the sun never set on the Albion Empire, ruling the empire
was not without its travails. Indianapolis was the kind of city the
United Kingdom of Albion held up as a shining beacon. Only a
dozen or so cities in the American colony were larger. Many
discounted it entirely, only knowing it was a city somewhere in the
middle of the United States. But to Albion, Indianapolis was what
every city in the American colony should aspire to. A large city with a
small-town feel, Indianapolis was quiet. It knew its place.

THERE WERE certain sounds which became part of a familiar
cacophony for those who lived in Freetown Village. Pistons
pounded out the power to run the overcity. Steam hissed as it
escaped pipes and billowed through the manhole covers along the
streets. Sleepy shuddered when he walked past a sewage truck,
wanting to banish any reminders of his day job from his mind.
Daguerreotypes of the civil rights provocateur, known as the Star
Child, plastered every telephone pole in the neighborhood. His
sepia shadowed image highlighted by his green eyes. A street artist
painted the words "I am the change" across his forehead. News of
his capture swept through the community, a near tangible ripple of
anger, resentment, and frustration. Sleepy heard him speak at a rally
once. The man's words had a way of carving into a person's heart.
Shaking him from the inside. Stirring him. With eloquence, the Star
Child detailed the excesses of the policing force and instilled a sense
of pride into each of his words. Of course, the powers had to silence
him. Sleepy's heart ached. Heavy with the dull reminder of where
he stood in the greater schemes of Albion. He imagined it would be
the same for his fellow poets and make for a tough crowd. Still, he
needed to get into character.

Slats of metal lined the twin, six-paned doors of the Two-Johns
Theater. Security on the doors amounted to a coal-complected
former fighter, whose size suggested that he may have swallowed a
small truck. Beyond those doors was an open set of wood-framed
glass doors. A lesson in restored opulence, eight faux-wood pillars

lined the lobby. Ceramic tiles on the floor created a mosaic. Two massive chandeliers barely lit either side of the pavilion. The main hallway led directly into a small ballroom, candles illuminating each table. With a hiss of steam, like a fussy iron, a steamman took Sleepy's coat. Only older models, little better than government issued ones, were employed on their side of town. Not like the automatons of the overcity, with their porcelain parts and silent running.

Even as Sleepy attempted to find his bearings, a familiar figure of hair twists and sunglasses bobbed toward him.

"I can't stand places like this," he said.

Sleepy pretended to catch someone's eye and made off toward the stage.

Determined not to be left behind, the man followed. Not rushing, his nonchalant stride easily kept pace with Sleepy. "Today's mathematics is knowledge. Ten numbers constitute the language of mathematics. Ten. I am the sum of the cypher. (120 Degrees of) Knowledge Allah."

The words hung in the air between them like the pronouncement was supposed to bring all action to a halt. But the world kept moving, as did Sleepy. Knowing he wasn't about to call him that mouthful of syllables every time, he debated between calling him One or Knowledge Allah before settling on the latter. "Well, Knowledge Allah, this is the home of true revolutionaries."

"What do you know about true revolutionaries?" Knowledge Allah half-huffed, his limp becoming more noticeable as he kept pace.

"Submerged in song and poetry and stories, we bring the message, the fight, to the people. We awaken their minds." Sleepy recited the refrain the poets often bandied about. While high.

"Is that so?" Knowledge Allah made a point of craning his neck about. "Filled with self-important, neo-soul types. Look at them. An audience of nouveau Negro bohemians."

"Is there anyone you won't complain about?" Sleepy asked.

"I uproot the mind state. I'm not satisfied with anyone. We can all do better."

Pausing at the side of the stage, Sleepy held up his hand without touching Knowledge Allah. A nearby sign read "Performers Only." The man stopped short as if checked by an invisible force field. "Hold up. We about to start."

"Bring the funk, Sleepy." Knowledge Allah limped off into the curtain shadows.

Waiting until he made sure he was alone, Sleepy closed his eyes while he got into his mental place. He waited for the announcer to bring him out.

"'For our struggle is not against flesh and blood, but against the rulers, against the authorities, against the powers of this dark world, and against the spiritual forces of evil in the heavenly realms.'" The announcer spoke, low and breathy, into the mic, a seducing minister of the word. "The time for games is over. The mission is clear. We fight to survive. We struggle to stay alive. You're either with us or against us. The Cause is a state of mind. Some of us struggle with our past. Some of us struggle with our future. Some of us struggle with ourselves. We struggle against oppression. This is the good fight. Welcome with me a man who brings the fire. Who brings the soul. The government knows him as Hubert Nixon, but we know him by another name. He's our brother. He's our friend. Set it off for us, Sleepy."

Sleepy bumped shoulders with the announcer when they clasped hands. Stepping to center stage, the spotlight glared at him and the house lights dimmed. A gleam in his eyes, he inhaled and held his breath. He was in his moment, deep in his muse. When he opened his mouth, the words poured out from a different place.

"I'd like to do a new piece for you. This is the first time even I'm hearing it out loud. It's called 'Let it Flow.'"

The crowd applauded with encouragement then settled down to allow Sleepy a moment to gather himself.

> "Too many thoughts crowding in my brain
> I'm just so angry, so frustrated, I don't know where
>   to begin
> To unknot this cord inside my head.

I just need to sit back, relax, and let the chiba flow.

You see, my girl done left and I say I don't pay that
    no mind
The first time in a while I let myself relax
Been too long between girls. I got that charm. I got
    that smile.
I got them words that burrow into your soul.
I'm a mirror. Maybe they don't like what they see.
Or maybe it's just me.
I just need to sit back, relax, and let the chiba flow.

I got me a job and I got no right to complain.
Gonna work the same line, dawn til dark, all sweat
    and grime
In the end, I don't do nothing, don't amount to
    nothing
Ain't changed nothing. Day in, day out, just
    another cog
In a machine that grinds you up in its gears.
And would never know that I was here.
I just need to sit back, relax, and let the chiba flow.

I wake up in the morning with nothing but the
    craving
The need to chill out and let my thoughts rise high.
Just wanting to escape. Alone, not wanting to be
    alone, resigned to loneliness.
Looking all around me, my soul cries out for more.
I just need to sit back, relax, and let the chiba
    flow.

Every time I share my story, I create a new history.
Stuck with a ghost spell truth: builders build.
I'm wandering in the desert of our U-N-I-verse
    trying to overstand.

Didn't know my father. Couldn't save my mother.
Couldn't save my brother.
I need to get out so that I can at least save me.
I just need to sit back, relax, and let the chiba flow.

Where can a brother get a light?"

The pause when he finished was always the longest, most unbearable stretch of seconds. The held breath of the audience deciding if his piece was to be received well. But the roar of finger snaps and a series of *all right, now*s greeted him. Sleepy basked in their approval for several heartbeats before he tipped his hat. He returned the nod of the announcer, who prepared to bring up another poet. A few patrons passed behind him and clapped him on the back for his poem. Another poet took the stage, talking about the tragedies of her family.

Knowledge Allah remained locked in an animated conversation with a man not dressed in a too dissimilar manner from him. The man's long suit jacket, black tinted glasses, and bow tie gave him the intimidating appearance of a classic gangster. He carried himself with grim seriousness.

"Peace, sun. I heard you took on a new name."

"Peace, sun. One is Knowledge. Zero is a Cipher. Completion," Knowledge Allah said. "(120 Degrees of) Knowledge Allah."

"The tricknology of living mathematics." The man stepped back a bit, taking a fuller appraisal of him. "Two is Wisdom. One plus two equals three. Three is Understanding. Seven is the divine influence in the physical realm."

"Seven is wholeness," Knowledge Allah said.

"Seven plus seven plus seven equals twenty-one. Two plus one equals three. Three is holy because seven is God."

"G was the seventh letter made." When Knowledge Allah spied Sleepy, he crossed his hands to wave off the man mid-sentence and limped away from him. "You dropped some deep science there, Sleepy. It was like you were aiming your words right at me."

"I spit for me." Sleepy dabbed his forehead with his handkerchief. His pre-performance jitters kept him from eating, but after his success, both his appetite and thirst returned with a keen fury.

"You put words to something *real* right there. A hurt. It was like you knew."

"Knew what?"

"I think you're ready."

"Ready for what?" Withdrawing a small pouch from his jacket pocket, Sleepy tamped out a measure of chiba leaves into a pipe. He couldn't wait to let loose a long, thick exhalation of smoke to issue up and about him in a languid curl. The glow of his struck match lit up Knowledge Allah's face, distorting his features. His face drew, dark and ugly. Knowledge Allah waved him off from lighting it and ushered them to a table near the rear of the room.

"I need you clear-headed for what I want to talk to you about."

"What's up?"

"People underestimate you, Sleepy."

"Go on." Checking his pocket watch, Sleepy decided the man had three minutes to keep him from his smoke.

"I need you. We do. And part of you knows it." Knowledge Allah swept the room with cautious eyes before lowering his voice to a conspiratorial whisper. "The Cause you all talk about in your poems is more than rhetoric for hipsters and bohemians. It's a very real movement. With very real and committed people."

"I don't understand." Sleepy wrote for himself. His passion for words provided release. Like there was an anger in him he rarely admitted to, but when he put pen to paper, it bubbled out from a well he couldn't control. So much anger to go around. Himself, for settling in life. The system, for cutting him off at every turn until he threw his arms up and settled. His wasn't exactly a unique story. These were the dissonant chords of the measure of his life. Their life.

"The Cause actively moves to thwart our oppressors. The forces of Albion in its American colony. We move in secret. In cells, so that no one person could reveal too much if compromised."

"We?"

"I've been charged with forming a new cell. We work in threes.

Three is the Trinity. Father, Son, Holy Spirit. The Holy Spirit is a she. Three is a trimester. Three plus three plus three equals nine. Nine is the ninth letter. There are nine months of pregnancy."

"I don't know which of us is supposed to be high right now." Sleepy raised his hand to light his pipe again, anxious to let the smoke wash over him. With his head up, even Knowledge Allah's nonsense amused him.

"Welcome to The Cause." Knowledge Allah reached out again to hold his arm, keeping him from lighting it. "The chance to do more than just tickle the ears of a few. This is an invitation to do something real."

"Why me?" Sleepy asked a little too loudly.

"Your discretion for a start." Knowledge Allah rapped his cane against the floor as if calling a meeting to order. "Besides, that's the wrong question. The real question is why not you?"

Sleepy hadn't made up his mind whether he much liked Knowledge Allah. Admittedly, despite the air of crazy, Knowledge Allah had a charisma about him, a gravity that made one pay attention. He reminded Sleepy of his mother. She was a woman of dreams and ideas. And causes. "Life ought to be lived outside of yourself," she often preached. Drumming his fingers against the table, Sleepy tapped percussive melodies, losing himself in the rhythms of his thoughts.

"Am I boring you?" Knowledge Allah asked.

"Nah, just trying to get my head around what you're saying. And I'm waiting to hear the deal, you know, figure out what you want from me."

"Simple, we want your effort. We want your voice."

"I don't know, Knowledge Allah. I ..."

The front door rattled under a large boom as if it had been struck by a tree during a tornado. The Two-Johns Theater patrons froze in their seats, heads turned toward the source of the disturbance. The doors were slammed again, buckling under a sudden weight, and then broke free of their hinges with the third heavy thud.

A sea of blue uniforms trimmed with black streamed in. City

Ordained Pinkertons took positions blocking the exits. Many slapped their batons into their empty hands, ready for action.

"Everyone, stay where you are," the lead officer yelled. "You are in violation of the Gang Congregation Act. Get your national registration cards ready but stay where you are. You are all under arrest."

TWO

POLLYWANNACRACKA

Vox Dei *Data Files: The Jefferson House was a celebration of immigrant ingenuity. Designed by the famed architects Bernard Vonnegut and Arthur Bohn, it was constructed between 1894 and 1895 along the Central Canal. A twenty-one-room, mansard-roofed mansion built in the Broad Ripple neighborhood, famed for being a summertime retreat for Indianapolis dwellers. Not much is known about the home's current owner.*

RIDING PLEASED SOPHINE JEFFERSON. The wind swept through her hair as her mechanical horse sped madly across the field. Steam escaped in clouds as the beast snorted, the heavy bellows within its chest cavity thrummed, firing the gears and pistons that animated it. Many considered the animatronic steed old-fashioned to the point of being rather gauche. Young lords and ladies gravitated to the two-wheeled variety of metal conveyance rather than the kind with undulating brass shanks, a mane of metal shingles, and clockwork gears at each joint. Sophine appreciated the art, the craftsmanship, of the older ways.

Her skin like porcelain, her slight build gave the impression that a stiff breeze might snap her in twain. She crouched low over her steed, its brass flanks tensing beneath her. Ironically, horse hair padded her bustle beneath her dress. She pressed her ride harder. Designed to work in tandem, teams to draw carriages, the mechanical horse chuffed impatiently. The rolling landscape sped by in blurs of green and brown. Everything seemed so much smaller since her return from school.

Sophine slowed the horse to a trot when she wound the bend toward her home. The sun set in the cloudy sky; the western heavens drew to a nacreous gray. The iron steed squelched; its pistons idled. The workmen rushed out to meet her, anxious to get the horse put away before her father could see what she'd been up to. They implored her to be careful, as the Colonel would have their hides fashioned into rugs for his study should anything happen to her. But the daughter of Colonel Winston Jefferson was not to be denied. When she wanted to ride, she would ride.

Hopping down from the horse, she strode to the front door. A Victorian mansion built in 1875, its recent refurbishing had returned it closer to its original state, down to the forlorn gaze of the windows. The Doric portico, whose massive columns supported an outside walkway meant to instill a sense of terror and magnificence but only added to the singular shroud of gloom. A veil of melancholy hedges hid the side of the house. The voices of the trees spoke their dark whispers in the rustling leaves. Virginia creeper choked the surrounding sugar maples and smallish elm trees, its berry bedecked red leaves winding about the young trees' leaves. The throaty croak of bullfrogs reverberated from between the house and the carriage house. The front steps were reduced to scree along the edges. The woodwork, upon closer inspection, was rotted from years of neglect, glossed over to preserve the memory of a great home. Vines threatened to overtake the eaves. Taking in a deep breath, she took a moment to collect herself and rang the doorbell.

An automata opened the door. Its brass fixtures beamed, but it moved with a jerky clunkiness. When it came to automata, it wasn't that her father appreciated history and older ways; he was simply cheap.

"May I take your coat?" Its garbled voice speaker squawked—it also lacked facial recognition or else it surely would have fussed more—and announced, "Lady Sophine."

"Thank you." She didn't know why she maintained the art of civility with the automata, save perhaps that she didn't want to fall out of the practice of graciousness. She casually noted the lines of the machine. Her mind dissected it and re-assembled it a half dozen times, improving its design and movement with each pass. She couldn't help herself. Machines had a way of speaking to her.

A life-sized portrait of Sophine's mother, the Lady Trystan, though poorly lit, loomed over the mantel of the front parlor. Lady Trystan had stood at a formidable six feet tall. Olive complected— only slightly darker than Sophine—long brown hair framed aristocratic features from her piercing brown eyes to her aquiline nose. Despite the distraction of her peculiarly-framed glasses, her features favored the Negro. In a wide-brimmed hat, garnished with tall feathers, her mother preferred to let the world take her as she was. Because she died when Sophine was young, she never really knew her mother. All she had was this portrait, her heart, and her father's stories of their life together to define her mother in her mind.

"I'm glad you made it home safely," Lyonessa Jefferson said. Outlined by the parlor doorway, Sophine's father's second wife (she steadfastly refused to even think of Lyonessa with the overly familiar term "stepmother") was a coiled ball of repression and restraint; a tightly wound polar opposite of who Sophine imagined her mother to be. Lyonessa's stiff wardrobe failed to completely hide the bulges left over from "the trauma of carrying a child," as she once described her pregnancy. She insisted that having a child aged her ten years, thus the flecks of gray in her long brown hair. From the time of her son's birth, nannies raised him until he could be shipped off to boarding school. Just like Sophine, the very next week after her father and Lyonessa pronounced their *I do*s. They never tried to have another child.

"I'm glad to be here, Lyonessa." Sophine kissed the air beside her stepmother's cheek but regarded her with suspicion.

"Oh, look at you. You must have taken a steam horse out for a gallop. Your dress in a crumpled mess." Lyonessa grasped each of Sophine's hands and swung them wide for a fuller inspection. "You will have to hurry if you're to be ready in time."

"In time?" Sophine withdrew her hands and took a wary step backward.

"For the dinner party. The Colonel arranged for Lord Leighton Melbourne and his son, Gervais, to join us."

"That doesn't sound like the Colonel." Sophine poured herself a glass of sherry rather than wait for an automaton to be summoned. She watched her father's second wife begin to mouth a protest, then purse her lips with disapproval. "That young fop, Gervais, wants nothing more than a trophy to become his wife."

"You should aspire to so much." Lyonessa sniffed. An otherwise still-faced and taciturn woman, she shared the Colonel's bed only when it suited her. He didn't care because his heart belonged to Lady Trysta. After Sophine's mother passed, it was as if all the things in him that loved or dreamt of love—other than Sophine—were put under glass and kept on a top shelf in his study. Lyonessa stood in a frozen pose as an automaton poured whatever delicate drink she favored.

"May I see the Colonel?" Sophine asked.

"It's been a rough time for the Colonel of late." Lyonessa sipped at her drink.

"He's my father."

"He's also my husband and a busy man." Lyonessa turned her back in dismissal, her words to be the final comment on the situation. "There may be a moment before dinner. Do be easy on him. But you must hurry if you are to make yourself presentable."

Presentable. Like she was some show pony.

An automaton shadowed Sophine as she made her way upstairs. Sophine's room had been maintained with the care and perspicuity of a museum exhibit, her father its lone curator. She held out her arms as the machine deftly worked its mechanical fingers to unfasten her dress. Sophine hated the spidery traipse of metal fingers along her skin, but such was the natural order to a woman of her station. Stripped down to her modest underthings, she opened her closet door. The closet was larger than many people's bedroom chambers. She refused to attach an image to exactly which people she meant.

Her chifforobe was filled with lavish gowns and sumptuous dresses, each dress purchased in guilt. A gift commemorating an event her father missed in her life. Sophine pressed the first dress to her body. White silk taffeta with pink silk trimming and a narrow waist, she last wore it when she graduated from Lady Churchill's Finishing School for Girls. The Colonel was off closing some deal and she had to waltz with some pimply-faced graduate of Mr. French's Finishing School for Boys for the father-daughter dance. The boy's hand slipped to her bodiced breast one time too many to be an awkward accident, so her knee accidentally grazed the delicate, dangly bits he so identified with. The perfect dress for a lady. She would perform for her father, try to be the girl he wanted, rather than the daughter he had. Though she doubted he would notice either way. This was why she preferred the confines and comfort of a laboratory.

Slipping a black-grooved disk into her Reginophone, she waited for the faint strains of music to begin. She imagined aged, black fingers—wizened by years of fieldwork, matching a voice grizzled by ages and hardship—plucking at guitar strings in lament to his life. The music fit her spirit.

THE COLONEL'S sanctum's sense of forlorn seclusion encapsulated the spirit of the house in the one room. Elegant draperies covered the large windows, blanketing the room in darkness. A large, lonely room, with plenty of space, but few memories to fill it. The faint hiss of gaslight signaled another late night. A cigar butt smoldered in an ashtray, the smell of stale smoke filling the room. A fireplace faced the couches at the center of the home, a stairwell wound behind and around the column of brown stones. A stack of magazines piled onto the pianoforte bench. Her father sat behind his huge desk. Sophine and nearly a half dozen of her schoolmates used to be able to fit into the knee well of the clawfoot desk. Ensconced in his chair of Moroccan leather, he didn't see her at first. He got up from his study's desk and stiffly walked to greet her.

"How is my favorite science rogue?" Colonel Winston took her by her hands and inspected her. Nearly sixty now, the white of his mustache and beard made him debonair, as men were wont to be judged. He returned both of his hands to rest on the open-mouthed copper dragon's head, which topped his lacquered black cane. Copper fittings ran down from the hilt to the midway mark of its shank. His walking cane allowed him to mask the slightest of limps.

"I'm doing well, Father." Sophine embraced the Colonel with a *pro forma* wrapping of her arms around him. Without much warmth, little more than how she greeted a stranger, and exactly how he preferred it. "Rogue?"

"You and your scientific dabblings." The Colonel scooted to the drink cart and raised a snifter of Scotch toward her.

"Dabblings are they now?" Sophine poured herself another glass of sherry and tottered it toward him in response, feeling as though she'd brought a butter knife to a duel of pistols at dawn.

"I don't appreciate your tone." Keeping his back to her, the gentle clink of ice cubes bumping against each other the only indication that he was about to fill a glass.

"I don't appreciate your dismissal of my pursuits."

"That's interesting. I don't appreciate your 'pursuits' getting you expelled from Oxford. What so noble a cause do you slave toward now?"

"Do we wish to talk about our family's history with slavery?" Her sentiment was so barbed, she immediately regretted making it, as if seeing his pistols and meeting them with grenades. A renowned businessman, he had inherited an estate of $750,000 credits from his father. As family lore went—meaning the story he had passed along to her—it was a family fortune earned in trafficking indentured servants. The weight of the shame profiting from his people being sold into indentured service was not worth his soul. At this point in the telling, the Colonel would make sweeping gestures with his hands, proclaiming that he vowed to make his own way. He knew he was meant for greater things and wanted to be beholden to no one. What money he didn't just outright give away, he used to free others from indenture. Airships would be where he'd make his fortune. Funny, every time he gave that speech about independence and determination, he failed to mention where he got the starting capital for his ventures in the first place. But everyone was the hero in their own story and history was spun by the victors. Or at least those still around for the telling. She lowered her gaze to avoid his eyes. "I began tinkering while at school."

She hoped her demur withdrawal and subject change would be enough space to allow for an apology.

The Colonel waited a few heartbeats, her words sinking in for them both. He cleared his throat. "What sort of ... tinkering?"

"Electromagnetics has been an area of research, but biomechanics has been my focus. Improving the human condition through machines."

"Picking up where God left off?" He raised his glass to her.

"I wouldn't put it that way." Though it had been years since she darkened the doorway of a cathedral, she still respected the idea of church and God. For some, faith was a life preserver, and life preservers had their place. She was simply more interested in learning to swim. "Anyway, are you well, Father? You seem rather piqued."

"The perks of a life well met. By the way, the dress looks lovely on you."

"I trust I'll pass Gervais's scrutiny." Sophine took the davenport across from the Victorian loveseat, leaving the smaller couch or the chair for him to adjourn to. Leaning forward, she couldn't quite find a comfortable posture. She hated the way her torso felt thrust into an oncoming breeze due to the latest fashion of corsets. Men never seemed to have to abuse their bodies for the eye of the opposite sex. The grand insanity of it all was that women ended up drawing men whose eyes were drawn to fleeting beauty and fashion. Thus, their heads easily turned when another beauty caught their inattentive gaze. And few men were more inattentive than Gervais was rumored to be.

"Not even a blind man could miss the beauty you've become."

"So, why the rush to get me married off?"

"I don't know what you mean." Despite having the lady's lounge, he availed himself of the seat without any comment.

"Father, I love you, and I respect you. But I also know you. You have seven reasons why you make any move. And this dinner strikes me with ... dubious curiosity."

"I'll admit. I'd hoped you and young master Gervais would become better acquainted."

"He's a boor on his best days."

"You see most eligible suitors as boors."

"Only the boorish ones."

"Well, he's a well-monied boor. It would be good for our families to finally be more closely aligned." The Colonel had little time nor patience for the intrigue of social politics. The jockeying for position among the noble houses was more the sphere of Lyonessa.

"Why not simply trade me for two goats and a prize cow?" Sophine poured another finger of sherry. Her face flushed with heat, she'd become resigned to the pointed bickering that met their every conversation of late, as if nothing she said was right enough for him. "That strikes me as more seemly than pimping out your little girl as a peace offering to strengthen the family name."

"That's awfully ..."

"... on point?" Sophine arched an eyebrow.

An anguished expression overtook his face. His arms parted as if reaching out to embrace her before thinking better of the idea. "Sophine, I only want the best for you."

"And, in your judgment, Gervais is the best for me?"

"He can take care of you."

"I can take care of myself."

"I know you can." The Colonel's voice lowered to its version of a whisper. "But a father wants to know that, even when he's not around, things will be provided for."

Sophine stopped herself from delivering the obvious retort,

questioning how much he'd been around so far. However, the tenor of his voice, this entire conversation, was all wrong. Like a familiar dance to the wrong tune. "Father, is everything all right?"

"I ..." The Colonel averted his gaze. A grimace fluttered across his face, though he hid it quickly. When storms prepared to roll in, his old aches always began to act up. Shoulder aches from where he took a bullet during the rescue of the actress, Cassandra Moore. Pain along his wrist from where he broke it in three places during the Kilimanjaro expedition. The joint pain from when he was wounded during the Five Civilized Nations uprising, which led to his military discharge; not to mention his other innumerable adventures, more than a few shared with her mother, Trystan. Adventures he did a poor job of keeping secret, in the name of protecting Sophine from that life and its inherited tragedy.

Lyonessa strode into the room without knocking. She took one glance at the posture the two of them sat in, then began her *tsk*-ing harangue. "Will you two move along? Our guests have arrived."

SOPHINE LOATHED the gamesmanship of courtly life. An open-topped carriage trundled down the long driveway. Their butlers, maids, a seamstress, cooks, stable hands, and automata streamed out, all in a processional adorned in the colors of the Jefferson house: black, white, and red. The regalia and pageantry presented to their guests in a show that their needs would be well attended to.

Gervais Melbourne nodded in approval as the servants were dismissed. He held a long, white box, patting it as he walked. Tall and broad-shouldered—with the build of an athlete too bored to play sports, or even break a sweat—he possessed a curious softness about him. His thick blond hair was sculpted more perfectly than the Jeffersons' topiary, and they paid quite the kingly sum to maintain their bushes. His gaze lingered on Sophine in a far-too-familiar way.

The elder Melbourne exited last. A bulbous man in a white suit, a sour expression on his face, which recalled the image of a spoiled onion. Whatever business imbroglio the Colonel had found himself in must have been quite dire for him to entertain his longtime rival as a dinner companion.

"It's good to see you, Lord Melbourne." The Colonel outstretched his hand.

"Ever the magnificent liar, eh, Colonel?" Lord Melbourne met his grip.

"When dining with Romans, as it were."

The two continued to smile at one another while hurling barbs. The more exquisite the dig, combined with how smoothly one dealt with it, only heightened the game and erstwhile respect. The only thing Sophine hated more than courtly life was the dynamic of male posturing. The constant need to be in competition with one another —jousting with words, in business, at sport, even with the women they consorted with—amounted to a preening sport, which bored her.

"May I formally introduce my son, Sir Gervais Melbourne?" Lord Melbourne's mouth twisted in disgust; a sneer crossed his face. Sour and disappointed, his voice was without warmth and seared with contempt.

"It is an honor to meet you, Colonel." As if not hearing the disdain in his father's voice, Gervais stepped forward and bowed slightly. "Any man who has proved such an intractable thorn to my father's side is truly a man to be reckoned with."

The Colonel nodded. "Well met. Allow me to present my daughter, Sophine Jefferson."

"She is as beautiful as described." Gervais took her gloved hand and kissed it; his fingers lingered to stroke the underside of her hand.

Sophine withdrew her hand quickly as if an asp had snapped after her.

"Here, these are for you." Gervais made a show of retrieving a silver case from his vest, removing a cigarette and lighting it before presenting her with a long box. Inside were a dozen long-stemmed roses.

Sophine hated roses. She considered the flower trite and too full of treacly sentimentality. She understood one thing about men: the best way to distract them from their quarrel was to give them a new objective to fix their attention on. And she didn't like the way the group of them studied her. Their eyes filled a little too much with the gleam of lions tossed a fresh kill. "Thank you. They're quite lovely."

Sophine curtsied, more from muscle memory prompted by the weight of the Colonel's and Lyonessa's keen gazes than anything else.

"I see you have inherited your father's gifts," Lord Melbourne leveled a cool, yet approving gaze at Sophine, as if appreciating an unspoken joke.

"Melbourne?" the Colonel asked.

"Oh, nothing. Though I'd suggest Miss Sophine not take up poker," the older Melbourne chuckled without humor. "Shall we go inside?"

Gervais set his business card in a silver tray when they entered the house, then winked at Sophine. She unfurled her hand fan and fluttered it in front of her.

Lyonessa had arranged a sumptuous banquet that filled the table. Chicken Fricassee served with rice, scalloped oysters, a brown soup removed with fish; a rump with greens later removed with a roast turkey with dressing. Boiled eggs and fresh dinner rolls with sweet cream butter, jams, jellies, and sweet pickles. The smorgasbord of food represented such gluttony, such debauchery of appetite, that Sophine soon lost her hunger.

"Is something the matter with the food, my dear?" Lyonessa's voice had the slightest hint of irritation to it, as if she had prepared the food herself. Undoubtedly, she perceived her time and effort in choosing and coordinating the courses as the real work of executing such a dinner.

"No, my time away at school dimmed the eyes of my stomach." Sophine scooped a few spoonfuls of rice and chicken on her plate to give herself something to push around as they ate.

"In my experience, most ladies eat sparingly as birds, even on their best day." Gervais heaped a pile of potatoes onto his plate.

"That's not the proper way to hold a fork." Sophine unfurled her fan with a snap of her wrist and fanned herself rapidly. The art of fanning had a secret language all its own. In this case, the message was simple: *I have doubts about you.*

Lyonessa arched an annoyed eyebrow at her and rapped her closed fan. *Don't be so imprudent.*

Oblivious to their argument by the fan wave, Gervais grinned. He must have taken it as a good sign that she tried to correct him, unaware that Sophine had dismissed many a prospective suitor for their poor table manners. His customs at the table were only the latest addition to the stack of issues that worked against him. He shifted the fork between his fingers, using Sophine's face like a cutlery divining rod.

Sophine carved a thick slice of turkey and plopped it on her plate.

"Sophine!" Lyonessa held to the same gospel held by most of her society acquaintances: what-will-the-neighbors-think. She clung to the rules and values of her polite society, despite her knowing that the word "friend" could never be applied to any in her circle. But appearance and propriety meant everything to her.

Sophine relished upsetting her rules. "I seem to have found a measure of my appetite."

"Let the girl eat in peace." Before anyone could further comment on the matter, the Colonel turned to Lord Melbourne. "What did you think of the latest regent appointment, Lord Melbourne?"

"Regent George II has assumed his rightful place in the line of succession." Lord Melbourne daubed his forehead to pat away a sheen of sweat. He moved as though fatigue leadened his limbs. This great man, whom so many trembled before when in the same room. He even had the Crown's ear.

"It will be good to attend his investiture ceremony. I wasn't sure about his father, either. A good man, but he had amassed some powerful enemies."

"The quality of one's enemies defines a life well lived," Lord Melbourne said. "Wouldn't you agree, Colonel?"

"True." Referring to him as the Colonel was a source of great pride for him. He began his career as a soldier when he was seventeen. For ten years, he served Queen and Country, earning a battle-field promotion to colonel during the Five Civilized Nations uprising. Not that the title was anything more than honorific since one of his station couldn't hope to command men. A moot point; wounded as he was, he was soon discharged for his troubles. The Colonel smiled. "Still, better him than that rapscallion, Sir Clinton, again."

"I don't know. Rogues have their charms." Gervais turned to Sophine. "And gifts."

"We've always had difficulty telling our heroes from our monsters." She rested the closed fan over her forehead. *I am ignoring you.*

"Perhaps you should leave the talk of politics and business to the men," Lyonessa said.

With sculpted poise, fixed with furious resentment, Sophine's ungiving jawline retained perfect composure. Lips pursed tight in a moue of disapproval, she toyed with her fan quite consciously, often pressing it to her left cheek under her father's careful scrutiny. *No.* She wondered how many times she'd have to press her cheek until he received the message.

"You must excuse me. I am feeling poorly and faint," Sophine said finally, pushing away from the table.

"Ah, the idle vapors. I understand the fairer sex." Gervais dabbed his mouth with his napkin. Bits of food sprayed out of his mouth in his excitement to make his observations.

Lord Melbourne made a show of drawing a large pewter watch from his waistcoat pocket. "Well, we shan't tarry. We will take our leave soon."

The Colonel eyed the watch with mild scorn.

Noting the Colonel's attention, Lord Melbourne closed the watch. "Gervais, why don't you see the young lady to her chamber?"

"I don't ..." Sophine protested.

"Sophine, perhaps if I could escort you." Gervais pushed his chair back as he stood. With a mild flourish, he offered his arm.

Sophine sighed. "If you must."

"Sophine," Lyonessa began without turning to meet her eyes, "do try to be a lady."

The two of them passed the library. Sophine's gaze lingered with longing on the respite she had hoped to find in there. There would be no comfort in books this night. Gervais and his ceaseless nattering would see to that. The burgeoning stillness would prove too much, and he would feel the need to fill the quiet. Some people didn't know how to enjoy a peaceful moment. His sharp inhalation signaled him finally screwing together the courage to interrupt the silence. Sophine leaped in to beat whatever topic he had at hand.

"Do you listen to much music, Gervais?"

"Oh," he said, caught off guard by her abrupt interest in him. "Mozart. Bach. The usual suspects."

"That doesn't tell me much. That's what the people of our station are expected to listen to."

"Sophisticated. Classic. The music of the elite. My taste may be pedestrian, but only among my equals."

"Yes, but are you moved by it?" Sophine didn't know what she hoped to find by digging into his tastes. Music struck her as a rather personal thing. A revelation of who a person truly was; a certain level of intimacy risked not only to share their tastes but achieved when they were matched. Like books, there were those carefully arranged on one's library shelves to give the appearance of what one read and was formed by. Then there were the books on one's nightstand which one truly read.

"I appreciate the beauty of its construction. Where do your tastes lie?"

"I've developed quite a fondness for the form called the Blues."

"You definitely like to rebel from the expected. Far too guttural for my tastes. It's barely music," he clucked noisily.

"Too much a product of the people?" Her tone didn't bother to mask the trap her question presented. She knew he barely cared and would stumble blindly in with his answer without thought.

"It may have its peasant charms, but it lacks any kind of sophistication. Wholly unlistenable." Gervais paused a heartbeat after the words left his mouth. "I hope I didn't offend."

"I found your answer quite illuminating." Her fan dabbed her left cheek.

"Good. After all, I am ever your devoted admirer." His eyes traced her with an intensity designed to make her feel like the only woman in the world. He stepped closer, a one-man pack of hyenas threatening to corner her. She couldn't escape the feeling that she was little more than another backroom deal orchestrated by the men in her world, meant to be served up on a silver platter.

"Perhaps you could admire me from a greater distance." Sophine pressed her hand against his chest to give herself some room.

"Nonsense. The whole point of this little gathering was for us to get better acquainted." Gervais stepped nearer. She could feel the heat of him. He took her hand and traced patterns along it.

"Sir, you begin to upset the equilibrium of my nerves." Sophine drew her hand free of his.

"There is still all manner of areas for us to explore our compatibility." Gervais pressed in on her. He wanted her to feel the state of his arousal for her.

She took a half step backward. "I was unaware that ... compatibility was a sport one had to practice."

"Practice makes perfect," he whispered. A well-rehearsed bon mot no doubt used to weaken the knees of many a debutante.

"Then practice on the harlots. I'm sure you've already spent far too much of your father's money on them to vent your beastly lusts."

"Do you know who you are talking to?" Gervais reared up and stepped back. Not used to being denied anything, a trace of indignation crept into his voice. This pleased her.

"Yes, yes. The spoiled son of yet another powerful man. Truth be told, you all begin to look alike after a while."

"You are lucky I even stooped to consider sharing my bed with you. Your family is not so carefully placed to be able to afford your ... spiritedness."

"Stooped? I doubt the stiffness of your gentleman's gentleman ever since I walked into the room would allow you to bend in any fashion."

"It speaks to my constitution that it was able to remain at full attention once you started speaking." Gervais turned on his heel to head back toward the dining room but paused to have the final word. "You'll be an iron-handed crone whose husband would rather will himself to early death rather than face the slow emasculation of your withering glare."

This, too, pleased her.

THREE

100 MILES AND RUNNING

Vox Dei Data Files: Originally called Indiana Street, early settlers avoided Indiana Avenue because of its proximity to the White River. Like all right-thinking citizens, they feared the disease-carrying mosquitoes. Only poor laboring families wanted to live there. The stretch was a blight within the city, in desperate need of renovation, and needed to be reclaimed by its rightful citizens.

THE TWO-JOHN'S THEATER erupted in confusion, the crowd in a frenzy, knocking over tables, even bowling over chairs. A wave of City Ordained Pinkertons waded into the rushing throng. Holding clear plastic shields, from shoulder to knee in length, the charging line of COPs marched in lockstep. A formation so tight their shields mimicked a charging translucent wall. They made sure people could plainly see their insignias. On each shoulder, a black patch trimmed in gold embroidery featured a gold eye, wide open, with the word Pinkerton above it. With their faces hidden behind gas masks, batons drawn as they crept along, their presence alone had the desired effect.

Patrons surged toward the exits against the undertow of retreating patrons scrambling for other exits as more COPs barred those doors. Blurs of bodies dashed about, turning tail if they encountered a group of Pinkertons covering another exit. Screams like a siren's report squalled from every direction. Candles tumbled to their sides, spilling wax and catching tablecloths on fire. The scattered flames spurred further panic. Like a bully attempting to maintain their reputation, the Pinkertons relentlessly, inexorably swam against the tide of bodies. If any gentleman or lady strayed too close to them, the Pinkertons broke their turtle shell formation to batter them.

"This way." Sleepy locked his beefy hand around Knowledge Allah's arm and steered him toward the rear of the room.

"What?"

"We can't just stay here. Look at them. They're out to bust some folks' heads."

"Standing while black is an offense against the peace now." Knowledge Allah tensed, his hand gripped his cane, ready to wield it like a bat.

"I don't want to risk being thrown off the employment cycle or, worse, end up at The Ave, classified as an Unperson. Besides, do you want to go through the front, right where the Pinkertons just came?"

"They're probably round back, too," Knowledge Allah mused, though seemingly not to anyone.

"Probably. Which is why we're going through the side."

"I don't understand."

Sleepy raised his index finger to his lips then continued in a whisper. "COPs don't know this area that well. Two-John's Theater is a maze of doors and corridors. I'm guessing most are out front in a show of force, with maybe a few out back to round up any strays."

"You sure about this?"

"You got a better plan?"

"Lead on." Knowledge Allah bowed and gestured forward.

Sleepy pressed himself against a wall and peeked around the corner. A Pinkerton slammed a man dressed in a finely tailored suit against a wall. Yanking him back, the agent slammed him again, sending the tails of the man's jacket flapping in the air. The

Pinkerton cuffed the man's hands behind his back and sat him against the wall.

Sleepy skulked down the hallway with Knowledge Allah trailing.

Two-John's Theater defied the local prohibition ordinances regarding alcohol being served in Negro establishments. A group of Pinkertons busied themselves by running their batons along the shelves behind the bar. Fine liqueurs in ornate glassware toppled from their berths. The agents paused to enjoy their handiwork when the glass exploded on the ground. The walls vibrated with the mad thrashings of the Pinkertons during their "investigation."

Huge fans whirred from a few floors above Sleepy and Knowledge Allah, both circulating the air and generating power for the building. A metal grate blocked their way at the end of the hallway. The pair huddled in as much of the shadows as the corner could accommodate. Sleepy worked his fingers around the grate until satisfied that it couldn't be pulled free. He tested the spacing of the bars, first by stepping a leg through—then by squeezing his head and a shoulder through—the grate. The metal bit into his chest, stopping him cold.

"I'm stuck," Sleepy said.

"You didn't see that coming?" Knowledge Allah inspected the bars.

"You want to help instead of offering less-than-helpful insight?"

"You want to get acquainted with a salad?" Knowledge Allah grabbed the edge of the grate. He tried to squeeze his other arm against the opposite side but couldn't circumnavigate Sleepy enough to find sufficient leverage. Untangling from the nest of arms and legs, he ducked under the man, positioned himself between Sleepy's legs and pushed against both sides of the grate from below him. "I got this."

"Almost ..." Sleepy crawled forward, pressing his crotch against Knowledge Allah's face.

Knowledge Allah turned away as best he could, the seam of Sleepy's trouser zipper smashing his cheeks.

"I'm through. Come on." Sleepy turned to wave Knowledge Allah along. "I appreciate the help."

"Let us never speak of this again." Knowledge Allah slipped through the bars, pausing only to retrieve his hat and cane.

The two scurried into the shadows. A lone Pinkerton checked the hallway, pausing to study the shadows in their direction. Sleepy held his breath. His sides burned from his exertions, not to mention squeezing through the metal bars, and knew his labored breathing brought to mind defective bellows. Satisfied, or not willing to explore a dark corridor on his own, the Pinkerton moved on.

Sleepy and Knowledge Allah inched along, unable to make out much in front of them. The shadows deepened in impermeable pockets of darkness. The walls were neither smooth nor even. The rough-hewn stone works scraped their clothes. The seams of the mason work ran like a thick thread between the bricks. Sleepy hated the way the unseen walls pressed in on him in the dark. It reminded him of a cave, the very thought of it being underground clawed at his mind like a tortured dream. Behind them, the wails of his fellow poets and audience faded under the chorus of COP brutality. Even they brought to mind the image of people trapped in a distant cave in. He pushed it all from his mind and concentrated on moving forward. Eventually, a hint of an electric phantasm shimmered in the distance. The light flickered above an access door, gas-fueled flames dancing in an errant breeze.

"This leads to an alley. It's not used very often," Sleepy whispered.

"I didn't realize the building went so deep."

"That's the idea. It was used more during Prohibition."

Knowledge Allah peeked through the door. "All clear."

Sleepy took a deep measured breath, attempting to calm his pounding heart. Poking his head out, bumping Knowledge Allah out of his way, he studied his side of the alley. Several Pinkerton steam vans lined the block across from the Two-John's Theater. The large blue behemoths, the driver sat in an open bay behind the idling engine, puffs of steam coughing up in regular intervals. The Pinkerton's symbol emblazoned on the side. Guard rails along the top encircling, seating for COPs. Ramps lowered to easily walk citizens into their holds. "Yeah, we clear over here, too."

"We're going to need some transportation."

"Any ideas?"

"One. Come on." Knowledge Allah led them.

A black man huddled on the curb's edge on his knees. COPs stood around him, making jokes, congratulating one another, ignoring his existence. He'd already been judged guilty of the crime of being. What halted Sleepy was the look on his face. Not fear. Not hatred. Not anger. Resignation. The people streaming out of the surrounding buildings didn't need the COPs' cordon to hold them back. The sight of the man on the ground—who could have been any of them—made them avert their gazes to continue about their business.

The parking lot was largely under-lit because the city didn't devote much by way of infrastructure maintenance to Freetown Village. Knowledge Allah skulked toward the nearest car. Polished to a glassy sheen under someone's tender ministrations, the metal gleamed even in the wan moonlight. Twin brass tubes formed the body of the car, curving down on both ends and stitched together by copper rivets. Knowledge Allah crawled into the passenger side to gain better access to the underside of the steering wheel. These new hybrids—electrical and steam-powered vehicles—were all the rage, but not very secure. Tugging a few wires free, he adjusted several gears then twisted the free ends of the wires together. A small hand crank popped loose. Sleepy scrambled into the driver's side. Knowledge Allah pointed frantically at the freed hand crank and Sleepy spun it for all he was worth. Headlamps, like jutting cans, burned to life, as pistons hopped under the hood of the vehicle. Several spouts released steam with a slow hiss. Sleepy threw the car into reverse and backed away from the sirens of the Pinkertons. Throwing it into *drive*, he slammed his foot onto the accelerator.

"So, about your little club, what would I have to do?" Sleepy asked.

"We just did it."

"Stole a car?"

"Commandeered," Knowledge Allah yelled. "For The Cause!"

COPs vehicles had much of the street cordoned off. Sleepy had hoped to drive past the rest of the COPs before they had a chance to get into position to lockdown the entire block. Sleepy approached a blockade of COPs vehicles. He turned up the alley that ran adjacent to Two-John's Theater and floored the accelerator. The suspension bounced and lurched in a frenzy of steam belches, jolting them up and down. When they emerged at the other end of the alley, the sewage vehicle blocked the road. Sleepy and Knowledge Allah screamed in unison as Sleepy spun the driver's wheel. As much as he hated the water company and had dreamed of smashing it, the reality ready to crash into him was a different matter. Overcorrected, his steering sent the car careening. Sleepy turned the wheel the other direction to avoid fishtailing, but the rear of the car slammed into the truck. The back fender well caught against the basin of the tanker. Tires squealed in protest with no traction to be found.

Knowledge Allah turned around in his seat to inspect the damage. His voice raised, noting the advance of COPs. "Go, go, go!"

"Hold on." Sleepy bounced in his seat, his weight rocking the bumper loose.

They drove off with the shallow whine of metal in their wake. The car left a dent that looked like three triangles in the side of the sewage truck.

"We clear?" Sleepy asked.

"You can admire your handiwork later."

Just beneath the scar they left on the tanker, a crack began to wind along its base. Liquid seeped from the weakened area further straining the bin. Finally, the canister bulged then gave way and like an opened hydrant over a dirty well, grayish brown water poured out. Gallons of sewage burst from the side, spraying its contents onto the COPs vehicles parked beside it. Thick, murky filth stopped the charging Pinkerton agents in their steps.

Sleepy eased off the gas, the pit of his stomach emptying with the dawning realization of what they'd likely be accused of. When he glanced around to see if any COPs were chasing them, he felt the weight of stares from the patrons of Two-John's Theater held in custody along the sidewalk.

"For The Cause!" Knowledge Allah raised a fist and shouted to them.

The 24-inch rims—whirring fans—continuously shuttered like retracting shields. With a roar, the car sped off, spumes of steam left in its wake.

VOX DEI *DATA FILES: "Haughville: A Dreamed Deferred."* *When Benjamin Haugh moved his iron foundry from the Mile Square out to the farmland west of the White River, a community developed around it. A few years later, the village incorporated as Haughville, but Indianapolis annexed it within two decades as the great city expanded. Originally settled by Slovenes, the Polish, and Hungarians, they were widely derided as "honkies" by the influx of Negroes and moved out. This caused many of the local industries to shut down.*

AN OVERLAY of smog and thick plumes from the manufacturing towers continued to billow well into the night. Spotlights lit up the gleaming spires of the overcity, the Mile Square of downtown Indianapolis. Colored gaslit tubes illuminated the buildings. The Indianapolis Sleepy knew faded in a swirl of darkness, the way familiar streets seemed totally different at night. The shadows created by the evening sky almost hid the grayness of their world. Crossing the railroad tracks, the meat markets and salons had shuttered for the evening, though the fruit cart and penny sheet stands were already unloading their stock in preparation for the next day. Near the border of Old Ward Number Four stood church after church: faith parceled out by lot so that no one denomination or meeting had too many attendees at one time. The White River canal, clotted with rotted carcasses, reeked of dead animals, dumped and sunbaked by day. A skim of filth frosted any still surface. The rising tide of odor carried by the breeze served as an olfactory reminder of what side of town they were on.

"What do you think they were after?" Sleepy asked. "The COPs, I mean."

"Did they need to be after anything? Or anyone?" Knowledge Allah asked. "They exist to threaten and intimidate to keep us in our place."

"They've been raiding a lot of our night spots lately. Where there's a party, they crash it and shut it down."

"Every life form has its predator. For the poor, it's the COPs."

"It's the circle of life." Sleepy's voice trailed off. An easy silence settled between them. He steered the car further and further from the furor of downtown. His idle thoughts turning to the idea of home.

"Where are you heading?" Knowledge Allah asked.

"Back to my place."

Knowledge Allah shook his head. He seemed to lower his head as a windup to him preparing to climb into his pulpit and deliver a sermon from Mr. Blackness. "You think you done did something living up by Eagle Creek? One of those upper west side Negroes, too afraid to be among your own, but still only renting your place. Just like the rest of us."

"How did this turn into a referendum on my commitment to the community? I'm supposed to turn down a chance for my own place in a safe neighborhood based on your principles? I have to work and I have to live. Principles don't fill my refrigerator."

"Safe," Knowledge Allah sniffed. "You just saw how they treat a roomful of 'safe' folks? No matter where you live, you just as safe as the rest of us. But you keep on. You passing through Haughville?"

"I can. You want me to drop you off?" Sleepy failed to hide the relief in his voice. Knowledge Allah was frustrating, constantly setting Sleepy's nerves on edge, a condition which would require a great measure of self-medication to correct. His meaty hand patted the pouch of chiba leaves in his vest pocket.

"Yeah, I want to check in with some folks, let them know the revolution has begun." A manic glee filled his eyes. "Maybe we can reconnect later."

"Uh, yeah. *Mi casa* and all that." Not knowing what else to say, Sleepy mumbled, "Power to the people"

SLEEPY CLOSED his eyes under the steady stream of water. It had been a long night and he wanted to wash the memory of it from him. A two-shower night meant the next day's labor would feel particularly arduous. He longed for his bed, but more so, he desired the sweet smoke of chiba leaves to unwind him first. Unable to delay his gratification any longer, he shut off the water valve. As his feet padded across the linoleum floor toward his kitchen, a sense of disquiet filled him. He couldn't quite put his finger on what made him so anxious. Nothing had been amiss when he arrived home, but he was aware that something wasn't right now. Sleepy tightened his grip on his towel.

The cabinet containing his dry goods wasn't closed all the way. The dishes left drying on the counter had been shifted. Little things, but Sleepy knew his space had been violated.

He examined the area for any other details but felt vulnerable. He cast about for a weapon, only finding an umbrella next to the door. Grabbing it, though he didn't know what good it would do, he pressed his back to the wall. He strained to get his breathing under control before the excitement sent him into cardiac arrest. Clutching the umbrella like a rifle, Sleepy crept up the stairs to his living area. He hated the way the shadows loomed and danced in his house. Every shape seemed like a many-fanged beast waiting around each corner. But he didn't want to announce his presence nor the state of his undress by turning on the light either. Pausing on the landing of his stairs, he tightened the towel about his waist. He edged toward the top of his stairs, not terribly anticipating the singular moment of thrusting his head blindly into the room to face down any intruders. It wasn't as if he had much to steal, besides his electro-transmitter and his recording equipment.

"Damn it," he whispered far louder than he wanted at the thought of his stuff gaining legs and marching out of his place. He pictured cartoon ants at a picnic, parading past his indifferent neighbors who valued "no snitching" above looking out for one another's stuff. Especially *his* stuff. A year's worth of credits.

"That you, Sleepy?" A familiar voice called out from the steeped shadows.

"Allah?" Sleepy relaxed and moved toward a light switch. Once flipped, a sole gaslight hummed to life.

"I prefer *Knowledge* Allah. If my name has to be shortened for convenience at all. Names are to be respected." Knowledge Allah's thick braids bobbed as he took the measure of Sleepy's approach, a bowl of cereal in one hand. His attention lingering on the umbrella to the towel back to the umbrella. "What, exactly, were you going to do with that?"

"Man, what you doing up in my crib?" Sleepy tucked the umbrella into the corner.

"Eating a bowl of cereal, if it wasn't plain." Knowledge Allah scooped up a spoonful with a nonchalant air. "Your showers take forever."

"That's cause I enjoy my alone time." Sleepy emphasized the word alone, then noted the flakes of cereal scattered along his sheets. "You must be hungry like a hostage."

"You did tell me that your place was my place."

Mi casa? Sleepy reconsidered using polite language ever again. "How'd you even know where I lived?"

"When you move out to avoid the rest of your kind," Knowledge Allah stirred the contents of his bowl. "You the easiest chocolate flake to spot in the milk."

"You a literal mother—"

"Language." Knowledge Allah cut him off with his raised spoon.

"It is still my house, right?" Setting the umbrella in the corner, Sleepy tightened his grip on his towel.

"And with me being a guest in your home, I know you'd want to conduct yourself with the befitting civility. Speaking of," Knowledge Allah rose, "may I use your facilities?"

"You may." Sleepy bowed in overacted graciousness. "If you're planning on taking a shower, you're going to have to get a towel or something. I'm not trying to have you drip on my hardwood floors. And my apologies for the smell."

"I don't intend to deposit roses myself. But for the love of Allah the Magnificent and Most High, please put on some clothes."

With that, Knowledge Allah departed. Sleepy stood in the center of the room, still clutching his towel. Screw it, he thought to himself and let the towel fall free. If Knowledge Allah came back without announcing himself again, he could kiss his naked black behind.

Sleepy slipped into his undergarments, enough clothes to satisfy matters of polity before reaching for the drawer of his nightstand. He withdrew a small bag of dry leaves and began to place them in the bowl at the base of what appeared to be a pitcher with a small hose attached to it. He moved with all due deliberation, almost a sacredness to his ritual.

"You smoke to escape the oppressive ways of Babylon and the toll it takes on your soul," Knowledge Allah interrupted from the doorway.

"The more you smoke, the more Babylon falls." Sleepy held his match in the air ready to strike it.

"Where'd you hear that?" Knowledge Allah began to walk about the apartment, picking up a knick-knack on occasion for closer inspection.

Sleepy could see the gears of Knowledge Allah's mind spinning with the fury of an addict casing the house and set down his water pipe to follow him around. "The Rastas."

"You can't even spell Rastafarian," Knowledge Allah said.

"Don't matter none, long as I respect their beliefs."

"Which are?"

"Who gives a shit as long as it gives me an excuse to smoke."

"Not a book in the place. You should never have more friends than books." Knowledge Allah studied the furniture, especially the equipment, gesturing toward a glass-fronted cabinet containing a rotating cylinder that gyrated up and down. A series of antennae lined the top of the device, electricity arcing between them. The charges climbed the spires like tendrils of ivy. Pipes splayed like the pleats of a fan, groaned and gurgled. "But look here, enough transmitter equipment to be your own broadcasting station. You are a walking opiate of the masses."

"Here we go."

"Exactly. Here we go. Again. You are clearly a product of the white man's largesse." Knowledge Allah warmed himself by the home kine. In the undercity, Fortune—as much as the government allowed—favored a neighborhood possessing a single kine or two. A home laying claim to its own was nearly unheard of. "They have you living in a one-room pen, a twelve by twelve space, conditioning you for a jail cell, yet you act appreciative to have it."

"Compared to your palatial estate?"

"Not the point, brother. I don't accept it."

"Don't you ever get tired of always fighting? Or at least talking?" Sleepy asked.

"The fires of revolution fuel me."

"Like hot gas in an airship."

"Joke if you must, but you've been trained that this is your lot. Your place stinks of chiba leaves. These despicable cigarettes smell like burned vegetables and field work."

"Yeah, sweet, ain't it?" Sleepy reached for his water pipe again.

"The pretentious devil cloves are a foul-smelling affectation," Knowledge Allah said.

"Every man's got to have a hobby." A phlegmatic gentleman by nature, Sleepy didn't care if some mistook his somnambulant demeanor for muddle-mindedness. Given nuanced consideration, this was rather true after a fashion.

"That weed is not your pastime, it's your lifeline."

"Finally, something you've said that makes sense."

"It is. The part of you which knows life isn't as it should be, can't face the horror of your existence, so you blunt it to numb the pain."

"You just determined to take the joy out of getting high." Knowing Knowledge Allah was not going to allow him peace enough to smoke, Sleepy ambled his considerable girth toward the faded tapestry that concealed the descending spiral stairway. Wide-shouldered and bulbous framed as he was, each step creaked under his weight as he slowly made his way into the subterranean hollow. Another box lined with an array of antennae hid in a corner. He adjusted dials and the speakers whined to life.

"What are you doing?" Knowledge Allah trailed after him.

"Scanning for any transmissions. I may as well put on some music or else I'll have no other choice but to continue to listen to you."

Sleepy scrolled through the various channels until the clear voice of a news alert caught his ears. Though the national penny sheet, the *Vox Dei*, competed with *The Indianapolis Star* and *The Indianapolis Recorder* for print news, the *Vox Populi* transmissions might as well have been called Albion sponsored news.

... of the Pinkerton Agency are in search of two men in connection to tonight's disturbance at the Two-John Theater. One of whom had performed at the illegal gathering. Patrons of the Two-Johns Theater are being detained for questioning about the thieves and suspected saboteurs, with the hopes of more information being learned. The city curfew has been extended until the two fugitives are apprehended.

"Look at that: we're famous." Brushing lint from his jacket, Knowledge Allah leaned against the wall.

"They looking to pin that whole mess on us?" Sleepy couldn't stem the rising panic in his voice. "We've got to get out of here."

FOUR
WHO STOLE THE SOUL?

Vox Dei Data Files: [OP-ED] Various social justice crusaders seek to address inequality in science, technology, engineering, and mathematics (STEM) education. Their new system aims to develop consistency among technology students by most likely placing enrollment caps seeking to keep men, especially non-minority men, out of math and science classes. To these radical elements, gender disparities are only troublesome when they disfavor women and so-called minorities. These reverse equality measurements will only lead to subpar education and produce subpar practitioners. They must be rooted out before they organize, become political, and actually gain footholds in the societal discourse.

LIGHT FILTERED from the crack under the door of her father's study. She opened the door without knocking, though he didn't notice. Slumped over his desk, he focused on a stack of papers. He seemed like a ghost of himself, frail and old. It was the first time he looked fragile to her. She wondered if he was sicker than he let on.

"You might as well come the rest of the way in." His chair rasped as he pushed back in it.

"I, for one, would consider that another successful Jefferson family dinner." Sophine sat down across from him.

"Girl, don't make me take you over my knee."

"I see your sense of humor hasn't abandoned you." The Colonel had only ever laid hands on her once to discipline her for being insolent to her teacher. He must've cried more than she did when he spanked her. She refused to put him in that position again, thus she excelled at school. She knew the Oxford University expulsion broke his heart.

"I imagine I won't be walking you down the aisle anytime soon," he said.

"Not to that lout."

"You certainly got his nose all opened up."

"Father, what's going on with you?"

The question hovered between them as unresolved as smoke.

"My interests face a hostile takeover by the government. Combined with Lord Melbourne, we can stave them off, but, in turn, I would risk an internal takeover."

Lord Melbourne was a powerful figure in the city. With his ties to the Pinkerton Agency, his reach extended to the national stage. He graced no doorstep without purpose and his purpose was always the acquisition of wealth, if not power. He brokered deals and broke people for his amusement. To be in his sights was worse than the fate of the stag in Gervais's hunt.

"Then why risk it?"

"He, too, would be equally vulnerable to internal ... machinations."

"Old men and their games." Before she thought about it, she swept around his desk and tightly hugged his neck. His hands rose in the instinct of defense, before returning the hug.

"All I ever wanted was for you to be happy." The Colonel closed his eyes.

"I know, Colonel," she whispered into his ear. The word "Daddy" stuck in her throat. "But I have to go my own way."

"You are so much like your mother."

"Really?" She released her hug and crouched beside him.

"Yes, but don't let Lyonessa know." He closed the folder he had been studying and focused on her. "Determined. Stubborn. Free-spirited. Passionate. Beautiful. I risk squandering the family fortunes in my gambles, so I've come to a decision."

"What sort of decision?"

"Oh, I'd rather surprise you. Just follow your passions and do something worthwhile." He piled the papers on his desk. "And, for the foreseeable future, you should probably give young master Gervais wide berth."

"You say that about every man."

"Once scorned, men—especially men like him—can be dangerous and need time to cool off. His family has never been afraid to tread the line of criminality."

"I would say the same about his father."

"Indeed." The Colonel took another swallow of whiskey. "I fear you're probably right."

VOX DEI *DATA FILES: The Knights of the White Camelia, despite the propaganda of agitators, is a well-respected organization made up of the wealthiest members of the United States of Albion. Their splinter organizations have had difficulties due to appeals from lower-class citizens and compromised leadership. David Curtis Stephenson, a prominent member of the Republican Party, was the subject of a smear campaign by liberal sympathizers. Indianapolis Chancellor John Duvall was jailed for 30 days as a part of that scandal. Having disbanded the splinter groups, the Knights of the White Camelia has revitalized, becoming a valued organization on the fore-front of stemming the tide of declining social values, urban riots, and industrial restructuring from resident aliens who erode the job cycle. Half of the General Parliament proudly has ties to the White Camelia.*

LORD MELBOURNE OWNED the Algonquin Tower on the Governor's Circle in the heart of the Indianapolis overcity. So, when

Sophine was summoned to his office, she couldn't help but be reminded of being called to her headmaster's office at Oxford University. The last time she was called to her headmaster's office, she knew exactly what that meeting was about. She spent the morning practicing the proper face of contrition in the mirror. Not that she considered herself in one bit of need of anyone's idea of forgiveness. She went to uni to learn, to innovate, not to be strangled by some Puritanical notions of morality. Besides, there was no face imaginable that was proper to demonstrate contrition for reanimating the corpse of a former roommate.

Sophine believed that her intelligence and talents spoke for themselves. Despite anyone's taunts of her being someone's bastard legacy to Oxford or accusations of her being an example of others pursuit to proffer a policy of the school's equanimity of admission, she knew the truth. Being both a person of color and a woman, she had barely accepted their offer of admission before she was photographed, and her image used to mollify advocacy groups that Oxford University was indeed a school with a vision toward the future. Some might have bristled under such dubious scrutiny but Sophine focused on her greater objectives: using the resources of Oxford University. In the end, it was the same reason she accepted Lord Melbourne's invitation.

"Am I early?" Sophine stood in the open doorway, having been escorted back to Lord Melbourne's office by his receptionist. She didn't have to re-visit every conversation or gesture for any possible infraction since she was undeniably clear in her dealings with Gervais. Not wanting to scuttle her father's ambitions, she began to rehearse something approximating an apology and hoped her tart tongue would comply with the effort.

"Not at all, my dear. We were just wrapping up." Lord Melbourne cradled a glass of brandy in his hands. Nodding toward his other guest, he settled back in his seat.

Chancellor of Indianapolis, Lucas Pruitt, paced back and forth, pausing mid-stride at Sophine's entrance. A heavily built man, he stood unsteadily, his belly hung from him like a deflated tire. He had a boxer's face, which despite him being in his fifties, prematurely aged him by more than a decade. A tweed cap tottered on his head as if he'd just come in from a spot of hunting, but his hands hadn't seen a day's worth of honest work, nor did he own the bearing of someone who shot anything. When he spied her, a flash of disdain flittered across his face before he caught himself.

Not much was known about Chancellor Pruitt before he leaped onto the political scene in spectacular fashion only a few years ago. A speaker of marginal skill with a less-than-magnetic personality to match, his isolationist rhetoric and general denunciation of all things different made him a formidable politician. "One Hundred Percent Americanism" was his campaign slogan, but in practice, he "out-Negroed" his opponents. Fomenting white people's fear of blacks to garner votes, he blamed all of Albion's woes—from the lack of jobs, the rise in crime, and the degradation of societal morals—on Negroes. A distasteful practice, to hear her father wax on about it without any particular ire. It was always easier to blame the "others" for people's own complacency, boredom, laziness, or hard times, the Colonel argued. Already Lucas Pruitt prepared for a run for General Parliament, with his representatives testing the slogan "automata doesn't make it auto-better."

"It looks like you're pressed for another meeting." Lucas cut his eyes from Lord Melbourne to Sophine back to Lord Melbourne.

"No, no, you were quite worked up and had a point to make. I'd hate to have you carry that burden around any longer." Lord Melbourne raised his glass to him. Though a smile crept across his face, there was a malignant twist to the curl of his lips. "Please ... get it off your chest."

The Chancellor appeared to suffer from a bout of severe gastronomical distress, becoming increasingly nervous at the prospect of continuing the conversation in front of Sophine.

Sophine suppressed the budding pleasure she felt at causing his discomfort.

"Did you lose your train of thought? You were saying that casks of untaxed whiskey waited at the warehouse with not enough staff to unload it. And your same lack of control of the labor unions was preventing you from moving merchandise along the train line." Lord

Melbourne, too, seemed to relish in the Chancellor's discomfort. It was one thing for her to enjoy it, but this was how he treated his associates. Why her father was involved with such a man, she never understood. Every time she neared him, she felt like the proverbial toad about to give a scorpion a ride across a river. "Are preparations nearly complete? Who on the council would be in need of renumeration to facilitate our dealings?"

"Are you sure we should be discussing this so ... freely?"

"Nonsense. Sophine is like family," Lord Melbourne said.

Sophine glanced at him. He tipped his glass to her.

"All I'm saying is that there are dangerous elements operating in the city." Like a man stripped of his clothes emboldened by the idea of embracing his nudity, Lucas Pruitt set his glass down and strutted about like the politician he was. "This 'Star Child' fellow was the tip of the iceberg. I hear rumors of an entire network. I am simply putting you on notice that I am taking steps to not only isolate this network but rid the city of them once and for all. 'By any means necessary' as they like to say. Because animals don't know any better. They don't understand the ways of civilized people and enjoy resorting to threatening honest, hard-working citizens." Pruitt was proud of his ties to the Knights of the White Camelia. They had been operating in the area for decades but were now coming into their peak. They used offertories to gain access to church pulpits, which soon became their chief recruiting centers. Pruitt's coffers quickly filled. The 1853 Horse Thief Law, originally intended to authorize citizens associations to arrest and punish individuals without bringing them to trial, was the legal loophole exploited to justify Camelia raids. He co-sponsored a bill allowing them to be officially deputized to work alongside the City Ordained Pinkertons.

Conscious of Sophine's presence, Pruitt cleared his throat. "Further details we can discuss another time. I have a few ... black sheep in my family. I am not nearly as trusting as you."

Chancellor Pruitt extended his hand. Lord Melbourne feigned having a runny nose by exaggerated snorting and reaching for his kerchief. The Chancellor turned on his heel but kept his head upright as he left the office.

"The Chancellor didn't seem too pleased to see me," Sophine said.

"The Chancellor is rumored to be a lover of the Duchess of Edinburgh, with the well-known proclivity of snorting snuff from her belly. Oh, the things that get repeated over electro-transmitters when one forgets they are on. The famous palm reader, Lady Emma Bennett, once pronounced that he would die of a syphilitic seizure while sitting on a commode in prison convicted of a rape charge."

Sophine stifled a giggle. "I hesitate to agree with him, but he had a point. Should you have been so forthcoming in front of me?"

"I wanted to demonstrate my trust in your discretion." Lord Melbourne returned to his beverage cart and refilled his glass. "In any budding relationship, someone has to venture forth in risk."

"And it conveniently reminded the Chancellor of his place ... in your world." Sophine side-eyed him.

"You have your father's sharp mind." Lord Melbourne waved his hand toward the empty seat across from his desk. "And impertinence."

"We just don't like to be told what we can and can't do. By anybody." Sophine perched on the edge of the seat, undecided if she were uncomfortable in her dress or if she were poised to bolt in a moment's notice.

"Not even your own?"

"Any. Body." Sophine emphasized each syllable for clarity.

Lord Melbourne leveled his cool gaze on her. The corner of his mouth twitched upward in approval. "Good. That's exactly the attitude I want for the sort of person I'm looking for to fill this position."

"Position?"

"All in good time. Help yourself." Lord Melbourne dipped the nib of his stylus into the inkpot to compose whatever letter he needed to wrap up his business with Chancellor Pruitt. Sophine traced his furtive gesture to the cart with glass decanters on it. Picking up the first one, with its raised crystal bumps along the side, she removed the top and sniffed. A rich scent of brandy wafted to her nose. She poured herself a finger's worth. Enough to occupy a glass without turning her head. She swirled her glass as she took in the collection of animal heads arrayed along his wall. Elephant. Bear. Rhinoceros. Tiger.

"Your décor is quite ... striking." She studied each face, frozen in the moment it realized it was trapped or mortally wounded. The death masks were meant to intimidate, remind a person that each of the beasts assumed they were the top of the food chain until they encountered their true predator.

"Do they disturb you?" Lord Melbourne didn't raise his head from his papers.

"No, it strikes me as very masculine."

"Do I detect a hint of judgment?" he sniffed. "Don't be so ... common."

"I am many things. Though this is the first time I've ever been accused of being common."

"They are my totems and I have taken their power." Lord Melbourne set down his stylus. "It is no mean feat to track a beast from its lair to its dealings. To remain still for days on end, watching your quarry, studying its habits, insinuating yourself into its world so that it takes little notice of you. To draw near to it, until you get it within your sights and take that final breath before you squeeze the trigger." Lord Melbourne closed his eyes and fired his imaginary rifle. Again, his mouth curled in the briefest of satisfied smiles. Then, as if caught in an all-too-private moment, his eyes sprang open and he moved to change topics. "Tell me about Oxford."

"What about it?" Sophine nearly dropped her glass with the unexpectedness of the question.

"I understand you did some breakthrough work there."

"I ..." She scrambled, not knowing which direction the conversation might turn. She wasn't in the mood for either lecture or sermon condemning her. The familiar sense of déjà vu from when the head-master began to interrogate her washed over her. Well-connected, well-monied, well-bred, none of that would save him from being well-covered by the contents of her glass.

"I read your paper with great fascination." Lord Melbourne patted a stack of papers.

Only then did she notice the journal *Science Frontier*, what many scholars considered fringe science. With her lone published article, her name credited as S. Jefferson, as not to alert the editors to the fact that its author was a woman. Beneath it, a copy of *The Indianapolis Recorder* where she had placed an ad to raise money to further her research. He had certainly completed much research on her. She swallowed most of her brandy, suddenly relieved, but moved to pour herself another fat finger's worth before she began to speak. "My specific area of inquiry was the joining of the organic with the inorganic."

"Man and machine."

"Quite. The human body's capacity to adapt never ceases to surprise me. Life is a precarious balance of energy and mechanics. All life has evolved along patterns and yet I wondered if some adaptations could be augmented."

"Such as a mechanical bracer for an appendage." Lord Melbourne planted both elbows on his desk, his hands danced about whenever he spoke. The subject woke within a child-like enthusiasm he couldn't quite contain.

"Yes, though such an external skeleton only touched upon what I thought was possible."

"Such as your encephalagrammic research?"

"Yes. The brain is nothing more than energy across a field, information transmitted along membranes."

"If I understand it, you designed an engine to spark the brain. And used it on your dog."

"A dog. My K-9 series."

"Yes, yes. That's marvelous." A genuine grin spread across his face. He pushed his seat slightly away, leaning back into it. "But then came the messy business leading to your expulsion. I understand the story isn't fit for polite company, so I didn't bring it up at dinner."

"That was another matter entirely. Molly Fairborn." Sophine swallowed. Closing her eyes, she carefully weighed whether or not she wanted to delve into the account. Her heart still ached when she pictured her dormitory roommate's face. The silence deepened, both patient and inviting, until with a barely audible sigh, she continued. "There were only a dozen ladies studying science in all of Oxford. Fascinated though I was with biology, my area of interest was in engineering. Molly had a keen mind and would have made an excellent biologist. We stayed up long into many nights discussing the intersection of biology and mechanics. It was she who helped me fine tune the neuroprobes I used in the cortex of the K-9 series brain. As long as the body had not been dead longer than six hours, the probes stimulated the latent energy of the brain, providing it a jump start, as it were. We were still in the preliminary stages when ..."

"... the accident occurred?"

"Yes," she said. The accident might as well have occurred yesterday. All of the bitterness, pent up tears—and righteous fury—returned in an instant. She never understood the energy and focus so many of the boys in her class poured into harassing the female students. Taking every opportunity to belittle and minimize them. Hazing was one thing, but their constant little torments were designed to remind them of their place and drive them out. "Small-minded ruffians. Oh, how they harangued Molly. They would burst into our room and blindfold her. They spiked her water with spirits and forced her to drink until she vomited. Another time they stripped her naked and used a stylus to circle areas of her body in need of firming."

"And where were you when these ruffians absconded with your friend?" Lord Melbourne arched a knowing eyebrow.

"I was quiet. I drew the covers over my head and held my breath hoping they wouldn't notice me. I prayed I had enough 'darkie' in my blood for them to not be bothered with me. And then one night I returned to the room to find her hanging from a banister. And I had to ..."

"You had to what?" Lord Melbourne leaned forward.

"They had taken away her voice. *I* had denied her the reality of her own voice. So, I was going to make sure she was heard. I broke into the hospital basement and brought her body to my laboratory. I was ready for Stage Three testing of my procedure anyway. I wired her brain and jolted it. When her eyes opened, she stared at me without recognition. She brushed past me to head back to our room. She stopped in the hallway outside of our room. She stared at the door, at her hands, at the faces of her friends as they approached. Scared. Lost. Alien. She let out the unholiest of cries. The women screamed and scattered as if chased by the hounds of hell themselves. But Molly just stood there and wailed until security subdued her and ... undid my work."

"And so ended your tenure at Oxford." His words landed softly, without judgment, an almost regretful tone to them.

"They all but called me a necromancer. Accused me of necrophilia. At the hearing, the barrelhead trial that it was, the term I chose to most fully describe myself was necromechanic. I told the faculty—in no uncertain terms—exactly what I thought of their delicate social mores and their antiquated ideas of what a woman's place was." The brandy worked its magic on her, emboldening her tongue.

"Given how you dispatched my son the other night, I can only imagine your, how did you put it, terms."

"Well," Sophine twirled her glass, with sudden fascination of the brown eddies created. Not wanting to meet his gaze, but acutely aware of it. "That may not have been my finest hour."

"It may have felt good in the moment, but there are prudent ways to speak to the wealthy."

"I'm all about truth to power." Surprising herself, Sophine gulped down the rest of her glass and stared directly at him. His face attempted to portray openness and kindness, but it was clear he had little practice at it.

Lord Melbourne leaned back in his chair and bridged his fingers in front of his face. "If you're not careful, you're going to end up on the wrong end of *the power* of power."

Sophine shuddered slightly when she heard his words. She originally intended to keep her head down as much as possible during the conversation to divine Lord Melbourne's agenda. He was a power broker and business magnate. Meetings and socializing with the elite filled his time. Certainly, he had more pressing considerations than the doings of an expelled university student. She felt she'd managed to paint a large bull's eye across her backside.

Lord Melbourne interrupted the stillness which had settled between them. "And what of your work? I've heard tell of brains floating suspended in liquid in jars. Your handiwork?"

"No, that's more the handiwork of the scientists in Jamaica. I never could manage the preservation of consciousness. The demands of power to facilitate that transfer was beyond my resources."

"I think you and I come from similar stock. We're dreamers, dreamers in search of a place to belong. To call our own." Lord Melbourne straightened in his seat, the chair returning to its upright position with a mechanical click. Suppressing the manic air of a young boy whose attention had been lured, he returned to the quiet, dignified posture befitting a man of his station. "Despite my national prominence, this is my city. I want what's best for her, but I also look to the future. Beyond the hiss of steam. Perhaps harnessing the power of the sun. Of automata. Merging the mechanical with man. Communicating through the ether. Tapping eldritch energies unthought of."

"You are indeed a man of vision." Sophine set her glass on the table with an air of finality.

"It is not for me to say."

"But you enjoy it when others point it out."

"Ha!" Lord Melbourne collected the papers on his desk and tamped them loudly to straighten them. "My son is wasted on you."

"What did you say?" The second glass of brandy clouded her head. She wasn't sure she heard what he couldn't possibly have said.

"I have a proposal for you." He focused the weight of his full attention on her. The power of his gaze had a near physical quality to it.

"Lord Melbourne, I don't ..." Sophine feared whatever offer he was about to make. She fought back the image of a Venus flytrap closing all about her.

"Hear me out. I wish you to come work for me. At one of Melbourne Industries subsidiaries, ZeroDyne Corporation. Think of it: the chance to innovate without restraint. To have all of the resources you could ever want at your disposal."

She froze for a moment, double-checking to make sure her brain absorbed what her ears captured. ZeroDyne Corporation was a small division of Melbourne Industries. It was once a competing lab, specializing in the budding field of cybernetics, but was now part of the Melbourne Industries complex. Inhaling sharply, she parsed her words with all due caution. "And what would you have of me?"

"Ever the pragmatist. I do this in exchange for you giving up intellectual claim to what you discover."

"So, I innovate, you take the credit?" She pictured her head alongside the other animals on his office wall. Stalked and hunted, walking right into his trap, waiting for the jaws to spring shut.

"Nothing so blasé. You innovate, I could care less about the credit. The whole world can know it was your invention. You can research, publish, and go lecture. Under your full given name, if you desire."

"But you own the patents." Sophine glowered with the realization.

"There's the catch." Lord Melbourne tipped his glass to her. "I do, after all, run a company that I would like to see make an obscene profit."

"You could have hired me into you employ and had me sign contracts tricking my rights from me."

"I could have. And, mind you, there shall come contracts so binding you'll have to loosen your corset to sign them, but as I also said, I want there to be a measure of trust between us. I put all of my cards on the table in order to be ..."

"The first to risk?"

"Any relationship requires honesty if it is worth sustaining. What say you?"

Sophine tapped her glass with her forefinger while she considered. His laboratories and resources must far outstrip those of uni. And no one could deny what she was able to accomplish there. Still, Lord Melbourne hid agendas within agendas, and whatever contracts would have to pass through her father's barristers. "Let's see this lab."

FIVE

RIGHTSTARTER

Vox Dei Data Files: Described as a social safety net, our citizen's welfare system only manages to encourage people to not work, reducing them to worthless drains on the system. Even animals learn to fend for themselves in order to survive and thrive. If we keep feeding those who don't work for it, we only teach them to become dependent. Maybe the poor should go through the effort of harvesting their food from dumpsters to learn the value of handouts. The entire program essentially amounts to bribes by insurgents within the General Parliament.

SLEEPY'S HAND hovered over a blue jacket, not quite ready to commit. After a few seconds of mental debate, he tossed the jacket onto the growing pile on his bed. This was not an occasion for blue.

"I thought you said that we've got to get out of here." Knowledge Allah skulked in the doorway, popping his head out into the hallway on the lookout for unexpected company.

"I did." Sleepy flipped past a purple ensemble and a brown one, both with jackets whose length ran to his knees.

"And yet you find yourself buried in your closet."

"We're about to set out on a journey. We don't know how long we'll be gone." Sleepy pressed another outfit to his chest and checked his mirror.

"That is the very essence of fleeing," Knowledge Allah said.

"Well, the journey is moot if one isn't ..."

"... accessorized?"

"I was going to say dressed appropriately." Sleepy stepped out of his closet having selected a red velvet frock coat to wear over his gray waistcoat. He hastily wrapped a black silk cravat around his neck and tucked it into his vest. He donned a red top hat to finish his look. "What do you think?"

"I think any COP within a mile will be able to spot you just fine."

"It's called color. The world doesn't have to be dreary," Sleepy said.

"And what's the harm if there's one more peacock strutting about. Is there anything else you need as we prepare to flee the authorities? Pedicure? Sponge bath?"

"Just my electro-transmitter equipment."

"All right. Let's pile it in the trunk and backseat." Knowledge Allah turned toward the living room.

Sleepy paused at the door and turned to Knowledge Allah with sudden suspicion. "That's it?"

"That's what?" Knowledge Allah slapped his thighs and turned back with a sigh.

"No argument? No protest?"

"It took you an hour to fashion yourself after what's left of a clown once having leapt from a downtown spire. Why waste more time arguing?"

Sleepy sniffed the air around Knowledge Allah. "What's that smell? It's mighty familiar. Rather like that one cologne, *l'eau de bullshit.*"

"Fine. If you must know, I'm thinking down the road. Your equipment may come in handy."

"How?"

"As I said, I wanted your voice. That includes the ability to broadcast it."

"You could've just said so."

"A man's got to have his secrets."

Knowledge Allah reminded Sleepy of someone he knew from secondary education, 5th Form. Football star, smooth, easy way with the ladies, he had a raw charisma about him that made everyone in his orbit fall in lockstep behind him. The gentleman never gave him the courtesy of a glance, yet Sleepy couldn't help always trying to associate with him as if on the off chance he ended up spending enough time with him, he'd find Sleepy positively delightful. He hated 5th Form.

Sleepy backed the vehicle down the alley between rows of the townhouses, which faced their rear patios. They carted the equipment to the car. This lessened the chance of a nosy neighbor deciding that Sleepy was robbing his own place and calling the very COPs they were trying to avoid. Knowledge Allah slammed the car trunk shut. Sleepy draped a few more of his outfits across the equipment piled in the backseat.

"We need to head to the Second Marion County Courthouse, and then somewhere to stash your equipment," Knowledge Allah said.

"We have to chance a trip into the beast's bureaucratic heart, despite the fact that every blue-suited tentacle of the beast is on the alert for us?" Sleepy crossed his arms. "Why, pray tell?"

"It's the first of the month," Knowledge Allah said. "I need traveling credits. I'm not on the work cycle and can't afford my own place. Bad enough they had me over in Meadows Towers."

Sleepy spent time in the Meadows Tower. A pioneering concept at the time, a government project to house the city's poor and otherwise forgotten, which required tenants to accept any work if offered. It proved a convenient source of cheap labor, though the rise of automatons had pushed aside citizen and immigrant alike.

"Fine. We can head over to Stylez barbershop after that," Sleepy said.

"The wardrobe change was one thing, but a haircut?"

"Coming from the man needing to collect his first of the month check?" Sleepy slid into the driver's seat. "It's where we're stashing my equipment. My dude Sugar will take care of me."

"Melvin Knight?"

"You know him?"

"Everyone knows Sugar."

THE SECOND MARION COUNTY Courthouse stretched along Washington Street between Alabama Street and Delaware Street. Between the red granite pillars on the second floor and the mansard roof was the massive central clock tower. Its limestone façade excavated from Indiana quarries, its five three-story bays the picture of mannered stateliness. Or Second Empire pretension.

"I feel like we're zig-zagging across the city." Sleepy kept checking over his shoulder as they approached the building. A row of COP vehicles lined the street.

"We've gone from your place to the overcity. Twice. So more just the same zig. Besides, at this point, we want to keep moving."

"Yeah, but where are we heading?"

"Looking for the proper clerk. Then somewhere quiet to be still for a minute and think," Knowledge Allah said.

"I suspect we'll have plenty of time to think here. Especially if we get caught."

The building seemed designed to belittle and humiliate all who entered its halls. The lobby of the Courthouse nearly spanned the entire length of the building. Looming frescoes depicting scenes of charity, the queen's largesse, the shining empire of Albion. The gingerbread-trimmed hallways all looked the same and seemed to shift if one didn't pay close enough attention. Laid out to make finding the right building, the right department, the right person to talk to as difficult and frustrating as possible. A retired Pinkerton agent sat behind a desk reading a penny sheet.

Brown and black, poor and dirty, children with disheveled hair and mismatched clothes rifled through charity bins. Their parents milled from room to room, each resigned to the long waits. If there was one thing the poor learned, it was patience in the face of bureaucracy. Given the way the *Vox Dei* reported, Sleepy was surprised to see the number of white faces among the sea of brown and black ones. With their pale complexions and high cheekbones, their straight brown hair draping their square heads, they all vaguely resembled each other. No matter their color, years of distrust and isolation built up like cataracts in their dark eyes. They all shared the same haunted look which made them seem like kin.

They were the shattered.

Like most citizens, they bought into Albion's social experiment they called the United States. They strove for the dream of independence, creating bubbles of control. They chased after enough credits to pay their bills, put food on the table, and build their bourgeoisie lifestyle of garages and fences, the perimeter defense against the intrusion of neighbors. Their bootstraps and efforts were their sovereign kingdoms of class and influence. Dedicated to their cinemascopes, hobbies, or social cause célèbre for distraction. They lived for the delusional dream of middle-class mediocrity because they didn't need anyone other than themselves.

Until the shattering.

The shattering took many forms. Being dropped from the work cycle. Crossing the path of the wrong COP and ending up an Unperson in The Ave. Injury. Accident. A missed bill. The slightest hiccup to the delicately maintained machinery of their lives, which kept their heads bobbing above the waters of circumstance, and they fell like so many surprised angels from heaven and found themselves circumnavigating the system for the underclass.

"Name," said a woman with a sour face, porcine nose, wide mouth, and eyes deep and recessed while her attention focused on a stack of forms. Her coarse, broomstick hair would shred any attempt by a comb to run through it.

"(120 Degrees of) Knowledge Allah."

Her head stopped bobbing over her paperwork, and she straightened in her seat. After a moment of intense scrutiny, she laid her pen down and crossed her arms. "As much as I'd like to believe that you popped out of your mother's womb, she took you into her arms and said 'my precious baby. You look like a (120 Degrees of) Knowledge Allah to me,' I'm going to guess the government knows you by a different name."

No matter how friendly the words were on the surface, the public servants' voices were tinged with a mix of pity, boredom, and condescension. Their knowing eyes dissected all who came before them, assuming their story sometimes without judgment. An able-bodied adult black male, Knowledge Allah had to be shiftless and lazy. Since he certainly appeared fit enough to work, he must have several babies running the streets or sold narcotics. Either way, he had the nerve to walk in for a handout. Luckily for the commonwealth, these bureaucratic arbiters of public alms—who neither provided help nor a safety net—guarded the governmental largesse with the fierceness of duty to face down barbarian hordes coming over the gates to pillage their village. Or to simply stay off the unemployment rolls themselves.

The corner of Knowledge Allah's mouth twisted into an uncertain frown. Leaning toward the glass which separated them, he muttered, "Carlton Drayton."

"Identification papers, Carlton?"

"Here." Knowledge Allah passed the papers to her with all due speed and discretion. He scanned about to see if anyone heard her.

"Second form?"

"The only other piece of identification I have is this." Knowledge Allah produced a cracked and frayed card which read Lost Nation ID.

The lady's face bunched even tighter. She scrutinized the card a second time. Flipping it over, she glanced up at him with an expression of mild annoyance before handing the card back to him. "Carlton X?"

"I'm on a journey of self-discovery. As I peel back enough new layers, I feel the need to change my name."

"Yeah, well, we'll need something a bit more official than your neighborhood passport. Birth certificate. Ident card. Here's the full checklist."

"Fine." Knowledge Allah pulled out an ident card from a hidden fold in his wallet.

"Was that so hard?" she asked.

"To prove who I say I am?"

"Well, to be fair, you say you're a lot of people. It must get confusing. Fill these out and turn them in at the next window." She leaned over to shout past him. "Next!" She waved the next empty-store-having person over.

Knowledge Allah stepped in front of her, blocking her eye line again. He leaned heavily on his cane. "We go through these same hoops every month."

"Then you'd think you'd be used to them. Next!"

"Look around you, Sleepy. This is what it all comes down to. The last refuge of citizens when they fall off the work cycle. The Vox would say it's the first rung up."

"The Vox also hinted that I could stand to lose a few pounds, so we already know it's a damn, dirty liar. A paper not fit for me to wipe my ..." Sleepy took notice of several young women fanning themselves in nearby chairs. "The view ain't all bad."

"You can't be serious." Knowledge Allah glanced over the top of his glasses.

"Look around you." Sleepy lowered into a half bow and tipped his hat when a young woman slid by him to take an empty seat. He resumed his conspiratorial whisper. "It's a smorgasbord of mostly single women."

"Mostly with children," Knowledge Allah added with mild, chastising disdain. "Anyway, I'm dark meats only this week."

"Whatever, man. Don't matter the flavor of the ice cream, just as long as I get a taste."

"You're a pig."

"Oink, oink, Mr. Dark Meats Only." Sleepy tugged at his pants. "You got this? I need to make a run."

Ducking into the nearby public water closet, Sleepy struggled to an empty stall. He had held the pressing weight in his bladder for as long as he could until it was the sole focus of his concentration. He hated public restrooms, preferring what he called "his home court advantage." What struck him most as he stood half-gazing out of the eye-level window; was how no one said "excuse me" in the bathroom. Outside its walls, a sneeze may be met with an "excuse me" and a "bless you." Here, men were a collection of grunts and farts and plopping sounds with no polite retorts. He closed his eyes to concentrate on not hearing.

When he opened his eyes, two COPs walked along the street below him, checking a piece of paper between them, stopping the occasional black gentleman as he strolled along. They weren't near the side street they had parked on, but it would only be a matter of time before they stumbled over it. Sleepy slipped out of the room.

"You done?" Sleepy sidled up to Knowledge Allah, keeping an eye on the security guards.

"They're cashing me out now. Two hundred credits. They make you work each month with their bureaucratic bumbling. The most inefficient waste of time ever conceived ..."

"We got to go. COPs are patrolling this area. I suspect looking for men matching our general description."

"You sure?" Knowledge Allah whispered as he collected his credits.

"Sure as biscuits going with some gravy."

STYLEZ HAIR SALON was one of the few privately owned businesses in Freetown Village. The name of the business would have been Knight's Barbershop, but city ordinances prevented such prominent declarations of private ownership by a black family. A seven-seat shop, Rochester chairs lined the west walls. Two older gentlemen played chess in the front corner of the shop.

"What's up, fellas?" Sugar's voice boomed like a thunderclap, startling the men playing chess. Tall and proud, he reclined as a customer in a chair. Since gray speckled Sugar's mustache, he rarely allowed his beard to grow out beyond stubble before he trimmed it. The gray would seem premature on him if it wasn't for his eye. A patch covered his left eye, leaving his right to a knowing glare about it as if it had seen death so close, it scalded it. Just behind him, a small capuchin monkey—in a white pinstriped suit identical to Sugar's—frolicked about him.

"Sugar, my man. How you been?" Sleepy said.

"Steady slinging, boss." Sugar nodded to the barber to get him started. "He'll be with you in a minute."

With a dramatic snap of his drape cloth, the barber covered Sugar and ginned up the lather on his face. Leaning the seat as far back as it could go, the barber turned to the array of razors on a tray beside him. This was Sugar's station. Each blade had a day of the week engraved on its handle. Sugar watched the man draw the blade near his throat. With delicate grace, like his life depended on it, the barber scraped through the lather.

"Don't know if I'd trust any man with a razor to my neck. Don't know how you can tell a threat when you have depth perception issues." Though his tone remained light, visions of Sugar's thugs visiting him one night if a joke landed wrong filled his head since Sleepy knew Sugar's reputation. Word on the street was that Sugar lined the pockets of politicians and COPs officials in order for them to turn a blind eye to his activities. Little business was done in Free-town Village nor in The Tombs without his fingerprints on it. He just as easily had thugs carry out his business orders as did the dirt himself. Most days he operated out of a backroom of his family's church or the barbershop, explaining that churches and salons were, respectively, the sacred and secular meeting places for the community. Sleepy had grown up with weekly visits to the barbershop, though made a point of avoiding direct business with him. "No offense."

"None taken. I see more truth with my one good eye than most brothers do with two. You can best believe that." Sugar smiled, his focus shifting to Knowledge Allah. "It's been a minute, Carlton."

Sleepy glanced from one man to the other. A spark of familiarity and ... something passed between them. "You two know each other?"

"Man, I been knowing, brother Carlton-crazy-X-Abdullah or whatever he's calling himself these days since forever."

Knowledge Allah upticked his chin toward him. "(120 Degrees of) Knowledge Allah. He knew me before I saw the light."

"Yeah, he used to come around back when he was in foundation school." Sugar's tone changed as he slipped into neighborhood historian mode. "Sleepy, by the time you was in secondary school, you hung more with the burnouts and artists. My man here ran with a rougher crew. Back then, Carlton Drayton would just as soon plant a fist in someone's face as say 'hello.' And Carlton was rarely too keen on 'hello.' Once he 'saw the light,' we ran into each other again and just sort of fell into each other's orbit. Common interests and all. You know how we do."

The barber slapped his chair when Sugar vacated it to signal to Sleepy that he was next. Throwing the drop cloth around Sleepy, he was careful to slip a paper collar around his neck and tuck the cloth around his shirt. Not one hair would end up on his suit.

"Thought you weren't getting a cut," Knowledge Allah said.

"Well, I mean, while we're here," Sleepy said. "Thought I'd let Sugar handle his business."

The chess-playing old men grumbled louder because they needed to talk and Sleepy wanted to hear the latest. Neighborhood chatter as communal therapy.

"You hear about Trevon?" Sugar asked with the nonchalance of asking about the weather.

"Nah, man. What's up?"

"He got himself killed."

"Oh damn." Sleepy raised up a bit. Another one of his childhood friends had met death. No matter how tough, how immortal, they believed themselves to be, death drove home the temporary nature of their place in the universe. The barber pressed two fingers into his shoulder to hold him still. "What happened?"

"That boy was minding his own business," one of the old men glanced up from the chessboard to comment.

"Good kid. Good kid. No angel, but he wasn't too far gone. Not like some," the other man added.

"You know Trevon," Sugar continued. "Always had to be the smartest man in the room, but he had that charm about him though.

Could get a room full of people to believe any nonsense he came up with. So, he was out working with his knucklehead crew, you know how they be on them corners waiting for life to jump off around them. When some City Ordained Pinkertons rolled up on them."

Sugar spat the words "City Ordained Pinkertons" with an extra bit of venom. During his campaign for Chancellor, Lucas Pruitt dubbed the COPs "medical constabulary" because "crime was a disease and the City Ordained Pinkertons were the orderlies." Low-level criminals—everyone from disorderly conduct to illegal assembly—were often "rehabilitated" through the use of drug collars, which dosed them during the course of the day, meant to keep them sedate and out of trouble. Higher level offenders—everyone from excessive debtors to murderers—were simply ware-housed in facilities like The Ave.

The barber spun him around to approve of his work-in-progress. Sleepy nodded his approval.

"The civil ordination of Pinkertons was one of the worst laws ever passed." Sleepy closed his eyes. He hated the way his eyes watered when the clippers brushed against his nose hairs.

"I didn't exactly see you up at Parliament lobbying against it," Knowledge Allah said.

"Anyway, you know how they do," Sugar continued. "Some woman in upper Naptown probably misplaced her earrings or some nonsense, so the COPs came tearing through Freetown Village to search for them."

"They've been pretty active lately," the old man said.

"End of the month quotas," the other man added.

"I don't know. Something's up. They've been extra intense," Sugar said, in a tone which didn't invite further interrogation. "This gets us back to Trevon who gets to running his mouth. So, one of the COPs shove him. But you know Trevon. He got that anger in him. Got all up in the Pinkerton's face. Talking, talking, talking. The Pinkerton took out his billy club, but Trevon wouldn't back down. I don't know who put hand on who first."

"I got a guess," the old man said.

"Damn COPs," the other man chimed in.

"By the time it was over, Trevon was dead."

"Damn," Sleepy said. "What's everyone doing?"

"What do you mean?" Sugar asked.

"What's the word?"

"Man, that barely made the paper. How did the *Vox Dei* put it? A street urchin gets put out of their misery. That's not even man bites dog territory."

"I know. You were waiting for the Star Child to rally the community. That's why they got him in The Ave. Muzzle the voice of the community," Knowledge Allah said. "Keep us quiet and knowing our place."

The barber spun Sleepy about one last time to allow him to study himself in the mirror. He was the epitome of what Albion told all of its citizens to aspire to. Clean. Respectable. Yet no part of his life felt like it was supposed to. Dissatisfaction ate at him like a tapeworm. The clothes, the job, his place, it was all part of the same veneer of a lie. Sleepy's life was comfortable enough to avoid complaint. Working his little 9-5 spot. Hitting the Two-John's Theater on Friday, Saturday, or both. Getting his praise on every Sunday morning in church. Every now and then splurge on a new suit. Maybe mix in a girl and a walk through Military Park. His was the life of an ordinary citizen. He made the most from the hand he was dealt. Yet he couldn't help but think that he was a person caught somewhere between the lie of citizenship and an Unperson at The Ave. If he strayed into the wrong neighborhood, he'd be seen as just another member of the undifferentiated menace the poor represented. Should the COPs notice him, they'd judge him as someone out of place. A suspect stomped by birth. Sleepy's stomach soured.

"You know they're talking about tearing down the Madame Walker building?" Sugar said. "They say they got plans for urban renewal."

"Urban renewal? You mean their ongoing plans for Negro removal," Knowledge Allah said.

"Does he ever stop?" the old man said.

"That boy would talk to a busy signal if he thought it would listen to him," the other man said.

"Of course they want to tear down the Madame Walker building," Knowledge Allah said. "They ought to leave well enough alone. Let money stay here in our community before our people have had enough and there's another rebellion."

"By 'rebellion,' you mean 'riot'?" Sugar voice rose with skepticism.

"The white man's 'riot' *is* the black man's 'rebellion.' When people resist a racist and oppressive power structure, it's a rebellion."

"Listen here Ramadan Raheem," Sugar said. "The last time we 'resisted' a Roselyn Bakery to the ground and all we managed to do was 'rebel' all the windows out of the laundromat."

"This is why we can't have nice things," the old man said.

"Sho you right," the other man said.

"Wait, hold up," Sugar pointed to the screen. "Turn that up."

The old man slowly scooted out of his chair and began to shuffle toward the electro-vision. Knowledge Allah dashed past him to turn up the volume. He cranked a knob and the signal control to adjust the picture. An image of Sleepy sharpened into view. Sugar's monkey screeched.

"*... of the pair has been identified as Hubert "Sleepy" Nixon. He is considered a person of interest, a fugitive in connection to domestic terrorist activity. Authorities are searching for him and his partner throughout Indianapolis. They will be apprehended, and the security of the city restored.*"

"What daguerreotype of you did they find? Could they make you any darker?" Sugar asked.

"You look like an inkblot test," Knowledge Allah said.

"A terrorist?" Sleepy asked. Not that he or most anyone he knew believed anything that came out of either the *Vox Dei* daily paper or *Vox Populi* broadcasts' propaganda machine, it disconcerted his spirit to see such a crude caricature of himself as well as hear the aspersions to his character. "Terrorist? I ain't terrorized anyone since my little brother was a baby."

"They got you good, man," Sugar said. "What you going to do?"

The more he stared at his image on the screen, the more Sleepy found that he couldn't simply abide. He hated the way his black skin, pixilated and smeared, automatically consigned him to a status he could never hope to escape. No matter how he dressed, no matter how he behaved, he'd always be marked. "I need a favor."

"Don't know if I want to be doing business with a future Unperson," Sugar smirked, already beginning his negotiations. It was nothing personal, strictly business.

"I'll pay in advance." Sleepy started counting out credits. "Mind if I stash a few things with you?"

Sugar had significant real estate holdings all about the area, buying up his relatives' homes if they were about to be evicted. Speculating on vacant properties. Secretly purchasing a few corporate properties using partners and proxies he'd buy out later. "No problem. What sort of access you need?"

"Off the beaten track, where I can check in on it from time-to-time."

"I got you. Anything else?" Sugar scribbled an address and handed him the piece of paper.

"I may need a place to crash 'til I figure out my next move," Sleepy said.

"We," Knowledge Allah limped beside him. "Where he goes, I go."

SIX

ALL ALONG THE WATCHTOWER

Vox Dei *Data Files: The United States of Albion shone as the most prosperous colony in service to the Albion Empire. With its plantation farms and free labor force, America was considered the dirty sweatshop engine that propelled the Empire. Even the upper crust of the American social strata was held in tacit contempt by the Albion proper, with them being unwilling to acknowledge how they managed to keep their hands so clean. The force of her colonialist spirit had long ago reduced the issue of slavery to a low simmer and the much talked about threat of a United States Civil War never came to pass. With the rise of the automata, however, the economics of the unseemly endeavor proved too deleterious and the slaves were released.*

A VOICE SQUAWKED from the speaker box on the ceiling of Sophine's lab. Dimly aware of the metallic thrum interrupting her, her mind immediately leaped to the mechanics of running lines from a central computing system to a miniaturized speaker box, pistons translating vibrations into the approximation of voice. The tiny voice repeated its interruption, now with a hint of irritation to it.

"Sophine, were you expecting a visitor?"

"No, Dr. Yeager." Sophine straightened in her seat, her aching muscles letting her know exactly how long she had remained hunched over the valves, cogs, and coils that lay scattered before her. Her workbench resembled an automaton having regurgitated its insides. Raising her goggles to her forehead, she shut off her hand-held torch, the reflection of its blue flame arcing across the surfaces like brewing lightning. Every surface of her metallic workbench had been wiped and wiped again. Not an instrument out of place nor the slightest accumulation of dust. Sophine pressed her hands to the small of her back, teasing out the tensions which had migrated there over the last few hours. "Who is it?"

"He claims to be your father." The metallic voice contained a sneer to it.

"Not many would dare make so bold a claim. I'll be right there."

"You do know that I'm not your secretary, don't you?"

Sophine ignored the last comment from Dr. Yeager. As Principal Investigator, he headed up their department, but he also ferreted out information like an addict. Curiosity alone drove him to find out who might be inquiring after her. As Principal Investigator and head of the department, Dr. Yeager could stall the publication schedule of any member of their team. Everyone in the department competed for patents, status, resources, lab space, and above all, Lord Melbourne's attention. The division reported to Dr. Yeager, he reported to the board, and the board to Lord Melbourne. With Lord Melbourne's ties to the Pinkerton Agency, rumors began to float about a possible cabinet position as head of the Ministry of Defense. All department heads scrambled in anticipation of the leadership changes due to be created should Lord Melbourne leave.

Much to her father's chagrin, she had accepted the position at ZeroDyne Industries. He now groused about the house like a child pouting that they had been chosen last for a game of football. The Colonel had hardly spoken a word, locking himself away in his study, making his mysterious phone calls and receiving communiqués at all hours of the night. He turned away most of his meals. If he passed her in the hallways during chance encounters in the night, he greeted her with a furtive grunt and chose to study the minutiae of the carpets. She hated the growing chasm between them as it reminded her of how distant he became before he sent her off to Lady Churchill's Finishing School for Girls. Or to Oxford University. It was his ritual of letting her go.

By the time she reached the ZeroDyne Industries welcome desk, Colonel Winston leaned against his trusty cane, chatting amiably with the receptionist. Three security guards positioned themselves about him, crawling from whatever cubby-holes they were usually stationed in. The receptionist, a sallow-faced woman with hard cheekbones and graying hair, glanced nervously from him to the guards. With the slightest turn of his eyes, Sophine saw a flash of the man he used to be. Defiant. Unafraid. Calculating the best way to take down all of the guards, old man or not.

"What are you doing here?" Sophine made quite the production of wrapping her arms around him, an exaggerated picture of Daddy's Little Girl, which seemed to put the guards at ease.

"Meeting with Lord Melbourne." He stiffened at the contact, as if measuring her potential as a threat, unused to so public a display of affection.

"Another one? People will begin to whisper." She squeezed again. Until he relaxed in her arms—and she was certain he wouldn't overreact—she held on before releasing him.

"I'm certain they already are." The Colonel turned and glared at the guards without apology, long used to going through life as a suspect of one thing or another. He had a manner about him, an implied threat to his steps. Like he never attempted to fit in and took pride in being where he wasn't supposed to, daring people to deny him entry. "Is it a crime to visit my little girl before my appointment with her employer?"

"Not a crime, but they do love their protocols." Sophine absently led them back toward her lab, her steps now guided by muscle memory. She hated drawing attention to herself in any new situation, preferring to learn the lay of the land before riddling it full of divots.

"What kind of work are you doing?" The Colonel exaggerated

his limp as they walked along. He loved it when people underestimated him. His eyes, however, missed nothing.

"I can't talk about it."

"Big picture stuff; not state secrets," the Colonel said. "I just want to know how my little girl spends her days."

"That's twice."

"Twice what?"

"Twice you've called me your 'little girl.'"

"There a crime in that now?" The Colonel probed her in the annoyingly knowing way of his.

Sophine had no idea why the words disturbed her as much as they did. Perhaps the implication that he saw her as the same pigtailed child who ran about the house, taking apart any device before putting them back together. A girl to be protected, shelved on a mantle, admired, but never touched. Or perhaps sarcasm hid behind them, a young lady playing in a man's world, never to be seen as anything more than a cute affectation. The thought of the words approaching true affection was not in her top five list of possibilities.

"Robotics. Think of me as a professional tinkerer. They pretty much just want me to explore my curiosities. I have my own assistant, Alejandra Lopera. Young. Smart. Pretty. You'd like her. My Principal Investigator is a bit of an ass, but nothing I can't handle. My work keeps me focused. I'm dabbling with the interface between brain membranes and mechanical housing to direct robotic parts."

"Hmph," he sighed.

"You disapprove?"

"I didn't say anything."

"You say volumes in your sighs. I fluently speak your many nonsyllables of disapproval. You think this more of the ethical slippery slope which led to me being expelled from Oxford. That I tread none-too-lightly on creating an abomination against man and God."

"I realize that a highly learned *young woman*," the Colonel overemphasized the words, "such as yourself, already knows pretty much everything. That's the purview of youth. But perhaps, just perhaps, there is the slightest of possibilities that the breadth and scope of what all you do might take a moment to digest. Especially by a dinosaur such as your father, so woefully out of touch with the ways of young people these days. And, in the throes of digesting, his mind may race, in the protective manner of fathers to such *young women*, to calculate how a place like ZeroDyne may take advantage of even so knowledgeable a *young woman* of the world."

"Hmph," Sophine snorted.

"You doubt me?"

"I doubt everyone." Chiding herself, Sophine wanted to lower her walls. Defenses erected by necessity to protect her from a world she never managed to quite find her place in. Including her family. She wanted to believe that her father's eyes weren't filled with disappointment over her expulsion, that the quiet flame of pride he nurtured in her honor hadn't been extinguished. She wanted to believe she wasn't alone in this world.

"I just want you to be careful." The Colonel touched her arm, stopping her in her tracks.

Sophine stared at his hand on her arm. "Of what?"

"Whom. Lord Melbourne."

"He employs me. His motives are quite transparent."

"To spite me?"

"How narcissistic. You might want to make room for the slightest of possibilities that someone might find value in the 'breadth and scope' of what all I do."

"I have no doubt." The Colonel craned his neck about to check for any potential eavesdroppers. "What did your barristers say?"

"Anything I do and discover in this lab falls under his control. And ability to patent. Anything I work on for my own interest needs to be done away from here with no relation to what I do here."

"So, you have limited rights to your own thoughts as long as they don't compete with your thoughts at his company which he owns."

Sophine stood in impatient silence. Her lips pursed before she caught herself and returned her face to stony inscrutability. She conceded that he was correct but didn't want to give up any ground. "You don't trust him?"

"Not him. Not his kind."

"What kind is that?"

"A businessman with political connections, if not intentions." The Colonel's shoulders slumped. Again, so tired. So worn. So ... fragile. "Lord Melbourne is an agency man. High clearance due to corporate greed, political patronage, and military corruption. Alchemists, transcontinental alliance, Pinkertons, gangsters, and high-level intelligence operatives. He's untouchable. An invisible man."

"Not nearly that invisible," Lord Melbourne said. His ruddy complexion caused the illusion of thick creases in his face. Dabbing his sweating forehead with his handkerchief, he regained his composure. A woman trailed behind him with an odd bearing. Her rifle frock coat draped nearly to her ankles. Her double-breasted vest gave her the appearance of a sheriff. She carried a black gambler hat, twirling it around her hand. Her eyes, like shards of broken beer bottle—green and hard—studied them. Tall and statuesque, she had a cold kind of beauty most at home in a museum. The woman's long hair was a delicate orange, stained light by exposure to the sun's rays. Her freckles arrayed in an angry pattern on her face.

Without turning around, the Colonel said, "And he has a penchant for dramatic entrances."

"Not so dramatic. Not with my ears burning so."

"If your ears burned every time someone talked about you, all of downtown would be set ablaze. Though, I suspect, that's exactly how you like it." When he finally turned, the Colonel backed up a step from the woman even though she stood behind Lord Melbourne. "And who's this?"

"She's my escort. I'm an old man and she sees me from place to place."

"Does she have a name?" the Colonel asked.

"No," the woman said.

Sophine realized the particular distribution of the woman's body weight. Similar to the Colonel, despite appearing relaxed, her easy stance positioned for the easiest way to subdue all threats in the vicinity. She hard-eyed the Colonel. Satisfied in whatever appraisal she made, she donned her cowboy hat, turned, and departed.

"Cayt Sirango. She's always been a charmer," Lord Melbourne remarked once she was clearly out of earshot. "If you'll follow me, my private dining hall is this way."

"I'll head back to my lab," Sophine said.

"Nonsense." Lord Melbourne halted her with a touch to her arm. "You're already here."

"I don't know. You'll probably be bored by all of this business blather," the Colonel insisted.

"Why not join us? We have no secrets from family." Lord Melbourne held the crook of his arm out in invitation.

Sophine's inclination was to head back to her lab; to be secluded from others, surrounded by her ideas and equipment. But, despite his earlier words, she heard that unmistakable condescension in his voice. She hated the way her father kept shutting her out and calling it shielding her. "I am a little peckish."

"Wonderful."

The three of them had the dining hall to themselves. The staff cleared all the tables from the room save theirs. A servant filled their glasses with tea. Black, fresh-faced, a country innocence to his oval face, uniformed in a tight-fitting black suit. The Colonel watched the man without suspicion, but with something closer to pity mixed with disappointment, like he wanted something better for him. That was the look Sophine feared might be aimed at her.

"Ishmael, go ahead and serve the main course. I don't want to keep Ms. Jefferson away from her lab for too long." Lord Melbourne commanded the head of the table. His words caused businesses to rise or fall; banks to raise or lower their lending rates. As the American colonies of the Albion Empire teetered on the brink of war with Jamaica or the Five Civilized Nations, as it struggled with the internal tensions of the nation-state of Tejas, he had the ear of the United States' Regent. He was not one to be kept waiting.

The butler placed a plate in front of Sophine and lifted the silver dome. Roasted pheasant with red potatoes in a brown sauce. He nodded to her as if they shared a secret.

"You make people nervous, Winston. The wrong people." Lord

Melbourne started in as if continuing a conversation he'd been having in his head.

"I do that every time I stroll the streets at night," the Colonel said. "You get used to it."

"Don't be flippant. It's beneath you," Lord Melbourne scolded him in a tone reserved for children. "You have spurned every government contract that has come your way. Despite the fact that you've thwarted several espionage attempts to give our forces operational advances."

Unperturbed, the Colonel sipped his tea. "Surely you don't condemn me for keeping my business just that? My business."

"Surely *you* can imagine that it would only be a matter of time before those same potential friends got around to act against you, if only out of a sense of self-preservation."

"That's hardly what it is. Her Majesty's government needs no pretense to operate in its best interest. It simply hates any inconvenience."

"And you pride yourself on being as inconvenient as possible."

"Is that how you see me?" the Colonel asked.

A silence briefly yawned between them. The Colonel sipped his tea and Lord Melbourne stifled a glare. Sophine studied each in turn. She made a point of clinking her knife against her plate as she sliced into the pheasant. The smell of the food encouraged her appetite and distracted her from the notion that she was a trophy these two men quietly wrestled for. With all eyes on her, she gestured with her knife for them to continue.

"I see you as someone smart enough to understand the game yet filled with his own special brand of hubris to not play along," Lord Melbourne said.

"It's all about positioning. If you play their game, by their rules, you've already lost because the game is rigged in their favor from the beginning. So, you stake out a position for yourself, first learning all you can, then carving out your own space, and play by your own rules." The Colonel may have met Lord Melbourne's eyes, but Sophine had the distinct impression his words were for her.

"Admirable, but ultimately futile. It's naïve to believe that any space you carve out isn't still on their playing field." Lord Melbourne raised his glass to Sophine and gestured for the desserts to be brought out. "Have I ever mentioned that I knew your father briefly. A man of vision."

"Vision without character," the Colonel said, with an all-too-defensive sharpness.

"You judge him too harshly."

"Only as harshly as the light of history." The Colonel bristled. The topic of his family's history was a sore spot. Few dared make mention of it for fear of the Colonel's reprisals. Even if it jeopardized his own interests, he harangued any who tried to use it against him until he drove them into bankruptcy.

"He understood commodities knew no morality."

"He trafficked in his own people."

"See? Even now you hint that his so-called crime was worse because he dealt his own people."

"That's not what I mean ..." The Colonel's voice trailed off, not wanting to give up any ground yet conceding the point. Sophine recognized the signature look on his face as he cataloged this breach in etiquette. If he and Lord Melbourne were rivals before, the Colonel just dedicated the rest of his life and fortune to frustrating any deal of Lord Melbourne's he could.

"That's exactly what you meant. He understood that one had to do what they must to create the life they want."

Sophine had that uncomfortable feeling again but this time it was Lord Melbourne's words, which—while directed at the Colonel —were actually aimed for her consumption. She watched the two of them poke and jab in the way of not-quite-friends but without the hostility of enemies. More like brothers with irreconcilable differences, each marching down their own path. A measure of respect, jealousy, and resentment, all caught up in a miasma of male jockeying. She wondered why Lord Melbourne dared go where few others ventured. Perhaps he felt protected by their years of sparring. Perhaps he felt slighted over something. Even so, there was something else under their words. She was more certain than ever that the two competed for her interest. Her loyalty. That she was caught on an intricate, tenebrous web, with two spiders waiting on either side of it, wanting to draw her to their side. Each worked their own perverse machinations to turn her into a knowing and willing conspirator in their agenda. Though she wasn't sure if it was to protect her or devour her. Either way, she hated being anyone's plaything.

Lord Melbourne's mouth formed a fishhook of a smirk. "Some may believe that if you won't play ball, they will simply clear the board and try again when the new pawns emerge."

"We can't live forever," the Colonel said.

Sophine heard a tinge of resignation to her father's words. And an echo of sadness. She turned to him, but he kept his attention rapt on Lord Melbourne.

"Now, see, that's where I disagree." Lord Melbourne's voice raised to lighten the mood and change topics. "Some people choose not to. I simply don't accept it."

"Is it that simple?"

"That simple." Lord Melbourne eyed Sophine with the salivating stare of a man breaking a fast and spying the last biscuit. "With enough dedicated resources."

"Why are we here?" Sophine asked.

"Beans." Lord Melbourne let the words hang in the air for a heartbeat too long, overplaying his need to be dramatic. "Specifically, coffee beans. I've never understood the U.S.'s fascination with coffee. Completely uncivilized drink. Do you play the futures market?"

"We all should look to the future," she said.

"Quite. History casts a dim light on those who don't." Lord Melbourne gestured, and Ismael seemed to appear from the shadows to refill their glasses. "Your father always looks to the future."

"How so?" Sophine leaned in with interest. The Colonel reclined in his seat; his face placid, not anxious about where the conversation might end up.

"Well, let's take coffee beans. If a company controlling the sourcing of said coffee beans through Company A suddenly has a bumper harvest, what happens to the market?"

"Prices drop through the floor. Too much product over demand," Sophine speculated.

"True. But what if Company B, which controls distribution, chokes off the supply of beans, despite growing demand in China and India?"

"Are Companies A and B working together?"

"Funny you should ask that. The government started asking such questions. Wondering who, despite all the shell companies and proxies, may be behind those companies. Colonel, as I recall, you may have sold short on coffee, just before supplies flooded the market."

Sipping his tea, the Colonel leveled heavy eyes at Lord Melbourne. "Yes. Quite a fortuitous go of things."

"Quite so." Lord Melbourne took his time to dissect the piece of meat on his plate. Nearly smacking his lips with the effort, he savored the bite with exaggerated flourish.

"One thing I know about the Colonel," Sophine offered with hesitancy, treading lightly between speculation and—sharing too much—accidentally betraying family trust, "what you're looking at with him is never what you should be paying attention to."

"Splendid. Too bad the government can't examine things with such alacrity. I started thinking this seems like a pretty sloppy and heavy-handed maneuver. Almost ... distracting."

"Misdirection." Sophine turned to the Colonel, intrigued and seeking approval. He picked at his salad coolly.

"Exactly what I thought. So, I started wondering, what should I be looking at? Backed by an influx of hard cash, a suddenly flush and shrewd investor could make an offer on a fraction of a company's shares. This sort of commitment works rather like a promissory note to purchase securities in said company. Even if the shares are offered through a shell company. If that offer succeeds ..."

"... the rest of that company's assets become the collateral to finance the rest of the acquisition," Sophine finished.

"You raised a smart one." Lord Melbourne tipped an imaginary hat to the Colonel.

"I always thought so," the Colonel said with an odd beam of pride in his eyes.

Ishmael cleared the plates, then brought out the dessert. Bread and butter pudding, layered slices of buttered bread covered in custard. Raisins dotted the mix.

"Luckily," Lord Melbourne took a bite of the dessert and closed his eyes to fully experience the taste. A moment later, he opened them and continued. "That company was able to call in many of its long-term notes and, aided by a banking hiccup which delayed things, was able to fend off the hostile takeover."

"There was nothing hostile about it. Just business," the Colonel said.

"Just business. Never personal." Lord Melbourne paused, his spoon hovering above the pudding, considering his words. "One has to love the spirit of capitalism. Still, a long way to go because someone doesn't know how to pick up the phone and play nice with others."

"Sometimes we have to communicate in the language in which we'll be best heard." The Colonel used his smile to fend off the thrusts of his barbs.

"How ..." Sophine feared she knew the answer to her question even as it formed in her mind; however, she had to hear it for herself. "How long ago was all of this?"

"I believe the maneuverings began soon after you began your employ at ZeroDyne. Though, to be fair, the maneuvers with the coffee price would have taken months to engineer. Pieces put into place as a contingency on the off chance that certain events occurred."

Whatever meaning hid buried in those words were the first to truly stir the Colonel. Shifting in his seat, he ground his forefingers into the table as he spoke. "You play too many games, Leighton."

"Just making a point." Lord Melbourne took several more spoonfuls of pudding. "We both know your hands aren't as clean as you'd like to claim. Men in our position rarely get here ... unsullied."

"You didn't call me over for lunch just to rub my face in a failed venture or else we'd be dinner companions every week." The Colonel used his fork to slice potatoes before popping them in his mouth. "What is it you want?"

"The air. Specifically, your airships."

"No." The Colonel dabbed his mouth with a napkin.

"We can do much more together, rather than constantly striving to outmaneuver one another."

"No," the Colonel said flatly, not inviting further debate.

"Why be so damned intransigent?" Lord Melbourne dabbed his mouth before wadding his napkin and tossing it to the table.

"We each draw lines for ourselves. I drew two very specific ones for me ... and my family. One, we would not traffic in human indenturtude. Two, we would not be a part of the military complex. I don't care how tangentially."

Not wanting to give either man the satisfaction that she paid any attention to their game of one-upmanship, Sophine pushed the raisins about in her bowl of pudding as if making do with it having not being prepared to her liking. With their insults, venom, and sudden heat, she could no longer tell where the rivalry ended, and true enmity began.

"You live somewhere south of the ideals you express." Lord Melbourne jabbed his empty spoon at him for emphasis. "While you remain engaged with me, your other enemies, and you have plenty of enemies, O Righteous One, become entrenched. You need me."

"Need you?" The Colonel's arms nearly thrashed apart in disbelief and protest.

"Need my resources. Need my connections. Need my will."

"Listen here and listen close," the Colonel said. "I will go my own way, be my own man, alone if need be."

"Leaving you flailing at shadows."

"Better than dancing by another's strings."

"This is a one-time offer," Lord Melbourne said.

Sophine stopped chewing and turned toward him. The finality of his tone left her unsettled.

"Is that a threat?" The Colonel slowly leveled his steady gaze on Lord Melbourne.

"Hear what you want. You are running out of time. There are forces moving against you ..."

"... including you?"

"We all must do what we must to survive. It's just business," Lord Melbourne said, his voice thick with entreaty and something ... sad.

"Never personal," the Colonel agreed.

IN THE MORNING ROOM, Sophine read next to the fireplace. The Colonel still hadn't arrived home for the evening. At a clatter from the front door, she set her book on the end table and glided through the hallways to meet him just as their automata took his coat and hat. When he noticed her, he paused, fully taking her in. With the slightest of upturns to his lips, he cocked his head to the side, indicating for her to follow him. He swept open the door to his study, allowing her to enter first. He made his way to the table cart of drinks, but his manner seemed distracted. Tilting his head like a dog sniffing the air at something amiss, he strode over to the grand bay window and latched it fast. He returned to the cart and poured himself a drink.

"Brandy?" he offered.

"No, thanks." The fire of righteousness filled her. Her father called it the affliction of youth. That heady time of invincibility and fearlessness, the sheer potential for anything, before age, world-weariness, and cynicism doused the flames of passion. For her part, Sophine always believed herself born in the wrong time or place. She wanted so much more out of life, this world. Not to be confined by other people's ideas of who she was and who she was meant to be. This wasn't her world. She was meant to resist it, perhaps even reshape it in some tiny way. At the very least, she didn't have to tolerate it.

"I'll pour you one anyway for when you change your mind."

Sophine crossed her arms across her chest. She hated the way they fell into their usual patterns. She so wanted to push past the years of accrued nonsense and simply share a real moment with him. But sometimes it seemed that the groove they fell back into was where he was most comfortable with her. In argument. She resumed her part of their dance. "Why'd you ask then?"

"You still had a choice." The Colonel squeezed behind his desk, the very act itself seemed to wear him out. His chair sighed as he settled into it. He hunched over his drink.

With something akin to pity, Sophine eased into her role rather than unleash all salvos. "Like me choosing to accept the job at ZeroDyne?"

"It was your choice."

"And it was yours to attempt to buy the company," her rebuke remained gentle.

"It was a solid investment."

"And not the act of an overprotective father seeking to guard his daughter."

"Ever a father's prerogative." The Colonel's voice softened, thick with warmth. Finding strength in her words, he toasted her and drank. "Don't take it for granted. I'm not always going to be around and one day this will all be yours."

Sophine picked up the glass he had poured for her and walked the perimeter of the study. She meandered to the Colonel's desk and casually glanced at the papers scattered there. The communiqués from Panama, legal briefs from his barristers regarding trades and purchases.

A glass shattered against the floor.

The Colonel slumped in his chair; his arm dangled off the side over the shattered remains of his glass.

"Colonel?" Sophine dropped her glass and crouched at his side. Pressing her fingers to his wrist, she checked for a pulse. She lowered her cheek against his hoping to feel his breath. Desperate tears filled her eyes as she shook him. "Daddy?"

SEVEN
CAUGHT, CAN WE GET A WITNESS

The Indianapolis Recorder: *The Old Fourth Ward was the oldest African American settlement in Indianapolis and among the oldest land developments of the city. When it was first established, the 1870 census estimated a population at 30,000 people. Once slavery was abolished, the people were allowed a measure of autonomy and the residents took to calling it Freetown Village. The other major concentration of black people was within the Mile Square, specifically the undercity people called The Tombs. In Freetown Village, people still clung to the illusion of the dream of a better life. In The Tombs, the dream—even the hope to dream—had died.*

Despite its nickname, Freetown Village was occupied territory. The people were at the mercy of landlords because most people rented their houses; at the mercy of crime lords, who monetized desperation and powerlessness; at the mercy of COPs, who policed the territory in the interest of the state, which merely needed the "problems" contained. This was even more true in The Tombs.

THE OVERCITY of Indianapolis could afford sunlight, with its tall, gleaming buildings jutting into the horizon. Air tram cars ferried passengers from skyscraper to skyscraper so that their feet were never despoiled by the taint of touching the streets of the undercity.

Graffiti close to the undercity entrance decorated many of the building walls, both pictorial history and guide to the city. Murals covered the surrounding concrete walls. Local heroes—Madame C.J. Walker, John Freeman, Father Justice, Rev. Andrew J. Brown, the Star Child, Rev. Moses Broyles, Mari Evans—stared down on the block like apostles on stained brick panels. A damp umber settled over the city blocks, a dreariness to mood and spirit which grayed the world around them. People sat in their windows, legs dangling over the side, watching the world parade by. Avoiding the Arclight glare of street lamps, they stepped into the shadow of a billboard for COPs. An accusatory finger pointed at them under the words "Respect the law."

"The law is meant to serve, not be masters. It licenses our torturers. To respect the law is to surrender," Knowledge Allah opined to no one in particular. "They don't want us here. They're done with us and here we are, swept up under the rug."

Sleepy entered a theater at the west end of the City Market and descended a large stairwell. Knowledge Allah, with his red-tinted hair tightened into a series of twists, like arthritic fingers dangling from his skull, limped alongside him. Wind-blighted brick walls gave way to limestone. A series of cantilevered brass tubes ran along the ceiling. The walls thrummed as large fans behind them whirred to circulate the air. A cast iron steamman, with a top hat and a cadaverous smile, loaded coal. The hydraulics of its pneumatic legs wheezed with each movement, its features a cold caricature of a person. Tanks on its back powered it; its pressure gauge crept higher as it exerted itself.

The Tombs—the undercity of Indianapolis—languished in the eternal night of the lower avenue. Its residents lived in the shadows of the downtown spires—sunlight parceled out in dribs and drabs—in the reflections of a better life. The tunnels beneath the city were old when Indianapolis was founded. Some whispered that this was the original Indianapolis and the overcity was built over it like some steam-fueled clockwork tombstone burying its past. Before the

Pinkertons received their localized charter, the police used the underground alleyways as a shooting range. During the winter of 1912, the homeless slept down there. In 1913, the tunnels flooded, so by that winter, black people who were off the work cycle or who would otherwise be labeled Unpersons took up residence down there. Each week a non-descript city vehicle deposited a load of Unpersons released from The Ave, most of whom were elderly or had health issues severe enough that it cut into the prisons profits to house them. With no place to go or money to get there, they drifted down into The Tombs.

In The Tombs, gas-lit lamps illumined every intersection, showering huddles of men in their flickering light as they shot dice. Old men huddled in puddles of light, drinking brandy and smoking cigars blunted with chiba. Their garrulous conversation of the most impolitic kind filled the night with the bluster of oafs. A twinge of jealousy at not being able to join in fluttered in Sleepy's chest.

"The key for us is to lay low." Sleepy took a tone much like explaining something simple to a child with Knowledge Allah. "I figure that we're a couple of needles in a needle stack down here."

"Down here?" Knowledge Allah let the words drip from his tongue as if measuring how sour they tasted. "You make it sound like we're lost on a safari. The reality is that your place on the west side, where you ran off to in order to distance yourself from your people, is no longer a safe option for you. So, it's time to get over whatever sense of shame you feel and get comfortable among your own. If we'll still even have you."

Though Knowledge Allah delivered the words in an even, matter-of-fact tone, they landed on Sleepy with the weight of a downtown high rise collapsing on him. Lips pursed into silence, Sleepy withdrew into his own thought space, his long-ago learned coping strategy for dealing with conflict. Especially in The Tombs. He mentally pieced together retorts while keeping his face implacable, as to not give whoever caused him to retreat there the satisfaction of witnessing him spiral.

The Tombs was his birthplace. Part of him never truly left. His parents signed their marriage contract formally granting them licensure to start their unipod while in The Tombs. Marriage was doled out in five-year increments among the poor to "protect the sanctity of the institution" the politicians insisted. Unipods, the license to have children, was only granted to two-parent households. To have children outside of a contract risked the children receiving Unperson status just for being born. The Tombs were filled with Unpersons who managed to escape being sent to The Ave. But they lived as refugees in their own country. His earliest memories involved running through the musty catacombs, heedless of the rats, playing tag with his friends through the alleyways. He spent many a night bundled in hemp blankets. After a few years, his parents managed to move to the Meadows and later to Freetown Village. Once he moved to the northwest side, he never looked back.

"Here they are. I got 'em.

Sweet gapes, watermelon, watermelon, watermelon,

Sugar bananas, pe-eee-aches,

I got 'em.

Red, ripe tomatoes, I got 'em."

A fruit vendor led a horse-drawn cart, its red and yellow hues flared against the dreary backdrop of the streets. His sing-song holler fell into an easy tune. Sleepy and Knowledge Allah scooted past him without making eye contact, lest they receive his full sales pitch.

"What's the plan?" Sleepy asked, not in the mood to hear any more of Knowledge Allah's opinions. "I don't have much beyond disappear in The Tombs, like we've entered some sort of ghetto witness protection program."

"Who can we reach out to?" Knowledge Allah's limp became more pronounced.

"Lost Nation? They've been doing some good in the neighbor-hood. Organizing like a community version of the Pinkertons."

Knowledge Allah stiffened at the mention of the name.

"You all right?" Sleepy asked.

It fluttered for a moment, like a wisp of steam curling up from a grate before disappearing, but something deep and sad crossed Knowledge Allah's face. "I've ... had some dealings with the Lost Nation. I know some of their leaders, but I've no inclination to be around them. Even though I called some of them friends, and some of them carried me through my worst time, seeking them out would serve to only remind me of that time."

Almost hesitant, not wanting to scare Knowledge Allah off when he sounded on the verge of revealing something real and true about himself, Sleepy said, "It sounds like there's a story there."

"I wasn't always so ..."

"... ridiculously militant?" Though he wanted to draw the man out a bit, Sleepy couldn't help but launch a barb delivered with the same matter-of-fact tone he had been injured by.

Knowledge Allah's face darkened with a glower, then seemed to reconsider it. "Conscience. My so-called 'militancy' is simply my cultural nationalistic awareness and the resulting constant vigilance required to resist an oppressive system."

"You never turn off, do you?"

"Ever. Vigilant." A storefront meeting place between a liquor store and a speakeasy. Red brick building with yellow trim, its top like a bulb, painted green. Black curtains covered every window. Knowledge Allah slowed his steps as they passed it. A couple of gentlemen exchanged peace on its doorstep before catching sight of him and eyeing him with suspicion. "You never know where your enemies may spring from."

Too many people pushed creaky carts full of discarded junk, artifacts from the city above or a life that once was. The corridors kept everything close. Conversations echoed, like whispers of ghosts long passed. Despite the fans and ventilation, the smells clung, a miasma of cloying body odor, a splash of piss, and the sinking stench of the overcity that seeped into clothes.

"Do you know that dude over there? He seems to be avoiding your attention in particular." Sleepy nodded toward a gaunt gentleman who took special pains to not appear to be observing them. A thick layer of pomade coated his hair, to the point where the hair paint looked like tattooed finger waves. His suit jacket was freshly pressed and impeccably tailored down to its long tails. "What's up with his hair? It looks like he smeared shoe polish over ramen noodles."

"I see they package self-hate in a jar now." Knowledge Allah leaned heavily against his cane. "Yeah, I know that fool. That's Tigga. He's one of Sugar's soldiers."

As if he knew he was being discussed, Tigga donned a top hat—cocking it to a side like a bird distracted by prey—and disappeared into a crowd.

"A friend of yours?" Sleepy asked.

"I ain't studdin' him." The word "studying" collapsed into two syllables. The words sounded like they came from someone other than Knowledge Allah but from someone born and raised in the fury of The Tombs. "He's like too many Nubian brothers I know. Negroppeans, identifying with their oppressors like they have Stockholm syndrome. He exists in the well-charted territory beyond pain, beyond shame, in the wilderness of self-hate. His whole life through school, until he dropped out, he'd been told something was wrong with him. That brand sunk deep within him, the same way an automaton was programmed. The stigma gestated within him until it blossomed into him getting in trouble. Fulfilling the expectations and beliefs of those who programmed him."

Knowledge Allah slumped as if suddenly tired.

"You all right?"

Knowledge Allah composed himself. "As I said, I haven't always been on an enlightened path. I was once just another lost, knot-head kid running around these streets. What the government would label an Unperson. Didn't know my father. My mother, either, since they refused to sign a unipod contract. The Tombs raised me. I was already sliding into the life—an operator, hustling, slick, working every angle—ready for Sugar to scoop me up and make me one of his lieutenants, when Father Justice found me."

"You know Father Justice?"

"For a time, I was his favored sun."

"Then what happened?"

"The way of fathers and suns, I suppose." Knowledge Allah let the words trail off, an unspoken understanding passed between them. In those few words, Sleepy heard a similar uncollectable debt owed to his father. His heart hardened to the idea of his father because fathers had a way of continuing to disappoint, even in their absence.

"That why you want no part of the Lost Nation?"

"Reasons. Still, though, they took me in, gave me purpose and direction. Even if we no longer walk the road together, I owe them a debt I cannot repay."

Sleepy wasn't sure he actually liked Knowledge Allah and failed to understand why he stayed with him. Surely, he'd be able to navigate his own well-being in The Tombs without him. Every conversation felt like an interrogation, a scolding, or criticism. At every turn, Sleepy wanted to suggest an auto-anatomical storage idea for what Knowledge Allah could do with his opinions. At the same time, it was as if he also wanted the man's approval. Like Knowledge Allah saw something in him, something worthwhile, that he wanted to draw out. Sleepy really craved his pipe and the opportunity to smoke right about now.

"My father was physically there for us. I can say at least that much about him. In every other way, he remained a stranger to me. I never knew, much less understood, the man. I think he wanted it that way. To not get too close to me. I might have embarrassed him. I did that sometimes." Despite the high vaulted ceilings, whenever Sleepy walked The Tombs, he had the sensation of being trapped in a labyrinth. Sleepy leaned against a pillar girding the side of the avenue opposite a storefront. Knowledge Allah sat on the curb, using his handkerchief as a cushion. With Knowledge Allah out of his eyeline, Sleepy continued talking. "So, I never really knew my father. I was one of the lucky ones. My father remained within our unipod. He wasn't one of the 'breeders' forced into insemination ranks or one of the rogues who abandoned their unipods. When the marriage contract expired, Pops left. Mom held the unipod together until her death. My brothers and sisters got shipped off to relatives."

"Leaving you alone and adrift," Knowledge Allah said in a flat tone.

"I wouldn't say all that."

"I recognize the fire that burns in you. It gives your work its spark. But there's a danger to it, a dark edge. Like any flame, the more you feed it, the more it grows."

"Sometimes you're a little too ... on point."

"Then let me ask you this: what do you want?"

"To be left alone, so I can get high."

"No. I mean, how can I put this?" Knowledge Allah sighed deeply, his face scrunched as he grasped at how best to come at a puzzle. "A hero in a story has to want something. Have some goal he wishes to accomplish. Have some greater purpose or vision for his life that he strives for. What's yours?"

"To be left alone, so I can get high."

"You weary me sometimes."

"Then my job here is done," Sleepy said.

Along the plaza, men in grungy clothing slept off the previous night's elixir of forgetfulness. The night pilloried by screams of women in obvious mental distress berating no one in particular. A wrought iron fence bounded the far end of the block, the thick bars dividing the view of the overcity. The fruit stand man ambled along, parking in an open lot tucked between vacant structures. His hair in cornrows, his beard groomed to a severe point, he kept a cigarette tucked behind his left ear. His blue denim overalls hung from his thin frame.

"Wat-oh, wat-oh ... got your watermelon.

Wat-oh, wat-oh ... got your watermelon.

Uh-oh, uh-oh ... got them strawberries.

Uh-oh, uh-oh ... got them strawberries.

See them pretty ladies? Make me wanna holler again.

Wat-oh, wat-oh ..."

The fruit vendor slowed, nearing Sleepy. "Looks like you could stand to mix in a few fruits in your diet." The man's tone was jovial and light, his words filled with a casual thoughtlessness.

"You calling me fat? Is insulting potential customers some sort of new selling technique?" Sleepy mustered as much vitriol as he could in the moment, but given his to-the-bone weariness, barely made him sound piqued.

"Come on now," the vendor protested. "I was just messing with you. I didn't think you'd be so thin-skinned about it." The vendor turned to Knowledge Allah in quiet entreaty.

Knowledge Allah raised his hands to signal that the man was on his own.

"I have half a mind to ..." Sleepy's eyes lit up. "Oh, you have bananas."

"What are you doing?" Knowledge Allah asked.

"Impulse control has never been my strong suit." Sleepy plucked one from a bunch. He met Knowledge Allah's accusing eyes. "Besides, I'm a little peckish and a brother could use some potassium."

"That'll be four credits," the fruit vendor said.

"Four credits? For a single banana?" Sleepy turned the banana over in his hands. Perhaps gold laced its skin because that was the only thing that could demand such rates. "Topside I'd pay two for the entire bunch."

"Well, you're not topside now, are you?" The fruit vendor's voice shifted, a measure of steel entering into it, signifying that play time was over. "Laws of supply and demand."

"Laws of the crab bucket is more like it," Knowledge Allah said.

"Look here, keep your banana. That's what I get for veering off my natural dietary inclinations." Sleepy tossed the banana back into the cart. He pivoted in an attempt to turn on his heel, when he lost his balance. His arms pin-wheeled until he found the cart's edge to rebalance himself. The cart tipped due to Sleepy's sudden additional weight. Several fruits toppled out and bounced along the ground. The trio watched the fruit in silent unison until they rolled to a stop.

"My bad, man." Sleepy beat over to help pick up the bruised fruit.

"Your bad? I don't even know what that means." The fruit vendor pressed his fists into his sides, posing like an indignant hero. "Twenty credits."

"Twenty credits? For what?" Sleepy stopped mid-scoop to protest.

"Damaged merchandise."

"It's fruit. Wash them off, good as new."

As Sleepy turned to demonstrate, a couple of kids scurried from the shadows, grabbed the scattered fruit, and dashed off down the corridor. Sheep-faced, Sleepy turned back to the man and shrugged. Kids would be kids. He remembered many times when he was their age scrambling after a fruit vendor, hoping for him to hit a bump and possibly jostle a loose piece of fruit free. It was all part of the survival games played in The Tombs.

"Thirty credits." The vendor spit to the side.

"What?"

"Can't wash fruit that's not there. And Sugar demands his cut. Thirty credits."

Sleepy understood that the man had to re-coup his loss and he must strike him as an easy mark. But he hasn't been gone from The Tombs so long to just be punked out. "They're kids. You need to adjust for inventory loss. That's the cost of doing business."

The man patted about his neck until he withdrew a whistle. He blew several shrill notes while pointing at Sleepy.

"Are you for real now?" Sleepy shifted his weight. His bold and cheerful, slightly formal, manner turned into something irritated and solid.

"Brothers," Knowledge Allah stepped between them. "Surely this misunderstanding doesn't need to escalate into anything more."

"Who you blowing that whistle for?" Sleepy stepped closer until Knowledge Allah's hand met his chest, halting his advance. "It's not like COPs ever come down here."

Every organism had their parasites and predators. The citizens of The Tombs were trapped between gangsters like Sugar and the arrogant autonomy of the COPs. Emerging from the far avenue, high boots and then black jackets descended the stairwells. A squad of COPs parade-marched in straight-legged step. They patrolled the sidewalks, casually scanning faces with a glare of suspicion. Their guns aimed toward the ceiling, scattering any kids who scrambled along the rafters. Their slow march a reminder to the residents that they lived in occupied territory.

"How did the armed will of the state get here so quickly?" Knowledge Allah asked.

"Knowledge Allah," Sleepy tugged at his arm without taking his eyes from the approaching COPs. "Given our ... dubious relationship with law enforcement at the moment, perhaps a strategic withdrawal may be in order."

"Any act of resistance in occupied territory can only be met by the full flexing of said occupying forces."

"And discretion is the better course of valor." Sleepy yanked at his arm.

There was a tell-tale look some denizens of Freetown Village had, like an advanced case of The Shattered. One that spoke of having been broken by their circumstance. A hardness in their eyes he'd not noticed when he was young. The need to meet the everyday aggressions of life head-on. Anger and defeat passed down from parent to child, another story to serve as institutional memory. Lessons imparted generation after generation, as the system crushed their parents and their parents before them. The shards of their pride patched together unable to form the most threadbare of cloaks. The ones who scavenged through their lives, without hope, without community. Climbing over one another or dragging another underfoot in order to make it another day. Curious onlookers gathered, close enough to watch but not so near as to be caught up by the arriving COPs. The bodies pressed closer as the crowd thickened. The fruit vendor whistled again, pointing in their direction.

One of the COPs spoke to the vendor, who pointed out several of the kids. The COPs began to round them up roughly. Sleepy backed Knowledge Allah away, about to disappear into the nearest alleyway, but found their route cut off by the massing throng. They stayed within the crowd, just out of COP attention. One of the kids darted behind Sleepy. A COP followed. The kid clutched at Sleepy's leg.

"Hey, no need to be so rough." Sleepy paused, the optics of him standing between the COP and the child dawning on him.

"Get out of our way and let us do our job." The COP unholstered his baton.

"Sleepy," Knowledge Allah said in a cautioning tone, "you know they'd be happy to overreact to anything you say or even the hint of you demonstrating resentment or resistance. It's all the excuse they need."

"I'd hate to let a snide comment be my death sentence," Sleepy said. All around him, he recognized another look. The anger that bubbled just beneath the shattering.

"Get over here," the COP yelled at him.

"What for?" Sleepy asked.

"Detention. Interference with law officials during the commission of their duties."

"I ..." Locked in paralysis, Sleepy turned to Knowledge Allah with a questioning expression, not knowing how to react. In The Tombs, even in Freetown Village, citizens were baptized in self-hatred. One of the reasons he left was his fear of what would happen to him—to his mind, left to marinate in the culture and propaganda of inferiority—if he stayed. The secondary education teachers had been long trained to give up on people like him, and merely went through the motions of teaching or even bothering to encourage them. The main lesson absorbed was to at every turn to learn, and stay in, their place. Sleepy was always a lousy student. Sleepy knew the power of hopelessness, anger, and grief erupting in a wail of angels weeping. The weight he carried with him—like the ballasts tied to slaves to dump them overboard when the illegal ships were threatened with capture. He settled snugly into the blanket of fear that enveloped him. Fear wasn't bad, if it didn't paralyze you. His jackrabbit pulse beat so hard he had trouble breathing.

"Let go of me!" a man shouted, turning to scream at another man.

"Get away from me!" another yelled, drawing everyone's attention. Sleepy recognized Tigga, who shoved the man. The human turbulence rippled through the crowd like a contagion. The crowd began to grumble and surge forward. Sleepy felt it, too. Pressure built behind the eyes. Blood raced through their veins in an adrenaline rush. The throat tightened, as if locked in a silent cry. The mouth dried. Thought dissolved to mental static as frenzy overtook the crowd. Buried in the shards of broken glass was the purging of their souls. The pent-up rage of every slight, every hurt, every indignity ever suffered, the turning snarl of an exasperated dog at the hands of a cruel owner. The grumbles turned into raised voices. Sleepy released short, sharp breaths, in barely controlled hyperventilation.

"Enough," he yelled, shirking off the COP and voicing the collective thought.

Tigga was the first to throw a stone.

People picked up anything nearby to hurl at the COPs. Rocks, garbage, fruit. The officers huddled with their backs to one another, forming a wall of blue, anxious for the opening to use their batons. Finally, the crowd surged toward them. People lashed out in every direction. The melee spread further with each passing moment. The crash of windows echoed into the bleak darkness of The Tombs. COPs launched flash-bang grenades to disperse the crowd. Smoke poured from everywhere. People made their escape between the rocks thrown at windows. The crowd dared the fruit vendor to move. His cart was set aflame. Men, women, and children ran about, unafraid, handkerchiefs over their mouths. The frenzy wasn't without purpose.

The parade of humanity—all patched hand-me-downs, gray clothes, frayed cuffs—marched with the inexorable force of anger. A presence much larger than any one single person. They had simply had enough and were ready for a new order to reign. But to usher in the new, the old had to go. Not that many had thought through their intentions beyond taking the opportunity to beat some folks or break some stuff. A scream echoed in the night; another grief-stricken wail drowned out by the cacophony of directionless rage.

Knowledge Allah became a symphony of rage in E minor, his perpetual black eyes reflecting burning fires.

An orchestra leader sitting back and enjoying the music he directed, oddly detached from the efforts of his labor. The Tombs was on the brink of being reduced to smoking embers and piles of brick. Windows smashed. Doors kicked in. Looters ran amuck. The madness was only an excuse. The frenzy seized them full borne with white-hot rage. Black faces and brown faces and even a few white faces, all caught up in the throes of fury.

COPs scattered, battering any stray members of the surging crowd, hoping to take out the main rabble-rousers to take the steam out of them. Two COPs slammed into Sleepy, pinning him against a wall.

"You're coming with us." A COP placed Sleepy in handcuffs. "Staging an illegal gathering. Failure to disperse. Inciting a riot. And anything else we can think of."

EIGHT

I'LL BE MISSING YOU

Vox Dei Data Files: The Indianapolis City Hospital began when a smallpox epidemic prompted the city to build its first, 75 bed, charity hospital. It opened its doors in 1859, with its first building at Locke Street and Indiana Avenue. It offered medical and surgical treatment for those who couldn't be attended to by a doctor's house call. Dr. William Niles Wishard expanded the facilities, and the "Flower Mission Training School for Nurses" graduated its first class soon after. In 1887, its ambulances delivered the sick and injured to its doors, one of the first of its kind. As poverty increased, so did its patient population. Once a state-of-the-art medical facility, it opened its doors to treat the poor, who failed to recognize that chronic disease was a consequence of their lifestyle choices. Rather than give an individual the tools they would need to manage their own health needs, it fostered a system of dependency. Soon the hospital was overrun and fell into a state of chronic disrepair.

THE INDIANAPOLIS CITY HOSPITAL ambulance raced through the streets. Sophine now wished they lived in one of the downtown high-rises since then they would have been whisked to one of the many hospitals down there by air tram. New hospitals sprang up downtown like wild dandelions, competing for quality of care, the latest technology, and the patronage of the overcity dwellers. The City Hospital existed for the poor and indignant, but it only needed to keep the Colonel stable until its doctors could consult with the Jefferson family physician and be transferred somewhere proper. The clang of the ambulance's bell threatened to drive her mad. Its constant toll distorted by the speed of the vehicle, blurring into a long keening.

An ambulance attendant hunched over the Colonel, holding the cot he rested on whenever the ambulance took a corner too quickly. Machines clicked and beeped. An automaton stood in the front of the ambulance between them and the driver. Cool to the touch, due to its obvious state of disrepair, it had long been deactivated. Without its assistance, the attendant moved with a frantic air.

"Ma'am, I need you out of my way so that I can do my job." The ambulance attendant's tone was stern, both from urgency and condescension. His tone recalled her earlier hysterics.

"Do something!" Sophine had screamed at the attendants once they had arrived. Her constant harangue followed them as they raced through the house to collect her father. Not quickly enough by her estimation. She insisted that she accompany the Colonel. Ever the height of decorum, Lyonessa offered to meet them at the hospital once she composed herself. As far as Sophine was concerned, dignity and decorum be damned. She wasn't going to leave her father's side.

"Of course." Sophine shrank into herself, trying to accommodate the attendant, all the while feeling like a little girl banished to the corner. A thick line of sweat edged her father's hairline. He looked so small. So helpless. She dabbed his forehead and brushed his hair absently. She knew that he hated to look disheveled under any circumstance. The only thing a man had was his name and how he carried himself, he always said. She wasn't going to let him out of her sight and was going to make sure he was treated with respect.

The attendant maintained a controlled fussiness, checking the Colonel's pulse, monitoring his temperature, going through the motions of lifesaving measures. The Colonel's social position demanded that they spare no effort. A look passed between him and the driver. The attendant slipped a mask over the Colonel's face. What appeared to be a squeezebox in a plastic tube forced air into him.

"I'm sorry," he said.

"Why?" she asked sharply. His apology left her more disconcerted than him being stern with her. She flexed her fingers, winding them like a spider folding into itself. She needed someone to fight with. Someone to rage against. Anything to relieve her feeling of helplessness.

"He ..." Taken aback, the man seemed to reconsider his words. "It's all right if you hold his hand until we get there."

"I don't want to be in the way." Sophine found herself hesitant, a dire trepidation came with the thought, as if clutching his hand might hurt him.

"It's no trouble, miss." His tone had softened, his words almost consoling. Bracing her for what was to come. Truth was hard to disguise. She knew what was coming from the moment her father collapsed in his den.

THEY BURST through a set of double doors into the emergency room. Limestone porticos filled the pavilion, supported by huge Corinthian columns. Steam hissed along the vents. The exposed rivets along the entrance way provided evidence that the building saw no recent remodeling. The waiting bay was filled with shipwrecked souls washed upon a beach of medical need. A forlorn harbor of bodies waited, their injuries and maladies pressed close to them in an attempt to keep their business to themselves. Eyes filled with worry and grief, welling behind a dam of no news. Soul-weary folks tracking her with the interest of breaking the tedium of their existence.

Sophine believed them to be in a health desert, where the poor ended up by default because no one else would take them. An older black woman, her joints swollen, shifted in her seat, one leg having been amputated. Sophine wondered how long the woman waited to come in, how great the pain must have built to, the vomiting, the coughing, or whatever symptom drove her. Or how many trips back this made for her because she couldn't abide previous long waits for a doctor or nurse to acknowledge her existence.

"This is Colonel Winston Jefferson," the attendant announced to the nursing staff. "Let's move it, people."

Orderlies rushed her father through another set of double doors. The privilege of wealth purchased a different level of medical attention. Though once the emergency room doors closed her out, a nurse ushered her to the same waiting area as everyone else. Through the glass partition, she watched them lower him onto a bed under a fluoroscope machine. She half expected him to rise up and yell ...

"...YOU can't go off to Oxford like this." The Colonel stormed from his desk, wringing his hands as he paced back and forth in front of Sophine. He would pause, study her up and down, shake his head, then begin his angry striding again.

"I thought that was the whole point of this ridiculous exercise." Sophine froze in still repose, quite pleased at the lather she'd worked her father into. It served him quite right for wanting to sweep her under a rug an ocean away and out of his life. "Their" life.

"The whole point of this ridiculous exercise was to provide you with the best education money could buy."

"You've been sending me off to boarding school in an obvious need to get rid of me. I'm just taking the next logical step." Sophine watched him with cool eyes.

"Speaking of ridiculous notions ..." The Colonel tutted without breaking stride. He moved at such a pace, the gaslit sconces fluttered when he passed.

"Do not dismiss my notions. Once you married *her*," Sophine nodded toward Lyonessa, who continued to sew and not acknowledge either of them, "a woman several years your junior and not so many my senior, I've become all too aware of just how inconvenient my presence has been."

"Inconvenient how?" The Colonel stopped in front of her, almost daring her to air her laundry list of suspicions about him.

"Inconvenient for one determined to re-live the days of their college youth. You cannot gallivant about freely with her if I lurk the corridors. Surely she has been whispering that in your ear all these days."

"Don't drag me into you two's games of who gets to be right," Lyonessa said without glancing up. "It's no fun being the ball: all I get is hit."

"She's right, this is between you and me," the Colonel said.

"A *family* matter," Sophine said.

"Nice try." The Colonel wagged his finger at her. He could never resist an opportunity to *tsk* at her. "One, Lyonessa is family and has every right to be a part of this discussion ..."

"For the record, over my protests." Lyonessa drew a long thread through her work.

"Two, this digression into motives and family won't work as a distraction. You're not wearing that outfit to Oxford."

"I repeat: what's wrong with my outfit?" Standing, Sophine held her arms out and twirled. A black stocking mini-dress clung to her body like a velvet glove over her figure, stopping just past her hips. Gold fringe edged the dress, matched by the gold fringe of her long black boots. In between, black tights ran the length of her legs. A men's suit jacket fitted loosely about her, and a matching black top hat cocked at an odd angle on her head. A gold ankh brooch clasped at her neck. "You can't see my ankles."

"I can see a darn sight more than your ankles, young lady!" On the verge of an apoplectic fit, the Colonel adjusted his cuff links, not meeting her eyes nor conceding any ground. He took several measured breaths to calm himself. "It's an affront to all modern rules of decency."

"Who exactly is in charge of writing these rules?" Sophine arched a knowing eyebrow. To be fair, she did enjoy any opportunity to eyebrow arch.

"Not you. Nor do you get a say in re-writing them."

"As I am reminded of so very often, I have few rights and a litany of wrongs," Sophine said.

"As you say. So for now, change." The Colonel turned his back to her and clasped his hands behind him.

"Winston, if I may?" Lyonessa set her sewing pattern in her lap.

"You might as well, you're clearly the woman of the house now," Sophine said.

"Sophine! Manners. She's your ..." The Colonel whirled back toward her.

"My what? Please, finish that sentence, Father, and condemn me to my place like any magistrate to one found guilty." Her eyes dared him to replace her mother with this woman as the object of maternal affection and respect in her life.

Only willing to fight a war on so many fronts, the Colonel relented. A little. "Such high strung theatrics isn't like you. You go on as if ..."

"As I was saying," Lyonessa interrupted. "It seems to me a rather trivial matter to raise up in arms about. Sophine is a grown woman and the minute she steps out that door, dear husband, you'll have no say in how she dresses. Nor, sweet Sophine, do I think this row is about your manner of dress, no matter how much time you painstakingly spent putting together such a provocative outfit. You two simply can't find any other way to say good-bye. So why don't I take my leave so that you two can simply have at each other with no audience to perform to."

Lyonessa gathered her things and withdrew.

Sophine and the Colonel squared off against one another like two armed gentlemen preparing for a duel. Sophine was not going to admit, if she even realized it on a conscious level, that she sought out his long harangue of disapproval, if only to bask in the familiarity of it. His ways, however maddening, were comforting in their predictability. Taking a few steps toward the door, her bags waiting in the hallway, she hesitated.

Sophine lowered her head with the weight of letting go and

saying good-bye. When she glanced back at him, he had adopted the same posture. Neither one of them was ready to say ...

<hr />

"...'SCUSE me, baby, do you have a light?" The word baby had a careless quality to it and thus managed to not offend her. A tall man with a broken-toothed smile sprawled out over several chairs. When Sophine neared, he retracted himself into one to allow her room to sit.

"You shouldn't smoke in here," Sophine said.

"I shouldn't do a lotta things. But I was planning to take my nail outside to smoke it. The only civilized thing to do. Just needed a little light to get going."

"I'm afraid I don't have one."

"Number forty-two." A woman in all white, with a flower pinned to her lapel, held a door open.

"Number forty-two ... come on down!" the broken-toothed man yelled with a booming, showman's voice. He stood to follow the nurse.

Sophine attempted to puzzle out the stories of the people around her. How many worked just enough to avoid Unperson status? Foundry, coal cleaner, dishwasher, janitor, anything that hadn't been replaced by an automaton. Yet. How many loved to read or go to plays or travel or ride horses when they had the luxury to dream for themselves? How many dropped out of school to work to support their families and were lost when it came to modern technologies? Stuck in a cycle of too little work, no health care, their body breaking down, thus preventing full-time work, and not enough credits to their name. The stress of mounting bills added to their health problems. She closed her eyes and pictured herself in her father's library, reading. A calming ritual; forced herself to breathe deeply. The room became safe again.

A little girl, a smudge of ash on her left cheek, clutched at the hem of her mother's dress. The fabric was cheap, often-mended, but presentable. She stared at her with suspicion, as if Sophine were the one out of place. The little girl risked a smile from behind the curtain of her mother's safety. Even the poorest people smiled. Sophine had no idea why that observation sprang to mind.

"What a pretty dress," Sophine said. The little girl's intense scrutiny reduced Sophine to an awkward gawker with only the barest grasp of English. She had spent little time among children even when she was one and was told on many occasions of her lack of maternal instincts. Still, Sophine chided herself. She always hated the way people older than her focused on her beauty, what she wore, or how she did her hair as if her presentation was all she had to offer. She waved her hand in front of her as if erasing her conversational start in order to begin again. "What's your name?"

"Farin."

"Farin? What a lovely name." Sophine crouched low, pausing to catch her mother's eye and tilted her head in her direction for approval. The mother nodded. "I'm very pleased to meet you."

"I'm pleased to meet you, too." She tilted her head in that child's way of mimicking adults.

Scrambling for something to latch onto to continue the momentum of conversation, Sophine took care not to ask what injury brought her here, or, worse, brought someone she cared for there. "What do you have there?"

"A book." The little girl clutched it to her chest like it was a prized stuffed animal.

"A book? I love books."

"My mother said we may be here awhile, so I needed to bring something to keep me busy."

"You have a very wise mother. I wish someone had warned me about how long it would be. It seems so much longer when you're waiting to hear about someone you care about."

Farin nodded in thoughtful sympathy. "I could read you my book."

"That would be lovely. But only if it's all right with your mother." Sophine looked up. With the thinness of smiles accompanying it —not so broad as to unleash the storm of emotions she otherwise had to keep in check—her mother nodded her approval.

Farin read her a tale about a little girl who lost her brother. About the magical place in the woods they had created together, which seemed so much darker without him. Sophine interrupted her to ask her questions or have her re-read passages because she really enjoyed a sentence. And Farin was delighted to do so, answering all of her questions about what certain words meant. Or why characters behaved the way they did or made the choices they made.

"Farin," her mother interjected, some unseen time clock alerting her that their time together had elapsed. The rules of societal convention dictated that there be only so much time to presume a stranger might entertain one's child. "Leave the pretty lady alone."

The way she pronounced "pretty" made her sound like an alien of some sort. Sophine half curtsied and went back to her seat.

A doctor pushed through the set of double doors. "The Jefferson family?"

Sophine stood up and smoothed out her dress before approaching him. Farin brushed her hand when she walked by. Sophine returned a thin-lipped smile, then met the doctor's gaze. "Is there any word about my ..."

From the doctor's expression, she knew her father's fate before she finished. In his downcast eyes were conversations her and her father would never have, questions she'd never have answered. In the exhausted manner in which he removed his mask, she saw arguments they'd never settle, apologies they'd never be able to make. With a forlorn snap, he pulled his gloves free, she knew suppers they'd no longer partake together and inventions she wouldn't be able to show him. The gleam of pride in his eyes when she'd demonstrate them, that she'd never see.

"I'm sorry, Ms. Jefferson. We took every measure that we could, but he was already gone."

"I ... see." She gave herself a moment to collect the emotions that threatened to shrivel her mind into a desperate cry. A wordless roar longing to find its voice.

The doctor stepped near, his arms at the ready for when her legs gave out and she fainted dead away. To clutch her heart or perhaps tear at her clothes. Anticipating her emotions to get the better of her the way men often presumed. He was irrelevant. Oblivious to her fury. "Are you all right, miss?"

"I'm ... fine." Sophine struggled to control her rage, to not let it seep through the cracks in the mask. She wanted to lash into him, but she remembered that he was not the villain here. She pressed a crease from her dress. "Do you know the cause?"

"Not yet. We won't know until the autopsy. Perhaps his heart ..."

"... was just fine. He was in the peak of health. His heart as strong and stubborn as a mule's."

"Any recent malady?"

"Not so much as a sniffle. Perhaps a little run down, of late, but that comes from running a business with so many interests."

"Like I said, I'll know more when I've had a chance to examine his body. His systems just seemed to have shut down."

"I won't rest until I find out why," Sophine said.

SOPHINE CLIMBED the back stairwell of her house. The Colonel's house. These stairs ran down to the basement. The wave of renovations hadn't reached this back corner yet. The wallpaper peeled, revealing the original greens that bled into orange, as the quarters met the stairwell of the original house. The renovations resumed with a fresh coat of white paint that led to the next floor. Sheets of drywall, some broken or cut into workable bits, two by fours, tools, and workbenches collected rubble from any demo. The original servants' quarters were hidden behind the back stairwell, like pantry closets embedded in the walls. The third floor was a cramped space containing one bedroom and a door that led out to the widow's walk.

On her right was her doll cabinet, a three-tiered glass cabinet, reminiscent of a doll's transparent apartment. Her childhood dolls filled the display to overcrowding. The antique toys of her youth, preserved behind locked glass. Not to be touched. The top tier showed off her miniature dolls. Fair-skinned, blonde moppets dressed in elegant ballroom gowns. Except for a brown-haired doll in a blue riding suit, which brought to mind a soldier with a riding whip. The second tier held her animals. A motley crew of cats, bunnies, and horses, with the occasional dish or cup from a long incomplete tea set. The bottom tier, tall as the first two combined, preserved the true treasures. A baby doll, perched in a wicker chair, easily a century old, surrounded by princesses arranged like court attendants. One, in a yellow hooped dress, had an intricate hairstyle of blonde curls and braids that must have been labored on for hours.

At the end of the hallway, black tapestries covered the windows. Their heavy folds puddled onto the carpet. Lyonessa spent her mornings on the widow's walk. She played to societal expectation with her last breath. When a husband died, the widow wasn't expected to appear in public for at least a month. So she went out on the roof for air. A guard railed path wound the periphery of the roof. The paint chipped in huge flakes. The railing led to a smaller deck. Working on some ceramic piece, Lyonessa hunched over a wrought iron table. She paused in mid-action, certainly aware of Sophine's presence. Concluding who it must've been, she resumed working. Sophine plopped down in one of the matching wrought iron chairs opposite her.

"The doctors suspect that he was poisoned." Sophine turned to her side, her back not quite to Lyonessa. "It was the natural conclusion, once everything else had been ruled out."

"Poisoned? By what?"

"Does it matter?"

"I suppose not." Lyonessa's mud-slickened hands caressed the figure taking shape on her spinning wheel. Her foot nudged a pedal, adjusting the speed of the gears controlling the wheel. Mud smudged her face when she wiped the sweat from her eyes. She was both stubborn and not wanting to deal with her grief and poured herself into making pottery. Her body centered and locked over the wheel; the form of a vase slowly took shape.

"I suspect cyanide," Sophine started again, as if talking to no one in particular. "Its telltale olfactory notes hidden by the taste of brandy."

"But who?"

"I don't know. The Colonel had his share of enemies. And friends."

"Sophine, don't say such things."

"It's true. I know we've never been close." Sophine paused to see if she'd be contradicted.

"I suppose not."

Sophine almost wished she could see Lyonessa's eyes, but her stepmother's grief on top of her own would be too much. Too soon. "Still, what would you do if you knew who murdered ..." The words stuck in her mouth. It was one thing when it was a matter of suspicions. This was the first time she allowed herself to say it out loud, and it sounded far too real to her ear. "... the Colonel. My father."

"And my husband. As far as what I'd do, inform the police, I suppose. And you?"

"You have more faith in our constabulary than I. Besides, they require proof. The kind that would stand up in a court, supposing it got that far."

"And you have none."

"Only suppositions and conjecture." Less than a week ago, her father would have been the first to argue the point. Now she was alone, her decisions unchallenged.

"But you have an idea. Someone in mind."

"More the idea of someone. So far. None of it seems quite real to me yet."

"You are so much like your father. Your mind has to work out the puzzle like it's a secret to be kept until you can lay it out like a chef presenting a dinner plate." Lyonessa wiped her brow. "You're all I have left of him."

Sophine didn't know what to say to that. She took additional interest in Lyonessa's labors. "Looks like you got quite the job ahead of you."

"I told you, I like taking broken things and fixing them."

"I've never been particularly good at playing family."

"Me neither." Lyonessa returned to her ceramic pieces. "Stay for tea?"

"I'd ... like that. I'll be along in a moment."

HER FATHER'S death left a wound in Sophine too deep to staunch. She needed to escape the house. Sophine needed to get back to work, to the safety and comfort of her laboratory. For as much as she begrudged life in a corporate setting, right now, she was glad of it. Computations, paperwork, design, seclusion, her mind occupied in solitude. Away from people's endless sympathizing and their delicate clucks of pity. But she couldn't yet. Not until she dealt with her father's unfinished business in his office.

The largest room in the house, save for the parlor, her father's office was tucked away and yet sealed off with its own water closet and a couch deep enough to double as a bed. A matching couch sat next to the first so that the couch appeared to run the length of the room. He only had to leave to eat and, even then, the automata often brought him his meals. The beverage cart remained at attention next to his desk. Sophine desperately wanted to crawl into the decanter and not leave the room until she had drained it and all of its companions dry. Anything to numb the pain and let the world carry on without her. Reaching for the bottle, she froze. An itch at the back of her mind needed scratching. She removed the lid and sniffed the glass, waiting for the telltale scent of cyanide. She lost patience with herself. She thrashed the glassware from the table. An automaton hurried into the room, but Sophine waved her off. Her rage would suffice and keep her for another day.

Sophine piled the last of the Colonel's papers into a box. Stripped of the fruit of his endless endeavors, the room felt barren. She tried to distract herself from the emptiness of the room. She hugged the box of his papers to her. His cane canted to one side in the corner of the room. She scooped it up on her way out, wanting it as a memento mori. She considered burying it with him, but that, too, felt final.

She walked the box across his expensive Oriental carpet and down the long hallways to the basement and loaded it next to the other boxes. Neither she nor Lyonessa had the stomach to sift through them nor did they want his office remaining as some sort of memorial sarcophagus. There would be time enough for her and his barrister to go through them. For now, they would be out of sight.

"I'm going to get your murderer," she said. "Whoever that might be."

NINE
CLAIMIN' I'M A CRIMINAL

Vox Dei Data Files: Under the stewardship of Chancellor Lucas Pruitt, Indianapolis expanded its territorial jurisdiction from 82 square miles to 402 square miles. The policing of the city was split between the Indianapolis Police Department, which served Indianapolis proper, and the Marion County Sheriff's Department, for those districts outside of the Indianapolis police special service district. This split service continued until the Pinkerton Agency expanded its federal contract to allow city ordination of its federal agents. Privatizing government services, once again, allowed the free market to solve government inefficiencies.

THE UNIGOV ADMINISTRATION Building at 50 N. Alabama Street was a dull spire of concrete and glass, setting it apart from the many gleaming buildings of downtown Indianapolis. The East Wing of the building housed the City Ordained Pinkerton's main offices, though the department recently opened five district operations around the city. The UAB functioned as the division headquarters for Indianapolis proper. The mechanized velocipede and horse patrols aided the officers who still walked their downtown beats. The "Flying Squadron" aerial copter units docked along the top of the building known as The Aerie.

On the fourth floor of the East Wing of the UAB, a series of small rooms faced the west. The rooms never had to worry about the blinding light of the setting sun because the rooms were windowless save for the twin panes which spied into the adjoining room. The rooms were decorated the same: a lone black table situated far from the door, two seats behind it nearly against the wall, two on the other side. Pale blue, nearly gray, paneled walls. Taupe colored tiles for flooring. No ashtrays. No clocks. Once a person sat down, their back against the wall, they lost all sense of time. A corner of their reality uprooted, the better for a COP to gain a foothold in them.

The operatives were all smiles and cordiality before they ushered him into the room. Now Sleepy sat in one. He knew somewhere along the corridor, Knowledge Allah waited in a similar room. Sleepy had been reminded of his rights as a citizen of the United States of Albion. He still had the option of a barrister, though not only would invoking one escalate matters, it wouldn't much help. He might languish for years without one. He had to scrape together the $500 credit bond to prove himself a responsible citizen. That might get him ten minutes with a public defender who would urge him to accept whatever plea offer was tendered by the state. Not willing to roll the dice on actual jail time, he'd likely leap at probation, though it had a steep cost. It meant more fines, court costs, and probation costs. Then, being branded a felon, he'd become an Unperson. If he lost his job, he likely wouldn't get another. If he lost his home, he wouldn't qualify for public housing. If he had children, they'd be removed from him, but would inherit his Unperson status as wards of the state. And a repeat offense, even for poverty, demanded mandatory imprisonment. And so it goes.

If Sleepy stared at the blue-gray paneling in just the right way, they seemed like a series of doors which stretched off into infinity. He'd already counted the twelve square inch tiles (260 if he included all of the half tiles) as well as the larger square swatches on the floor (111). He wondered if Knowledge Allah had done the same and divined some meaning from them.

Sleepy laid his head down and began to drift off.

The door opened. Sleepy opened his eyes without moving his head. The first officer in was an auburn-haired woman with a thin, angular face, a constellation of freckles high on each cheek. A red-piped dress trimmed in white peeked from beneath the unbuttoned folds of her long, red coat. A badge was pinned to her dress above her left breast. An empty holster belted her. She dropped several file folders on the table.

A bull of a man followed her. He folded his long, gray coat over a chair and set his black bowler on the table between them. His badge was pinned to his black vest, a silver chain trailed from the middle button of the vest into his right pocket. Bald, and with a thick mustache in need of trimming, his red-tipped, squat nose had a crook to it, as if it had been broken several times but never set properly. Eyes the color of frost on a murky pond studied Sleepy with the careful intensity of another pat down.

"What's his mood?" she asked. She had a slight European accent Sleepy couldn't place.

"Calm. Indifferent. Had the nerve to go to sleep. In our house." The bull officer made a show of talking about Sleepy as if he wasn't present. "Only the guilty sleep."

"Or the really damned tired." Sleepy raised up, recognizing his cue to join the conversation. He wiped the tired from his eyes, determined to be as alert as possible.

"Did he just curse?" she asked.

"In our house?" the bull responded.

"Where would we be without the civil manners of polite society?" She cocked her head in expectation.

"My ... apologies," Sleepy found himself saying, raising his voice at the end as if asking a question.

"Good. Just so we get off on the right foot, we accept your apology, do we not?" She turned to her partner.

"We do. In the spirit of right-footedness." The bull moved to the corner opposite her, remaining just within Sleepy's eyeline, like a subtle threat.

"My name is Assistant Lesia Tudor," she announced. Not many

women rose to the rank of assistant in a Pinkerton office. Only two assistants were assigned to any station and each oversaw five general operatives, as well as the clerical and other operational staff. "I'm the lead investigator on this case. This is my colleague, General Operative Logan Breedlove."

"This is an ongoing investigation." Breedlove's penetrating gaze bore into Sleepy.

"Ongoing?" Sleepy asked. Even without representation, he knew enough to keep his answers short, volunteer nothing, and give them as little as possible to work with. Though he'd stayed out of trouble, the reality of how and where he grew up required a certain familiarity with the workings of the criminal justice system.

"The ground constantly shifts. Events moving quickly. New evidence uncovered. More people talk. Witnesses come forward," Breedlove said.

"Good police work. Continue to talk to people," Tudor said with deference.

"Leave no rock unturned."

"My partner here is a rock turning specialist," Tudor said.

"Practically a geologist. Not afraid to get my hands dirty." Breedlove intertwined his fingers and popped his knuckles.

"No, you're not." She nodded in agreement.

"A lot of heads out there are simply thick as granite."

"I see what you did there," Tudor said. "He's a geologist and a wordsmith."

Sleepy straightened in his chair. His eyes bounced back and forth between their bobbing, chatting heads. Their rhythm was nearly dizzying, which he was certain was the intended effect.

Breedlove notched his neck back and forth. Like a shadow shifting in the light, he settled into his seat directly across from Sleepy.

"For the record, what's your full name?" Tudor scooted down to Sleepy's left, at the end of the long table.

"Hubert Marcellous Nixon."

"But your friends call you something else."

"Sleepy."

"I can see why," Breedlove said.

Sleepy stared at him.

"You're not very talkative," Tudor continued.

"I'm inconversable," Sleepy said.

"Whoa. You hear that? He's inconversable." She turned to her partner. "He's giving you a run for your wordsmithing title."

Breedlove glared at him without comment. COPs hated even the hint of being showed up. Sleepy made a note to tread lightly with him.

"Well, Mr. Inconversable, says here that you reside at 3906 Gateway Court." Tudor read from the first file.

Sleepy folded his arms along the table, not quite getting comfortable, but bracing himself for a long round of questioning. "Yeah."

"How long have you lived at that address?"

"Seven years."

"You're twenty-three now. Move out at sixteen?" she asked.

Sleepy held his tongue. His first instinct ran along the lines of wanting to compliment the police officer's math skills. But there was one door in this room of four gray walls and they formed the barricade between him and it. "Sixteen. Yeah."

"Where did you reside before then?" she asked.

"With my mom. Our unipod."

"How many kids did we approve?"

Sleepy flinched at the idea that she had any say in the matter. "Two. One brother."

"Two boys and two parents."

"Two and two." Breedlove held up two fingers. Flashed them twice. "Very symmetrical of you. Your dad in the picture?"

"That's how we got permission for the unipod." Sleepy kept his face angled at the lead investigator, but occasionally side-eyed her partner.

"Standard five-year contract?" Tudor focused on the file in front of her, flipping pages like she went down a checklist of pro forma questions.

"Yeah."

"Renewed how many times?"

"Once," Sleepy said.

"Ten years. That's a good run."

"No shame in that," Breedlove offered.

"You married?" she asked.

"No," Sleepy said.

"Ever been engaged?" Her voice lilted, almost inviting. The near flirtation of a detective, an assistant at that, was a trap he wouldn't fall for.

Sleepy felt the sting of judgment. The berating questions a steady drip of humiliation. "No."

"Go to church?"

"Sometimes."

"You believe in God though?" She glanced up at him then.

"Yeah."

"What religion are you?"

"Was Baptist. Now a little Rastafarian."

"That's an excuse to smoke chiba, not a real religion," Breedlove interjected.

"My colleague brings up an interesting point. Do you smoke chiba?"

Sleepy didn't answer.

"The lady asked you a question," Breedlove repeated.

"I claim my right against self-incrimination," Sleepy proffered.

"That's cute," Breedlove said. "I'll take that as a yes."

"But you didn't lie. Good." Tudor went back to her file. "You have any friends?"

"I know a couple of folks."

"I'm just trying to get a feel for your social network." She closed the file folder with a mild sigh of bored exasperation. She put on the air of someone who didn't want to be there any more than him but had a job to do. Another trap to lull him.

"I hang with a few poets."

"Down at the Two-Johns?"

"Yeah."

"Don't see your family much though?" Her tone took an oddly sympathetic turn.

"No." Sleepy stared at her, not flinching.

"Mom?"

"Dead."

"Brother?"

"With family."

"Dad?"

"Don't know."

Tudor made a notation in the file. "Any other family?"

"Not really."

"You have no friends and no family, that about right?" she concluded.

Sleepy said nothing and began to study his fingers.

Reopening the folder, Assistant Tudor turned the page in her file. She ran her finger along the next page. Setting on her next point of inquiry, she began again. "What do you do for a living, Mr. Nixon?"

"Why stand on formalities? Call him Sleepy," Breedlove said.

"And what do I call you?" Sleepy asked.

"General Operative Breedlove." His face hardened, without a trace of anything jovial. "Anything else earns you a beating, you got that?"

"Yeah." Sleepy turned from him. The man was hard to look at anyway, like a cement block a failing art student tried to chisel a face out of.

"So," she continued, "place of employment?"

"Commonwealth Waterworks."

"How long have you been there?"

"Seven years," Sleepy said.

"There's that number again," Breedlove said. "Practically biblical."

"You like it?" Tudor asked.

"It's a job." Sleepy wouldn't give them the chance to worm into his thoughts.

"What do you do?"

"Steam engineer."

"We have a hardworking man here. Not afraid to get a little dirt under his nails." Breedlove grinned without warmth.

"So, you're a hardworking man, spending your day scrubbing coal and what not. You have something against other people earning a living?" Tudor asked.

"No." Sleepy reared up in his seat at the strange turn in questions.

"You must have something against folks out there trying to make a living. Why else roust a fruit vendor?"

"I didn't roust anyone." Sleepy sucked his teeth.

"Maybe its fruit vendors in particular that you have a problem with."

"I'd say he's not had much use for fruit in his days," Breedlove said.

Insults. A tried and true tactic. Taking a silent breath, Sleepy pressed his hands flat on the table in front of him.

"I think we've touched a nerve," Tudor said.

"Maybe he's just sensitive about his weight."

"About the fruit vendor, are you one of those folks who don't think highly of them? Think of them as, what you say, Breedlove?" Tudor's accent thickened a bit. Definitely Eastern European.

"Vagrants." Breedlove popped his knuckles again. When he craned his neck, a thick vein bulged and throbbed along it.

"Yes, vagrants. Told you my partner has a way with words."

"I don't think of them one way or another." Sleepy swallowed hard but hoped neither COP noticed.

Tudor smiled a predatory grin. "You mind their prices?"

"Seemed a little high."

"It's a market economy. Higher price, fresher produce. Yes?" Tudor asked.

"That comes to you. Down there," Breedlove said. "It's not like there's a supermarket down in The Tombs."

"Why were you down in The Tombs?" she asked.

"Man has a right to go where he pleases," Sleepy said.

"That's not strictly true," Breedlove said.

"Besides, man works hard like you, he can afford his own place."
Tudor closed the file again and rose out of her seat.

"His own clothes." Breedlove twisted slightly to pop his back.

"No need for him to go undercity. Unless he's hiding." Tudor
strode behind Sleepy while she spoke. "You hiding from anyone,
Sleepy?"

"Nope."

"That's strange. That sound strange to you, Breedlove?"

"It sounds a mite hinky."

"Indeed. A mite," she repeated.

"A smidgen, as it were."

Tudor picked up another file. "See, we have here a district-wide
dispatch about a pair of Negro gentlemen, one about your age and ...
disposition. Says they were involved in some mischief the other
evening."

"Mischief and vandalism," Breedlove corrected.

"Destruction of government property, I do believe."

"I daresay you are correct."

"It was pure luck that we rumbled you in the first place," Tudor
said. "Did you ever run with the 42nd Street rioters?"

"I have no idea who they are," Sleepy said.

"Tell us about your friend," Tudor said.

"Who?" Sleepy asked.

"The man we picked you up with."

"He ain't my friend."

"What does he call you?"

"Sleepy."

"I thought only your friends call you that?" Breedlove asked.

"So do you." Sleepy regretted his tone but couldn't help himself.
"General Operative Breedlove."

"We have a smart one here." Tudor pointed at him with her thin
thumb.

"Yeah, I'd like to see how smart he looks picking his teeth off the
floor." Breedlove glared at him until Sleepy turned away.

"About your friend ..." she continued.

"What about him?" Sleepy asked.

"What's his name?"

"(120 Degrees of) Knowledge Allah."

Breedlove whistled. "Damn, that's a mouthful."

"Now, Breedlove. That's not fair. We wouldn't want to give Mr. Nixon here ..."

"Sleepy," Breedlove corrected. "Since we're all friends and all."

"Yes, we wouldn't want to give Sleepy the impression that we were above our own rules."

"True. My apologies. I shouldn't have cursed."

"See? We're all civilized people here." She closed the folder with her index finger holding her place. "Now do you say all those numbers and such every time you call him?"

"Knowledge Allah."

"Not Knowledge for short?" she asked.

"Or Know?" Breedlove smirked. It was an ugly, derisive grin.

"Knowledge Allah. I respect the man's name and what he chooses to call himself."

"But that's not what the government calls him," she said.

"Not what his momma named him," Breedlove said. "Not that she stayed in the picture long."

"Carlton Drayton," Sleepy said.

"Now Carlton, this isn't his first run-in with the law, is it?" she asked.

"I wouldn't know. I just met him."

"He has quite the rap sheet. As Carlton Drayton, numbers running, drug dealing, well, possession with probable intent, same difference. Petty burglary. As Carlton X, disrupting the peace, unlawful trespass."

"And now as 120 Degrees of Bullshit, we can add vandalism and inciting a riot."

"Language, Breedlove. Besides, I'm sure we can add a few other things to that list before we're done." Tudor re-opened the second file. "Back to the fruit vendor, you work for Melvin Knight?"

"Who?" Sleepy asked.

"Don't play coy. It doesn't suit you," Breedlove said.

"You work for *Sugar*?" Tudor repeated.

"No."

"You sure you and your boy, Mr. Allah, weren't down there negotiating a protection fee on behalf of Mr. Knight?" Breedlove asked.

"No."

"Because it seems like you went through a lot of hassle to get our fruit vendor's attention," Breedlove said.

"Hit him up for free fruit. He comes back with a price. Negotiations don't go well. You overturn the cart. When COPs enter the scene, you incite a riot," Tudor said.

"That's ridiculous," Sleepy said.

"You calling my partner a liar?" Breedlove asked, his voice thick with threat.

"No."

"Which is it: she a liar or are you working for Sugar?"

"Neither."

"What do you think your little buddy is telling our colleagues right now in the next room?" Breedlove asked.

"The truth." Sleepy hoped his words came across with the strength of conviction he intended because slowly his mind began to tick off what all Knowledge Allah could possibly say. Then it occurred to him that Knowledge Allah probably only spoke to them in sacred mathematics. Probably why they spent so much time with him. But they said something, let something slip, if they'd just give him a moment to think about it.

"How do you see it ... going down?" Her words halted as if trying them out for the first time.

"Me and Knowledge Allah minding our own. Vendor catches our attention. He tries to get me to buy fruit. I didn't want to, but I changed my mind. But his prices are too high. We negotiate. I decline. I trip and knock over a couple of items. He wants me to pay full price. Full price, plus damages. I decline. He pulls out a whistle and starts blowing his fool head off. COPs arrive. Then things get ... complicated." Sleepy cursed himself for going on so long with his answer.

"Complicated?" Breedlove asked.

"Should we take a break?" Tudor asked.

"Yeah. I need a cigarette. What about you?" Breedlove asked.

"I'm good." She finally turned to Sleepy. "You thirsty?"

"I'm good. We about through?" Sleepy asked.

"Ha! That's good. We're taking a break," she said.

"We're a damn sight sure not done with you yet. Not for a country mile." Breedlove headed toward the door.

SLEEPY SHIFTED IN HIS SEAT, wishing he was high. He waited for the next round of humiliation, the assault on one's dignity that came with a COP interrogation. He wondered if his self-respect was an illusory construct in the first place. Sleepy recounted the tiles, both ceiling and floor. He drummed his fingers, then began to pound out rhythms with his hands against the desk, improvising rhymes about his situation. Despite the pleasure of rhyming Breedlove to a menagerie of increasingly violent demises, he tired. He put his head down again, simply to pass the time. The weight of the judicial system stepping on the back of his neck.

He could hear his mother *tsk*-ing at his situation. Over Sunday dinners, she'd have him set an elaborate table no matter what the meal was. Three different forks, two spoons, two knives, napkins in a brass ring holder set on a separate saucer. Classical music played from a gramophone despite the fact that no one in the house particularly liked it.

"You must know the rules of proper society," she chided at her children's complaints.

"When are we ever going to an extravagant dinner party?" Hubert asked (he was Hubert back then).

"That's not the point." Her voice a constant *tsk* at him.

"No, the point is that I'm hungry and don't care which fork I use as long as its close."

She glared at him with her "I wish you would" face and his hand backed away from the fork. Out of sheer muscle memory, he found himself reaching for the correct fork.

"The point is that you never know where you'll find yourself. Or when. And better to be prepared than look like some ... some ... street mongrel."

"I don't even know what that means." Sleepy carved up the small piece of meat, his huge hands nearly swallowed the knife and fork in their grip.

"The more you're exposed to the more refined things in life, the less likely you'll end up as an Unperson."

"I know, I know." Hubert turned to his brother. "Go to school. Work hard. Get a job. Make something of yourself. Support your unipod. Support your neighborhood. That is the secret to a better life."

(That reminded him of his pops. The man worked, came home, ate, slept. Every day until one day he was gone.)

Following all of her lessons, he'd never gotten in trouble. He worked his entire life, associated with the right people. He did everything an upstanding citizen was supposed to. For all of his effort, in the span of one day, he still ended up here. A police interrogation room. Next stop, jail. Then court. Then The Ave and Unperson classification. Her disappointment at where he was ringing so real, she might as well be breathing on his neck.

As his thoughts fragmented into shards of nonsense, the two operatives re-entered the room.

"Do you know why you're here?" Tudor asked without preamble.

Sleepy had a theory, more like a nagging suspicion, that their arrest was a matter of show. A symbol of the Pinkerton's reach, even in The Tombs, to silence future possible unrest. But it was just a theory, one best left unvoiced. "No."

"You have no idea?"

"No."

"The incident at the Two-Johns jog your memory any?" Breedlove slammed his meaty fist against the table once. Sleepy jumped.

"You vandalized a lot of COP property during your little

getaway adventure. That's a lot of public property demanding someone pay recompense," Tudor said.

"Then there's The Tombs ..." Breedlove stared at Sleepy like he'd spent the last hour disparaging the operative's mother.

"Whew. The Tombs. That's quite the mess. Lots of conflicting reports. But the general consensus points to you and your friend instigating the problem," she said.

"That's not true," Sleepy protested.

"You hate COPs," she said.

"I don't ..."

"Now don't lie. We've been doing so well," Tudor said.

"Hate is a ... strong word," Sleepy said.

"Would it be fair to say that you feel something just short of hate?"

"Maybe somewhere around the loathe area." Sleepy hoped his words came off cute, almost charming.

"You worried about hurting our feelings? Don't be. We're like barristers. We already know the answers to our questions. We're just seeing how honest you're being. So, somewhere between loathe and hate?" Tudor smiled. "So, it stands to reason that you might wish to vandalize COP property given the proper occasion."

"Maybe," Sleepy said.

"See? Was that so hard to admit?" Breedlove popped the joints in his knuckles again. He focused on Sleepy with his knowing eyes.

"You have a problem with authority figures. You must challenge them. Defy them. Disrespect them. It's the mark of a boy with an indifferent father."

"You don't know me." Sleepy bristled at the word 'boy.' And his voice sounded less confident.

"Are you angry, Sleepy?" Tudor asked.

"About what?"

"Your job. Your dad. Your unipod. Your life. Take your pick."

"Blame the COPs for any of it?" Breedlove asked.

"You didn't have no call," Sleepy snapped, then caught himself.

Tudor paused for a moment like a hunting dog catching a fresh scent. "No call for what?"

"To hit them kids." Sleepy lowered his voice, reduced to the tone of a child reluctantly admitting a wrong-doing to a parent.

"What kids?"

"In The Tombs. The way y'all burst in. No questions. No warrants. Just start swinging."

"Like at the Two-Johns?" she asked.

"Yeah."

"It made you angry?"

"Yeah."

"We spoke to your friend," she said. "He seems to think you're this righteous man."

"Stand up for the little man," Breedlove said.

"How did he put it? 'The oppressed must leap like lions,'" she said.

"You leap like a lion?" Breedlove cocked his hand slightly, ready to swat some unseen insect.

"I don't even know what that means," Sleepy said.

"You believe in justice and injustice, don't you?"

"Yeah."

"And when you see an injustice, what does a righteous, upstanding man, like yourself, do?"

"I stop it."

"How do you stop a COP from swinging at a kid?"

"I step between them," Sleepy said.

"You take the hit?"

"Yeah."

"COP hits you, how does it make you feel?"

"Angry."

"And what do you do when someone acts like you don't belong, like you're less than them just for being you?" Tudor piled on, a rhythm building with her words. "When you're angry? When you're tired of the injustice, when you're tired of all the pain, when you're hit?"

"I hit back." Sleepy closed his eyes and slumped in his seat.

"You hit back," Tudor repeated in a near whisper.

"You hit a COP," Breedlove confirmed.

Sleepy seemed to catch the weight of his words. "In self-defense."

"There is no self-defense when a Pinkerton agent is carrying out their duly sworn duty." Tudor closed her file. Her voice drained of any trace of sympathy. There was only Pinkerton in her tone.

"There's only compliance." Breedlove rose, a similar tone of professional nonchalance to his voice. "No overturning carts. Not inciting a mob. No hitting."

"You're being charged," Tudor said.

"With what?" Sleepy asked.

"We'll be filing three charges against you: assault and battery against the fruit vendor; destruction of private property, specifically the fruit cart; and, most damning, assaulting a COP."

"Enjoy your newfound Unperson status," Breedlove said.

TWO GUARDS SHACKLED Sleepy to a metal bench inside of a large box truck. He awaited transfer to the Marion County Lockup Facility a few blocks away. After a few minutes, the metal doors opened again. This time the guards deposited Knowledge Allah.

"I bet you are used to putting black men in shackles. Just loading us up in another cargo hold to take us on the next leg of our journey in the judicial triangle trade," Knowledge Allah shouted, while the guard fastened him to the truck. "Black bodies sold to prisons for free labor."

The guard checked both of their sets of chains before he left. A heartbeat of awkward silence passed between them.

"They're locking you up, too?" Sleepy asked without turning to him.

"What did you think? You were in this alone?" Knowledge Allah turned his wrists over, inspecting the chains.

"Didn't know what to think. About any of this. They got my head so turned around."

"It's a pretext derisoire," Knowledge Allah said.

"A pre-whatnow?"

"Pretext derisoire. They're filing charges against you to discredit you as a potential witness down the road."

"What about you?"

"I am guilty of *lese-majeste*," Knowledge Allah said.

"You certainly love your words today."

"Basically, inciting a riot. Civil rebellion is always seen as an assault on the crown. They make it sound like I called for Queen Diana's head. If it wasn't for the fact that they're going to try to bury us under the jail, I'd wear that charge with pride."

"I am guilty of a crime against fruit." Sleepy slumped over.

"I wouldn't go around saying that too loudly. Or often."

The truck lurched forward. It rumbled along the streets, each bump or chuckhole hit with such precision that it sent the two of them bouncing out of their seats. Then Sleepy's stomach pitched. He knew they descended along a steep road. He couldn't help but think they were on their way to hell. When the doors flung open, Marion County Lockup facilitators hard-eyed them as they got out of the truck. "Follow our trustees. They'll show you where to go."

Sleepy took two steps forward, then stopped so abruptly Knowledge Allah stumbled into his back.

"Well, well, well. Look who we have here," a man said.

Sleepy stared at him. "Hey, Pops."

TEN

THEY REMINISCE OVER YOU

Vox Dei Data Files: Melbourne Industries stands as a pillar among Indianapolis businesses. Founder Colonel Josiah Melbourne, an Army veteran during The Struggles, earned a chemical engineering degree from Rose Hulman Institute of Technology. The company developed and manufactured "ethical munitions" for defense contractors. From a small, two-story, brick building on Pearl Street, the company has grown, recently moving a second time. Its headquarters occupies the buildings collectively known as The Pyramids, which also houses several of its divisions, most notably ZeroDyne Corporation. The company continues to innovate and expand its reach in service to Albion.

TASKS WERE the only thing that gave order to Sophine's world. Invitations sent out. Flowers arranged. A service to order. Seating arrangements organized. Music selected. Bible passages chosen. Task after task checked off a list in lieu of thinking, feeling, or living. Merely motion, somnambulant and empty. The service proffered little except formal distraction.

Lord Melbourne told Sophine to take as much time off as she needed to arrange her father's affairs. With so much to slog through, she could only take a few hours of his voluminous papers per day. The first few weeks were the most difficult. She retreated to a simple routine beginning at ten in the morning; two hours poring over her father's work, lunch with Lyonessa, and then gardening in the afternoon. Grief had a way of creeping up on Sophine when she least expected it. One moment, she pruned a bush, the next, lost in some memory of her father, tears spilling down her cheeks. She spied her father in most visitors that attended the house: postman, delivery men, utility engineers—all had either a familiar likeness or bearing to her when strolling up the walk. Not even her sleep was free of grief. Every evening she went to bed after an early supper, only to be besieged by dreams of her father collapsing, his death throes all the more grotesque behind the imagery of her subconscious. Though she could remember no specifics upon awakening, she was left with feelings of acute helplessness, vague horror, and dull melancholy. Yet she learned to live with loss until it became a part of her.

Sophine dreaded returning to work. She stood outside of Building A, dubbed Little Giza by its employees, for several minutes steeling herself to enter. The reception lobby was designed to be reminiscent of walking along the canal of downtown Indianapolis, smooth marble walls with water trickling down them into small gulley ways filled with koi fish.

The weight of eyes pressed in on her. Studying her face, pouring over her for any signs of lingering grief. Searching for weakness. She fixed her eyes on a distant point, careful not to meet anyone's eyes. Armed with a slight smile plastered on her face, if someone's gaze lingered too long, she simply nodded. Her numb smile shielded her through the obligatory conversational dances of "Glad you're back" and "Sorry about your loss." Her heart grew heavy with the motions of "Thank you" and moving forward. Her sole goal was to make it to the familiar space of her lab's office, close the door behind her, and declare the day a victory.

"Miss Jefferson?" Dr. Anson Yeager called after her. His thick brown hair, gray just beginning to sprout behind his ears, bobbed down the hallway toward her. He wore a simple white shirt, buttoned up to his neck, though without a tie. The distressingly tight-fitting shirt was tucked into his pants, the bulge of his gut on proud display. He moved with the additional arrogance which came with height.

"Hello, Dr. Yeager." Sophine froze, swearing silent oaths that she hadn't avoided his attention. She chided herself for failing to remember to not walk down the hall of his lab, even though it was a convenient shortcut to her own facilities. Whoever he spied in the hall he took as an opportunity to update on the details of his personal life. Unfortunately, most details amounted to encounters and dalliance he'd had in response to ads taken out in the back of local periodicals. She turned to him.

"I'm sorry about your loss, Miss Jefferson." Dr. Yeager always emphasized the word Miss as her title to point out her missing doctorate. Dr. Yeager had a way of speaking that on the surface seemed convivial, yet scraped like well-placed blades. The conde-scension in his tone was thicker than usual. Though a principal investigator who oversaw his own lab, he resented Sophine's appointment by Lord Melbourne. She still had to generate a certain number of publications and prototypes to achieve greater autonomy, but she was fast-tracked for becoming a PI. Left to Dr. Yeager, she'd be reduced to general maintenance, changing machine oil, and washing labware. A maid in a lab coat.

"Thank you." Sophine hoped to end the conversation.

"My sister is sick, so I understand what you're going through." He tilted his head to the side, awaiting some sort of reciprocated sympathetic gesture.

"Yes," Sophine said awkwardly. "I'm sorry to hear that."

Dr. Yeager caught her arm before she turned to continue down the hallway. "I really saved your reputation the other day while you were out."

"Oh, did you now?" Not letting her eyes completely roll when she stared at him, her shoulders tensed as she braced for what was sure to be a pile of ridiculousness.

"Don't look at me like that. Lord Melbourne himself paid a visit to your laboratory. I think he was looking for an update on your ... what do you call that device?"

"Cybernetic membrane. Once I have the sheath to the point of passing information along it, the membrane will go a long way to perfecting human-automata hybrids."

"Quite. Well, he wanted an update and was quite insistent. I took the liberty to cajole the location of your journal from your assistant and go over the details with Lord Melbourne. He seemed quite pleased."

"Those lab journals are proprietary." Sophine's anger flared. A snarl crept into her voice.

Dr. Yeager smiled, almost pleased. He made a point of straightening his collar to demonstrate his cool control. "Nothing is proprietary around here. You should know that. Everything belongs to the company and Lord Melbourne is the company."

"Thank you for letting me know." Sophine stiffened, knowing that he was correct.

"We're all on the same team."

ALEJANDRA LOPERA STOOD atop a step ladder pouring a batch of solution into a large chamber. Barely five feet tall, she was stretched on a precarious edge. Her raven-black hair trailed down to her waist. A gold cross broach ornamented her lab coat.

"Out of Keene Buffer again?" Sophine asked.

"You know how *his* lab does." Alejandra rarely let the word "Yeager" trip from her lips unless she had to. "They all but empty a chamber so that the next lab has to restock it."

"Our lab, you mean."

Alejandra made a non-committal noise, stepping down from the step stool. "In your absence, he's been in rare form. Leaving notes on equipment reserving it, then not bothering to show up. Re-scheduling the time of meetings with the department head to when I couldn't attend. And I won't tell you about the state he returned your Frammerston unit, which he didn't ask to borrow in the first place. I'm positive that any piece of equipment you can't find is over in his area."

Alejandra muttered in her native language. She caught herself, then turned to Sophine. She grasped Sophine with both hands and, in her flawless, unaccented English, said, "I'm truly glad to have you back."

"I'm glad to be back," Sophine said, doubly grateful Alejandra said nothing about her father, loss, nor offered any sympathetic condolence. "I heard Lord Melbourne was inquiring about our progress?"

"Is that what *he* told you? I returned from lunch one day to find him in the common hall outside of our lab in a heated conversation with Lord Melbourne. He's waving about your lab journal, crowing about how much he's accomplished in your absence, and that he could provide the results Lord Melbourne was looking for."

"That doesn't make any sense." Sophine rubbed her temples, already wearied by the morning. "One cannot make science give the results they want. One gets the results, draws conclusions, and makes adjustments."

"There's your problem. While you're being a scientist, he's being a politician. He's carving out time with the board and with Lord Melbourne. He's angling to get his name on papers. Requisitioning more lab space. Getting greater shares of grant money."

"I don't care about any of that." Sophine retreated to her desk. Things had been waved about, cluttering her space to the point where she didn't recognize it. Papers piled from one side to the next. Stacks of reports. The latest journal issues. Assorted memoranda. Her chest hitched for a moment, reminded of her father's remaining papers to sort.

"Well, you should. You're not much of a salesperson, I get that, but if you're going to be a Principal Investigator ..."

"I know. Right now, I just find it difficult to care."

"Is this too much, too soon?" Alejandra slowed down enough so that her smile faltered for a moment.

"No. Honestly, I need the distraction of work." Sophine knew she couldn't begin to work until she had reclaimed her space.

Clearing the papers into a tray, she angled a framed daguerreotype of her and the Colonel toward her.

Alejandra smiled. "Good. Because you're smart and pretty."

"As are you," Sophine said absently.

"Thank you." Alejandra leaned against the desk. Biting at her bottom lip, she brushed her hair back over her ears. "That reminds me, you know what I heard him tell one of his assistants the other day?"

"Do tell."

"The assistant had remarked that I looked good that day, so *he* chides him saying, 'When one of your female colleagues starts to look attractive to you, then you know you've spent too much time in the lab.'"

"Yeager resents us." Sophine ducked below her desk, her words full of an echoing quality. "How many times did he mention that we were 'social experiment hires'?"

"We're the future." Alejandra attended an escuela secundaria in Medellin, one of Colombia's largest cities. Her mother developed early onset Alzheimer's disease. Her sister dropped out of school to take care of their mother so that Alejandra could finish school. The only reminder of them was a framed silvery daguerreotype on her desk of her sister wearing her First Communion dress, while her mother was hunched over in a chair.

"Which *that man* perfectly well knows, reminding his assistants with his snide commentary: 'Don't rile up the ladies, they have Lord Melbourne's ... ear.' He can't stand the fact that we are treated as his peers so early in our careers. His, dare I say, equals." Sophine snapped to attention, snitching a pen from its well and waving it like a pointer. "Meritocracy is an illusion, never forget that. The company would have you believe that the playing field is level, that its rewards go to the most successful, with that alone as their criteria, but ... why are you smiling?"

Alejandra wiped the grin from her face and put on a façade of mock seriousness. "It's good to see the spark of your usual self."

Alejandra turned around and dug through the pile of papers

Sophine had stacked away. She withdrew a small, unadorned envelope.

"Why are *you* smiling?" Sophine asked. "What have you been up to?"

"Nothing. When this letter arrived by messenger, I took the liberty of surreptitiously burying it in case *that man* dropped in to abscond with it. I may have overheard *that man* tell Lord Melbourne that he'd be happy to join him at the séance tonight."

"Séance?" Sophine crossed her arms, a sneer gave way to a look of boredom on her face. The bottom of her heart tumbled into a deep well at the very idea. The idea that there was another side, a side where her father now resided, was nearly offensive to her. But anger wasn't what nearly choked her. It was hurt. And longing. "I don't go in for that foolishness. And I would think, given your faith practices, neither would you."

"My faith isn't so soft that attending a séance would be an assault on it. Science would be a difficult course to pursue if that were the case. Besides, this is about the practicality of networking. Think of it as a themed dinner party, the séance as little more than eccentric entertainment."

"And if I were so inclined," Sophine tapped her pen on her desk, wishing she had her fan, "how would you find yourself on the invitation list?"

"As your plus one."

———

VOX DEI *DATA FILES: The Tuckaway House derived its name from being "tucked away" among the trees at 3128 N. Pennsylvania Avenue. From 1920 to 1930, the house was a famed salon, home to one of the most famous couples in the country, George and Nellie Meier. George made his fortune designing women's apparel. Nellie became a famous palm reader. Their patronage supported all manner of writers, artists, actors, dancers, and musicians. When they sponsored a colony of degenerates in the name of art, they fell out of favor with the local government. The property has since changed owner-ship several times.*

SOPHINE AND ALEJANDRA walked along the winding drive toward the house. The dreary estate, with its pervading iciness and the cool, aloof atmosphere of untended wealth, cast a pall over them. A dull and soundless evening, the tree frogs curiously mute, the cicadas' song stilled—the verdant chiaroscuro of the landscape had prematurely buried the sun. The oppressive landscape reeked of decayed trees in need of felling. The branches of an encroaching tree scraped against the corner of the manse. The bungalow-style cottage had a two-story salon in front and a complete second floor in the rear. A great, open porch led into a sunroom of latticed walls and ceilings. Tulips lined up like sentries at attention at the foot of the brick walls of the house. Great ceramic pots guarded each ledge. Latticework covered the windows along the basement. The number 1906 was etched into one of the stones at the front entrance.

A tall, thin lad, barely out of his teens, with his mustache trimmed to a severe angle, greeted them as if he expected them. Alejandra handed him Sophine's invitation. "Of course, of course. Right this way. Madame Bennet will be right along."

The thin man led them to the drawing room. In the corner was a pianoforte, surrounded by nearly a dozen paintings, including a large portrait framed in gold leaf. The not quite vaulted ceiling allowed a chandelier to hang without the threat of anyone bumping into it. A clock inside a glass dome ticked away moments from a nearby table. Curtains cordoned off the next room. Chairs were angled randomly throughout the room.

"Good evening, gentlemen. I hope we're not disturbing you," Sophine announced.

Lord Melbourne, Dr. Yeager, and Lucas Pruitt all stood up. The Chancellor nearly dropped his hat but recovered, however awkwardly.

"I didn't expect to see you here." Lord Melbourne took Sophine's hand, pressing his other hand over it.

"At a séance?" Sophine's face rendered elegant by the keen intelligence which laid in wait behind the beguiling playfulness in her hazel eyes. Mischievous humor hinted about in her lips. Glossed to an exaggerated redness, pursed tightly, not betraying a hint of her feelings. A blue accent mixed into a green kente cloth pattern; crinoline supported her dress as it flowed into a slight train. The image of her mother.

"Anywhere, actually." He lowered his head in a thoughtful nod, squeezed her hand once, and released his hold.

"I am anxious to be about my work." Sophine drew her hand to her neck.

"I'm glad to hear it," Lord Melbourne said. "Ms. Bennet purports to talk to people on the other side."

"The other side of what?" Sophine asked.

"Don't be dense. The great veil that separates this world from the next," Dr. Yeager said.

"She's a great consolation for those who have experienced loss," Alejandra said in a tone between whisper and reverence.

Sophine's suspicious eyes narrowed at her assistant. She had the feeling that her assistant had her own ulterior motives for luring her to this meeting.

"I've never heard a bigger load of rubbish." Pruitt assumed one of the chairs angled away from the ladies but toward Lord Melbourne.

"Be still, Lucas. It's all a diverting lark. Relax and enjoy the show." Lord Melbourne settled into a large, high-backed chair.

Victorian couches positioned back-to-back were covered with throw cushions and blankets. A fireplace at the far side of the room spat the occasional ember like seeds from a watermelon. Three Oriental rugs spanned the distance from the fireplace to the couches. Sophine and Alejandra adjourned to the nearest couch. Sophine tucked her dress under her as she sat. She ended up on the side closest to Lord Melbourne, almost face-to-face with him given the peculiar arrangement of furniture.

"I wonder how much room you make for spiritualism, for one with such a scientific bent." Dr. Yeager scooted next to Alejandra rather than take a chair that faced away from Lord Melbourne. Alejandra inched closer to Sophine.

"I suspect it is much the same for you," Sophine said.

"Oh, take no offense. I understand you come from a very spiritual people." Dr. Yeager announced in a way signifying his worldly understanding and progressiveness.

"Hoosiers?" Sophine asked.

Lord Melbourne chuckled.

"Some consider there to be a war between science and religion, was all I meant," Dr. Yeager said.

"I don't see them as at war with one another. Both are pursuits of truth with different methods. Even one of my simple spiritual people can hold two paradoxical viewpoints in her head without undue perplexity."

"Is that why you're here?" Lord Melbourne inquired. "Exploring truth through more spiritualist methods?"

Sophine inhaled. Matters of social engagement and polity did not come easily to her and she needed to quell the fount of anxiety threatening to erupt from her chest. "In truth, when Alejandra informed me of your gathering, I hoped it might permit us a chance to chat in a more informal setting."

"About what?"

An automaton rolled in with a serving tray. It stopped in front of each guest, offering a cup of tea with the options of cream, sugar, and digestive biscuits. Its blank face nodded with approval as each person took a cup. Sophine considered it a matter of her imagination that the mechanical servant met her inquisitive gaze, almost cocking its head at an angle, the way a dog might at the sound of its master's voice. The automata withdrew as silently as it arrived.

"I was told that you had an interest in my notes." Blowing across her tea, Sophine did not bring the cup to her lips. Rather she enjoyed the warmth of it in her hands. Only then did she realize how cool the room was.

"If I may," Dr. Yeager interrupted and shifted further in his seat toward Lord Melbourne. He would have jumped up and completely blocked her from view if he could. "I took the liberty of informing Miss Jefferson about your visit the other day."

"Yes, I was curious about your progress and wanted to discuss possible applications of your work," Lord Melbourne confirmed.

"Applications?" Sophine asked.

"Practical use."

"Beyond medical?"

"That's a start. I was curious about possible military uses."

"Such as what? Implanting the brains of soldiers into automatons? Men of metal controlled by human thought?" Sophine asked with a sharp rise to her voice. The shock of such implications staggered her.

"You see? Your mind has a natural facility for such imaginings."

"I couldn't live with myself if my work was used to harm another." Sophine unfurled her fan and held it open in her right hand. *You are too willing.*

"Presuming you could get your project to work," Dr. Yeager interjected.

Sophine made a point of ignoring him. "My goal is to heal, not have my work aid the baser instincts of humanity."

"Science is neither moral nor immoral, but merely a method. A method that sometimes produces useful tools which are, again, neither base nor given to a higher calling."

"The short answer is 'no.' I cannot see my work having any useful military uses." Sophine eased back in her chair as if hers was the final word on the subject. "I can guarantee that."

Maybe it was a play of the light, but Lord Melbourne's face flickered for a moment. A hint of hostility beneath his surface charm. In his eyes laid something dangerous.

"My, don't you all look tense," a woman announced from the doorway.

"Ladies and gentlemen, allow me to present our hostess for the evening." Lord Melbourne's easy smile returned in a heartbeat as he stood at attention. The other men rose. He stepped to the woman, took her hand, and led her down the carpet runner. "The legendary Emma Bennet."

Ms. Bennet's black dress hugged each ample curve of her body. Despite the graying of her thick blonde hair, a vitality infused her every movement. Her eyes thick with blue mascara, too much rouge on her cheeks, she took a long drag from her cigarette before leaving the holder on the mantel place. She strode the length of the room, enjoying everyone's captivated attention. The elegance of her bearing could not hide her Adam's apple.

"You really aren't good at this whole 'politics' thing, are you?" Alejandra whispered.

"I fear I may have done more harm than good." Sophine set her cup on the end table.

"A prudent fear."

The pair ceased their murmurs when Lord Melbourne and Ms. Bennet drew near. Lord Melbourne appeared giddy, a smitten schoolboy light on his feet and effusive with his charm. He took her from guest to guest. He began to introduce his companion, but she held up a finger to cut him off. She took in their full measure. Dr. Yeager attempted an awkward buss with her which she finessed with aplomb. When introduced to Alejandra, she half-bowed in deference. Ms. Bennet paused in front of Sophine with an extended stare. Sophine became so self-conscious of the woman studying her, she feared that a loose bit of salad clung to her teeth. Ms. Bennet pressed her hands to her chest as if overwhelmed and moved on.

"You hardly look like any medium I've ever seen." Pruitt swallowed a hint of disgust.

"Looks can be deceiving. I assure you, Ms. Bennet has been a spiritualist and trance medium for nearly four decades," Lord Melbourne said.

"That's an impressive resume for one so young," Dr. Yeager attempted flattery. "What's your secret?"

"I have the appetites of a woman half my age," Ms. Bennet said. "I'd actually say a quarter of my age is more likely, but then I'd be putting you in the uncomfortable position of admitting that young ladies might have appetites of their own." She smiled at Alejandra and Sophine.

"My dear, you are a delight," Lord Melbourne said.

"You're too sweet. Come, let us prepare ourselves."

Ms. Bennet led the way toward a table underneath a four-paned window. A lone candlestick remained unlit on the table next to a metal urn. Adjacent to the table was an array of books in a cabinet. Stands filled with thick and musty books had a layer of undisturbed dust. The shelves were thick with clutter, from vases with tiny flowers in them to figurines. So many fringed doilies lined every surface, the entire room felt smothered. Bookended by busts of an infant. In front of the books was a framed daguerreotype of a man and next to it, a large magnifying glass. A light holder stood taller than Pruitt. Three cherubs, each a foot tall, formed its gold-trimmed base. Another young man appeared from a cul-de-sac and beat Lord Melbourne to pulling her chair out for her. He did the same for Sophine and Alejandra before taking his leave through a door half hidden by the alcove.

"So many ... young men," Sophine remarked absently.

"Were I your age again, I'd be sitting on a throne of boys," Ms. Bennet said.

"Should we take our seats?" Lord Melbourne smiled. Pruitt and Dr. Yeager each had the curdled expression of having eaten a bad piece of fish.

"Yes. Lord Melbourne to my left next to ..." she gestured toward Sophine.

"Sophine." She gave a curt nod of her head.

"And you ..." Ms. Bennet flourished with her whole hand as if waving him away.

"Dr. Yeager." He sat on her right between her and Alejandra.

"Yes, you on my right next to our other lovely guest." She winked at Alejandra.

"And where do I sit?" Pruitt asked.

"There's only one seat left. You'd make a poor detective." Ms. Bennet sniffed. She took a moment to inspect the table. Satisfied, she stretched out her hands. "Good, good. We have a complete circle. Alternating men and women allows the psychic energy to balance and is greater that way. It will make it easier to pierce the veil. Come now, hands flat on the table."

"Then what?" Pruitt asked.

Annoyed, Ms. Bennet scrunched her face as if smelling something foul. "Then we wait. Clear your minds. Prepare your hearts. Concentrate on what you would ask of the spirit realm."

She gave them a stern look and they placed their hands flat on the table. Soon the room fell into a dreadful silence. While they stared at one another waiting for someone else to be the first to do something, another young man entered the room and sat down in a chair near, but angled slightly away from, Ms. Bennet. The young man brought out a notepad and began to write.

Not knowing what to do, Sophine closed her eyes. She considered the entire exercise a waste of time. Such spiritualism seemed out of place, but she wondered if it took such fringe activity to amuse certain types of idyll rich. Personally, her time would be better spent with a book. She chanced a peek at the rest of them to check if she were within expected decorum. Lord Melbourne pressed his eyes shut. Dr. Yeager modeled himself on Lord Melbourne, down to his posture. Pruitt fidgeted in his seat. Alejandra kept her head bowed; her gold cross dangled in the cleft of her décolletage.

The wind picked up and rattled the window panes with a start.

"There's definitely someone there. Everyone, stay very quiet," Ms. Bennet said. "Allow the spirit to feel safe." She inhaled deeply, then let her breath out slowly. She repeated it until they all found themselves breathing in lockstep with her. "Don't be shy. Come forth."

A series of bracelets slid down her wrist when she moved her arms. She took Lord Melbourne and Dr. Yeager's hands. They, in turn, took the ladies hands and so on until the circle was complete. Ms. Bennet tensed; her eyes closed. She lifted her face toward the ceiling. A low groan escaped her lips. She raised her chin and shivered as if a mild shock passed through her. Lord Melbourne's grip tightened on Sophine's hand.

"Look above my head. I feel a presence," Ms. Bennet intoned.

A wan light flickered above her. The ends of her hair raised, caught in a static charge.

"Someone here has suffered a great loss. Someone close to them. Her."

All eyes fell on Sophine. A twinge tightened in her chest in response. She buried it as fanciful foolishness she refused to entertain. The weight of the attention pressed on her; became a conscious thing in the room.

"A brother." Ms. Bennet shook her head, her eyes still closed. "No, a father. Spirit, are you there? I can't hear you."

Lucas and Dr. Yeager leaned in, straining to hear better.

"Have you a message for the woman?" Ms. Bennet's face contorted, struggling to understand the whispers only she could hear. "A rift? A gift? You ... have something for her? But she must wait a little while longer. Spirit, are you still there?"

Anger flared like a struck match within Sophine. The idea that her father might be in the room rose to the level of offense. Her lips pursed, unsure how much to let her fury show. She had already risked offending Lord Melbourne with her challenge to his plans. She closed her eyes to not betray her thoughts and to consider her next move.

A single knock emanated from underneath the table. Everyone except Ms. Bennet flinched as if jolted. She gripped the hands she held tighter, the blue veins in her hands became more pronounced.

"What is it, spirit?" Ms. Bennet leaned forward. With her eyes clenched, she turned to each of them in turn. "Someone here has blood on their hands."

The group turned to one another, their eyes more questioning than accusatory. The strange knock repeated. And again. It reverberated through Sophine's arms and filled her ears. A slow building banging that increased in fury. A burgeoning wave, like guilt. Of time wasted and memories and promises unfulfilled. Despite herself, she strained to sense any hint of her father.

Pruitt jumped up. "Enough of this nonsense. I can't stand it anymore. You wicked charlatan. Preying on the grieving. I won't be a party to it any longer."

Sophine couldn't help but sigh in relief. A part of her somewhat angry that even an ember of hope smoldered because of this effrontery.

"Spirit?" Ms. Bennet cried out, her voice an echo of itself. Sweat dabbled along her forehead. Her mascara began to smear. Her dress clung to her in a sloppy fashion. She weaved back and forth, craning about as though searching for someone, though her eyes remained shut. Finally, she slumped in her seat. "He's gone now. And I'm ... tired. So very, very tired. You must go."

Most of the group rose, taking concerned steps toward her but she waved them away. She mumbled about the strain of fighting against the force of doubt in the room. All eyes focused on Pruitt, who ran a finger along his collar.

"You must understand, I'm a good Christian," Pruitt exclaimed in mostly hushed tones as he excused himself. "I shouldn't have come here in the first place."

Lord Melbourne shooed him away before turning back and offering a hand to Ms. Bennet. "My apologies."

"No need." Two young men rushed to attend to her. One brought her a cup of tea. After giving her a moment to sip, the other helped her to her feet. "I fought against his negative energy the whole night. Ultimately, it proved ... exhausting."

"Then we'll take our leave." Lord Melbourne brought her hand to his lips.

Sophine rose. When she walked past Ms. Bennet, the older woman snatched her and drew her close.

"Your father ... he has something for you."

ELEVEN
LIKE FATHER LIKE SON

Vox Dei Data Files: [OP-ED] *The soft-hearted liberal elite cannot seem to fathom one simple fact: criminals behind bars cannot harm the public. The best way to deter crime is to enforce existing laws and hand down tough penalties. Upstanding citizens don't need any strikes: a first crime demands mandatory sentencing. A robust constitution and a strong political will allows for the repeal of citizens' access to government programs by those classified as Unpersons, as well as the mandatory sentencing for Unpersons, debtors, degenerates, and dangerous felons. In addition, said persons should be housed in prisons without amenities in order to make the threat of jail itself a deterrent. And make them appreciate the privilege of civil society. The confiscation of assets and privatizing prisons allow the criminal justice system to fund itself. All of which leads to a safer United States.*

PART of Sleepy still clutched to a few fantasies about his father. Back when he was in 5th Form, he liked to think that his father was a spy working for the Pinkerton Agency at a level they couldn't acknowledge. Deep undercover, perhaps infiltrating the Five Civilized Tribes or deep in the heart of Tejas. Not that he shared any of these ideas with his classmates for fear that they'd ridicule him. As the years wore on, his daydreams simplified, settling on the possibility that his father had been killed in a shoot-out or explosion—something dramatic—which explained why he couldn't contact them. Incarceration was just so ... common.

Marion County Lockup served as the secondary education for many poor, young men, with The Ave as their finishing school. Once someone had been incarceration's student, it infected them like a virus. It bore into their psyches, defining how they dressed, how they walked, how they talked. Prison trustees lined the walls of the processing area, each one assigned to a new arrival whom they watched with the careful scrutiny of a hawk tracking a field mouse. Each new detainee took one somnambulant step after another, making their way from one checkpoint to the next. A Pinkerton attendant took Sleepy's hand, rolled each finger in ink in order to print them onto indexing cards. Sleepy barely had a chance to wipe the ink from his hands when he was directed to face a camera for his daguerreotype. A few steps behind him, Knowledge Allah was soon caught in its sharp glare.

"Here you go," Sleepy's father handed him a paper sack. A low cropped tangle of hair and a thick, black mustache framed deep, inset brown eyes, slow to focus on anything in particular, like he stared out at the world from within a cave. His mouth twisted into a half sneer. A keloid etched along the base of his neck. He smelled faintly of cigarettes—Kools brand, if Sleepy remembered him right— and sweat. A big man, but not as big as Sleepy recalled. The man who loomed so large in his memory had hands so large they could slap the entire expanse of his butt with one careless swat.

Two Pinkerton guards trailed behind them at all times, the silent authority to the trustees' role as overseers. In The Ave, guards had been replaced by large, mechanical spiders. Eight-limbed automata with metal nodules, the bottoms of canisters, budding from their chassis, ever ready to subdue their prisoners at the slightest infrac- tion. Here, since trustees wanted to retain their status, they policed their own with greater vigor and severity than a guard ever would.

This way the Pinkertons rarely had to sully their hands with contact.

Sleepy opened the bag to find a bologna sandwich, potato chips, and a cookie. "What you got?"

"Beans and tofu," Knowledge Allah peeked inside the sack handed to him by his trustee. "Why? You want to trade?"

Sleepy turned up his nose and took a bite of his sandwich. With his mouth full, he rumbled, "Nah, man, I'm good."

"You a friend of Hubert's?" Sleepy's father swung his leg over the bench and joined them. He nodded to Knowledge Allah's trustee, dismissing him.

"I think he prefers to go by Sleepy." Knowledge Allah took a spoonful of his beans.

"Booker Nixon. My friends call me 'Bird.'"

"(120 Degrees of) Knowledge Allah."

"Ah, you one of them Lost Nation boys, ain't you?" Booker tapped his index finger along the table.

"Something like that."

"That'll serve you well in here." Booker bent over to grab a bundle. He handed each of them an orange jumpsuit. "Here. Change into these."

"Why? I can make bail." Sleepy turned to Knowledge Allah. "For both of us."

"If they're having you change into these, they expect you to be with us for a while."

"But ... bail," Sleepy repeated as if no one understood the definition of the word.

"Boy, I can tell you ain't had no brush with the system. Bet you expected one of them public defenders to show up, too. They will. And you'll get a bail hearing. Shouldn't be more than a few months."

SLEEPY RAN his fingers against the cool of the freshly painted walls, steadying himself as Booker led them down a long corridor. The dawning reality of his predicament gave him a sense of vertigo.

Gaslit fixtures hid behind protective grates. Their shoes squeaked against floors which had been mopped to a shine. Gates clanked at every juncture, each trustee/new arrival pair stopped about every fifty feet or so.

"I don't look bad in orange," Sleepy whispered.

"No one looks good in these ... outfits. And I'm not talking from a fashion sense."

Knowledge Allah limped along. Considered a weapon, the jail kept his cane with his other belongings. His limp wasn't pronounced enough to make any sort of medical allowance. He loped slowly along, trying to hide his limp as much as possible. The last thing he wanted to show a hall of predators was any weakness.

They arrived at an open bay. Two rows of cages, one atop the other—like the jaws of a huge beast clamped shut by braces—stretched on for several city blocks. There was no telling how many detention levels there were. Despite the open congregating area, Sleepy couldn't shake off the sensation of being trapped in close quarters. His breath hitched in his chest, the air thick and heavy as if it had been re-breathed through a dozen bodies. Bodies which carried the stink of The Tombs on them.

COPs filled the jail like they were on a mission. Vagrancy and nuisance laws such as "mischief" and "insulting gestures" were enforced vigorously among the Unperson population. This pipeline to Unperson status opened up a flood of convict leasing—prisoners contracted out to private firms. The rise of crime became the excuse to crack down harder. The law and order rhetoric sounded so reasonable, several prominent leaders joined in, not seeing the trap until it was too late.

Men leaned over metal railings, leering at them as they walked beneath them. It was like Sleepy was in his last year in primary school. Not sure who liked him. Not sure if he was doing school right. Convinced everyone was teasing him. Uncomfortable in his own skin. They stopped at an empty cell. Sleepy and Knowledge Allah carried their jumpsuits to the nearest bunks.

"You look good." Booker smiled. Not too eager but he pressed none the less. He followed Sleepy into the cell.

"Surprised you could ..." Sleepy started keeping his back to the man.

"... pick you out of a lineup?" Booker leaned against the bars, allowing Sleepy his space. Knowledge Allah also kept a discreet distance to allow them a measure of privacy. He stood between them and any passing eavesdropper or would be troublemakers.

"Heh. Whatever." Sleepy sat on the bottom bunk, bouncing slightly to test its springs. He studied the bed frame, the open toilet in the corner situation, the tiles, the bars, anything to avoid making eye contact with his father.

"How's your mom?" Booker asked.

"Dead." Sleepy delivered the news like he intended to slide a blade between the man's ribs.

In silence, Booker absorbed the news. The thin smiled disappeared, replaced by something older. And angrier. "Always thought you were better than me."

"No, I didn't."

"Yeah, you did. I could tell then and I can tell now."

"I was thirteen when you left. How would you know what I thought?"

"I saw it in your eyes from the time you were eight." Booker sighed wistfully and took a step backward. When he spoke again, his voice held less edge to it. He tried to fix the smile back onto his face. "You probably were. I don't blame you. I know I wanted you to be better than me."

"What do you think we're going to accomplish with this little chat?" Sleepy leaned forward, not even glancing toward his father's side of the cell.

"You need it."

"How do you know what I need?" Sleepy hated the defensive tone in his voice.

"I can guess you might have a word or two to say to me."

"I don't need anything from you."

"Fair enough. You seem to have grown into a fine young man without me." With a measured breath, he seemed to be reading from some rehearsed script and was determined to stick to it. Booker examined him again, something close to pride in his eyes.

"Without. You." Sleepy echoed, hoping the words landed like the blows of a hammer.

"I deserved that."

"This where you been?" Sleepy asked.

"Some of the time." Booker shrugged.

"But not all." Sleepy pounced on the gap in his story as if he were now a Principal Investigator interrogating a suspect he knew was determined to lie to him. "You could've reached out."

"It was easier not to."

"Easier on who?"

"Me, I guess." Booker took the bunk across from Sleepy. He was tall enough that even seated, he had to hunch to keep from banging his head on the top bunk. His muscles coiled and tensed with each movement, fluid and powerful, still a strong man who knew how to use his body.

Sleepy remembered the only time he feared his dad. He couldn't have been much more than twelve when left alone in the house. His school let out earlier than those of his siblings and long before his parents arrived home from work. Sleepy made a habit of going through his parents' stuff out of simple curiosity. Parents were always such a mystery. As if in their drawers or in their closets, they hid secrets only adults were allowed to know. The story of who they were. His dad's closet was a treasure trove.

Sleepy only had an hour and a half each day, and he excavated the closet with the care of an archaeologist on a dig. He'd uncover a shelf, memorize the place of every object, rifle through it, and replace everything the way he'd found it. One day he uncovered an old shoe box filled with all manner of pornographic pulp novels. Though many of the books had their covers removed, what few remained intact had racy covers. Sleepy stayed on that shelf for a long while.

When he reached the top shelf of the closet, he found a black suitcase, the kind he imagined espionage agents carried. Inside were all manner of penny sheet clippings. His father at sports meets, running track or playing football, a star in his day. Yellowed daguerreotypes of him with his mother and father. It was the first time Sleepy had seen any image of his grandparents. Paperwork from past jobs, resumes, school transcripts, the sum of who his father was contained in a briefcase.

In the inside pocket of one of the suit jackets—he'd never seen his father wear a suit—was a baggie filled with chiba leaves. Sleepy didn't know what they were at first. He inhaled deeply, taking in their loamy odor. He described his find to his schoolmates who immediately propositioned him to sell some of the stash to them. Their prices seemed reasonable, besides it cost him nothing to sell someone else's stuff. Two or three times a week for nearly a month he parceled out a few leaves and sold it to his friends. One day he came home to find his father standing in his room holding a half-empty bag.

Sleepy's heart sunk. So deep was the feeling, he was pretty sure the sensation bottomed out somewhere near his testicles. A bead of perspiration formed at his hairline. His armpits grew warm and moist and itchy. The anger simmering in his father's eyes terrified him. It was the first and only time he thought his father might actually seriously harm him.

There was no trial, no questioning, no going through the motions of explanations. His father drew back his huge hand and swung. Sleepy braced for impact. The hand seemed to arc at him from several states away with a speed and force that might knock him into the next building. Then at the last instant, his father caught himself and pulled the slap short. It landed as little more than a pat on his cheek. Still, the shock rippled the boy. An emotional wave of his father's fear at his own anger lashing out, the disappointment, the hurt, and the overwhelming sadness.

"Don't touch my things ever again," Booker whispered. The words carried the threat of a storm.

"Yes, Pops." Tears welled in Sleepy's eyes as if he'd broken something he didn't know how to fix.

They never spoke of it again. Not to each other, not to his

mother, not to the unipod. It wasn't but a few months later that his father left. Part of him always blamed himself for his father leaving.

"Ask the question." Booker fixed his dark, cavernous stare on him.

"What question?" Sleepy asked.

"The one you've always wanted to ask."

Sleepy braced both his arms into his bed as if to steady himself. "Why did you leave?"

Booker relaxed a little. The way a man eager to take the stand to defend himself walked when he finally had the opportunity. Especially knowing it would do him no good. "I don't expect you to understand. I lost my job. I don't know—I never want you to know—what it's like for a man to be off the work cycle. It eats at you. When company after company passes on you, you start to feel ... not good enough. Not worth anything. You come home to see your family struggling. Hungry. Looking for you—depending on you—to take care of them. The powerlessness that you feel. The worthlessness, the emptiness, the uselessness—the feelings gnaw at you until you convince yourself that they'd be better off without you."

"You left."

"Companies may not have wanted me, but that didn't mean there wasn't work for me to do. I got hooked up with Sugar. Ran numbers for him."

Word on the vine was that a janitor on Wall Street studied the Federal Reserve Clearing House report number totals in the daily penny sheets. The numbers came out each day, random. They couldn't be fixed. The system became the basis of a daily street lottery: a three-digit winning number was a combination of the last two digits of the "exchange total" of the New York Stock Exchange and a third from the last number of the "balances total." The winning total paid at 600 to one, so a tenth of a credit bet netted 60 credits. Playing the numbers was part gambling, part social event. Everyone joined in from the speakeasies to barbershops to beauty salons to grocery stores to churches. Bets, placed by everyday citizens, added up to millions. Part of an underground economy that grew under the tender ministrations of the "policy operators." Sugar was a bank, bankrolling the entire operation.

"COPs bust you?" Sleepy asked.

"A couple years back. They've been cracking down on activity, especially along Indiana Avenue."

"I know. They raided the spot I was doing my poetry at the other day."

"You spitting rhymes now?" Booker's face lit up with interest.

"Been writing for a while. Last year or so, I been getting on the mic, mostly down at the Two-Johns Theater."

"The Two-Johns? That's tight," Booker said. "You know, back in the day, I fancied myself a trumpet player. We couldn't afford lessons, but, man, in my heart, I could blow."

Sleepy shifted in discomfort, not knowing what to do with so personal a revelation. Like when he found himself staring at the daguerreotype of grandparents he never knew. "So, they got you in lockup? How long they keeping you here?"

"Don't know. I been doing whatever it takes to keep out of The Ave."

Everyone heard stories of the private prison facility known as The Ave. Some spoke of work farms, others of mechanical spiders serving as guards. Of holes so deep within the prison, that Unpersons thrown into them never returned.

"What does that mean? Snitching?"

With an unexpected suddenness and force, Booker snatched Sleepy and dragged him to the back of the cell. "Don't even joke like that. Not in here. Never in here. Careless talk like that can get someone killed." Booker lightened his grip and smoothed out Sleepy's shirt. "Besides, it ain't like that. I'm just trying to keep out of The Ave. Here, I at least have a name and the clothes on my back. There, they strip you of everything and put you to work until you drop. Now me? Here? You know how I do. I got that charm. Got put on as a trustee."

"You still working for the system." Sleepy further smoothed out his shirt, brushing away all evidence of contact with his father.

"Getting by to survive. I'm trying to earn enough to buy a court date. This system ... it's like I don't exist. I'm just waiting on the official notice that I'm an Unperson. I ..." Booker stopped, reconsidered his words, then started again. "I didn't want to be reunited like this. Not in here. But the universe moves in mysterious ways. You don't know how many times I wanted to reach out to you. Check in on all of you."

"I get it."

"You do? Really?" The side of Booker's mouth tightened in a disbelieving smirk.

"You thought you were failing as a man, so you left. That about it?"

"Something like that."

"Thing is, you didn't fail as a man *until* you left." Sleepy let the words hang between them for a while. The three of them stared at one another in silence, the confines of the cell closing in on them. "Don't you have somewhere to be?"

"You'll need someone to look out for you in here. You'll need friends."

"I needed a father. Friends I have. See you around, Pops."

Booker fixed his eyes on Sleepy, then to Knowledge Allah, then back to Sleepy. "That how it's going to be?"

"That's how it is," Sleepy said with finality.

Booker stiffened. His tone shifted to that of a disinterested professional carrying out his duties. "Count's at eight. Lights out at 9:30 pm. Count again at 3:30 a.m. Then breakfast."

With that, Booker pushed past Knowledge Allah without so much as a grunt.

Sleepy stared morosely after his father as he walked out. Again.

"You good?" Knowledge Allah patted and rested his hand on Sleepy's shoulder.

"Yeah, I'm good."

SLEEPY CONSIDERED how much this stay would cost him. Convicts had to pay court costs and fines, and, in some situations, the cost of guards. Legs dangled from the bunk above distracted him. Knowledge Allah slowly lowered himself to the ground, a spider easing itself down on an invisible strand, before steadying himself on his bad leg. He took a few tentative steps to test the strength in his leg before putting his full weight on it. Out of habit, he stretched out his hand for his cane, but it wasn't there.

"Your knee bothering you?" Sleepy asked.

"The pain is a reminder." Knowledge Allah's face contorted with each step. Each morning was the same, the slow rise and the deliberate pacing, pushing through the pain until most of the stiffness loosened up.

"You have a lot of reminders in your life." Sleepy watched the routine with distant fascination.

"I never want to forget any lesson, no matter how hard it was learned." Knowledge Allah kept his back to him, attempting to use the toilet with as much privacy the small cell allowed. "Otherwise the tricknology of supremacy will get your mind state upset and out of balance."

They headed down to the cafeteria. They had barely settled into eating before a trustee stood at the end of their dining table. Sleepy scanned the room for any sign of his father. He couldn't help a twinge of disappointment that his father had simply given up and disappeared when the conversation became difficult. "You two have a visitor."

Sleepy glanced up from his plate of what he presumed were scrambled eggs. The headcount had them awake and out of their cell by four a.m. and he was far from adjusted to their new schedule. He'd read once that the Marion County Lockup facility had been sued by its inmates a few years back. That in and of itself was newsworthy since so many prisoners had to combine their earnings to purchase a court date over the matter. They claimed the living conditions violated their civil rights. In the end, they prevailed. The facility hired a new food service vendor and even contracted with a healthcare provider. Sleepy couldn't imagine what the food must've been like before the lawsuit.

"What visitor?" Knowledge Allah said.

"Someone who requested you. Since you two share the same case ..."

Knowledge Allah wiped his mouth. "Let's go."

The trustee led them out of the cafeteria to the visitor's reception area. A large, open room with several tables in it. On the far side of the room, small rooms partitioned off by glass doors were available. Inside one was a tall man with deep sepia skin. Black tinted glasses hid his eyes. A black pinstriped suit jacket draped to his knees. A blood red bow tie clung to his neck. The man looked vaguely familiar, though Sleepy couldn't place him.

"Who's he? Your barrister?" Sleepy whispered.

"Something like that." Knowledge Allah grasped the man's outstretched hand before turning to introduce his friend. "Sleepy, this is Majestic Jamal, Minister of Propaganda for the Lost Nation."

"Sleepy? Like so many brothers locked up in here. At least you admit your condition with your name." Majestic Jamal tucked his suit jacket under him as he sat down.

"I'm already tired of your bullshit," Sleepy said with bored nonchalance, not extending his hand for any sort of greeting. He couldn't figure out why Knowledge Allah was suddenly acting so out of sorts. Just then, Sleepy placed Majestic Jamal as the man who had been at the Two-Johns the night of the COPs raid.

Majestic Jamal returned his attention to Knowledge Allah. "Seems every time the Lost Nation finds you, you're in some sort of lockup."

"*Father Justice* was the one who found me. In a county lockup."

"'His beloved sun' he always called you. He still talks about you. Even after all that transpired." Majestic Jamal brushed lint only he could see from his jacket's shoulder. Without glancing up, he said, "You broke his heart."

Knowledge Allah shifted uncomfortably, half-turning toward the door before remembering that he couldn't leave. The awkward dance and scurry to depart was familiar. "What do you want, Majestic Jamal?" Knowledge Allah asked.

"To see if we can help our wayward sun." Majestic Jamal's voice bit with malevolence as well as a genuine concern, as if he were bound by duty to support Knowledge Allah, not out of actual concern for him. Faith always created strange bedfellows.

"Not gloat after how far that sun has fallen?"

"I am here. How's your brother, Keith?" Majestic Jamal asked.

Knowledge Allah grew coldly silent. Almost embarrassed. "We still haven't spoken."

"After all this time? Even once you left the Lost Nation?" Majestic Jamal reveled in whatever knife he turned in Knowledge Allah's belly. "I figured once you left our—how did you put it? 'Cult of grand delusion'—you'd have reunited with your 'real' family."

"Lost Nation was my family when I turned him away. Seemed only right that I face the consequence of my choices."

"I am here." Majestic Jamal uttered the words as if they pained him. "I am here because Father Justice still cares. About you."

"All of his secrets are safe with me, if that's what you're wondering." Knowledge Allah flinched whenever the words Father Justice were uttered. A twinge of pain strained his face.

The Lost Nation wasn't a gang. They were a way of life, taking in citizen and Unperson alike. They were an identity, their ways like a religion. Their words like a convicting spirit in The Tombs. Their message like the practical application of the dream preached by the Star Child. Father Justice was their head and if Knowledge Allah was his favored sun, leaving them had to be traumatic on many levels. Knowledge Allah rubbed his leg.

"Some within the Nation still see you as a potential threat."

"Wise Abu wouldn't be Minister of Defense if he didn't."

"Then you understand his concern."

"When caught in the jaws of the beast, some might be tempted to spread ... any lie ... to save themselves." Knowledge Allah had a faraway gleam in his eye, recalling some lesson.

"You remember him well."

"I remember you all well. I remember who I was with you. My oaths, my duty, my heart. I was with you. But there were some things I could not abide as a matter of conscience. It broke my heart to leave the Lost Nation. My family. You remain my brothers even in exile. I know who I am now. Why are you here?"

"As I said, some see you as a potential threat. But you still have friends. You may need them. In here, the message of Father Justice has not reached some of our brothers. Gangs still run this place. Untain Boys, City Boys, Ghetto Boys, Gimmie Boyz, Ridin' Boys, Wretched Boys. If your friends were to believe you did not hold their best interests at heart, they'd have no choice but to see such a false prophet buried out of sight. And hearing."

Sleepy heard whispers of some of these gangs from when he lived in the Meadows. And The Tombs. Only the biggest fool was surprised when a stigmatized group embraced their stigma as a coping strategy. The danger for the overcity, any overcity, was when hands of Unpersons united. For protection against COPs to do commerce outside of its system. They walked a line between prey and predator even among their own. Listed together like this, however, he couldn't help but think they could use some sort of brand management advice.

"For such staunch allies, your assurances all seem to have the intimations of a threat," Knowledge Allah said.

"You are paranoid. You have been ever since you broke with us. You know us. You know our ways better than most. The penalty for such a break is isolation. Yet, here I am. My job is to assess and, if you don't represent a threat, bring you home."

"I ... don't know what that means."

"Because you're too stubborn to see with your heart. I'm here as a friend, simply carrying the words of your friends. You may be done with us, but we're not done with you. You have and may always be his favored sun. He won't see you caged. Be safe. Be patient." Majestic Jamal stood up to leave. "Peace, sun."

"Peace, sun."

THE NIGHT COUNT was due to happen in a few minutes. Knowledge Allah hobbled over to his cot. Sitting on its edge, he rubbed his weak leg. Sleepy waited for him to reach for a book, but he kept massaging his leg, lost in thought. Sleepy left him to his silence for most of the day, though he hovered nearby like a mother worried about her child battling a fever. He plucked a hair from his chin. Closing his eyes at the fresh sting of pain; a nervous habit he'd developed to remind himself that he could still feel. His world turned upside down, he lost the thread of who he was. His mother was a woman of dreams and ideas. And causes. "Life ought to be lived outside of yourself," she often preached. The soft footfalls in the hall betrayed an approaching trustee.

"All right, you two, time to go," Booker called out, not meeting Sleepy's eyes. Two Pinkerton guards stood sentry behind him.

"Go where?" Sleepy stirred. It had been a couple of weeks, and the routine of incarceration had become familiar. He joined Knowledge Allah in standing at the rear of the cell.

"You're being transferred."

"To where?"

"The Ave."

"The Ave?" Sleepy asked. "You have to be kidding me. We're bound to have a court date before too long."

"No, you're not," Booker said.

"That's not fair."

"What are you? Five? This ain't a negotiation. This is the way things are done, especially to Unpersons."

The words wounded Sleepy almost as much as if the man had gone ahead and slapped him. Booker, biological father or not, was little more than a stranger, yet wielded both personal and administrative power over him, and Sleepy reached an emotional impasse on how to react to him. Knowledge Allah rested a hand on his back, a momentary brush of solidarity.

"Let's go," Booker repeated.

The gates opened, a series of clockwork gears grinding against one another. The metallic clang a constant reminder that they were all caged. Booker led them along the rail past several cells. No one called out to them, insulted them, or made any comment on their passing. Joined in grim silence, the prisoners all knew a late-night transfer meant a trip to The Ave. No one wished that on even their worst enemy. Any of them could be next. The hallways seemed to stretch in more serpentine patterns at night. The shadows of the dimmed corridors made the halls appear unfamiliar. Different. Sleepy shuffled along, his legs not wanting to carry him where they were heading. Any promenade through the bowels of the jail tempered Sleepy's demeanor. The place imposed itself on his spirit, almost a physical thing which weighed upon him to the point of him struggling to take in a full breath. They descended a set of stairs leading to the receiving bay where they had first been unloaded. A bus idled, a blue behemoth of firing pistons, long flutes along each side issuing steam, warming the bay.

"Just two," Booker said to the Pinkerton guard. A middle-aged man whose bald head shone like burnished bronze. His mood and temperament easily read in his sallow complexion, he turned florid at their approach.

"I had transfer orders for twenty." He opened a log book and inspected the men as if Booker fulfilled a livestock order.

"Don't know what to tell you, boss. I was only sent to get two." Booker slipped an envelope to the guard.

Sleepy kept his eyes downcast, pretending not to take too much notice or interest in the transaction. With his head lowered, he glanced over at Knowledge Allah who caught his eye and gave a barely perceptible shrug.

"It don't matter to me." Thumbing through the credits, the agent pocketed the envelope. "If there was an error in the paperwork, I'll just make another run. You're up, trustee."

The bus was made up of two compartments: the swollen belly which housed prisoners and the twin slotted cab which drove it. Booker entered the bus and got behind the wheel. The guard took out a set of shackles and clipped one to Knowledge Allah and the other to Sleepy. The chains jangled with each step, though their stride had long since adjusted and accustomed to a chain length. The Pinkerton escorted them to the rear of the bus, fastened the shackles to the rear bench, and then got into the shotgun slot of the cab to watch over his prisoners. Booker shifted the bus into gear and drove away. The bus rumbled along the roads. The spires of downtown Indianapolis loomed over them, the bus remained in its shadows for miles until they left the Mile Square of the overcity on the way to the outskirts of the city where they would be deposited and forgotten in the belly of The Ave.

———————

VOX DEI DATA FILES: Originally founded as a separate village from Indianapolis proper, Broad Ripple was the result of a merger between two rival communities—Broad Ripple and Wellington— each vying for expansion. The White River wound along its north side; the ever-crowded thoroughfare of Keystone Avenue pulsed along its east; Kessler Boulevard meandered on the south, and the officious Meridian Street stood rigid guard to its west. Indianapolis residents built homes in Broad Ripple, using it as a summer retreat from the city. It even once sported its own amusement park built to rival Coney Island's, though, by criminal shenanigans, it burned to the ground two years after its construction.

THE TRANSPORT WAGON held an oppressive heat. Its steam-mount engine pistoned and hissed as it growled along the streets. Only a thin grate separated Sleepy from the driver—his father—not that he bothered to consider the man. Each pothole landed with such a jarring force, Sleepy's joints ached. He hunched along his bench, turning his hands over, studying the way the manacles fastened to his wrists and jangled with his movement. He imagined a musicality to them, different movements producing different notes, until he decided it was only his imagination and it was the same note of bondage. Knowledge Allah folded his arms across his body as best as he could, lost in the mathematics of his thoughts. The large Pinkerton bus slowed.

"Boss," Booker said, "I think we have a problem."

"What is it?" The Pinkerton guard first craned about in his seat, then peered through the windshield, using his hand as a visor against the glare of street lamps.

"Something in the road." Booker's voice rose with insistence.

"Where?" The guard braced himself against the metal grate of the cage, nearly rising from his perch.

Booker turned the steering wheel with sudden violence and stomped on the brakes. The guard slammed against the metal wall of the wagon. The vehicle careened, sliding along the road, the tires unable to maintain their grip on the street. It overturned, continuing to skid along its side until it came to a halt. Over a stream of oaths, Sleepy clutched his chains, holding onto them in fervent prayer that the laws of physics would not have him tumbling out of the bus. Knowledge Allah flew into the air, a distant shadow lost in the thuds and banging of the bus. Booker reached between the slits of the cage and freed the baton from the barely conscious guard. He whacked the man twice in the head until he was satisfied the guard was unconscious.

"You two all right back there?" Booker yelled.

Sleepy slowly unfurled from the chained ball he had curled into. Each movement accompanied by a pause to make sure everything was in working order. "Knowledge Allah?"

A low moan came in response. "What the hell happened?"

"You two have friends. More than you think." Booker strained to reach the keys secured on the guard's belt. The guard's body had tumbled away from him, dangling precariously from his seat, half-slumped out of the window. "I can't reach the keys, but you need to go."

"Go where?" Sleepy asked.

"You want to go to The Ave?"

"No."

"Then anywhere but here," Booker barked.

"What about you?"

"Hopefully they'll buy that he received his injuries in the crash. Otherwise, I suspect I'll be tossed in The Ave."

"But ..." A conflicting mix of feelings began to well up in Sleepy.

"... at least you'll know where to find me. Now go." Booker cut him off. He jerked his chin toward the rear door. "Go on now."

Examining his shackles, Sleepy stomped at the joint which fastened them to the transport bus. Given the angle, damaged sustained in the crash, and his weight already straining it, the bar gave way quite easily. Both sets of chains tumbled loose. He scooped up Knowledge Allah, wrapping an arm around him. Sleepy turned back to his father. The man waved him on. He tossed the baton into the seat well of the guard and positioned himself in a pose of unconsciousness. Already sirens wailed in the distance. The rear door popped open in the crash. They scrambled out and headed into the nearby bushes.

"This is going to be awkward." Sleepy held up his still manacled wrist.

"Where to?" Knowledge Allah raised his left hand to more closely examine the handcuffs. The movement tugged Sleepy's right arm toward him like some sort of chained marionette.

"Up there." Sleepy pointed to a lone structure atop a hill. "That's the Fall Creek lift station. I know those facilities."

They clomped up the hill. Much of the land around any waterway was as little developed as possible to preserve the landscape. The manicured lawn of the lift station was an open expanse. Sleepy felt too exposed. At the top of the hill was a concrete structure reminiscent of a military bunker. He led them around to the side of it. His hand hovered over the electro-chirographer pad. He punched in his code, each tap causing a hesitation in his breath. When the door clicked in release, he sighed.

"You know the code?" Knowledge Allah asked.

"I still work for Commonwealth Waterworks. Even if they terminated me when I was arrested, it takes forever for paperwork to push through cancelling everything. The employee codes work for all facilities. Come on."

Sleepy accessed the first tool closet. He rifled through the equipment until he found a set of bolt cutters. After a few fumbled attempts—eventuating in him passing the cutters to Knowledge Allah who had a better angle—the cutters snipped the chains.

"What's that sound?" Knowledge Allah held the bolt cutters up and close to him like they were a rifle.

Sleepy cracked the side door open. Spotlights crisscrossed the hill. A low-flying airship hovered nearby, deploying men. Two more Pinkerton vans screeched to a halt. The distant bays of dogs soon followed. He closed the door. "We won't be going back that way."

"Any other exits?" Knowledge Allah asked.

"Plenty. But most take you back to street level."

"Most?" Knowledge Allah pointed to the chimney. "How about up there?"

Sleepy sighed. "Do I look like Father Christmas?"

"Well, you lack a certain jolly quality to be certain." Knowledge Allah shrugged since they had few options.

Leading the way, Sleepy climbed the ladder. The tube enclosed around him. With each step, he feared the channel narrowing and him becoming wedged in it. He focused on taking the next rung, not considering how high they must have climbed. Even through the walls, he felt the rumble of the waterway rushing alongside the station. The faraway thrum receded with each step, but he didn't know if it troubled him more or not. The hatch opened into a narrow access hallway. Sleepy was becoming less and less of a fan of this plan, already imagining the safety and comfort a small cell would provide him. He shimmied through the tunnel until they reached the end. The opening overlooked Fall Creek. Though described as a creek, from his vantage point it had the width and depth of a river. Its current bubbled white in the waning moonlight. The noise of it drowned out almost all other sounds. To the south, COPs cordoned off the street. A bridge spanned the north. At the backside of the facility along the hill base, dogs barked. They were running out of options.

"We need to jump," Knowledge Allah said.

"Jump?" Sleepy peered over the edge of the railing. "I live by a code. One of them is that I don't go leaping off perfectly fine buildings. Maybe if you'd said we need to take a hostage or said, 'shoot somebody,' I'd be down."

"We don't have very many choices. Or time."

"Time? It's 'fuck that shit o'clock.' Look, I'll turn myself in." Sleepy backed toward the tunnel. Knowledge Allah caught his arm.

"And spend the rest of your life in The Ave? Because once they add the very real charge of prison escape to their laundry list of made up charges ..."

"It's a long way down and this goes against my nature. Can we rock, paper, scissors this shit? Draw straws? Something?"

"It's time to change your nature. On three," Knowledge Allah said.

"One, two ..." Sleep counted off.

Knowledge Allah shoved Sleepy over the edge and then leaped into the night after him.

TWELVE

THEY USED TO DO IT OUT IN THE PARK

Vox Dei Data Files: George Kessler once said that, "planning should be comprehensive. Even though a grand urban design could only be realized in bits and pieces, and over a long period of years, still we should always know where we are going." His 1908 vision of nearly 3500 acres of extensive, interconnected parks was at the heart of Indianapolis's neighborhood planning. He lined the city's streams with boulevards which linked the major parks. After World War II, with the influx and increase of dissident voices, the park system fell into neglect.

THE DAY AFTER THE SÉANCE, Sophine wandered the corridors of the ZeroDyne Corporation labs in a slight daze, as if her morning hadn't quite come into focus. The open doors and glass walls design made every scientist appear like mice scampering through a maze. She passed white face after white face, not knowing why she was suddenly so conscious of their color. She wondered if she imagined the suspicion in their eyes. The jealousy. They may have thought this was the first time she had entered hostile spaces. Every day at school, being both a woman and "half-caste"—as the Oxford University elite often referred to her—made her the object of such attention on a regular basis. Every day at her boarding school, even her instructors would comment on her privilege. Every day she left her house, she ignored them, contenting herself to be lost in thoughts too advanced for them.

Her fashion sense had become a shield for her. An emerald tail vest over black zip leggings. She doffed her Baron top hat at Dr. Yeager as she passed him. When she entered her lab, Alejandra hid behind her workbench. Her leg danced up and down with anxious intensity, as if she was already six cups of coffee into her morning.

"How are you doing?" Alejandra asked from behind a row of flasks, a nervous quality trilled her voice.

"I'm still deciding whether I'm upset with you or not." Sophine donned her lab coat, a jacket of kente cloth patterns matching her tail vest. She slid a pair of magnifier flip goggles onto her head.

"Do tell." Alejandra sprang up from her seat. Her lab coat trailed behind her like a white cape. Her complexion seemed darker against it. Despite her high energy, she moved with a quiet elegance. A white blouse buttoned up to her neck. A simple ruche skirt. Much more in line with what was expected of a woman in her position. A measure of envy stirred within Sophine. There was something both stately and stalwartly feminine in her lab assistant's every gesture that part of her longed to have.

"I feel as if last night might have been a setup. A gathering arranged for your amusement."

"You mean me dragging you, my helpless prey, to a meeting of predators ready to pounce?" Alejandra smiled.

Sophine bristled at the grin. Her assistant obviously underestimated how serious the matter at hand was. And her feelings about the matter. "Yes. And I don't appreciate your mocking tone."

Alejandra allowed her smile to dim a bit. "I don't mean to mock. I do find this amusing though. I admit I was worried about whether it was too much too soon. Part of me hoped that putting you in the lion's den, so to speak, would distract you. Recall the you that spoils for a fight. A séance with those guests seemed like enough of an antagonism engine. I daresay that if you really thought me your enemy, you'd play your cards a little close to your vest."

"Perhaps I simply wanted to give you an opportunity to prove my assumptions wrong." Sophine suppressed a slight smile, robbing her words of any harsh edge.

"Perhaps." Pleased with the smile, Alejandra doubled back toward her desk. She grabbed an envelope. "By the way, this came for you."

Sophine took the sealed letter. "What is it?"

"I didn't open it. Another invitation, maybe?"

"I doubt either of us will be receiving invitations for any dinner engagements anytime soon." Sophine noted the lack of any return information. "Who delivered it?"

"Courier. But without any internal routing code."

Sophine opened it. She unfolded the piece of paper. In finely typed print were the words: Meet me in Holliday Park. By The Ruins at 3:00 p.m. Be discreet. Come alone.

"Well?" Alejandra asked.

"It is an invitation of sorts. Of the cloak and dagger variety. Has Lord Melbourne been around?" Sophine didn't want to outright lie to her assistant, but she was perfectly content to let Alejandra connect the two topics in her mind to keep her from too many prying follow-up questions.

"Yes. As a matter of fact, Dr. Yeager has been strutting about all morning in anticipation of his visit. I imagine they should be in his lab now." Alejandra leaned over her microscope. Her hands slipped into mechanical graspers in order to manipulate the specimen in her field of view. "Frankly, it's been unnerving having Lord Melbourne so active in the labs of late. Usually, if he were in the building once a quarter, it was enough to keep everyone in line for months. Whatever project has his studious attention must be quite important."

Sophine carefully folded the note, replaced it in the envelope, and slipped it into her pocket. She strode toward the door with determined steps. "I'll ... be right back."

When she arrived at Dr. Yeager's lab, two of his lab assistants rose to bar her way.

"This area's restricted." One crossed his arms and stepped closer, attempting to use his size to intimidate her.

"Since when?" Sophine calculated the amount of force to apply to drive her knee into his crotch if he inched any nearer. She locked defiant eyes with his and then with his companion.

"It's a private inspection. Level three security clearance only."

"Do you have any idea what my security clearance is?" she bluffed.

The two glanced at each other.

"Allow me to rephrase. Do you know what security clearance Lord Melbourne gave me when he appointed me to my position? Personally?"

The first man backed away to let her pass. The other was still uncertain.

"If you have any issues, put the responsibility on me. Consider this: I am about to have some serious words with our department head. Do you wish to stand between me and him when that occurs?"

The other one wilted. When she rounded the corner, Dr. Yeager glanced up at her immediately. His cravat fussily folded beneath his silver beard; a cruel smile stretched across his lips. He stepped closer to Lord Melbourne, almost like a protective mother bird, all too pleased to be seen with him. A disembodied brain, suspended in a liquid, seemed to float in a clear jar. A metal carapace protected it. Though humanoid in form, clasps were fixed to the end of each arm appendage. Its legs were the metal approximation of a horse's hind legs. At its belly, rifle and cannon turrets whirred as if targeting an object, then re-sighting with the next weapon. The monstrosity's herky-jerky movements reminded her of a puppet unsure which strings to follow.

"Are you here to bring me my messages?" Dr. Yeager asked.

"Do you need me to remind you where in your anatomy you can deposit your messages?" The metal beast turned awkwardly toward her, like a toddler learning to walk. Sophine stepped nearer. "That carapace. Is that ... based on my designs?"

"That's enough for now," Lord Melbourne said. "Father Justice, as you can see, we can change out your arm appendages. As per our agreement, we'll need you to come in once a week so that we can monitor how well the cybernetic control maintains over time."

The monstrosity turned to Sophine and then back to Lord Melbourne. A metallic voice called out, "Is our meeting still of the utmost discretion?"

"No one will know of our involvement in your ... resurrection." Lord Melbourne nodded to Sophine.

"I believe my refinements are worthy of Royal Society consideration." Dr. Yeager stepped forward, both eager to make sure he was seen by the subject and Lord Melbourne while blocking their view of Sophine.

"I'm positive Her Majesty, the Queen, will appreciate your responsiveness and your efforts." Lord Melbourne hooked his arm into Sophine's and began to walk away. "Walk with me, Ms. Jefferson."

"Wait." Sophine craned her neck, trying to more closely inspect the mechanical man with her engineer's scrutiny. The basic design was hers, but there had been numerous modifications. Even ... improvements. Her body slouched, allowing her to be redirected. "What was that?"

Lord Melbourne led them to an unoccupied meeting room. Away from too many ears. "A test. Further testing to be precise."

"That casing almost looked like automata. It is certainly reminiscent of my own designs."

"True. There have been some refinements. We work as a team here. Where one lab might hit a wall, so to speak, another might have great success."

"So, if I understand you, my project, my prototype has been turned over to Dr. Yeager?"

"He has been tasked with making adaptations to your original design, yes."

"You mean redesigning them for war."

"Don't play naïve, Sophine. It doesn't suit you." Lord Melbourne measured her. His manner shifted. The charm was still present, joined by a measure of steel to his tone. "ZeroDyne remains on the cutting edge of joining man and machine. *Our* designs, *our* breakthroughs have uses all across the spectrum. That man you saw was once a leader among his people until he was gunned down and left for dead. We were able to give him a new lease on life. To allow his memories, his lessons, his ideas to continue to inspire people."

"And the weaponization?"

"Well, those were just our laboratory technicians having fun with the design, seeing how many adaptations to the chassis they could manage. Although he had mentioned wanting to be able to defend himself should another attempt on his life arise. They were trying out different systems for him. He's a client, after all, not a lab rat."

"Here I thought you had lost sight of that." Sophine unhooked her arm from his. She paced back and forth. "Those were my designs. I should have been consulted. I don't care about patents or the machinations of business, but I care about my work. Being free to work as I see fit."

"There you go playing naïve again. You sound more like an artist than a scientist, and neither are thinking like a businessman, so let me be clear: I own all of your ideas here. Any idea you put to paper, any doodle of design, as long as you draw upon my resources to further your research or pursuits, they ultimately reside with me. And I will decide how those designs will be used."

A storm cloud drifted over his face. His posture stiffened. No longer the amiable rival of her father's, but feared CEO of Melbourne Industries. The man behind the Pinkerton Agency. A man who controlled much of the military industrial complex for Albion. The man who had the ear of Queen Diana herself. Lord Melbourne's tone turned icy. "Ms. Jefferson, don't let your familiarity or my fondness for you personally cause you to forget who you are talking to."

"I'm ..." Sophine was taken aback. There was something dangerous in his voice. The weight of a very personal, very immediate, very devastating threat to his words. She couldn't quite let an apology slip from her lips, but she demurred and lowered her gaze.

Lord Melbourne waved his hand, the spell of his fatherly demeanor cast again. "Think nothing of it. I simply wanted us to be clear about the business side of our relationship. I want you to be free to explore your ideas. Indulge your pursuits. Use my resources to follow your curiosity."

"But at the end of the day, you own everything and determine the applications."

"Well, yes. Many would be appreciative of the opportunity in front of them."

Yes, Sophine thought. It was a very gilded cage.

VOX DEI *DATA FILES: In 1916, John and Evaline Holliday donated 80 acres of their country estate to the city of Indianapolis to be used as a park. When the St. Paul Building in New York City was torn down to make room for one of its newer skyscrapers, three of its massive statues needed a new home. Known as "The Races of Man" in capitulation to the rise of so-called social justice crusaders, the statues were of an African-American, a Caucasian, and an Asian. The statues were placed in the heart of the park, near a reflecting pool with twin geysers, surrounded by two dozen Greek columns, all wrapped by a wrought iron fence in an area appropriately dubbed "The Ruins."*

EXCUSING HERSELF, Sophine said she needed a long lunch to get some air. Alejandra offered to join her, but Sophine begged off as being unfit for company. She took a horse-drawn carriage to Holiday Park. A sidewalk meandered along the periphery of the park, taking her past a thick, lush garden. Japanese lilacs and English hornbeams shielded a field of peonies and irises, their strong scent carried on the breeze. The wall of flowers bloomed pink, burgundy, and then purple, before meeting a wall of zinnias whose colors exploded like wildfire across the edge of the park.

The path wound its way through a copse of trees and opened onto a play area. A young father in dark breeches and a white shirt hopped on a spring-mounted platform to the giddy delight of three preschool children. They all shared the same caramel complexion and crooked half smile, as if they fought breaking into full guffaws. A group of young girls eyed her with suspicion, first to see if she were a truant officer ready to haul them in, next as the object of scrutiny as they commented on her fashion choices.

Benches were scattered within a maze of trees, as if the park's designers dropped them in wherever they could find space. Admitting to a morbid curiosity, the note and the idea of a clandestine meeting more than intrigued her. Walking in a relatively public place surrounded by parents and their young charges, she had no worries about her safety.

Children frolicked in the nearby fountain, splashing about without care. The breeze carried the occasional fleck of water to where she was seated. A dark-skinned man wandered toward the neighboring bench. An immense man who knew how to move, only a little of his heavily muscled body had gone to flab. A straw hat with a black band hung from his bald head at a precarious angle. An eye patch hid one of his eyes. A full mustache girded his face. A pink bow tie, pocket square, and flower in his lapel set off his coal-black suit. His capuchin monkey matched his attire down to a miniature straw hat clinging to his head. He withdrew a watch from his waistcoat, tsked to himself, then tucked the watch away again. Sitting, he fished a small paper sack from his jacket. He palmed a handful of its contents and let his simian companion snack from his open hand. So focused was Sophine's attention on the man and his marsupial, she didn't notice the man sidling onto the bench next to her.

"Don't you fret none," he said. The man favored a dark pinstriped suit that draped over his lanky frame with a shirt which rivaled the bloom of zinnias. Streaks of gray dappled his hair. He had strong hands and moved with the grace of a natural fighter. An unlit pipe dangled from his mouth. He clutched a tan-handled cane which reminded her of her father. He spoke in a low tone, not quite a whisper. His accent was difficult to place. The slight lilt of a Jamaican accent buried beneath years of living in the United States straining to blend in.

"What makes you think I would fret?" she asked.

"It might be assumed as the expected response of a young lady to the arrival of a strange gentleman."

"The note told me to expect someone. A man is as good as anyone else, I suppose."

"Do you often heed the instructions of surreptitious notes left by strangers?" The man stretched an arm along the back of the bench, his other hand firm on his cane. Despite the appearance of a relaxed posture, his body was positioned for readiness.

Sophine, likewise, appeared focused on the splashing children and the man with his monkey. However, her new friend she kept square in her peripheral vision. "This is my second time this week. The first led to a séance, which leaves plenty of room for me to not regret this."

"We don't want to go vex the spirits." He hid a smirk. "My name is Desmond Coke, Ms. Jefferson."

"Why did you ask me to meet you here?"

"Maybe I thought this garden needed a rose." Desmond set both of his hands on the handle of his cane now, making a point of looking away from her.

"You went through a lot of effort getting past ZeroDyne's security to deliver an invitation. I doubt it was solely to flatter me."

"It wasn't." Desmond shifted in his seat, angling more toward her but not encroaching in any threatening way. "I wanted to introduce you to some people."

"Who?"

"That gentleman for one." Desmond upticked his chin toward the large man feeding his monkey. The animal finished feeding and scampered along the back of the bench where it perched behind him. It sniffed at the air.

"It's rather difficult to make his acquaintance from over here." Sophine drew her fan and fluttered it in front of her face, obscuring her lips from casual view.

"Today, we observe if we wish to wrong-foot them. Listening will tell you a lot about him."

"Who is he?"

"His name is Melvin Knight. His people call him 'Sugar'," Every now and then, hints of Desmond's accent flickered to the surface. A broken thing, as if he fumbled for a way of speaking now no longer familiar to him. His natural ear for it lost due to disuse. "To hear his people talk, he was once a budding football player before getting into trouble with drugs and gambling. Among his legitimate businesses are a string of barbershops and a music troop with a roster filled with well-known singers. His numerous illegitimate dealings include everything from drugs to prostitution. The rude boy rules The Tombs with an iron fist."

"I don't think I'd much like to know him further. Or you, if this is a sample of the quality of company that you keep."

"He is over there." Desmond's voice dripped with disdain. "I am over here. With you. Ah, now here comes his appointment. I assume he is a devil you know. Him look vexed."

A familiar heavily built man waddled toward him. In comparison to Sugar, Lucas Pruitt's heavy frame seemed that much more ungainly. He perched on the opposite side of the bench, as far away from Sugar as possible to still be seated on it. Adjusting his collar, he scanned the park one more time. Desmond scooted closer to Sophine and draped his arm on her shoulder. She turned to him, her eyes hardened with displeasure.

"Remove your hand, sir," she said quietly, but with a firmness beyond misinterpretation.

"Pardon me, miss. I meant no offense. We need them comfortable enough to chat foolish. That's more likely if you're not staring at him and if we appear more interested in each other than them." Desmond canted his head at her in faux-study of her. "Not quite the gaze of two discreet lovers having a clandestine meeting, but it will do."

"Perhaps we're cross with one another and I'm here to end things." She tilted her head to his hand.

"Maybe something short of you ready to box me in the mouth."

Desmond glanced back over his shoulder. Removing his hand from her shoulder, he withdrew a small device from his jacket. A metal box with a miniature gramophone horn attached, he directed the device toward the two men. The cross-hatched circle was a speaker. The box squawked. Lowering the volume, he adjusted the interference until two tinny voices could be heard.

"I don't like this." Pruitt could not help the whine to his voice.

"Don't be like that. It's a beautiful day in the park. You should relax and enjoy the day more," Sugar said.

"He treats me like an errand boy. A man of my position can't just slip away from my staff and meetings at his whim."

"You jump at your master's command. He controls the purse strings of your campaign."

"You may be used to having a master, but I assure you, I am not." Pruitt's voice raised at the end, regretting his choice of words even as they leaped from his mouth.

"Then you're a fool," Sugar said with a smooth measure of calm. "Few people are their own men. They only have the delusion of such. I simply don't take it personally. It's only business."

"Still, he should have had his butler take this meeting. I'm too ... high profile for this."

"That's your real issue. You believe you're too good for this meeting. Well, for one, you're the Chancellor of this city, not in line to be Regent of this country. I'm sure part of his motivation was to demonstrate to you where you truly rank in the greater scheme of things. For two, you were sent as a sign of respect. To me. Again, to show you your place." Sugar smiled, revealing a full mouth of teeth. The visage brought to mind a shark preparing to devour.

"This is for you. I'm glad to be rid of it." Pruitt handed him a fat envelope. He cringed as the monkey leaped between them on the bench.

Desmond pulled a small box from his jacket. Recognizing its basic design and function, Sophine marveled at the craftsmanship. She'd never seen a camera so small before. He snapped a picture of the exchange.

"Well earned, I might add." Sugar slipped the envelope into his jacket. "Things moved apace better than expected. Do you know much about, I think I'll call it the endemic of unrest? Think of a group of people carrying the virus to become a mob. Mobs need time to fully incubate. One or two men looking to cause a ruckus may carry the contagion but said contagion has to be present at high enough levels to be symptomatic. A group doesn't become a mob until the contagion level reaches a critical index, a tipping point as it were, and becomes the collective will of the group. Only at this full fever does it attain the necessary bloodlust, dulling the minds and emboldening them. Your master wished to incite a mob with my help, just as I needed his strings to have the COPs appear so quickly. According to the *Vox Populi*, city officials 'feel the threat of siege in the offing.' Nice sound bite by the way."

"Our business is concluded." Pruitt stood and adjusted his suit jacket.

Sugar remained seated, content to enjoy a beautiful day in the park. "You should come by one of my clubs sometime. We can get you loosened up."

Pruitt walked away in a huff. Sophine turned to Desmond.

"What was that about? Why would those two ever associate with one another? They seem to be from two different worlds."

"They are pieces in one big chess game. We're still trying to divine the scope of their operation, if we want to wrong-foot them. Intelligence is hard to come by. We only got wind of this meeting thanks to one of our deeply positioned assets. In fact ..." Desmond hesitated. His head shone in the light. Not a dapple of sweat despite the rising temperature. Upon closer inspection, a tincture of silver sprouted about his cheeks, a gray five o'clock shadow. He gripped her hand, drawing her attention to the threat about them.

At first, all she saw were the shadows about the surrounding bushes. She feared that perhaps his paranoia was contagious. Then the bushes parted. Several augmented men stumbled from them. Their clockwork enhancements were military grade. More automata than men, they retained remnants of their humanity and much of their agility. Small packs on their backs issued thin streams of steam. They idly closed in on Sophine and Desmond with sure, lumbering steps.

The ornamented cane had a slight hook for a handle. Releasing his grip on her hand, he turned the shaft toward his pinky. It signaled a shift in his body language, preparing himself for possible danger. He rested backward, toward his hip, a posture she watched her father assume on more than one occasion whenever he took the measure of his opponents while playing the old man.

Desmond tucked the cane up under his arm. He clutched the underside of the hook handle. The half-mechanical men approached from both sides. Turning to his left, he stepped out on his left heel. No trace of an old man remained. His movements were smooth, controlled, fluid. The years peeled away from him with each step. A hint of a smile played across his face as if recalling the better days of his youth.

He circled his arms counter-clockwise, twin movements, and brought all of his power toward the back of his stance. He caught the nearest man behind him directly in the throat with the tip of his cane. He planted the heel of his thrust palm of his free hand into the bridge of the approaching man's nose. Desmond whirled into a stance much like a rearing cat, his cane still in position behind him. He twirled, using the cane to block the baton a soldier brought down upon him. Desmond stepped forward and swung the cane, smacking the third man across the face. The body crumpled, unconscious, before he hit the ground.

Keeping himself between the men and Sophine, Desmond whipped the cane into his body. Inching forward, he thrust it into the man's gut, jamming the clockwork gears which made up the bulk of his torso. Sophine gasped, both at the severity of the blow and the intricacy of the craftsmanship of the half-steamman. Their design had a ring of familiarity to them.

Desmond backed away, reversing the cane's position with a quick flip. The weapon moved like an extension of his arm. With legs crossed, his arm extending along with the cane, he held his other hand almost in salute. The old man crouched, avoiding their clumsy attack. The men stumbled about like newborn deer getting used to their limbs. They weren't prepared for this level of resistance.

No, Sophine thought, they were prepared for her.

Desmond herded Sophine behind him, keeping himself between her and their assailants. He jumped back to his cat-like stance. His cane slapped his free hand and he drew it back like he had just notched an arrow. With both hands, he clocked the first attacker out of the way, turned and blocked the other attacker. He turned around and dropped low again. He jerked the cane under his arm, smacking the person behind him in the process.

The last man circled them. He slowly slid a sword out of a scabbard. A deliberate movement, much like their initial approach, designed to intimidate. Bouncing on the balls of his feet, Desmond assumed a primary rear-guard position. He twisted the handle of his cane. He freed a sword from its shaft, handing the sheath to Sophine. The scabbard had a mild heft to it, its core reinforced by lightweight metal. She brandished it like a staff the way her father taught her in case any of the fallen men decided to rise up again.

Right foot forward—his sword aimed at his opponent's left eye— Desmond suspended his free hand over his sternum. He pivoted on his left foot, his sword held at shoulder level. The two of them squared off, staring at each other as if locked in a battle of wills, trying to control one another. It was like each one played out the fight in their minds. Move. Countermove. The steam soldier gripped and re-gripped his sword. Desmond remained deathly still. She wasn't sure he even drew a breath.

The steam soldier brought his sword forward and stepped closer. He slashed his blade downward. Desmond leaned back. He took a slight step to his left. In one swift movement, he brought his blade down with a sharp snap. Desmond reoriented his blade, twisting toward his opponent's throat. He paused, holding it there like a plea for the man to not to make him follow through. His opponent refused to yield. Desmond thrust forward. His blade plunged through the back of the steamman's throat.

"Come, nuh. We must leave before the cleanup crew arrives," Desmond said.

"The COPs will want to question us," Sophine said.

"No COPs will show up. This scene will be cleansed and us along with it if we do not get out of here." Desmond surveyed the fallen soldiers, ensuring none rose to re-engage them. He reached out to take her hand.

"Who are you?"

"A friend of your father's." Desmond locked eyes with her.

"My father?" Sophine allowed a moment for the revelation to settle in her.

"He'd been funding me and my associates for many years. He wanted to keep you out of this until you were ready."

"Ready for what?"

Desmond smiled. "Welcome to the revolution."

THIRTEEN
I AIN'T GOING BACK TO JAIL

Vox Dei *Data Files: The Fugitive Act states that*, "No person held to service or labor in one state under the laws thereof escaping into another, shall, in consequence of any law or regulation therein be discharged from such service or labor, but shall be delivered up on claim of the party to whom such service or labor may be due." *A law quite still on the books despite the efforts of the social justice crusaders. The same mob has also unfairly branded the law's enforcers, the White Knights of the Camelia, as racists and hatemongers. The group has also been demonized by rogue media elements. The White Knights of the Camelia simply stands for citizens of the American colonies trying to pursue The Dream. Oppressed by forces within and without of our borders, the fight to reclaim the civil rights of ordinary citizens. They simply want to protect our citizens' rights to work hard, keep the fruits of what they labor for, and secure economic prosperity for the nation. Subversive elements seek to disrupt the order of things. Those elements must be rooted out before they organize, become political, and actually gain footholds in the societal discourse. If the White Knights of the Camelia stand for anything, it's freedom and security.*

.   .   .

RAIN FELL IN THIN SHEETS, distorting shadows to a semblance of life. Branches, like skeletal fingers against the night sky, swayed to their own melancholy melody. The woods seemed alien, unnatural. The reflected moonlight gave Sleepy's skin a nearly translucent quality. He rubbed his hands along his rain-soaked arms. Mud sucked at his feet, devouring the jail-issued shoes he'd been wearing. Rocks and twigs, endless rows of teeth, gnawed at his bare feet. Tree branches scourged him as he ran. Frantic bellows in the night, Sleepy huffed with each step, each labored breath arriving in haggard shards. His joints ached, lumbering forward in an awkward gait just short of a jog. His legs, not used to such rapid movement, still struggled to remember how to work in cooperation with his other muscles. Finally, he doubled over, arms outstretched to find any purchase. Finding a tree within grasp, he leaned into it, nearly in full collapse, as if falling into a long-lost lover's embrace.

"You okay?" Knowledge Allah slowed. His pace, despite his limp, had been little more than speed walking to keep up with Sleepy. His head swiveled about on constant alert for pursuers.

"I've never been on the run before."

"Run is a strong word for what we've been doing. I can still see the lift station from here." Knowledge Allah wasn't even breathing hard.

"I have far too fragile a constitution for so much chase and adventure," Sleepy choked out.

Dogs brayed in the distance. Knowledge Allah cocked his head, his face braced with alarm. "We've crossed the creek ..."

"Creek? That was a river." Once he controlled his breathing, Sleepy began to shiver. "Look, it's night. The hawk's out. I'm wet, I'm cold, and this orange fashion abomination chafes in the most uncharitable of places."

"The dogs have probably lost our scent." Knowledge Allah hunched down. In a double take, he saw something in the distance. "Look, let's hole up over there. It's only a barn but it'll get us out of the open."

"And the wind."

"And we can figure out what to do next."

Leaves crunched underfoot as Sleepy jogged with renewed vigor. Any shelter was an improvement over being in the open against the unforgiving breeze. Under the wan glare of moonlight, the barn took on the color of dried blood. Paint had chipped off in large flecks, revealing dark wood under siege of rot. Its roof appeared intact, though faint seams could be seen among its lining. Sleepy wrapped his arms about himself as much as he could, bracing himself against the cold. The barn door opened easily enough. Its large wooden doors slid along a track for a couple of feet, then stopped. It had fallen into disuse and Knowledge Allah didn't want to try to force the track open any farther. Sleepy squeezed through, the effort tugging the damp jumpsuit in further discomforting ways.

"What are our options?" Knowledge Allah doubled over, his hands on his knees.

Sleepy closed the barn door and then found a convenient pile of hay to collapse into. "Let's see: the COPs have probably tossed my house and seized anything of value. The Two-Johns was raided and most likely shut down. If the police were after us before for giving them the slip at the Two-John's or for supposedly instigating the riot in The Tombs, I can only imagine what kind of force is hunting for us now after a jail escape. I'm betting Sugar and anyone else we know has been questioned or is under surveillance."

"We can't afford to be seen by anyone. Don't forget, your face is plastered all over the *Vox Populi*."

Sleepy glared at him with a sour expression. Knowledge Allah seemed to enjoy pointing out when he was the source of a problem first, then only begrudgingly admit that he was in the same boat. "Yeah. Thanks for that. So, we have no friends, we have no funds, and we have no freedom." Sleepy curled up in a ball, wrapping his arms as best he could around his drawn-up knees. "We need to get out of these clothes, get warm, and find something to eat. Since it's my face out there, do you have anyone we can reach out to?"

Knowledge Allah settled into a nearby stack of hay. He stared absently at the ceiling. "We got to get out of the city. State probably. Think we can make it to Canada or the Five Civilized Nations territory?"

"Canada would be a better bet. Closer anyways." Sleepy found it hard to breathe. Like the weight of the situation finally settled on him. He was a fugitive from the law. The life he knew was over. Sleepy's belly grumbled, reminding him of more pressing concerns. "What about papers?"

"One problem at a time. Let's make it out of the city first, and then worry about that later." Knowledge Allah guarded the door. "I still have a few credits stashed away. Maybe get us to the border."

A strange glow flickered across the rear window's glass. Movement flickered beyond the windows—hints of shapes, shadowy figures seen only from the corner of his eye. Sleepy ducked down against the barn wall and edged toward the window. He slowly raised up to peer out the corner of the window. Torches, distant pyres, tromped toward the barn. The furtive procession wound its way through the surrounding woods toward the clearing in front of the barn. He couldn't make out any individual figures.

"Who are they? COPs?" Sleepy crawled over to Knowledge Allah and crouched just under his shoulder like a strange outgrowth.

"I don't think so. The way the torches bob and weave, it's like they're being carried by men on horseback."

"Oh no," Sleepy whispered. "Look closer. They're wearing robes."

The air chilled, an ice pick scraping at the marrow in Sleepy's bones. A distinct scent crept along the floorboards just at the edge of his senses, like a thief evading detection. The smell of recently unearthed death. Sleepy turned to Knowledge Allah to double-check what he thought he saw. For the first time in their acquaintance, a flicker of fear registered on Knowledge Allah's face. That chilled Sleepy even more.

The Knights of the White Camelia. The simple phrase reverberated in Sleepy's mind like the tolling of a massive bell, squeezing out all other thoughts. After the Unrest, Negro people were allowed their freedom and equality. The backlash against the idea of their equal status was swift and severe. The panic and outrage over the fear of "black supremacy" led to the resurgence of the Knights of the

White Camelia. They sought "the abolition of political instrumentalities" put in place to ensure the journey to equality. Such a path, though it hadn't started, was bound only to raise Negroes above their ordained proper station.

The group's meetings were rumored to be matters of great secrecy. Beyond that, much of what was conjectured about their rituals fell somewhere between the fantastical and the ludicrous. The only constant about the tales was the undercurrent of violence. The indistinct voices coalesced into snippets of conversation as the group neared.

"Find them. Both of them."

"What if they make it past the wire?"

"Our sources in the Pinkertons say they must still be near this area. They hadn't the time to get much farther. Capture them if you can. Alive, preferably. If they make it to the wire, you have ... full discretion."

Panic swelled in Sleepy, threatening to overtake all reason. All he could think was that he had to get out of the barn before the men realized they were in there, surrounded it, and set it on fire. He imagined armed men daring him to come out so that they could riddle his body with shotgun pellets while flames lapped all about them. Before Knowledge Allah could reach out to calm his nerves, Sleepy bolted.

Trees blurred in the thinning night as he ran. The earth heaved and dipped. His ankles nearly buckling with each footfall, Sleepy had trouble maintaining his footing on the uneven terrain. His thoughts reduced to a gray haze of terror, the single survival note of "flee." After a few hundred yards, a patch of undergrowth rose up to meet him. His footing gave way and he tumbled into the thick underbrush. His lungs burned. His heart squeezed in erratic rhythms as if second-guessing the wisdom of prolonging the terror. A dirge-like noise emanated from him. He chuffed with each breath, desperate to slow his heartbeat as he sought to gain his bearings and catch his breath. The few hundred yards he dashed might as well have been an entire marathon. Sleepy shivered in the night's chilly embrace. If there was one benefit to the rush of fear, it should have been that he was too terrified to think about how cold it was. Sleepy pushed another branch from his path; it snapped back, slashing him across the cheek. He shielded his face as he peered through the woods. Knowledge Allah caught up and ducked into the bushes.

"Sleepy?" Knowledge Allah stared into his eyes, searching for anything familiar.

"They're coming for us. They're gonna get us." The words poured out of Sleepy in a babbling stream. "They're not going to be satisfied until we're dead."

"Sleepy," Knowledge Allah repeated in a reassuring, level voice.

"We can't let them get us. I ain't going out like that." Sleepy popped his head up and ducked again. Shifting, he gathered his legs under him. He glanced to the left and to the right. "I ain't the one. I'm not going to be another casualty. Not shot in the middle of nowhere. Not strung up from some tree. Not strapped to an autocarriage and dragged through the streets. Not ..."

Knowledge Allah slapped him.

Sleepy stared at him. Mouth slightly ajar as the pain worked its way from his cheek to the area of his brain which registered the shock. The message then traveled to the part of his brain governing how much to cuss the man out. His words came out even and low, a cold measurement of his building rage. "Did you seriously just slap me?"

"You just ... you were getting hysterical."

"I got a right to be hysterical. People are trying to kill us. The Camelia is after us. On top of the COPs. That's a righteous moment for hysteria." Sleepy touched his cheek. "You don't go just slapping brothers. I'll let you have that one for now. But I ain't forgetting it anytime soon."

Horns blared from Fall Creek Parkway. Early morning traffic, congested by COPs roadblocks, and the occasional large municipal vehicle that rumbled along the roadway. The gurgling croaks of tree frogs and the drone of cicadas reminded Sleepy how much he hated nature. Outdoors, actually. Underneath those sounds, many footfalls —firm and sure, not hindered by mud or woods—closed in on them.

An unseen bird fluttered from the treetops. Invisible figures rustled about them in the trees. Ghostly snorts erupted around him, powerful exhalations from barrel-like lungs. He fell backward in a blast of hot breath from the beasts that seemed to plow into him from all sides. Their foul breath was thick with the smell of rotted hay. Ethereal torch flames erupted from all about them, flickering in the night like spectral will o' the wisps. Sleepy groped blindly, his fingers sinking with quiet desperation into the soaked earth as he tried to steady himself. He lifted his muddied hand to shield his eyes. He imagined leering faces on the outlines of the figures surrounding them.

The first kick landed squarely in his solar plexus. His body wrapped around a heavy, mud-caked boot, dropping him into a fleshy pile. The horse reared back, its hooves narrowly missed Sleepy's skull. His fingers raked at the wet leaves about him. His lungs drew another breath, risking both the stench of decayed muck and the working of chest muscles which drove needles into his lungs. An angry succession of stomps landed about his ribs and arms as he desperately protected his face. The rain of footfalls stopped with his low, surrendering moan.

"That's enough," a man said.

"Why?" Hot, frustrated tears streamed down Sleepy's face. Large, calloused hands propped him up. Their fingers bit into his arms. His mind resigned itself to the swirling madness that closed in on him.

"Why what? Why am I doing this?" A hood muffled the man's voice. "You tried to run. Don't."

Frayed, moldy rope bound his wrists. They shoved a trussed up Knowledge Allah next to him. A momentary tittering from the shadows distracted Sleepy before his body suddenly jerked forward. He fell face down. Mud filled his mouth. Twigs and leaves raked past him. He spat as the earth rose up. Bound to one of the horses, the rope tugged him forward. They tromped through the woods. Time lost meaning. Distance lost meaning. Only the haze of pain remained. Even the thought of movement sent flames of pain to his brain. His body, little more than dead weight, staggered along for fear of being dragged through the woods. What muscles held his arms in their sockets as he was dragged were stretched to uselessness.

They passed through a gate to the rear of an abandoned church-yard. The building was a remnant of the rural community absorbed by the Indianapolis expansion. The nearly erased trail sloped toward a clearing. Surrounded by trees, Sleepy couldn't help but think that the area was haunted by the atrocities the Camelia performed in secret. The party stopped at the bank of Fall Creek, the clearing protected from view by a tall hedge. A small circular structure of aged bricks over five yards in diameter had been arranged to resemble the mouth of a large well. The raised banks of the creek's edge acted as a natural amphitheater. A theater of barbaric cruelty. The gathered men's taunts and jeers rang out like voices in a dream. Their eyes filled with sadism and greed. Lookouts stationed themselves at the four points of the cleared lot. They dragged Sleepy and Knowledge Allah to the opposite side of the field.

To their left, roosters squawked from a series of cages stacked on a cart. A couple of men wheeled the cart into position, causing a renewed eruption of clucking. The birds' combs and wattles had been removed. Two birds were brought out. One bird had a metallic patch protecting the hole where an eye had been. A bolt ran through its collar. The other bird had been fitted with a mask, a metallic frame over its beak, both muzzling and further weaponizing it. A harness slung over its wings, like a metal framed sling, clockwork gears cinching it closed. Its claws had brass spurs. Trainers shaved and sharpened the talons of their roosters. The trainers dropped the birds into a small plastic container set on a crude conveyer belt suspended over the pit. Through the trees, it lowered the cages into the pit.

Men yelled their bets and back slapped one another, their faces obscured by their hoods. Two robed men with red bands on their sleeves, presumably the officials of the sport, took the gamecocks out and paraded them about. The hoots and hollers of the gathered men greeted them. The applause and cheers peaked when the officials banged the birds together like two boxers bumping fists before the bout. Returning the birds to their plastic chambers, they faced one another. The boxes raised, releasing the birds.

A flurry of wings followed, along with the encouraging howls of the men. With an almost feline pounce, claws at the ready, the birds lunged at one another. Pecking with each thrust, one feinted, shielding itself with its wing. Blood splattered against the wall.

"This ... is the opposite of the beauty of wisdom," Knowledge Allah said.

"I don't know. It's brutal, but I could get into it." Sleepy watched in abject fascination. "You don't think they're going to make us fight one another, do you?"

"I doubt they have time to set up a Mandingo ring before they turn us in. Why damage the goods any more than they have to? Besides, no one wants to see you with your shirt off."

"You choose now to try to body shame me, sir?" Sleepy nursed the garden of bruises swelling on his side.

"Just trying to lighten the mood."

"Yeah, they're going to bury us under the jail this time."

"Shut up over there," a hooded man shouted. He strode over toward them, a small club in his hand. "COPs will be here any minute."

"Aren't you worried they'll bust your little animal abuse circle?" Knowledge Allah asked.

"Do you know how many elected officials are in attendance right now?" The man's voice thick with his sneer.

"No. All I see are hoods."

"Let's just say 'enough.' Think of this as a networking event." The man's attention focused on catching glimpses of the action. A commotion broke out where a couple of the lookouts stood guard. A series of shouts followed by a flurry of movement. In a slow wave, hoods turned toward the noise. "Well, boys, I think your ride is here."

"I ... don't think so," Knowledge Allah said.

More shouts erupted from the same place. Several figures scurried past the tree line. Several men milled about, still focused on the cockfight. A few hands, frozen in the air, still clutching credits.

Their raised voices changed tenor from enthusiasm to bewilderment. From the woods came the sounds of bodies being beaten. The familiar hollow thumps. A few men called out, their cries cut abruptly short. A number of hooded figures surged toward the confusion. The rest's attention remained on the activity, though their postures braced to dash off at any moment. Whatever appraisals they made, they all came to the same conclusions that their best interests rested in fleeing. As if a starter's pistol suddenly fired, men bolted away from the woods.

"No," Sleepy mewed. Shadows coalesced into shapes. Men bobbed toward them, their forms waving improvised weapons.

Still bound to the parked steeds, Sleepy and Knowledge Allah worked frantically at their ropes. The cord tightened about Sleepy's wrists. The horse snorted. He imagined an out-of-control, steam-powered juggernaut tearing off through the woods dragging him and Knowledge Allah across the earth. Stones, tree limbs, and the eventual asphalt of the road eroding the skin from their bones. Lynching by horse misadventure was a headline he wanted no part of. Heedless of the pain, he ripped the rope over his wrists. He tugged at Knowledge Allah's restraints. The horse reared once. Twice. Frightened, it snorted neighs of protest. The ropes barely loosened from Knowledge Allah before the horse darted off.

"Behind you!" Knowledge Allah shoved Sleepy out of the way as a couple of bodies barreled past.

"Come on." Sleepy hoped to use the confusion to cover their escape.

Men screamed. Bodies darted among the robes, armed with sticks, bats, or rocks. The ruckus overturned a few of the torches, setting part of the bird storage on fire. Men scrambled to douse the flames. Acrid smoke billowed through the encampment. A rooster with part of its vestments on fire skittered through the camp. The clearest route out of the churchyard was cut off by a mob of unarmed men. Sleepy and Knowledge Allah tip-toed through the tumult. Men stomped about chasing after the robed figures. They threw wild punches and swung sticks like disciplinary rods. Sleepy couldn't make out any of the attacker's faces, though they didn't wear hoods like the Knights of the White Camelia, nor protective visors like COPs. They were vigilantes who sought the reward for Sleepy and Knowledge Allah's capture for themselves. Another cloud of smoke burned his eyes, reducing the forms to obscured shadows. Soon the scuffling settled, like a bellows which had been snuffed. The Knights of the White Camelia had scattered into the night. Their assailants now encircled them.

Sleepy's body barely had the strength to offer even faint protest against the cord or the hands. The men grabbed him, raising him to his feet. Reduced to an absurd marionette with whom a child would soon tire of playing, Sleepy waited. He tottered, too weak to steady himself properly. One of the men stepped through the smoke and stared with uncertainty. He examined Knowledge Allah first, then Sleepy, an expression of astonishment mixed with awe washed over his face before he stammered.

"It's ... you."

FOURTEEN

REVOLUTIONARY GENERATION

Vox Dei Data Files: Indianapolis is the nation's first consolidated city. Fifty separate local governments run under a Unigov system (referred to derisively as "Unigrab" by the hysterical liberal opposition). Its unusual government system consists of a nine-member Common Council—one for each of the nine townships they comprise —and a "strong chancellor" separately appointed for a four-year term. The municipal government of incorporated cities (the cities of Beech Grove, Lawrence, Southport, and Speedway were not included from the consolidation decree due to their size and are collectively referred to as "the excluded cities") centralized various elements, including their public school system (already in disarray after the social experiment known as integration), as well as their fire and police departments.

SOPHINE HAD NEVER BEEN to any circus, much less enjoyed the spectacle of a soul circus. Jazz melodies by way of the bayou cast a spell on Sophine. The notes ran up and down the scale, weaving in and out of the melody. Just this side of dissonant, though she saw the thread of it, the off-beat harmony like the flight of a bee. Syncopated pain, sun-beaten and weathered. Sweat and sorrow etched into old bones. Joy and defiance above the brash rhythms. Life despite circumstance. Her kind of music.

The massive pianoforte had pitted brass and was in desperate need of a polish. A man in a woman's dress, attired like a Sunday school teacher, laid into the keyboard with a madman's intensity, stopping to fan himself between each song, much to the audience's delight. The overwhelming smell of popcorn threatened to crowd out all other odors. Parents purchased light up knick-knacks, from glow-in-the-dark necklaces to small glow sticks, which siblings immediately used as sabers to stab one another. The house lights dimmed, leaving the audience in pitch black except for the lights provided by the excited children. Sophine and Desmond blended into the circus's audience.

"Who are you?" Sophine turned to her companion.

"I already told you. My name is Desmond Coke. I was a friend of your father's since you were a pickney."

"Then let me stop you there. Since you seem determined to repeat your lie. My father didn't have friends."

"You judge him too harshly. Your father was a good man. A cautious man. He had many enemies. He feared them coming after what he'd built. Or, worse, coming after you."

"Probably in that order." Sophine sniffed.

"As I said, too harshly. Everything he built was for you. He wanted to create something for you to inherit. You were his truest legacy. He wanted to see you protected, make you proud, and leave you the resources to make your own mark."

"You do speak ... almost like you knew him." Sophine hesitated to voice the possibility because it meant there was a whole side to her father she never knew.

"We have known each other many years, your father and I."

"Then why did he never mention you?"

"He loved his secrets. He lived a, how do you say, compartmentalized life."

"Next you will give me the familiar apologetics of how he was a complicated man."

"Feh," Desmond said. "He was smart, and he was bold. He

loved his family. He chased after his passions. Not so complicated when you see the bigger picture of who he was."

"Then I fear that you knew him better than me."

A voice began to speak, cautioning the crowd about their approaching host known as Big Top. Imploring them to put their hands together, the spotlight danced across the crowd and the walls. Joined by smaller reds, blues, and greens, the lights swirled like the inside of a kaleidoscope. Back and forth, searching about, until all the lights met at the stage's entrance. Lights fixed on a silhouette of a female automaton projected onto a screen. From her mouth emerged a man wearing a white suit with gold epilates, white-rimmed sunglasses which covered his whole face, a white Kangol hat, and gold shoes. All three and a half feet of the ringmaster bounded onto the stage. The same man had escorted the two of them to their box seats before the circus started. He gyrated in sync to the heavy bass line of the music. The crowd erupted, clapping and dancing as he pranced about.

"Why did you insist on coming here?" Sophine asked.

"Many reasons. Here we are not in the open and we will not be observed or easily heard."

"Here, I smell of elephant dung."

Desmond leaned in and took a conspiratorial air. "Everyone poops."

Maybe it was the delicate hint of his Jamaican accent and the overly mannered way he spoke English. Maybe it was the sheer absurdity of his comment or their circumstance, but Sophine burst out laughing. "Everyone, indeed."

"You have a wonderful laugh," Desmond said.

"Thank you. I don't get to use it very often." Sophine brought her hand to her neck.

"As for the real reason why we are here, it's simple. We're no longer in the city."

"What do you mean? We're in the parking lot of a shopping center on the west side of town."

"True. And not true. The circus signed an agreement with the city to lease this space for the duration of their run in the city. Look at the performers. Acts from all around the world. Citizens from all around the world. Whose countries demand a guarantee of their safety and rights. So the language of the contract technically specifies that."

"How do you mean?"

"Think of this circus as sovereign ground. Legally, it's as if the parking lot was its own country. No COPs allowed on the grounds."

All long limbs and torsos, lady contortionists formed a pyramid. Dressed in similar costumes and all vaguely similar in appearance. Asian and if not quadruplets—though as it turned out there would have to be three sets of them since during the course of their routine more and more of them revealed themselves—they passed for sisters from afar. Their bodysuits covered them entirely other than a window highlighting their slight cleavage. They made no noise, only glided from position to position, bending and interlocking, forming intricate bridges with their bodies. The audience winced at the way they twisted their bodies, folding in a jointless way as if having no bones.

"So these performers are like ambassadors with diplomatic immunity," Sophine said.

"Exactly. It's as if the audience has entered their embassy. I like to stay off the beaten track." Desmond eased back in his chair. He offered her a basket of popcorn. All butter and salt, she waved him off, but the odor was delightful. Without looking, she reached into the basket, grabbed an indelicate handful, and shoved most of it into her mouth in a less than ladylike fashion.

"Is that how you and my father met?"

"We crossed paths on a couple of occasions. Back when I had my charge."

"Your charge?"

Desmond grew distant, his mind occupied by wistful memories. "There was a boy. A very important boy. We escaped from Jamaica, fleeing some people who wanted to use the boy for their own ends. You met some of them earlier. We spent some time in Tejas. Then among the *Niitsitapi*."

"Wait, you mean the Five Civilized Tribes?"

"They call themselves the *Niitsitapi*, the Real People. Anyway, soon after our time there, we crossed paths with your parents."

"The Colonel never talked much about his life with my mother."

"I don't blame him. When you lose someone you care about so deeply, even though all you have are those memories, sometimes it simply hurts too much to remember." A hint of sadness crept into his voice.

"And your charge?"

"He grew into a fine, strong young man. Dark skin with fierce green eyes, the spitting image of the man he was meant to be. Your father funded our efforts. My charge developed a reputation as a community leader. A mythology swirled about him. People started to refer to him as the 'Star Child.' Damnable name, but they listened. He stirred their hearts. He preached about their inherent worth and dignity. That their lives were their own and they didn't have to fall in line with others' plans for them. That they were more than cogs meant to be used and ground by the great machine known as the United States. That their lives mattered. Then our enemies found us and we were ... separated."

"I'm sorry." Sophine heard rumors of a civil rights rabble-rouser known as the Star Child even as far away as Oxford.

Stilt dancers took the stage. One wore green, one red, one black, and the last gold, their long legs crept about like a spider's. Flitting from one corner to the other, refusing to remain still, they crossed one another. Streamers trailed from them; shimmers of their color captured the light. Their herky-jerky movements like marionettes twice the size of humans. Each wore a leering monochrome theater mask matching the color of their outfit. A team of dancers in Jamaican regalia danced between their legs, Lilliputians to the stilted Gullivers. They limboed under flaming rods.

"What was it that I saw at the park?"

"A lot of violence?" Desmond smirked. "What did you think you saw?"

"Now you do sound like my father." Sophine closed her eyes and replayed the day's details in her mind. "I saw a meeting between an associate of my employer, Lucas Pruitt, and a man you claim is Melvin Knight, whom some people refer to as Sugar. A pleasant enough conversation punctuated by, yes, an exchange of violence."

"Sometimes the only way to deal with a problem is to box them in the mouth," Desmond said. "But what does it all mean?"

"Depends on the motives of the players, possibly a payoff. Pruitt is Chancellor of the city and, from what I gather, in the pocket of my employer."

"He's also a member of the Knights of the White Camelia."

"The group of racial terrorists?" Sophine's voice rose, though she wasn't really surprised. Most of the political movers and players in the state were.

"No lie me tell. Rumor has it that they have begun arming and training a militia."

"For their imagined race war?" Sophine sighed.

"The end times are upon us, don't you know," Desmond mocked.

"I don't know much about Sugar."

"No surprise. You don't really travel in those circles."

Sophine snapped to rigid attention, her demeanor frosty as she cast a stern gaze his way. She'd encountered this attitude, this casual dismissal of her heritage before. As if certain words, names, places were some sort of Shibboleth of authenticity. "Am I not 'black' enough to know him?"

Nonplussed, Desmond waved her off. "And I thought the color games were bad back home. I suspect that you aren't 'street' enough to know him. He has ties to everything from numbers to prostitution to drugs. He's a one-man criminal empire. Unless I misunderstand the circles you run it."

Somewhat mollified, Sophine relaxed. A hair. "Both Sugar and Pruitt claim to be associates of Lord Melbourne. I don't understand that part. Pruitt—any politician—is a necessary evil. I don't understand why Lord Melbourne would employ a ... street thug."

"A more street-level criminal shouldn't be much of a leap from a corporate level one. Different constituency and another proxy to allow him to not dirty his fingers."

"Still a businessman with ties to politicians, a militia, and a crime boss. What game is Lord Melbourne playing at?"

"That seems to be the question." Desmond turned in his seat.

A troupe of dancing dogs gave way to tigers prowling toward the stage. They performed against the threat of the whip. The gleam in their eyes showed that they hadn't forgotten who they were. They heeded the sting of punishment, but should the opportunity present itself, their instincts would take over. And everyone would remember who they once were.

"You mentioned you having ... associates." Sophine didn't consider herself well-versed in the subtleties of intrigue.

"We struggle against the oppressive systems in place." Desmond rubbed the bridge of his nose. "With the Star Child's abduction, we evolved from a ragtag group into a more organized movement. We are keenly aware that many in authority would love to ensnare more of our leaders and members, so we switched to operating in discrete cells. A few know bigger pieces of the puzzle, but no one person knows too much."

"Smart. Compartmentalized leadership." Sophine scrunched down in her seat to hear him better.

"Your father taught us well." Desmond took her hand in his. Strong, but not demanding. Protective, but unobtrusive. She didn't object. It reminded her of the rare occasions the Colonel would do so. "Your father was so proud of you. It would have been very easy for you to commit your life to the societal machine. You come from money, but even if you didn't, you grew up with the story that you could buy into the American Dream. That if you worked hard, played fair, carried yourself in a respectable manner, you could buy a house in Broad Ripple overlooking the canal, maybe a boat on Eagle Creek, and live the life. But you recognized early on that the dream doesn't work for you. No matter where you are, you can sense something rotten at the core of this world. You trust your instincts and grope around in the dark, hoping you find something. You are your father's daughter."

Sophine withdrew her hand from his.

Magicians and clown skits allowed the center ring to be prepared for the main act. They wheeled out a giant metal sphere. Riders on two-wheeled autocarriages, their engines firing gears, puffing clouds of steam, and pistons filling the air with the smell of ozone. The first one wheeled up the ramp into the cage. The rider rocked back and forth astride his metal beast until he attained enough momentum to whirl about the inside of the humongous ball-shaped cage. Around its sides. Along the inside of its top, defying gravity to the *ooh*s and *ah*s of the crowd. Then a second rider joined him. Then a third. Spinning about in close quarters, thrilling the crowd with how close they passed by each other, yet managed to miss.

"What do you fight against?"

"We don't have all of the pieces. We fight where we can, where we see the shadows, until something or someone reveals themselves. Any opportunity to thwart the agenda whenever we think it rears its head. Maybe there's a conspiracy of sorts. More like interested parties with similar agendas working if not in concert, then at least not against one another. Big pharmaceuticals. The military industrial complex. The blind media. Even today ..."

"Good-bye, Mr. Coke. Enjoy the remainder of the circus." Sophine sighed. Lured by this man with the bait of learning more about her father, she dared dream that something intriguing might be found by the end of this meeting. Now she had the sinking feeling that she dashed down the rabbit hole only to find a paranoid lunatic. She began to gather her things.

"Wait, your father left you something." Desmond fished in his pocket. He withdrew an envelope. "For you."

Sophine eyed him with skepticism. She opened the envelope. A piece of paper and a key. "What's this?"

"You may think me a madman, I understand. You don't know me. Trust is hard won, especially these days. Know that there is a lot more to the story." He pointed to the paper. "This is a starting place. Go to that address."

"Where is this going, Mr. Coke?"

"We need your help. Go see what your father left for you. He hoped one day you'd join him at the forefront of The Cause. We'll be in touch ... Lord willing and life spare."

IT SEEMED LIKE A DIFFERENT DAY—ANOTHER lifetime—since Sophine left her work. She hoped Alejandra would cover for her, but found that she ultimately didn't care. Not when such larger issues seemed to be at play. She was so close to something, some piece of the puzzle, even if she didn't know what it was. Sophine thought about taking a taxi to the address, but she had the strange suspicion of not wanting any third party associating her with the location for whatever may be there. She rode her mechanical horse for over a half hour outside of the city. She arrived at the address and trotted along the winding driveway until she reached the building. The tall structure stood stark and forlorn against the encroaching evening. Dropping the key once, she fumbled with the lock. She didn't know why she felt so nervous. She took a calming breath and slowly opened the door. Flipping the light switch, all she could do was stare, her voice reduced to a near reverential whisper.

"Thank you, Daddy."

The occasion needed a ceremony, she believed. Something to mark this transition in her life. Perhaps a naming ceremony of sorts, as she was no longer Sophine Jefferson. That was who she was when she traveled in the social circles she was born into. If she were born into a new cause, she would need a name that would be the story of herself that she would present to the world. It would be a label to define her and her mission. One that would connect her to her past, her heritage. She recalled the afternoons locked in her room, just her and her Reginophone. The strains of the Blues passing the long hours. The survival music of her people. The name came to her. Deaconess Blues. With that, she entered her new world.

FIFTEEN
BECAUSE I GOT HIGH

Vox Dei Data Files: Radicalized elements in the Old Fourth Ward district have forced the imposition of the crown by Chancellor Pruitt. This required a curfew of sunset for all right standing citizens to be off the streets so that authorized Pinkerton agents can safeguard them. These dark forces are street thugs with uniforms, propaganda, and hand signs to identify them, who go around attacking citizens with clubs, attempting to intimidate our police forces, and attempting to disrupt civil society. These brown shirt enforcers amount to a secret, private army that act as shock troops against the interests of the crown. This nest of unrest is trash needing to be swept out.

THE SMALL GROUP of young men skulked among the mud-slogged sidewalks and crept through alleys, navigating the maze of corridors within Freetown Village with a native's ease. Seasons in Freetown Village passed with a certain severe regularity. Unlike the dust in other areas of town cut down by the city's installation of street sprinklers, dust from the hot, dry summers swept into homes after being stirred by traffic. During winter, autocarriages and public trams were relatively rare sights, replaced by horse-drawn carriages sluicing through the streets. Store owners placed ashes on the sidewalk for traction, the lush white of a fresh snowfall quickly reduced the mix to bleeding gray, like a penny sheet doused with water. Springtime brought the rains.

This year reminded the older residents of Freetown Village of spring 1970. That year *The Indianapolis Recorder* reported that mud ran four inches deep along Illinois Street. The White River overflowed and flooded many adjacent neighborhoods. The muck made the streets impassable, miring horse carriages. Open gutters spilled into the White River, everything from horse manure to chamber pot waste to household garbage to dead animal carcasses attracting maggots and mosquitoes. Along the bridge over Indiana Avenue and the canal, people stepped in gutters or dragged the edges of their petticoats and jackets in the filth. Muddy shoes and worn boots became the current fashion. No one pointed out the peculiarity of the weather patterns, the taste of coal in the rain, or the sour stink of the steamworks with the snow. As if it were impolite to correlate the city's industrial waste to its impact on its streams and the like. Things hadn't much changed in the intervening years.

Sleepy and Knowledge Allah had been warned to be as silent as possible if they wanted safe passage. With the choice of traveling with this group versus the possibility of either waiting for the Knights of the White Camelia or the COPs to show up, they simply nodded and followed. Sleepy noted how every now and then one of them would cast a lingering, yet incredulous gaze, as if they had kidnapped a leprechaun and couldn't believe their good fortune. When Sleepy caught Knowledge Allah's eye, Knowledge Allah shrugged.

Their leader introduced himself as Ishmael Washington. Tall and gaunt—a handlebar mustache framing his jaw—his grave looks and air of authority gave profundity to his directions. He comported himself with a practiced noble bearing. With a lone raised finger, he silenced and froze them.

The early morning fog cloaked their furtive entry onto the streets. Smokestacks belched poisonous clouds, making the oppressive sky gray as prison-issue uniforms. The air, redolent with a ferrous rock, was heavy with the stink of coal and sweat. In the shadows of the air trams of the overcity, a COP trawler slowed as it neared them. Other denizens scurried away like rats caught in the light, quick to return to the burrow openings they called home. The pair averted their faces, unblinkingly side-eyeing the passing vehicle. Sleepy spat, a black-tinged wad of phlegm.

The United States practiced the conducting of arbitrary searches under general warrants. All in an effort to ferret out seditious activities. The Pinkerton Agency trained COPs to use pretext traffic stops and the stopping and frisking of less-than-random citizens—especially Unpersons—in what they called "consent searches." Searching for contraband, since COPs exercised civil forfeiture laws such that if any was found, the person's assets could be seized. Everything from their cash on hand to their vehicle to their home. Already forgetting that police harassment, arbitrary searches, and intimidation of its subjects were what inspired the failed United States Revolution in the first place.

The somber caravan avoided Illinois Street and its telescopic viewers. A trial project of Chancellor Pruitt, it stationed COPs at various intersections, equipping them with an "eye in the sky for the eye that never sleeps." Each surveillance station could nudge their telescope to the right or left, and zoom in on a scene by balancing an array of mirrors through a complex relay of cranks and gears. No one pointed out that cantilevered brass tubes jutting from "equipment sheds" might be conspicuous. At each station along their route, someone had painted three triangles which roughly formed a three-pointed crown. Sleepy recalled seeing the image several times across the ward as they loped through the streets.

The leader of the crew approached a young man who leaned against an alley door. Making a hand gesture by splaying his middle three fingers across his chest, the young man nodded and allowed them entry. The young man did a double-take when Sleepy neared him. Another chorus of "Is that ...?" followed by "Be cool" was becoming a familiar song to him. Other members of the crew lugged in large canvas bags strapped to their shoulders. The last two escorted Sleepy and Knowledge Allah toward the basement stairs.

THE INDIANAPOLIS RECORDER: *The Martindale area of Indianapolis was settled in 1874 by railroad workers who found work in manufacturing and machine shops. African-Americans settled the residential areas around Beeler Street. In 1922, the Paul Laurence Dunbar Branch of the Indianapolis Public Library, located inside Indianapolis Public School #26—an all-black elementary school—opened its doors. In 1927, Harlem Renaissance poet, Countee Cullen, read there at a tea hosted by the library in his honor. The library operated for 45 years before it and the school were shut down.*

THE DOOR OPENED into a small room, like an unmanned reception area. Splashed by mud, dry brush, and leaves from their jaunt through the woods and across the ward, the men removed their soiled outer garments. They slung their garments, some flecked with blood from the melee, along the wall. Sleepy and Knowledge Allah stood with their hands in front of them. Though no claims bound them, they shuffled through the corridors as if still shackled. Still damp, their clothes chafed with each stop. A desk barred another set of doors which were all-but-invisible in the dim light. The men scooted around to push through them. They opened into a space much like a warehouse.

A large banner hung along the far wall. In more stylized detail, three triangles formed the tips of a crown. Underneath were several enlarged daguerreotypes of Sleepy's wanted poster. On each one, an artist had painted over the image in some way. Sleepy stood in front of the one in the center. Sleepy's face had been chalked over in white except for a band about his eyes. The brown of his flesh in stark contrast to the white layer forced upon him. In the white of his forehead were the words "I am the change." On other posters were words like "Rogue?" or "Justice" or "No Peace."

Ismael led them into a room which had the arrangement of a library study hall. Old student desks were piled back toward the rear of the room. Knowledge Allah dragged one to the center of the room to sit in. Sleepy grabbed another. Exhausted after their cross-town consti-tutional, he made several attempts to plant his ample frame within the desk, until finally opting to instead lean against its top. The room compelled a certain hush to it but was made surprisingly homey by the scattered knick-knacks and trophies which dotted its walls. Framed photos of the first graduating class of the John Hope School, protest rallies, and a close up of the Star Child at a podium raising his fist.

"You've been gone a long time, Ishmael." A tall man strode toward them with a determined grace and somber dignity. His steps had purpose, the cane he ambled more affectation than necessary. Despite the weather and their location, the man wore a dark brown suit over a bright orange shirt. His gray-streaked hair had grown out and was about to lock. A pocket kerchief with the same floral explo-sion of color as his shirt, sprouted from his jacket pocket. He spoke with a hint of a Jamaican accent.

"We had complications," Ishmael said.

"What sort of complications?"

The leader stepped to the side to offer a better view of Sleepy and Knowledge Allah.

The man limped over to them. He studied them with an appraiser's eye. "What's your name?"

"Hubert Nixon."

"That's your government name. What do your people call you?"

"My friends call me Sleepy."

"Then I hope to earn the right to call you Sleepy." The man shifted his attention to Knowledge Allah, though it seemed like he remained keenly aware of where everyone surrounding him was located. "And you?"

"I give you my name and you have me at a disadvantage."

"You raise a solid point. My name is Desmond Coke."

"(120 Degrees of) Knowledge Allah." He hard-eyed Desmond.

"You're one of those Lost Nation boys," the man said. "We work with them quite a bit."

"I'm no one's boy." Knowledge Allah sniffed.

Sleepy chuckled to himself. Knowledge Allah never let up.

When his hardness wasn't directed at him, Sleepy loved watching it in action.

"There's quite the reward on your head," Desmond said.

"Yet I doubt we're in danger of you turning us in," Knowledge Allah said.

"Oh?"

"Considering your men just assaulted some of the ... fine, upstanding citizens of the White Camelia to secure our release, not to mention whatever goods they ... collected."

"We are entrepreneurs in the procurement business," Ishmael said.

"What did we 'procure' tonight?" Desmond turned to him.

The leader began emptying the contents of the bags along the table, as if creating place settings for an elaborate dinner. Over thirty weapons, including a machine gun, carbine, twelve rifles, and thousand rounds of ammunition.

"Defanging our adversaries." Desmond ran his hand through the shells.

"And giving teeth to our cause." Ishmael checked his pocket watch again. "You can't expect us to bring cricket bats to a knife fight."

"These teeth are our last resort. Men who depend on guns limit their options." Desmond spoke with the gentle, chiding tone of a teacher reminding a student. "I expect us to bring ideas, intelligence, and wisdom—our truest weapons and the ones they fear most. If we're armed, that gives them an excuse to send in their militarized Pinkertons. You need to get back to your employer before your cover is blown. Go on, I'll take things from here."

Ishmael nodded to him and then to Sleepy, before taking his leave, slinking off into the gloom of the abandoned library.

"You plan on destroying the weapons?" Knowledge Allah arched a knowing eyebrow.

"You must be mad. Sometimes you have to bring a gun to a gun fight. I just won't see us armed or parading about with arms. It's not the image the Star Child wanted to project, and image is another important weapon in our battle. It's dangerous for you, for all of us, out there."

"How bad have things gotten?" Sleepy tugged at the collar of his orange jumpsuit. He shifted against the desk, unable to get comfortable.

"We are under the imposition of the crown. Freetown Village for now, maybe all of Indianapolis by week's end. So ordered by our fine and upstanding Chancellor. Any gathering of three individuals or more, if not authorized by prior arrangement with the Chancellor's office—who, slimy coward that he is, denies all such requests out of hand—are considered treasonous activity. Perpetrators are labeled and dealt with as enemies of the state. Once declared an enemy combatant, you're stripped of all rights as a citizen and deposited in The Ave."

"An efficient way to create more Unpersons," Knowledge Allah said.

"Except they can bypass the private penitentiaries and be detained in state-sponsored black sites. Where they can employ all measures of inducements to extract information," Desmond said.

"All this has happened in the last few weeks?" Sleepy asked. Part of him sunk with pangs of guilt that his actions might be responsible.

"Things have been in motion for a while to vex them most proper, not that you'd hear it discussed on the *Vox Populi*. Look we can discuss this later. You're our guests. Let's get you a change of clothes and out of those state-sponsored shame rags. Give you time to rest and eat. Sleepy, I've been appraised that you may need some recreational alone time."

Sleepy remembered his collection of illicit daguerreotypes. "Who's been impugning my reputation?"

"Your reputation is that you get high." Desmond produced an unlit pipe. Hand carved, with the bowl being the head of a lion. He withdrew a baggie filled with dried leaves.

Sleepy all but salivated at the sight of the bag. "Can't do much about the truth."

"From my personal stash. It's a chiba strain called Instant Death."

"Good looking out." Sleepy reached out to receive the baggy.

Knowledge Allah grabbed his hand. "You're going to smoke something you know in advance is called Instant Death?"

Sleepy took a deep whiff of the herb. "This free?"

"I always keep enough to share with my brothers who partake," Desmond said.

"Instant. Death," Knowledge Allah repeated. "As in, kill you."

"Will you relax? If these folks wanted us dead, we'd still be guests of the Knights of the White Camelia." Sleepy considered himself long overdue to be feted in some way. He missed music in his life. He missed the play of words and the energy of poets in his life. He missed being on stage, holding the mic, spitting his truth. He missed getting high.

"When we get together for dinner, we can discuss the intersection of our mutual interests." Desmond clapped a hand on his shoulder, drawing him from his reverie.

"Such as?" Knowledge Allah asked. Sleepy was too preoccupied with the baggie to care.

"I want to discuss the state of the world and your role in it," Desmond said.

"Does this have anything to do with why your people keep looking at me like I'm my grandmother's dish of macaroni and cheese at the family reunion?" Sleepy asked.

"That's what happens when you become the face of the revolution."

"The ..." Sleepy trailed off. He snatched the pipe. "I really need to get really high to finish this conversation."

A FEW OF Desmond's people escorted Sleepy to a back room. They didn't have the vibe of a security detail, more like overly concerned hosts attending to him. Settling into the room, he found two sets of clothes: a long nightshirt to rest in, and a dress shirt and pants for dinner. Sleepy slipped out of his dank orange dungarees, enjoying the respite of the moisture drying on his skin. The night-shirt proved snug, but he didn't care. He kept the lights low and found the back corner of the room. He pressed his back to the wall. He tamped the side of his pipe to even the spread of chiba leaves. Instant Death. The last time he had a strong strain of chiba—called Slap Your Momma or some foolishness—he got so chill, he imagined himself on a beach counting the waves. All he could mumble was, "I'm too high."

It had been too long since his last blast of smoke. So much had happened. The Two-Johns. The COPs. Lockup. His father. Escape. The jump. The White Camelia. He hadn't slowed down to process any of it and definitely didn't want to with a clear head. Sleepy lit the leaves and inhaled. His first hit alone sent him higher than Slap Your Momma ever did. His thoughts swirled like animated images in a winding zoetrope, the band of sequenced images spinning faster and faster until ...

... THIS IS WHERE IT STARTS. All desert mesas and cacti blurring by. Long stretches of highway, the black asphalt shimmering like water, baked by the pitiless, noontime sun. I run. I always run. Maybe I know I'm being hunted, but I'm always being hunted. That's the nature of life, my life. To be hunted, or be the hunter, either way, but to always run. All I want to do is run and be free, to feel the wind on my face. Running is as close to flying as any ground bound mammal can achieve. I don't care because when I close my eyes, I might as well be flying. Kicking up dust in my wake, I know something chases me. Long and slim, emaciated, always hungry. Living, breathing Desire, as determined as a coyote. It's close now. Almost within arm's reach. A napkin dangles about its neck like a dining cravat, its lascivious grin spoiled by desire and drool. So close. Then out of nowhere a train screams by. Desire doesn't notice the tracks, nor hears the rumble of its approach. All it concerns itself with is catching me. But I notice. I notice everything. My thoughts flow free,

as fast as my feet, and send my thoughts soaring among the clouds. I give voice to my freedom.

Beep-beep.

A tension charges the air, the vibration of being hunted. Of being watched, as if through a telescopic lens. I know to keep my head down as I run. A massive boulder swings overhead; tethered to what, I don't know. Gravity is its biggest enemy. The boulder's arc defies the laws of physics and common sense. The large rock swings high, too high, and lands on the architect of my intended demise. The boulder slams onto its cliffside perch, and for a moment it's relieved at not paying the price for its efforts. Then a crack trickles under its ledge and the earth gives way. Gravity ignores it for a moment, allowing it an opportunity to meditate on its folly. Then it falls, feet pedaling in the air. Bouncing against outcrops and branches, bones snapping, skull splitting in its fall, it slams into the asphalt of the eternal highway. The boulder and its cliffside perch shatter on either side of it. Again, its battered body rises, Desire doesn't know how to quit, a glimmer of relief fills its eyes because neither object landed on it. Until a truck runs it over. I notice the truck. I dream of driving the truck. I stick out my tongue to taste the air before I redouble my efforts to run because I know the truth of this life. That the hunt never truly ends. I know it will still come after me. The tire treads across Desire's chest fade away. Intestines scoot across the pavement crawling back inside it. Blood trails reverse themselves and find their way back to its body. Lungs re-inflate. Bones reknit. Nerve endings fire up. Synapses re-charge. Desire rises, and the circling vultures' curse, deprived of their meal yet again. Desire begins again.

Beep-beep.

It pursues, inexorable, never stopping. Magnifying its efforts, though it has long forgotten its goal. Caught up in its endless cycle of violence and cruelty. It opens a crate of dynamite ordered from the Acme Company. It knows how this will end even as it assembles the dynamite strapped rocket. It cannot help itself. Given to elaborate contraptions, great machinations of thought, and effort for a simple plan: to catch, to consume in so convoluted a method. Too clever by half. All its plans backfire, but it won't learn through the humiliation of its continuous failures. Desire ends in an explosion as I run past. I taste the reek of sulfur and I give the devil its due with a tongued salute. I know what I must do. I must stay on the road. I must stay the course.

Sometimes I have to disturb the peace when I've got no peace. For us all to get peace.

Beep-beep.

SLEEPY BATHED for an hour and a half to scrub off any trace of soot and jail from him. Though a few hours had passed since he first sparked up, he remained lit. When he came into the room, his match flared in the dim light, casting haunting shadows across his face. He drew hard on his smoking apparatus, thick plumes of smoke eventually issuing from his mouth and nose when he exhaled. Knowledge Allah rolled his eyes at Sleepy's somnambulant strolling entrance, not that Sleepy cared. Knowledge Allah greeted him wearing what he assumed was one of Desmond's old suits. A carnation colored shirt against a dark emerald suit, with a pocket kerchief to match the shirt.

"You need a blast?" Sleepy's eyes, hazy as the smog-clogged skies, tracked Knowledge Allah re-entering the room. "Chiba is like fruit: keep you healthy. Keeps your mind clear."

Knowledge Allah squinted at the smoke with disapproval. "I don't pollute my lungs with such filth. It's the devil's trap."

"Then consider me all the way caught the hell up. But you stand much closer and you're going to get contact trapped." Holding the smoke in his lungs for the span of three heartbeats, Sleepy exhaled another thick cloud of noxious vapor.

Desmond stood, met his eyes, and then clasped his hands as if they were long lost tribesmen who at last found one another. Desmond gestured toward a seat at the table and Sleepy slid into it.

"Where to begin?" Desmond asked.

"How about with Sleepy being the face of the revolution?" Knowledge Allah seated himself across from Desmond.

"Yes. The two of you figure quite prominently in the story."

"What story is that?" Sleepy's words slowly tumbled out of his mouth.

"The ancient story of oppression. Exodus. Exile. Exaltation." Desmond's voice had a faraway quality to it, like a teacher winding up for a well-rehearsed lesson. "As slaves in Egypt, look how the Israelites had to rise up and decry the oppressive powers, looking to Yahweh as savior to an enslaved people. As slaves in Egypt, He heard their groaning. We see in the story of Israel the history of our own people—from their Exodus out of slavery to their Exile in a land not their own. During their time of Exile, the Israelites had been taken into captivity to Babylon, their best and brightest were re-educated. They had to adopt the Babylonian culture, learn the Babylonian language, learn the Babylonian religion, and take on Babylonian names. Those men were in turn re-enculturated: indoctrinated with new language, new customs, even new names. The ruling power weaponized its culture to brainwash and be a form of systematic control. They were only able to survive because of hope. Their hope of future Exaltation. It all began when someone shouted, 'That's enough.' You two began shouting that the moment you left your mark on the COP vehicle. And many have heard your call."

"Our mark? You mean when we dented that COP vehicle?" Sleepy asked.

"Your symbol. The crown." Desmond held up three fingers across his chest. He then slid a drawing over to Knowledge Allah. "I thought a Lost Nation brother would appreciate it."

"I'm no longer with the Nation." Knowledge Allah studied the sketch. "Wait, this almost looks like broken star points around a cipher."

"A what?" Sleepy leaned back as one of the men brought out several plates of food. Rice and peas, collalou, and jerk chicken. He didn't wait for Knowledge Allah to pick at his plate to complain about whatever he'd find to complain about before he began eating.

"How we'd describe The Universe." Knowledge Allah drifted on a memory. "The Creator names. The name is seventeen, consecrated by righteous anger. One is Knowledge. Seven is God. *Arm. Leg. Leg. Arm. Head.* One plus seven equals eight. Eight means to Build. Or to Destroy. Eight is evolution. Eight is change."

"That's all part of the story," Desmond said. "Do you know how to kill an idea? With a different idea. The big ideas start with your philosophers, your thinkers, your theologians. If those ideas make it to your artists, they get popularized. Transmitted. That's when they enter the culture and the minds of the masses."

"And we're the idea?"

"Freedom is the idea. You are our rallying cry. Our symbol." Desmond pointed to the graffiti images of Sleepy.

"Your ... voice," Sleepy said between bites, thinking on Knowledge Allah's words. Knowledge Allah smiled with budding approval.

"Freedom has a price for those who seek it earnestly. Blood, like our Messiah. Sweat, because yolks are heavy to move. Tears, where there is a steep cost, there is often tragedy. Are you willing to pay that price?"

"Damn!" Sleepy exclaimed. "Does freedom take coupons?"

"After all we've seen and done, your ability to be silent has been shattered. You've been woke to a new reality. You can't go back to your old ways." Knowledge Allah studied Desmond. "What did it cost you?"

"In this story, he's called the Star Child."

"You know the Star Child?" Knowledge Allah asked.

"He's my son." The words landed like a slap in the face. Sleepy's fork froze mid-scoop. He swallowed his current mouthful, the gulp sounded louder than he intended. Though he'd been slowly working himself up, the air seemed to be let out of Knowledge Allah. He cocked his head slightly, assessing and re-assessing the man in front of them. No stranger to scrutiny, Desmond picked at his food. "The Ave ... they plan to execute him soon."

"What do you have planned?" A sudden solemnity filled Knowledge Allah's voice.

"All we have to go on right now are rumors. Everything from the possibility of Breton Court being razed to a city-wide 'revitalization' plan. At some point, the government will realize that the vast majority of us have nothing to lose from violent unrest. Assuming they haven't already."

"They know. I'd be surprised if they didn't already have a plan in place. And needed an excuse to phase it in," Knowledge Allah said. "Like the imposition of the crown."

Desmond stared at him. "I don't think I like what you're implying."

"It all makes sense," Sleepy said. "When I was being interrogated, something the Pinkerton Assistant said bothered me. The way she spoke about 'our fruit vendor' and the way they seemed to have ears in The Tombs, to the point of the too timely arrival of the COPs. Almost as if people were on someone's payroll. What if someone is stirring the pot, moving everyone around like chess pieces to take advantage of what seems to be inevitable? What if they are setting the table? We need to be very careful."

"We need a revolution in our way of doing life," Knowledge Allah said. "And need to be loud about it."

"Ig'nant loud." Sleepy scooped the jerk chicken from Knowledge Allah's plate. "The first thing we need to do is make a run to pick up some equipment. I know exactly the kind of match we need."

"CITIZENS OF THE UNIVERSE, do not attempt to adjust your electro-transmitter, there is nothing wrong. We have taken control to bring you this special bulletin." The attenuated pulse of Knowledge Allah's voice echoed along the airwaves. A whine of feedback blasted through the speakers. The warehouse basement smelled like a privy pit, but it was the only space that had enough room to hold all of Sleepy's equipment.

A glass-fronted cabinet contained a rotating cylinder that gyrated up and down. A series of antennae lined the top of the device, electricity arcing between them, the charges climbing the spires like tendrils of ivy. Pipes splayed like pleats of a fan, groaning and gurgling as the home kine burned. Sleepy adjusted the controls of his electro-receiver, then gave Knowledge Allah a thumbs-up.

"The Albion Empire bloated itself on its own myth—a proud, corpulent pustule of wealth—spreading across the land, a decadent cancer of corporate greed and industrial indulgence, all in the name of national pride.

"Washington aristocrats with vested interest in our eternal domination, governing to their interests, not ours. The Empire is a corrupt federal leviathan, swollen and lazy, and we are the cheap table legs propping it up. We wake up each day to struggle. We work to live and pay taxes to the crown for the opportunity. We need more than that. Revolution is inevitable. We are the First Cause. In our tiers of rage, we call for direct action. We resist constituted powers through property damage. We impede the flow of goods and capital, using their system against them and making the cost of perpetuating domination prohibitive. And it is time to co-opt their instruments of military guarantor to free the Star Child. There's a party at the crossroads. Watch the skies. Freedom or Death.

"I exist between time, outside time. In the between places. I am the voice of truth in these troubled times."

Knowledge Allah removed his headphones. Sleepy rushed over to greet him. They clasped hands and bumped shoulders.

"That was hype," Sleepy exclaimed.

"Not bad for our first go out."

"How many of these broadcasts do you have in you?"

"As many as we need," Knowledge Allah said.

"Gentlemen." Desmond opened the door, interrupting them. Sleepy and Knowledge Allah turned to him like two teenagers caught smoking behind the school.

"We tapped into the *Vox Populi*'s feed. You know they're having a fit once the *Vox Populi* stopped issuing its special brand of nonsense," Sleepy said, a little too quickly.

"What do you think?" Knowledge Allah asked.

"Everyone heard the broadcast. Oh, we've vexed their spirits. Big up." Desmond bridged his fingers in front of him. "If God so chooses to favor me, I think that I have someone I want you to meet."

SIXTEEN
FUNKIN' LESSON

The Indianapolis Recorder: *After the Civil Unrest, those of African descent, no matter how much or little of that blood ran through their veins, were relegated to a state of vague emancipation. Not living in the massive, industrial overcities, but dismissed to ghettos—pacified by legalized, free-flowing drugs—a terra incognita somehow lost between the cartographer's calipers. Or they were imprisoned. Viceroy George II pandered without shame to the interests of the Empire. Though high born and privileged, he was no nobleman, but rather a spoiled bloodline of nine generations of insular breeding.*

NEWS of the Colored Folks section of The Indianapolis Star: *(reprint) "Negroes have always held the lowest jobs, the most menial jobs, which are now being destroyed by automation. No remote provision has yet been made to absorb this labor surplus. Furthermore, the Negro's education, North and South, remains, almost totally, a segregated education. And, the police treat the Negro like a dog." — James Baldwin*

VOX DEI *DATA FILES: James Baldwin was a radical socialist and a homosexual.*

"CITIZENS OF THE UNIVERSE, do not attempt to adjust your electro-transmitter, there is nothing wrong. We have taken control to bring you this special bulletin," Knowledge Allah said.

"Aw, hell nah." Sleepy paused mid-keystroke on the pianoforte. A system of pipes ran from the back of the instrument to the ceiling, steam billowing in mild tufts from the joints. The low, arrhythmic notes slowly faded into a dull echo as he turned to the gleaming carapace of the electro-transmitter with a countenance of mild exasperation.

Sleepy reached for his pipe, tamped the side to even the spread of chiba leaves, lit them, and inhaled. Holding the smoke in his lungs for the span of three heartbeats, he exhaled a thick cloud of noxious vapor. Only then was he prepared to amble his considerable girth toward the faded tapestry that concealed the descending spiral stairway. Wide-shouldered and bulbous framed as he was, each step creaked under his weight as he slowly made his way into the subterranean hollow.

"That's right, today's mathematics is knowledge. Let me break it down for you: know the ledge."

The voice emanated from the darkened corner of the chamber. Barely seated on the many-times-patched ottoman, was the spindly-framed Knowledge Allah. His strong face was eroded by despair. His distant eyes had stared into the abyss of anger and hate for too long. A gold band pulled back his thick braids. His thick cravat was tucked into his vest. Knowledge Allah was in full form, all he needed was a microphone and an audience, Sleepy thought. One had to decipher the code of his thought language before he began to make any sense, and such a task rarely proved simple while under the effects of chiba.

"You don't know who you are," Knowledge Allah's self-secure voice rang with steel. "Take on your true name. *Arm. Leg. Leg.*

Arm. *Head.* You are the original man. You are gods. Yet you sit there, blind, deaf, and dumb to your potential.

"Few realize who they are and those that do—and seek to wake the people from their neglected truth—are incarcerated by this grafted government. The time for revolution is at hand, brothers and sisters. The time is at hand. We only await a sign.

"I exist between time, outside time. In the between places. I am the voice of truth in these troubled times."

The clockwork gears ground to a gentle halt as the spindles of the machine wound down. The electric arcs sputtered, and the entire apparatus darkened. Knowledge Allah stooped from behind the glass cabinet, daubing his sweaty brow with a handkerchief, a smirk of zealotry on his face.

"What the actual fuck, man?" Sleepy asked, his insistent steps catching up to him as he found himself winded. He eased himself into the nearest chair. Knowledge Allah poured him some brandy from a nearby decanter, before pouring a glass of water for himself.

"Are the mysteries I strive to illuminate too deep for you, my brother?" Knowledge Allah clinked Sleepy's glass with his own, then downed his water.

"The only mystery is my need to get high." Sleepy ran his pick through his Afro, his hair barely tamed by a comb. Drawing and holding another blast, he puffed out another cloud. "Mystery solved."

"They set snares that have been prepared for you. Snares meant to lead you from your path of righteousness. You've let them cave you."

"They who?" Sleepy asked, forgetting his oft-repeated lesson of not asking Knowledge Allah any follow-up questions. However, Sleepy couldn't help but think there was a more pronounced undercurrent of derision to Knowledge Allah's tones these days, as if the other man stared down the thin beak of a nose at him. A shift in temperament which could likely be solved if Knowledge Allah would just get high. Or laid.

"Your so-called grafted government's behind it," Knowledge

Allah continued. "The next phase is to destroy us. You think it stopped with Tuskegee?" The Tuskegee Institute. One of the few schools allowed in the undercities. The name sent a chill along the spine at the memory of the experiments done in the name of science. "No, they just got slicker. We don't have poppy fields. We don't have dirigibles. We do have wills sapped by opiate clouds."

"Sounds like we don't have shit," Sleepy said. "Speaking of, I thought we agreed on no more broadcasts until we got our act together?"

"The truth cannot go unvoiced." Ever since they had hooked up with Desmond and his crew, a new fire fueled Knowledge Allah. It was like his purpose had been rekindled. As if he had once been adrift, but had found a cause to believe in. Again.

"Shit." Sleepy pronounced the word as if it possessed three syllables. "You one of them long-winded brothers who just like to hear themselves talk. What I don't hear is a plan. You got all this 'righteous knowledge' ... What we going to do?"

"That does seem to be the question." Desmond swaggered toward them with a lightness of step that made Sleepy think that at any moment he'd use his cane as part of a dance routine. Desmond's suit du jour was dark green against a pale blue shirt, a yellow kerchief tamped into its pocket, which stirred a pang of jealousy. Missing his own beloved wardrobe, Sleepy wondered how many suits Desmond owned and where he stored them. The old man issued a proud smile. "You have an answer?"

"I don't know. I'm just a rhyme sayer," Sleepy said.

"And yet you rally the people. Sparked a sense of hope. Still, what's your next move?"

"We need to free the Star Child," Knowledge Allah whispered.

"Wait, what now?" Sleepy asked.

"He's the match. The light that reveals this caste system in blackface. The politicians trumpet colorblindness, trivializing and disguising the depth of our plight. I can't afford to be colorblind. These days, I need all the sight God gave me without any handicaps. Once you learn to turn a blind eye to something, it gets easier to not see other things around us." Knowledge Allah stood up for maximum dramatic effect. "We need to free the Star Child."

"I ..." The idea intrigued Desmond, sparked hope so heady, he pressed both hands on the head of his cane. Not solely to steady himself, but also to focus himself while he chewed on Knowledge Allah's idea. "It's a huge gesture. It would grab everyone's attention. What's the plan?"

Knowledge Allah turned to Sleepy, who remained seated, the implications of the words still reverberating in his mind. Their import required a few moments to digest.

"It'd be, what, the two of you? Know the layout of The Ave? Gathered any resources? Any intel whatsoever?" Desmond's words held little trace of his Jamaican accent.

"No." Knowledge Allah slowly lowered himself, a deflating dirigible.

"Don't get me wrong, you're onto something. It's something I've dared not hope to attempt. I think it's time you met our latest operative. Maybe add some of the pieces you're missing." Desmond scratched on a piece of paper. "Here's the address. You're expected."

KNOWLEDGE ALLAH BEAMED, obviously quite pleased with himself, and wrapped his greatcoat around him and nodded. Sleepy fastened a cape around his long, blue, eight-button coat, the image of a flabby martinet. He opened the garage door.

The metal of their autocarriage gleamed even in the wan moonlight, polished to a glassy sheen every day. Desmond's crew knew their way around vehicles. Twin brass tubes formed the body of the car, curving down on both ends, stitched together by copper rivets. Headlamps, jutting cans, burned to life. The suspension bounced and lurched in a frenzy of steam belches, jolting them up and down. The bemused pair enjoyed the weight of stares from their neighbors. The 24-inch rims, whirring fans, continuously shuttered like deployed armor. With a roar, the car took off, spumes of steam left in its wake.

Passing one of the topside entrances to The Tombs, billboards of smiling brown faces endorsing opiate use sat next to adverts of money changers offering promises of quick loans, both preying on desperation and ignorance. The buildings crumbled into screes of pebbles along rotted sidewalks under an air of imminent decay. Gas lamps produced forlorn shadows from the steeped darkness.

The slow and winding White River neatly carved the undercity in half, as the homes of Freetown Village gave way to the Victorian architecture of the suburbs of Indianapolis, following a parkway to the Broad Ripple Village. Knowledge Allah directed him to a two-story brick, Queen Anne home guarded by a wrought-iron fence. The house stood out from the rest of the neighborhood. Drab green, with fine terra-cotta ornaments and lacy spindles, its conical-roofed turret had fish scale slate shingles. Stained glass sat atop curtained bay windows.

"Whose place are we heading to?" Sleepy asked.

"All Desmond indicated was an inventor's."

"He down with The Cause?"

"You need to be open to the mysteries life offers," Knowledge Allah said.

"Like what?"

"Like the inventor."

Knowledge Allah rapped on the large obsidian knocker. The door swung open. A poor simulacrum of a person greeted them with the smooth manner of a well-rehearsed marionette. Twin lanterns burned in empty spaces as optical receptors, a mechanical stare masking its inner workings. Its inner workings whirred—pistoning brass and steel gears—over the gentle hum of whatever powered it. Its face—dull, unpainted metal—held no expression and little attempt at humanity. Wondrous and intricate, a flawless design, it projected a knowing discomfort of the other. Sleepy suddenly grew terrified of the mind of its designer. With a mime's gesticulations, it offered to take their hats and coats and escorted the pair. Its disjointed consciousness lacked imagination, the ability to create story, the power to question its being or its place in the greater scheme of things. It moved without the gift of ancestors and the weight of history; at best it held the illusion of electric dreaming against the cold void of blackness.

Sleepy envied its uncomplicated existence.

The double door entry opened into the foyer of the opulent home. Walls, alight with whale oil-filled lamps created an erudite glow within. A lone settee perched alongside a fireplace on the opposite side of the room. A deck of cards sat on a piece of silk atop a table. Sleepy cut the deck at random and saw a card inscribed with the number XVI over the picture of a tower struck by lightning. The building's top section had dislodged from the rest of it. Two men fell from the crumbling edifice. Filled with sudden disquiet, Sleepy set the deck down.

The automaton paused, like a bellboy awaiting a gratuity.

"*One nation under a groove,*" Knowledge Allah said to no one as he studied the décor of the home.

A bank of books parted to reveal a maw of shadows. The automaton withdrew, closing the library door behind it. The civilized façade of the pews of books gave way to the vaulted chamber of the laboratory. Rows of work-benches lined with test tubes, flasks, and beakers gurgling over Bunsen burners. Though a clangorous whir of fans vented the air, the room roiled with the cloying smell of steam and coal, hot metal and ozone. A skirling of flutes emanated from a boiler groaned under the strain of power and settling. A lithe figure bent over a metal frame of eight jutting arms spinning from a central mass, a mechanical arachnid contraption. Sleepy expected rolled up sleeves, moleskin trousers, and a grimy leather apron. Instead, beneath a cap, the figure was goggled and draped in a lab coat. It welded a few more joints, testing the articulation as the work progressed, lit to a haunting blue hue behind the jet of the torch.

Once the goggles had been raised, the inventor took a step back and nodded. Only then, as he examined the delicate features of the eyes—wrinkles of fatigue filigreed the corners of them, belying the youthfulness of the face—did Sleepy realize he regarded a woman. A green velvet jacket peeked from beneath the lab coat, with no décolletage or hint of femininity; the inventor held the bearing of a strict governess. She admired her handiwork and snugged her gloves. Her face retained an aqua tint in the dim electric glow. A product of miscegenation, she radiated the afterglow of light-skinned privilege, despite her secretive life ferreted away in her laboratory.

Upon noticing them, she stepped to Knowledge Allah. The air in the room thickened. They circled one another like two feral cats, all but arching their backs.

"Sophine?" he asked.

"Carlton?" The woman appeared to not know what to do with her hands. Sleepy always enjoyed a good awkward moment. As their bodies tensed, his gaze leaped from one to the other, waiting to see who would make the first move. "Desmond said to be expecting compatriots, but I never expected ..."

Knowledge Allah stepped closer but stopped just short of her. Leaning in with a tentative approach for an embrace, the angle proved odd. She had hesitated, having begun to stretch out her hand, first two, then three, then back to two fingers extended. The resulting hug was a sad, awkward thing. Sleepy shook his head in sympathetic pity.

"Uh ... Carlton?" Sleepy tested the sound of the name from his lips. "You two know one another?"

"Sophine is someone I met once." Knowledge Allah's eyes tracked the curves of her face. "In another life."

"Those in The Cause know me as Deaconess Blues." She held her ground, unflinching and defiant. Unabashedly vital, her high cheekbones framed an Aquiline nose against her sallow complexion, tea with too much milk; just light enough to be on the fringe of polite society. With a rigidity to her face and a hardness in her hazel eyes, she possessed a noblewoman's airs. She probably had an A-level education, which meant her parents had money or connections. The mirth of aristocracy barely masked an anarchist streak. Her terrible impertinence of dressing like a man covered a repressed gaiety to her Victorian effect. She polished her safety spectacles in a handkerchief, as cover for her taking a full appraisal of him also.

"And me as (120 Degrees of) Knowledge Allah."

"That's quite a mouthful." She pursed her lips, restraining even a thin smile. "No more orthocopters then?"

"No more raiding airships as a rule, no. But I still drop that melanin wisdom." Knowledge Allah stepped aside as if embarrassed. He favored his knee as if remembering their past life caused it to now bother him. "This is my compatriot, Sleepy."

"You're a woman of odd enthusiasms." Sleepy managed to hold his affable leer. "'Bout time we got some ladies representing. The Cause has seemed like a huge sausage-fest."

"Cooking stuff up in the lab," Knowledge Allah said.

"Just like 'Yacuub,' good sir." Deaconess Blues smiled at whatever joke only the pair of them understood.

Bored of whatever history floated between them, Sleepy wandered about the lab. It seemed like a lifetime ago that he whiled away his days as a coal shoveler, rather than as an artist or poet. Sleepy never fancied himself an anarchist by any stretch. Not like Deaconess Blues, who decided that she was past the male supremacy's notions of womanhood and waited for the rest of society to catch up to her. Her body and mind were hers to do with as she will. "It's nice to see not all of us had to struggle."

"Do not talk to me about struggle while you thoughtlessly squander what money you manage to scrimp together on instruments and automobiles worth more than your hovel." Her wan smile soured to a grim line. "My stepmother tried to program me with how it was unbecoming for a lady to fill her head with designs and equations. Her ideas for me would have me join the societal ranks of the vapid and colorless. I had other ideas."

Sleepy pulled a hair from his chin, closing his eyes at the fresh sting of pain. He tapped percussive melodies, lost in the rhythms of his thoughts.

"Did my words strike too close to home or am I boring you?" Deaconess Blues asked.

"Neither." Sleepy turned to her, hiding any trace of having gotten to him. "I'm just waiting to hear the deal."

"All in good time." Deaconess Blues half-bowed and gestured toward the door. An automaton recognized its cue and met them to lead them back to the library. Midway down the hallway, they passed a silver tray with a large envelope on it.

Sleepy patted his pockets and in a mocking tone said, "I don't have a calling card."

"Do not trouble yourself. You are my first visitors here. I don't expect to entertain many guests here. Few know of its existence, so I am trusting in your discretion." She sniffed. "This way."

Strains of classical music reverberated from the large horns encircling the room, surrounding them with sound. Her automaton had spread out the accouterments of high tea. A silver teapot poured a heady brew, the aroma filled the room. A tray of crumpets and other delicate pastries lay before them, as the blank-faced automaton attended to etiquette in Deaconess Blues's fragile dance of civility. Going through the motions of refined breeding, appearances were paramount. This Deaconess Blues woman put him off. Made him feel like he wasn't civilized enough to sit at the same table as her.

"So are we supposed to be one of Desmond's cells?" Sleepy stifled a rheumy cough, slipping a trail of gray sputum into his napkin. A pretty woman snubbing him had a familiar sting.

Knowledge Allah shifted noisily. He appeared rather ... nervous.

"I do not know, sir. The way I understand it, we compartmentalize ourselves so that no one person knows too much about our organization." Deaconess Blues tilted her head with a glimmer of maternal concern. "You look troubled."

"I just don't know what we're doing and..." Sleepy paused. "What's the point?"

"I have often wondered the same thing about the world we live in," Deaconess Blues said. "Has it ever struck you that we aren't as ahead technologically as we should be? That great capitalist machine called slavery robbed Mother Africa of generations of scientists, artists, and creative minds. That same machine depended on slavery, teaching its wealthiest and most privileged to depend on others to wait on them, rather than do and innovate for themselves. The very tools of their oppression stunted their culture's development."

"Knowledge and the reflection of knowledge equals wisdom," Knowledge Allah said. "Knowledge and wisdom equals understanding."

"Then if you *knowledge* my wisdom, you will understand what I'm saying," Deaconess Blues said. He nodded as if they shared the same gibberish wavelength. "Knowledge is built on the back of itself. Those who come along later stand on the shoulders of those before them. Think of where we'd be without that holocaust."

"We'd have flying cars," Sleepy said, "and show tunes."

"We *have* show tunes," she said.

"We'd have had them sooner. You feel me?" Sleepy glanced from one to the other. Deaconess Blues and Knowledge Allah shared the same blank expression. "What? A black man can't enjoy show tunes?"

"He isn't ready. He still needs verbal milk," Knowledge Allah said.

"Who *are* you right now?" Sleepy asked him.

"This meeting is premature. I am ... resources. Not propaganda," Deaconess Blues said.

"Time is of the essence. Our agenda demanded this level of meeting." Knowledge Allah could not find a comfortable position in his seat.

"My job is to oppose the corporate structure." Deaconess Blues scowled. "I care about the liberation of my people."

"Your people?" Glancing around the house, Sleepy straightened in his seat, discomfited by how defensive he sounded. With another dollop of chiba, the pungent sting of burnt weed would have sent his mind adrift among the clouds and made him much more receptive to high flung ideas.

Deaconess Blues remained unflustered. An obviously delicate eater, she drew a long sip of tea, then set her cup back onto its dish. "I'm black like you. I resist. I seek to end the chains and the extermination of oppression."

"You don't talk like a scientist," Sleepy said.

"Apparently I come from a line of anarchists and insurrectionists. And I'm a scientist. A scientist searching for knowledge and proof. For truth and meaning."

"You're a scientist of God," Knowledge Allah chimed in with a tone of deference.

Sleepy side-eyed him again. If Knowledge Allah was in romantic pursuit, this was some of the saddest game Sleepy had ever witnessed.

"With the revolutions in engineering and science and industry, we have yet to see any in our social systems. We might as well dress up the automata in minstrel outfits and paint them with bright, white eyes and red, bulbous lips for how we are seen." Deaconess Blues poured herself another cup of tea. She stirred in milk and sugar as her words settled in their ears, their anxious eyes on her, though she remained unhurried. "We've been promised universal enlightenment, an end to war, and a rationalist utopian ... as long as everyone knows their place.

"Any class reduction will face critical resistance. We have sold our souls in the service of commerce. We toil in the embrace of the machine and become a concubine of industry. So we rage against the machine and we must take extraordinary steps to defend ourselves. We must develop solidarity among our people, a swell of anti-colonial resistance."

"I feel you, but what're we going to do about it?" Sleepy asked, not one for the intellectual stuff. "Black folks are in a state of emergency. Got to start wilding out."

"You are a ruin to language," she said with the exacting manner of a spinster aunt.

"You rebel in your ways, I rebel in mine." Sleepy chafed against the subtle condescension of her civilizing influence. The discussion, though somewhat diverting, left him with the sensation of being out of his depth. Or perhaps it was the disconnection between the lofty ideas of whatever it was that they were fighting for and the practical reality of their people. And the idea that they were "their" people. Sleepy's views boiled down to pragmatism: the theory of struggle was great only insofar as someone actually was helped. It wasn't further argument he wanted, but action.

"We have the beginning of a plan," Knowledge Allah said as if reading Sleepy's reluctance.

"As I hear, the plan is the paragon of simplicity. Free the Star Child from the local penitentiary ..." Deaconess Blues said.

"The Ave," Sleepy said.

"The Allisonville Correctional Facility is a wretched place," Knowledge Allah said. "Its serpentine bowels, and those of its ilk, incarcerate a third of our people. Little better than slave pens, with us little better than beasts."

"The Star Child is a powerful symbol of the struggle. Imprisoned for speaking of a better way. Of revolution," Deaconess Blues said. "But The Ave is ..."

"Impregnable? No, its design bears the flawed fruit of the very hubris of its designers. Think of it: the administrative offices of the Indiana penal system housed in a lone spire, defying the heavens like the tower of Babel. Only a few guards, the rest automata. Were it to come crashing down, our brothers and sisters would be free."

"If everything came crashing down, wouldn't the prisoners be trapped?" Deaconess Blues asked.

"Don't you see? The same underground shafts that entomb them would now also protect them. All we would need is a group of folks on the ground to shepherd them to safety," Knowledge Allah said. "And something to bring down the tower itself."

A silence settled on them as they considered the idea. Knowledge Allah and Deaconess Blues sipped at their tea. Sleepy's mouth itched to spark up a pipe of chiba. Instead, he picked up one of the cucumber sandwiches from the tray the automaton brought in. The exact sort of thing he would have made fun of for being siddity, but they were here. And free. And he always enjoyed awkward silences more when eating.

"Allow me to be blunt: you, I do not know," Deaconess Blues said to Sleepy. She then turned to Knowledge Allah. "You and I haven't seen each other in ages, and now you have a new name and have shifted allegiances. Yet, you ask me to join you in committing high crimes of treason? No, just ... no." Deaconess Blues shook her head as if the very act of reflection was a wasted effort. Her stiff, stately bearing was the picture of restraint. "In addition, on a more practical level, helping free the Star Child would be a great symbolic victory, but that's all it would be."

"I hadn't thought of it like that." Knowledge Allah eased back into his seat, his posture tight, like that of a rebuffed gentleman forced to remain at the scene of his rebuffing.

"Maybe that's why Desmond introduced us. So that I may temper your enthusiasm with ..."

"Wisdom?"

"As you say."

"Then what do you suggest?" Knowledge Allah asked.

"I have reason to believe there is a more pressing threat to our community. Desmond has gathered a few of the pieces, as have I, but neither of us can see the whole picture."

"Who are the players?" Sleepy said.

"I know two of them. Lord Melbourne is a family ... friend. He and my father have had dealings as long as I can remember."

"Lord Melbourne? Melbourne Industries? The media mogul? He owns the *Vox Populi* and *Vox Dei*." Sleepy reached for his cup of tea. Though he'd never developed a taste for it, he needed to imbibe something.

"As well as the ZeroDyne Corporation, where I am employed. And he has a vested interest in the Pinkertons."

"He's a family friend? We certainly have been traveling in different circles," Knowledge Allah said.

"You didn't stick around long enough to find out what my circles are." Deaconess Blues's words had the mild sting of rebuke. The two of them basked in the silence.

Sleepy relished the show of Knowledge Allah squirming in sudden discomfort. After allowing the moment to foment for several excruciating seconds, Deaconess Blues cleared her throat to continue.

"Next, there is Chancellor Pruitt."

"Another friend of the family?" Knowledge Allah asked, though his tone had softened significantly.

"Anything but. I suspect that he has ties to the Knights of the White Camelia."

"We've recently had ... an encounter with them," Sleepy said.

"Then you know the threat they represent. Especially, if they have their hooks in politicians. Chancellor Pruitt and Lord Melbourne are known allies, but that's to be expected with a politician and a potential major donor."

"But you suspect more."

"Desmond led me to a meeting between Chancellor Pruitt and a man named Melvin Knight. But I don't know him. He had some other sobriquet."

"Now you're into our circles. We know Sugar. He has The Tombs on lockdown and looks to expand his influence throughout Freetown Village. It terrifies me to think what Sugar could do with Lord Melbourne's resources. If he were to travel in your circles, gain any sort of legitimacy ..."

"The ball," Deaconess Blues said, as if a notion struck her like lightning.

"The what?"

"I have an invitation in the foyer. The Chancellor is having a fundraiser ball tonight. Everyone who is anyone will be there."

"And you're invited?" Knowledge Allah asked.

"I am still my father's daughter." Deaconess Blues stood up. She strode to the coat rack and donned a hat and gloves. Sleepy distrusted the cock of her hat.

"I don't want to be *that guy*," Sleepy began, "but you're proposing that we—two of us being wanted as terrorists and prison escapees—consider going to a ball which hosts the very people hunting us. That about sum up this plan?"

"Well, it's like when we went to the Second Marion County Courthouse..." Knowledge Allah said.

"Which was a dumb idea then. And that was when we were new to being hunted...AND HADN'T ESCAPED FROM PRISON!" Sleepy slumped into a chair as if worn out from having made his point. "You don't think they'll be on the lookout for terrorists to do terrorist shit where all the power is gathered?"

"You raise a fair point," Deaconess Blues started. "However, as I said. I am still my father's daughter. No one will be looking for suspects on the red carpet of invitees only. And, to be frank, we'll be in costume and out of context. No plan is without high risk. Desmond wants to forge us into a cell. Let's get to know one another ... via the dance floor."

SEVENTEEN

WELCOME TO THE TERRORDOME

Vox Populi: Chancellor Lucas Pruitt is expected to announce the appointment of Melvin Knight as the executive director of the 10 Points Neighborhoods Initiative. An experienced community organizer, civic advocate, and businessman, Knight is charged with bringing a new vision of engagement between neighborhoods and the Chancellor's office. The announcement is to be made at the Governor's Mansion at tonight's annual fundraising event to support several Indianapolis charities. The Governor's Ball has grown beyond the Chancellor's wildest dreams, to become the societal event of the season. Knight declared that, "Now is the ideal time for Indianapolis to realize its full potential as a place where history is made and measured."

This has sparked tantrums from the usual quarters of social justice crusaders protesting what they call "oppressive policies," chafing under the peace and order brought about by the recent imposition of the crown.

SLEEPY FUSSED WITH HIS CRAVAT. A bone-white fragment tucked into a gray vest and wrapped in a long, black jacket with tails. It reminded him of gearing up for a performance. Never wanting to sound pretentious when it came to his poetry, he admitted in his quiet moments that he had hopes and aspirations. He dreamt of erasing the barriers surrounding his community. Maybe shift people's ideas of what it meant to be poor, share stories, and create sympathy, if not understanding. He dreamt of changing minds, if not circumstances. He just wanted his life to mean something. Knowledge Allah stood in the corner, silent, arms crossed, scowling with the expression of one who had bit into a lemon.

"I don't care for this plan," Knowledge Allah said.

"Oh, you were all about the rebellion when you thought we would blow shit up, but if your community requires the sacrifice of you wearing a suit ..."

Knowledge Allah extended his arms to impress upon him his wardrobe. A black formal suit with a white studded shirt, standing collar with a tie, and black waistcoat. Desmond loaned him the ornamented cane to complete his ensemble. And gloves. White cotton gloves. "A servant's suit. I look like Her Majesty's butler."

"I would hope so. That's the look I suspect Sophine was aiming for. You know who the most invisible people are, especially among the wealthy? The servants. We'll be able to go anywhere. The executive wing. Their offices."

"She would have us slip into the corridors of power, mingle among the lords and ladies and parliamentarians, to do what? Glean scraps of information? If they find us down the wrong hallway, we'd better be holding mops because we ... what are those?" Knowledge Allah pointed to the open knapsack Sleepy attempted to conceal.

"Cans of spray paint. I plan to tag the Chancellor's office with our symbol." Sleepy tucked the cans into his jacket pockets.

Knowledge Allah's grim expression faltered, and a smile eked across his face. "Now that's something I can get behind."

"I want to ask you something." Sleepy lowered his voice to a conspiratorial whisper and looked over his shoulder to see if anyone —including automata—were within earshot. "What's the history between you and Deaconess Blues?"

"We once had a ... moment. I should say that Carlton and Sophine shared a moment."

"When you're around her, you sound ..."

"... like I don't know who I am anymore. I know." Knowledge Allah smoothed an invisible crease from his jacket.

Sleepy looked at him with a mix of pity and ... no, it was just pity. "Come on. Let's see how the Deaconess is doing."

They wandered down the hallway. Save for a few automata, they had the run of the house. Deaconess Blues had dismissed much of the staff of the Jefferson estate for a few weeks. A paid holiday, so no one complained. Sleepy rifled through the medicine cabinets of the first bathroom he came across for the sheer sport of it. An automaton stood sentry at the last door on the left, where Deaconess Blues was changing.

"Are you decent?" Sleepy pushed past the protesting automata and half-ducked his head inside the room before knocking.

"Not in any sense of the word. I can't believe my stepmother expects me to wear this." Having departed to run her errands, Lyonessa left a note expressing how excited she was that Deaconess Blues would be joining them. Planning on a rendezvous at the soiree, she took the liberty of buying a dress for her daughter.

Another wall obscured his view. He raised his voice to alert her to his impending arrival. "It can't be that bad."

"Judge for yourself." Deaconess Blues clutched part of her floor-length dress while she walked, lacking faith that it wouldn't drag along the ground. A vertically striped top with short capped sleeves and overshirt which fit snug about the torso, it opened at the waist to reveal tiered, shimmery brown ruffles. "Ruffles. I hate ruffles."

"It's the rare woman who can pull off ruffles," Knowledge Allah said.

"It looks like you've wrapped up your behind and put a bow on top," Sleepy said. "We need to adjust your corset a bit. Your bust line needs to balance your bustle."

Deaconess Blues raised her hands, about to protest.

"I'd defer to him. The man is an expert when it comes to bust lines," Knowledge Allah said.

"I've noticed," she said. "He takes keen enough observation of mine wherever we've gone."

"Think of me as a doctor." Sleepy circled her for final inspection.

"I think of you as a man with a leer behind your smile."

"Maybe, but I know my way around a corset. Large hands." Sleepy drew the strings and paused, adjusted the material and drew again. Deaconess Blues coughed with its tightening. "The thing is, we want to take advantage of your dress's low décolleté."

"Much lower and you could divine the status of my maidenhood," she said with a gasp.

"All the better to distract from my face."

"What's the matter with your face?" she asked.

"Maybe you have a different definition of the word undercover. I'm still wanted by the authorities. We don't want people remembering my face."

"But being able to pick my bosom out of a lineup is fine?"

"Exactly." Sleepy paused his corset ministrations while in front of her. His gaze lingered about her face. He cocked his head to one side, then the next. He *hmm*ed with great thoughtfulness. "There's the problem. She favors a high neck."

Sleepy reached for the array of makeup and powdered her face.

"You're a little too good at this," Knowledge Allah said.

"Don't judge. Simply appreciate my skills." Sleepy tugged a few strands of hair loose to better frame her face. He shifted to take her in from different angles. "There. Perfect. Take a look."

Not used to the corset, Deaconess Blues moved with an awkward gait toward the mirror. "I don't recognize this preening hen before me."

"All the better," Knowledge Allah said with approval.

"She walks like a drunk duck," Sleepy whispered. "But we can work on that."

"THE LAYOUT of the Mile Square was designed by Freemasons advised by alchemists. Those given to rumor and representation belied that the city was laid out along ley lines, the product of *advanced geomancy. An area bounded by North, East, South, and West Streets, diagonal roads bisected its heart. A brick-paved circular road surrounded the governor's residence known as the Governor's Circle. From above, it looked like the city was centered in someone's crosshairs." –from* The Secret Lore of Indianapolis

VOX DEI *DATA FILES: When Alexander Ralston and Elias Fordham planned Indianapolis's new capital, they had it in mind to place the governor's mansion within the circle of downtown Indianapolis. The residence was completed in 1827 (at a cost of $6,500). The fourth governor of the state, James Brown Ray, was the first to live and work out of Indianapolis. His wife, Esther, refused to live in the mansion, complaining that if she were to hang their clothes to dry in the middle of the city, the entire public could see their undergarments. No governor's family ever moved in. The mansion served as the home of the high judiciary offices, before eventually falling into disuse for thirty years, except by transient drifters and ladies of the night. Rumors circulated that a dark, menacing figure without a head —whose long, black cape billowed in the night—haunted the halls. The city council decided it was an embarrassment to the city to have the governor's mansion in such a state of disrepair. Since its restoration, though the official governor's residence lies on Pennsylvania Avenue, the restored governor's mansion serves official state functions.*

THEIR AUTOCARRIAGE LINED up behind the other coaches along the circular drive, waiting for their passengers to disembark. The Italianate yellow brick mansion basked in floodlights surrounding Governor's Circle. During the holidays, red and green lights replaced the standard lighting to cast the bracketed cornices and three-story bay windows in seasonal celebration. The ceremony surrounding the lighting of the governor's tree—placed atop the roof of the building—drew thousands of spectators each year.

Knowledge Allah departed the coach first, climbing down to

unload the step and hold the door open. Deaconess Blues ducked her head out and took his proffered hand as he carefully stepped her down. Sleepy gripped each side of the carriage opening and swung the bulk of his weight out. An inelegant near-tumble, but he both caught and righted himself with a nimbleness that surprised him.

The protestors drew out COPs in heavy regalia. A wall of armed COPs with masks and shields formed a wall, like Roman centurions in black, between them and the arriving guests. The men bore the Pinkerton's insignia on their chest. Nearly stumbling, Sleepy's heart leaped to his throat.

"Remember, in costume and out of context," Deaconess Blues whispered.

"What?" Sleepy steadied himself, though his eyes tracked every COPs' position.

"It wouldn't occur to anyone to be on the lookout for you here. Over there, among the protestors, maybe. Over here, in costume and out of context, no. You said it yourself about servants being invisible."

"Again, I don't want to be *that guy*, but that was before we were surrounded by COPs."

"It's too late now. We'd draw more scrutiny by attempting to leave so soon after our arrival." Deaconess Blues straightened and fixed a smile to her face. "Besides, trust in their ability to confuse any one of us for another."

"We're seriously going with the 'we all look alike' plan?" Sleepy straightened and fixed his gaze straight ahead hoping to not draw any further attention.

A guard halted the trio.

Florid and pale, freckles clustered thickly on his cheeks, a look of being mildly stricken frozen on his face. The way the man scanned them—studying them up and down as if they were small— Sleepy feared that his face would be recognized.

"Invitation?" he asked with the resigned tone of duty, indicating that he believed they had wandered into the wrong social event.

With fuss, Deaconess Blues handed him the invitation. "Lady

Deaconess Blues Jefferson. Daughter of Colonel Winston Jefferson and Lady Lyonnessa Jefferson."

"It says 'and guest.'" The man held the invitation up toward the light, double-checking its authenticity.

"I travel nowhere without my attendant." She nodded toward Knowledge Allah.

"It is customary that a lady has female attendants."

"As you may have noted, I am not a customary sort of lady."

"Be that as it may, a lady must be escorted."

"I am. May I introduce Hubert ... Pulliam. Of the Breton Court Pulliams." She slipped her arm into the crook of Sleepy's arm and tugged him close.

He glanced at his arm as if a snake lashed about him to squeeze the life from him but caught himself and straightened. Sleepy tugged a pipe from his coat pocket. He tamped it a few times to clear it and refilled the bowl with dry chiba leaves. He struck a pose of thoughtfulness as he began to puff.

"How do you do?" Sleepy said, in an accent of a country no one could quite place.

The guard eyed Knowledge Allah, then returned his gaze to Sleepy. He gave Deaconess Blues a second glance, eyebrows raised.

"Are you finished with your inspection or do you hold up all of the personal acquaintances of Lord Melbourne so long?" Deaconess Blues elongated her drawl of disdain. Her weaponized haughtiness identified her as of these circles, her arrogance designed to remind the guard to both know his place and respect his betters.

The guard stood aside.

"You really think you're doing something there, don't you?" Knowledge Allah whispered to Sleepy.

"I figured a pipe was better for my look."

"You may wish to re-figure."

"Walk behind us," Deaconess Blues cautioned Knowledge Allah. "And speak only when spoken to."

"I have no idea why I had such reservations about this plan," Knowledge Allah mumbled.

The mansion was designed for official entertaining, not family life. Wide, intersecting hallways separated four large rooms on the first floor. Led by Deaconess Blues, Knowledge Allah and Sleepy climbed the oak-trimmed, walnut staircase, but slowed as they neared the entrance to the third-floor ballroom. During the restoration, the designers modeled the third floor after the home of Regent Benjamin Harrison, with its butternut woodwork, parquet floors, and cut crystal chandeliers. When they reached the doors, Deaconess Blues presented her invitation again and her party was announced.

A waiter idled toward them, carrying a tray of snacks.

"Hors d'oeuvres," he said with a practiced nasal quality to his timber.

"I'll have your finest cigar, your best cognac, and an order of chitlins, my good man," Sleepy said.

Deaconess Blues took him by the arm and steered him away. "That is not how one remains inconspicuous at these events."

"What are we to do here?" Knowledge Allah asked.

"Enjoy the scenery. How often do we have a chance to get out like this?" Sleepy scooped a plateful of assorted meats from another passing waiter.

"If you want to find out what lies at the heart of the city, you must traverse the arteries of its power." Nodding and smiling to passing guests, Deaconess Blues walked with the grace and elegance of a ballerina. "You are surrounded by the elite who guide the city. Mingle and eavesdrop. Then we can re-group and compare notes."

"Who is that woman staring at you like you have tentacles sprouting from your neck?" Sleepy asked.

"That, gentlemen, would be my stepmother." Without sparing so much as a glance, Deaconess Blues kept her back to that side of the ballroom. "Do not, under any circumstances, engage her in conversation or we are done."

"She's checking us out," Knowledge Allah said.

"She wants to ensure that I'm mingling with the right caliber of people." Deaconess Blues made a broad gesture, dismissing Knowledge Allah.

"Now this is the Deaconess Blues I remember," he groused as he disappeared among his fellow attendants who lined the rear wall of the ballroom.

"Shall we waltz?" Deaconess Blues asked.

"Don't mind if I do." Sleepy led her to the dancefloor.

The waltz bored him with its languid steps. The music failed to move him. Its clean melodies and delicate instrumentals might have moved the other dancers on the floor, but he couldn't get down like that. With a quizzical expression, Sleepy closed his eyes to concentrate on finding any sort of groove to the music. Dissatisfied, he hummed a backbeat to the music. Taking Deaconess Blues's hand, he brought it to chest height. She allowed him a moment to show what he intended. He began a slow step to the music, giving Deaconess Blues room to twirl before taking her hand again. He held her hand and stepped back again, his free hand snapping the count for her to follow. Deaconess Blues moved with the steady grace of a woman trained in dance. She naturally fell into a movement opposite of him. She drove up as he dipped back, creating an almost see-saw effect. He came up, she stepped back, matching his steps.

"Stay in your lane," he cautioned a couple who strayed too near them. Deaconess Blues held her arms waist high with a slight bend of the elbow. He guided her with a slight grasp, paying attention to how she moved. His hand at the small of her back, he took her through a series of turns. A mischievous glint filled her eyes, Deaconess Blues shifted to lead, then directed him through the reverse of their steps. When the music ended, they noticed the crowd had given them wide berth. A few nodded in appreciation.

"This is not how one remains inconspicuous at these events," Sleepy lightly chided. "But nicely done."

Deaconess Blues smiled and gave a slight curtsey.

A tall and broad-shouldered man, who moved with the self-assured cockiness that came from being well-monied, sauntered over to them. His blond hair appeared as if he'd spent the better part of an hour torturing it into exact place. With more than a little jealousy in his gaze, he side-eyed Sleepy. Deaconess Blues whipped out her fan and hit her right hand with it.

"Look who decided to grace us with her presence." Gervais slid in front of Sleepy without waiting for an answer. "May I cut in?"

"It's okay, Sl ... Hubert. I am acquainted with Lord Melbourne's son, Gervais," she said to catch him up. "Why don't you mingle, and we'll reconnect later."

Sleepy straightened his vest, bowed slightly, and took his leave.

THE MUSIC STARTED UP AGAIN. Another waltz, but Gervais drew her close. She allowed his casual embrace, now thankful for the buffer of ruffles, which shielded her like a chastity belt. Several measures into the song, she relaxed. There was something both tender and melancholy in the way Gervais held her.

"Is he more your type?" Gervais asked through a false smile.

"I have no type, only people who interest me."

"Do I not interest you?"

"You've shown me nothing besides your vacuous attempts to woo me with the practiced lines I've no doubt you've had much prior success with bedding women. At least judging by the many glares coming from so many young debutantes right now."

"So, I need to show you something new?" Gervais parted enough to allow him room to dip her.

"Something true. My friend whom you so rudely dismissed is nothing but true. Even in our short acquaintance, I have a sense of who he is and what he's about. I don't have to guess. Or worse, protect myself from him."

"Protect yourself? From me? But you stride into the lion's den with him?" Gervais tilted his head toward his father. A thick slather of makeup covered Lord Leighton Melbourne. The stark contrast of how it painted him to the sheen of full health, drew attention to how poor his color had been previously. He shook hands with Chancellor Lucas Pruitt. Director Melvin Knight wore what appeared to be a kufi of badger fur in elegant contrast to his funereal black suit. His monkey wore a matching jacket—presumably, it had no patience to be fitted with a shirt and pants—but kept snatching its kufi from his head in an attempt to eat it. Another man stood behind Sugar like some brand of shadow security. Sleepy half-expected him to be in a matching kufi, pants or no pants. Lord Melbourne posed for daguerreotypes with each of them.

"It's Chancellor Pruitt's gala. Your father is an honored guest."

"My father pretends to play the feted guest, even though everyone here knows his money bought the show. He says it makes him appear relatable. Human, even."

"Because, even among the elite, it pays to appear human on occasion."

"Now you sound like me." Gervais smiled, a toothy yet hollow thing. "See? I'm not all bad."

"I never said you were all bad." She wanted to fan herself rapidly.

A spoon clinked against a glass. Another joined in. And another. The chorus of ringing glass captured everyone's attention. Lord Melbourne raised his arms as if to lower the guests into their seats as he took to the raised stage where the band played.

"On behalf of Chancellor Lucas Pruitt, I'd like to welcome you. I'd like to thank our city's fine and gracious Chancellor for indulging me. I wanted to take the opportunity to say a few words to this august assembly. Many of you know me, either as a donor or a rival. Sometimes both." The crowd tittered with polite laughter. Lord Melbourne smiled, but then began to cough. The coughing didn't subside. He gestured for a glass of water. Taking a drink, he set the glass down on a music stand and continued.

"We're in a new century. What moved me and the generation before me and the generation before them, those values, those mores, those mindsets, are almost a foreign language to this generation. It's time for a new dream.

"Let me give voice to the rising sentiment we all feel. Mother Albion can no longer hold the center. I have a vision, not just for this city, but for this country. One where these United States determine their own destiny. One where we redefine our relationship with our mother country.

"I remember when that time occurred between me and my

father. I had been married for about a year. My father called me into his office, as was his wont, to measure my accounts. My father was a hard man. He gave me nothing. Everything was a business transaction. Be it schooling or housing or a business venture, he kept a strict accounting. I had just cobbled together a proposal for a company. All I needed was the seed money. Looking back, in my arrogance, I figured I was due my inheritance. My stake so that I could launch out on my own. I went to my father like the prodigal son and demanded my share of the property that was coming to me. Unlike the father in the biblical parable, my father opted to cut me off entirely. It taught me some valuable lessons. One, you build your own future, it isn't handed to you. Two, to demand the opportunity to become my own man, I had to become my own man. Not depend on the privilege of position, that sense of entitlement, but truly make my own way. So I sought out my own investors and grew that idea into Melbourne Industries.

"Now I'm the parent. My children may argue that I haven't been much of one, as I've had to devote so much of my time, energy, and resources to my many interests. However, I also know, that one of the hardest things to do is know when and how to let go of your child. To make the transition from providing for them, guarding them, nurturing them, disciplining them, to establishing an adult relationship with them. As equals.

"Now is that time for Albion and the United States. It's time to reinvent our national dream. Time to reexamine our identity. Time to strip down to our core values. And that discussion begins tonight."

The applause began as a ripple among the gathered crowd. Soon it erupted into cheers and huzzahs. Gervais took a glass from the tray of a passing waiter. He downed the drink in a single gulp.

"Your father sounds ..." Deaconess Blues said.

"Presidential?" Gervais finished.

"I was going to say like a man with a larger plan in motion."

"The man who would be kingmaker is a fool. He's never spoken of his father, nor their relationship with me. He treats me like an afterthought, a prop for when he has to tell a story. Something to make him sound more ..."

"... human?" Deaconess Blues grimaced.

Gervais half-bowed in appreciation of her wordplay. "He likes to pretend he's above the fray of politics. He doesn't treat me seriously. Do you take me seriously?"

Deaconess Blues opened her mouth but reconsidered. She knew the first words out of her mouth were going to be a transparent lie if her answer was anything short of "no." "To be honest, to hear him speak of you, I had no reason to."

Gervais considered her words. He betrayed neither anger nor hurt. "That sounds right. He likes you, you know. Respects you. Some part of him measures himself by how you see him. Sometimes I think you're the child he wishes he had."

"Gervais, don't ..."

"Even now he has no idea how much I know. He doesn't think I see what he's doing. The way he's been buying up houses in areas the city will soon target for redevelopment. How he has the Chancellor's political goons on the city council rezone areas of interest for commercial use. How, through his shares in the Pinkerton Agency, his interests have extended across the country and inched their way overseas. He doesn't even know that I know he's sick."

"Sick? What do you mean?"

"I mean ..." Gervais stopped himself. He raised his glass. "My glass needs refilling and the night is young. I have other guests to ply with my meager charms. It is a party, after all."

THE GOVERNOR'S mansion had a back stairwell, once used solely by servants when it was built, so they could move about the manse without disturbing the family or their guests. The second floor held the governor's offices when the sitting governor was supposed to stay in the city for business. The stairwell had been cordoned off for the party, but security patrols paid little attention to them. Sleepy pressed his back against the hallway wall, checked both directions, and skulked down the darkened corridor. He halted every few feet to navigate around the gaslit wall sconces. None of them were on, but he imagined the hall to be a well-lit and warm space should all of them turn on. The office door was locked, but Sleepy quickly disengaged the lock and slid into the room. Inching his hand along the wall, he found the light switch. The low hanging chandelier quickly burned to life. He adjusted the illumination to its lowest setting.

A wall of handmade bookshelves enclosed a conference area. An Agra rug filled the forefront of the room, with a grand desk dominating its rear. A large, hand-woven leather chair faced two other chairs—neither of which were nearly as luxurious as it—separated by the desk. Behind it, a portrait of the governor hung. Smaller portraits of Queen Diana and Regent Bush hung on either side of it. Sleepy hefted the portraits down to reveal a wide swathe of wall to serve as a blank canvas. Withdrawing the two spray cans from the folds of his jacket, he imagined the message he planned to leave as he shook them. The symbol of The Cause would take up the most space. Tilting the first can toward the wall, he was about to spray when someone jostled the door handle. He ducked behind the desk.

The door creaked open and several sets of footfalls followed.

"Turn up the lights. The janitorial staff must've left them on."

Sleepy recognized the voice of Lord Melbourne.

"Won't our absence be conspicuous?" a second voice asked.

"I made my comments. By now the food and alcohol will have done their job, and people will be enjoying themselves too much to notice the absence of a couple of long-winded politicians."

"Is that what we are now? Politicians?" Sugar asked. That made the other voice most probably Chancellor Pruitt. Sleepy swallowed hard. The muscles in his thighs already burned from the awkward position he held. He peeked around the desk's edge.

"It's what we will be. We are men of grand vision. This country is broken at a fundamental level. It has so many wounds from its past and no hope of seeing past its very woundedness to allow any sort of healing."

"You speak of wounds like they were suffered in some glorious war. More like the scars left over from an abusive childhood," Sugar said.

"That's the problem with you people. Always with the whining," Pruitt said.

"And you are one 'you people' comment away from collecting your teeth from the carpet." Sugar hard-eyed him until the man sat down and turned.

"You two illustrate my point. Even as we three gather to solve the very dilemma, the very nature of it threatens to tear us apart. You'd think people would have learned after that fool Lincoln nearly split the country."

A banging came from the door. Someone pushed past the guards stationed at the door.

"Cayt, who's this?" Lord Melbourne asked.

"He won't say," a woman's voice said. "Found him skulking around the hallways."

"(120 Degrees of) Knowledge Allah," Sugar said. "You a long ways from home, boy."

At the mention of the name, Sleepy sprang up, bumping his head against the desk. The crack of pain caused him to close his eyes. When he opened them, a woman stood over him, the barrel of her gun trained at his forehead.

"Uh, hello." Sleepy dropped his spray cans and raised his hands. "It's not what it looks like."

EIGHTEEN
MIND TERRORIST

Vox Dei: [Op-Ed] *Indiana Needs to be Saved from Savages—A growing insurgency continues to demonstrate the reality that the United States is in fact made up of nations within a nation. These political radials constitute the greatest threat to the internal security of the country. They are quickly proving themselves to be a most dangerous, violence-prone, extremist group. The activities of any such organization—their leadership, spokesmen, membership, and supporters—need to be exposed, disrupted, misdirected, and discredited. Only by preventing the rise of any unifying voice, and preventing the violence sure to follow on their part, can our democratic society prevent such a coalition from gaining momentum.*

SLEEPY LEANED FORWARD in his chair and adjusted his posture before he cramped up from remaining in the same position for too long. Leaning against the bookshelves, the woman drew her large-brimmed hat low on her face. She cast a hard, sideways glance at him. Her fingers didn't flinch at his movement, but they remained at the ready. He knew if he made any movement which could be interpreted as threatening, she'd cut him down on the spot. Knowledge Allah studied the room with the intensity of memorizing each player, committing their every gesture, inflection, bearing to memory. His nostrils flared, and his body had a slight tremble to it, as if he strained against restraints.

Withdrawn to a corner, as if not wanting to be tread underfoot, Sugar attended his monkey. The beast squawked at the attention, wanting to concentrate on where everyone was, not knowing who might present a threat. Chancellor Pruitt skittered about the room like a nervous squirrel. He took several steps forward before glancing over his shoulder to check on Sleepy and Knowledge Allah. Whenever he locked eyes with Knowledge Allah, he averted his gaze, scampered a few more steps away, and checked him again. At the center of the storm, Lord Melbourne poured himself several fingers of Scotch from the governor's personal stock. He whispered something to his female guard. She nodded.

A knock came from the door. Deaconess Blues swept into the room, trailed by Gervais. Two Pinkerton guards stationed themselves at the door. Their gray on gray hats with black bills bore the metal emblem of a gold eagle over blind justice. Their matching jackets had blue bands at the cuffs. A lone blue stripe ran down the side of their gray pants.

"What's going on?" Gervais asked.

"Nothing you need to worry about, son. I need you to return to the gala." Lord Melbourne smiled a politician's grin, too broad and revealing too many teeth. He raised his glass to toast Gervais. "In my absence, a Melbourne needs to oversee things. Can I trust you with that?"

Caught off guard, Gervais withdrew half a step. Suspecting a trap of some sort, he studied first his father and then Deaconess Blues. He performed some mental calculation. From his expression, like that of a man who had a badger gnawing at his insides, he didn't like what he came up with. "Are you sure you wouldn't rather have me here?"

Sleepy couldn't tell if he was talking to Deaconess Blues or his father.

"Your place is seeing about our business. Can you handle that?" Lord Melbourne's eyes half-closed to grim slits.

"Yes, Father. Of course." Gervais dipped his head in a half-hearted bow and took his leave. The men stationed on the other side of the door followed him.

Reading the room, Sleepy sensed a dark cloud hovered over the shop. Anger bubbled just behind the men's eyes. Sleepy met Knowledge Allah's eyes, sensing they both missed something. In the ensuing silence, each player considered their next move. Deaconess Blues spied Knowledge Allah and Sleepy but registered no measure of recognition or surprise on her face. She focused her attention on Lord Melbourne. For his part, Lord Melbourne only observed her. With a keen survivor's instinct, Sugar retreated to the side of the room nearest the door. From there, he could keep an eye on everyone and make a hasty exit if need be. Chancellor Pruitt skittered between Lord Melbourne and the female guard, not sure where his proper place should be.

"Well," Deaconess Blues broke the budding tension of welling silence, "you summoned me here."

Before he could say anything, Lord Melbourne whipped out his handkerchief and coughed into it. Flecks of red dotted the sputum, but he quickly folded the cloth and stuffed it into his pocket before anyone else could see it. He caught Sleepy's studious gaze but turned back to Deaconess Blues. "Apparently, your friends were rather lost without you. We found them wandering the halls and rifling through the governor's office."

"They ... are my responsibility. They shall be dealt with. Most harshly." Deaconess Blues cast a stern frown in their direction.

"Do you feign ignorance as to their intentions?" Chancellor Pruitt mustered harshness and impatience.

"All I am aware of is that you found them trespassing."

"With this." Cayt tossed the spray cans. They landed at Deaconess Blues's feet.

"That looks like intent to vandalize," Lord Melbourne said. "You consort with known terrorists. Did you not think I'd recognize the two most notorious figures discussed on the *Vox Populi*?"

"What do you intend?" Deaconess Blues straightened, inhaling sharp enough to be audible to steel herself.

"You ask that like I'm some villain whose trap you fell into. Like I'm supposed to reveal my secret plans before doing away with you."

"So we're free to go?" Deaconess Blues arched a skeptical eyebrow, her voice not betraying any sense of hope.

"Yes. Though if I could trouble you to answer one question for me?" Lord Melbourne moved with a combination of determination and fierceness. A bold posture which made him a feared business-man. His careful eyes scoured every detail of the scene, his mind anxiously filing away every tidbit of information like a librarian hoarding books. Lord Melbourne's complexion took on a waxy sheen up close.

"What's that?"

"Why did you come here?" Taking special pains not to meet her gaze, Lord Melbourne held his glass to the light, intent on studying the color of his libation. The pause held the rapt attention of the entire room. Cayt repositioned herself. No one wanted to take their eyes from him, but they angled themselves to keep her in view also. With his slightest nod or gesture, he could signal her to end them all where they stood.

"The gala ..." Deaconess Blues ventured. She steadied herself against the table.

"Please, let's dispense with any such games. We're all grownups here. What were you looking to accomplish here tonight? You and your ... terrorist compatriots."

"I do wish you'd quit referring to them as terrorists." Deaconess Blues choked on the rage which rose up in her with such sudden-ness Cayt's hand moved to her waist. But Deaconess Blues was heedless of her. She could only stare at Lord Melbourne, only seeing his fortune, his privilege. Like her, born into a family of connections, inheriting the accumulated wealth of generations. The roads made smooth for him. Except that he could exploit the system to further his dreams. "They are voices. They are two men who love their people and just want to speak out against the treatment of them. By the COPs. By the system."

Sleepy's chest swelled at the description. Knowledge Allah nodded at him.

"They weren't here to vandalize?" Emboldened, Chancellor Pruitt sidled up to her, reminiscent of a Pinkerton Assistant conducting an interrogation.

Deaconess Blues issued such a withering gaze it caused him to backpedal. She unfurled her fan like a samurai drawing a sword from their scabbard. She kept it between her and him, fluttering it in warning. "If that's what it takes to draw attention to their struggle."

"They aren't a part of a conspiracy to foment dissent?" Lord Melbourne asked, low and tight, his jaw resolute.

"Conspiracy is a strong word," Deaconess Blues admitted. "They simply have been trampled upon and dealt with unfairly. I only wanted to help them plead their case. Their methods are misguided but ultimately harmless."

"Fair enough." Lord Melbourne raised his hand in mock surrender. "You may go."

Sleepy cast his eyes about the room. Slowly he stood up. With no one making a move to stop him, he pressed his suit jacket smooth and stepped toward Deaconess Blues. Knowledge Allah followed, standing and backing toward Deaconess Blues without taking his eyes from Cayt.

"Okay, we out." Sleepy flashed three fingers across his chest and grabbed the door handle.

"Wait." Deaconess Blues pressed her hand against Sleepy's chest, halting him.

Sleepy closed his eyes and stifled a mental curse. "We were so close to being out."

"Just like that, you're letting two wanted political agitators go?" she asked.

"They are symptoms. We will deal with the disorder in due course. No point in breaking a few fingers when we can chop off the head. Besides, their efforts were thwarted and we have business to discuss. As a courtesy to you, I would consider the matter at an end," Lord Melbourne said.

"I appreciate that. Just like I appreciated your toast tonight," Deaconess Blues said. "I was curious what you meant about the United States forging its own destiny. The way you said it, well, it reminded me of how my compatriots often speak of our struggle. We have a great measure of commonality."

"Struggle is struggle. I suspect, if I understand the propaganda of your cause, we have similar concerns for our respective peoples."

"Aren't our people a part of your people," she asked, "in these *United* States?"

"You tell me, though I suspect your heart knows what I mean. We need to discover our identity as a people. Identity is forged in fire. Our people need to define themselves. Identity as a nation comes slow to the United States. Even in calling ourselves that, we admit to losing the right to name ourselves. The reaction to being captured, subjugated, or the threat of such. Look at the relations between Albion and France. They are without antagonism, because after our failed 'Revolutionary War,' there were no imported ideas of successful revolution, no seeds of rebellion. The French never attempted their own revolution. They didn't have to rethink their national identity. They are allies with Albion in the same way a child is allied to its mother. Our people need to learn how to move from being subjects to empowered citizens, move from loyalty to a revolution to loyalty to country.

"To compound the issue, Albion has fallen into a position where the tail wags the dog, as it were. The United States has a greater population and the greater economy. It is the engine that drives the empire. Albion can't repress a nation six times its size, especially from so far away. It's why Parliament moved its capital seat to Washington D.C. and started doing things in the name of the states. Time will prove that Albion will need to become incredibly repressive in order to maintain control. War is inevitable."

"It sounds like you are advocating for a second revolutionary war," Deaconess Blues said.

Chancellor Pruitt hovered by the cart with the drinks. He fumbled at a decanter and poured himself a drink.

"Republics have a strange habit of going to war," Lord Melbourne said. "If managed correctly, they can be largely blood-less. The aim would be to cause just enough agitation to loosen

Albion's grip on the colonies. The United States is large, unwieldy, and too far removed to effectively govern.

"Change is the only constant, the Ultimate Principle. Railways take to the air. Horse and carriage give way to mechanical engines. The electric telegraph to instant wireless aethereal communication. The age of steam has nearly run its course. Giving way to the age of solar, if Jamaica has its way, or wind or some other primal force. We must be willing to adapt. Perhaps the United States could be the catalyst for and linchpin of a TransAtlantic Confederacy. Canada, United States, Albion. Much as how Mexico, with all of its gold and resources, negotiates with Tejas and the Five Civilized Nations to form a powerful confederacy."

Deaconess Blues considered his words. Her brow furrowed; the puzzle pieces still not quite fitting. Or worse, fitting all too well. Lord Melbourne's tendrils extended everywhere. The consummate chess master shuffling everyone along like pieces on a chessboard, because his vantage point allowed him to see the entire game. Every level of the Pinkertons. Technology and industry. His agents infiltrated The Cause, even the militia. Churning them, sparking them like his personal kine, heating up the elements to shape the future he wanted. However, flames, once stoked, were dangerous to harness. An errant spark and the whole operation could go up in an infernal conflagration.

"And you," Deaconess Blues considered her words with care, "are the man to lead this rebellion into this new era of relationship."

"I am well positioned. And as you no doubt are aware, rebellion is rebellion. And war is inevitable. Some of us seek to unite our people. Get all of that righteous anger, all of the need to correct injustice, harness that dissatisfaction of the status quo, and direct it at the real enemy: Albion."

"'Don't you see it, Deaconess Blues?" Knowledge Allah said. "There's profit to be made from war. Seed a rebellion, the United States versus Albion. The United States 'free' under his control. His government companies—from ZeroDyne and the rest of Melbourne Industries to his connections to the Pinkertons; doing biomech research and selling munitions to everyone with a budget—are a government to itself. Like the British India Company. He's going to conquer the country in the name of his company."

"Deaconess Blues now, is it?" Lord Melbourne asked. "Apparently, you're more in bed with this insurgency than you wished to portray. Now would be a prudent time to distance yourself from them."

The sheer scope of it all boggled Sleepy's mind. He was struck by the audacity of Lord Melbourne's plan and the cynicism in which he enacted it. Here was this man of wealth and means, who had everything at his fingertips, yet he was still never satisfied. Like an addict, with his drug of choice being power. Control. Money. Like any fiend, there was never enough. However, when it came down to it, Lord Melbourne was simply scared like everyone else. That at any moment everything could be taken from him. His position. His comfort. The illusion of his independence. And he was ready to do anything, sacrifice anyone, to make sure that didn't happen.

"You imagine yourself a civilized gentleman. A savior to usher in this modern age of enlightenment," Deaconess Blues said. "But you're angry. Angry because the world doesn't appreciate you for who you are. You reach and reach until you overreach in the hopes that their praise will somehow fill that hole in your soul. But you're also a coward, living in fear of change as death draws ever nearer. Do your confederates know that you won't be around to see this 'war' of yours through?"

All eyes turned to Lord Melbourne.

"You're mistaken," he said.

"Gervais let it slip. Alcohol loosened his tongue. And I can't imagine that you'd entrust your vision to Gervais."

"As I said, you're mistaken." Lord Melbourne strutted confidently about the room, heading toward the drink cart. "I will be here with your help. I've seen to that. I will prevail. The United States will prevail."

Chancellor Pruitt sighed as loud as he could.

"Why you insist on being in bed with these animals, I have no idea. You allow them to wander these corridors like they belong here? That is too far." He downed another measure of liquid courage. "This is exactly why ..."

"Why what, Pruitt?" Lord Melbourne stepped close to the man. He laid his right hand on the collar of the Chancellor's jacket as if smoothing out a crease. "What have you done?"

"I ... have ordered the COPs to deal with their like once and for all." Chancellor Pruitt gripped his empty glass.

"What does that mean?" A mix of fury and concern filled Lord Melbourne's eyes like a director whose lead actress had gone off script.

"Oh, *now* you take me seriously? *Now* you consider me a man worth listening to? Do you think I haven't been paying attention? That I haven't noted the information at my disposal." With a look of utter disdain, he upturned his nose at Sugar. His courage finding root, Chancellor Pruitt smiled the self-satisfied grin of a reptile sunning itself on a rock. "We plan to take out your headquarters."

"We don't have a headquarters." Deaconess Blues turned to Knowledge Allah to see if perhaps she'd missed a memorandum.

"You operate out of, what do you people call it? Freetown Village? The Paul Dunbar Library?" The Chancellor preened, quite pleased with himself. He toasted Sugar. "Isn't that right?"

"Is that your role in things, Sugar? You provide your plantation masters with information about your people in hopes that they make you an overseer?" Knowledge Allah asked. "You betrayed The Cause."

"I don't do causes anymore. Causes are for the young. They're still angry enough to demand change and hopeful enough to believe it'll happen." Sugar held out his arm. His simian companion crawled up to perch on his shoulder. He hard-eyed anyone who neared. "I'm too old for such foolishness. I just aim to make it through another day, claim the big piece of chicken when I get home, and hope for a peaceful night's sleep."

Angry as Sleepy was, it was difficult for him to view Sugar as a complete scoundrel. He never judged how a man chose to navigate this system. Survive by any means necessary and look out for as many of your people as possible was his credo.

"We are a city under siege and it's time for drastic steps to preserve our way of life. Our COPs make preparations." Chancellor Pruitt waved him off, trying to cut off the discussion and re-take center stage. A man so insubstantial he needed to bring an arsenal for anyone to even notice he was still in the room. A desperate, near froth filled his tone. "They will be armed with tear gas and thousands of rounds of bullets. Then one of our airships will drop an incendiary device right upon your heads. Our fire department will have their hoses ready, but only to herd the people back and make sure the fire doesn't get too out of control. This is how we handle enemies of the state: those who raise arms against us shall have no arms to raise."

Silence hovered over the room as they took a breath to consider his words. A wan smile crossed Pruitt's lips as if he had wrestled something away from Lord Melbourne. The moment. The narrative. Deaconess Blues knew how their story would end. The plan had the ache of haunting familiarity. An enclave in Pennsylvania, MOVE was bombed within the boundaries of its city and everyone acted as if it never happened. No one remembered the dwellers. Those with the power controlled the narrative.

"Do you ... hear yourself? You're talking about the callous decision to bomb a residential area occupied by men, women, and children. Innocent people, no, assuming you even see them as people. And you," Deaconess Blues turned to Lord Melbourne. "You disappoint me, sir. This is the madman you've allied yourself with."

Another lengthy pause lingered as Lord Melbourne contemplated how best to play his next move. Sleepy read the man's face and recognized a mortal danger when he saw one. This was a face that decided matters of life and death. A trickle of sweat wound down Sleepy's back as he fully appreciated the danger of the moment. Sleepy tensed, ready to take cover, but with the slightest of gestures, the businessman waved Cayt off. Taking a circuitous path away from Chancellor Pruitt, Lord Melbourne clasped his hands behind his back and wandered toward the window. The lights of the overcity twinkled. The autocarriages lined up in front of the mansion ready to ferry the ball's guests home. "We are at war and sometimes during times of war, tough decisions must be made. It's easy to govern during good times. Leaders are measured by how they deal with conflict. With betrayal.

"Some people are petty and, in their small thinking, enact their own agendas within the greater plan, hoping that in all the ensuing chaos, no one would notice. They buy up property. They remove people they deem obstacles. People who stand in his way. People I might be fond of in my own way."

Lord Melbourne locked eyes with Chancellor Pruitt.

The blood drained from the politician's face.

"What ... people?" Deaconess Blues asked.

"Go on, Pruitt, answer her." Though his voice was barely above a whisper, Lord Melbourne had murderous intent.

"What. People?" Deaconess Blues trembled, struggling to maintain control and dignity. Needing to make sure she had all of the facts and understood them before giving into the mounting rage. "Say the words."

Chancellor Pruitt downed a full glass of Scotch in a single gulp. His hands still shook as he refilled the glass.

"People like your father," Lord Melbourne said.

The words slammed into Deaconess Blues, but the weight of them hadn't sunk in. Confusion. Anger. Hatred. Deaconess Blues's face contorted, her wanting to maintain her cool façade while her emotions roiled in combat, waiting for the victor to arise to determine the next course of action. "And you have evidence of this?"

"I traffic in information. I have purchase orders for the poison. Correspondence between him and his accomplice. All kept in a safe place as insurance. To protect me against his ... poorer judgment."

Long past hearing, her eyes glazed over in feral rage. Searching about with frantic urgency, Deaconess Blues snatched at Knowledge Allah. She grasped his cane and with a slight twist as she had seen Desmond use to unlock it, she unsheathed the sword. She managed to squeeze out a single word. "Monsters."

"Oh, snap!" Sleepy jumped back behind the desk.

Knowledge Allah stared at the empty sheath. "Why didn't someone tell me I had that?"

Deaconess Blues strode with grim determination toward Chancellor Pruitt.

"Leighton?" A quiver crept into Pruitt's voice.

Lord Melbourne cut a sideways glance at his female guard. Her hand moved almost faster than Sleepy's eye could follow as she drew her weapon. She trained it on Deaconess Blues.

"What are you going to do? Kill me?" Deaconess Blues yelled. "Kill us all?"

"Hey, hey, hey!" Sleepy yelled. "She doesn't speak for all of us. Let's not do anything hasty."

"Don't be foolish." Lord Melbourne nodded.

The woman turned her gun from Deaconess Blues to Chancellor Pruitt. The man had a chance to hold up his hands with the word "No" beginning to form on his lips before she fired once. A small hole dotted his forehead. His head snapped back. Blood and gray matter splattered the wall behind him. His body crumpled to the ground.

"Oh shit! Oh shit! Oh shit!" Sleepy closed his eyes as he dropped behind Deaconess Blues, both to shield her from Cayt's inevitable attack as well as to not be a witness to anything else. "I didn't see anything!"

Deaconess Blues stopped her advance and stared mutely at the still body. Chancellor Pruitt stared at her with blank eyes and a grimace of uncertainty on his face.

"Pruitt was a madman who needed to be put down. I suspect the COPs will have their hands full by later this evening. And when the truth comes out, no one will look too hard at the death of a madman." Lord Melbourne waved an unconcerned hand. Cayt lowered her weapon. "At best, the Pinkertons will dismiss any of your reports as paranoid ravings. This will all be blamed on the monumental incompetence on the part of all city officials. From the Chancellor, through the managing director, to the COP commissioner. There may even be an opening to clean house, politically speaking. Mr. Knight is in line for a cabinet position. Maybe even becoming the first black Chancellor ... with my support. If he understands the ways of discretion."

Sugar nodded. As did his ape.

"What about us?" Deaconess Blues asked.

"Shit." Sleepy backed toward her, keeping himself between Cayt and Deaconess Blues. "Why you always got to be asking questions? How has that worked out for us so far?"

"What about the library?" Knowledge Allah asked.

"You, too?" Sleepy repositioned himself in front of both of them. "Why's everyone suddenly catching a case of undue curiosity when we should be tipping the fuck out?"

"If what Pruitt said is true, that's already in motion." Lord Melbourne poured himself a drink. "I don't think you understand the big picture. You have no ideological kin. No one will raise your banner. Your cause will fade into obscurity because there is no mechanism to preserve and tell your story. Especially if I control the *Vox Populi* and the *Vox Dei*. And because no one connects to your cause. To be frank, your lives don't matter. This incident will be lost both now and to history, because people will have larger issues to worry about. A criminal investigation may even be lost, but in the end, there will be a report filled with recommendations that will end up in a file somewhere. Unread."

Sleepy knew men like Lord Melbourne. He saw them as street urchins, objects to be pitied when not overlooked entirely. The objects of his beneficence, but only serving to make him feel better about his largesse. He could not be wealthy if there were no poor. Without them, he'd just be a man. They might shout and raise a ruckus, but despite their rage, ultimately, they were to be kept in their place. Without any real voice. Without any real power. Anything that moved in that direction was a direct threat to him. Like all of his vaunted technology, the bright lights, the arc of lightning, the thrum of engines, they were to be tamed and obedient. Until someone stood up to him.

"No," Sleepy said.

Not used to being told "no" about anything, Lord Melbourne turned to him as if noticing him for the first time. "What was that?"

"No," Sleepy said again. "We're going to stop Pruitt's madness. Or die trying."

"Go right ahead. Race down to Freetown Village. Become collateral damage. I won't stop you. See if that gives you the answers you seek."

Deaconess Blues froze in her steps. Her mind still sifted through the night's events. She arched a single eyebrow. "Wait, you know the name of the accomplice."

"I do, as much as it pained me to learn. I ..." Lord Melbourne's face blanched, suddenly stricken. His body shuddered. His hand loosened its grip on his glass and it shattered on the floor. His legs tightened, then simply gave way. Before he hit the ground, Cayt caught him and lowered him to the ground.

"Get help," Cayt yelled.

Knowledge Allah and Sleepy looked at each other and then dashed out the door. Deaconess Blues backed away.

"Get help," Cayt pleaded. "Please."

NINETEEN

BLACK STEEL IN THE HOUR OF CHAOS

Vox Dei Data Files: In 1913, industrialist James A. Allison established the machine shop, Allison Speedway Team Company. The firm began supplying tools, jigs, and fixtures for military engines. The company was renamed the Allison Steam Turbine and was awarded several Army contracts to redesign and retool their engines. Their experimental development revolutionized airship engines. By 1943, they merged with the Aeroproducts Airship Company and built additional plants. Only the Jefferson Airship Company rivaled them. James A. Allison went on to become one of the founders of the Indianapolis Airship Speedway, and the Indianapolis 500 mile race, in part to test airship innovations as entertainment.

THE AUTOCARRIAGE RIDE was long and silent, punctuated solely by Sleepy's fidgeting as he checked the rearview mirror to see if they were being pursued. Lost in a sullen cloud, Knowledge Allah and Deaconess Blues hunched over in their seats.

"You two act as if we're already defeated," Sleepy said.

"I ..." Deaconess Blues's façade cracked a little, tortured by whatever demons chased her. "I don't know what to do next. It's all so ..."

"... big," Knowledge Allah finished for her. The two's eyes met, then, almost embarrassed, darted away.

"Then we should go at this the way I do at one of our meals at a family reunion," Sleepy said.

"Sleepy, I'm not in the mood and now's not the time for your ..." Knowledge Allah snapped at him.

"... one bite at a time," Sleepy said, unfazed by the outburst. "They want to drop a bomb on us, they can't just do that spur of the moment. There has to be preparation. A staging area. A private airship maybe?"

"Dirigibles." Deaconess Blues sat up. "The COPs lease space from the facilities on Steambender Alley in Speedway. That would have to be where they would do it. The only alternative would be the Indianapolis National Aeroport, but there's no way they could use that for military purposes without drawing a lot of unwanted attention."

"We need to hurry. We have no idea of Pruitt's timetable," Knowledge Allah said.

"I need to get out of this ridiculous dress, and we need to pick up a few things from my laboratory."

––––––––––

ONCE AT THE front gate of her property, Deaconess Blues hiked up her dress and tromped down the drive to her laboratory. When she threw open the doors, her workshop still had the unmistakable odor of smelt metal from a soldering torch. She ducked into her office and rang for one of the automata to bring her some clothes. When she emerged, she was a completely different woman.

She wore gold-trimmed black boots and a green skirt with gold trim over black form-fitting pants, she wrapped a gold sash about her waist. A lighter green vest covered an emerald blouse. Her cuffs alternated black and gold. She donned a green wrap for her head but clutched a pair of black gloves in one hand. She snapped several tools into her utility belt. Lockpicks, a compass, a portable torch. A knife, a variation of the Swiss model.

Deaconess Blues fussed along a shelf until she reached a box smaller than the size of a cake tray. She handed it to Knowledge Allah. "Here, for old times."

"My orthocopter?"

"Not quite. It is based on a similar design as your original, except far more compact."

Knowledge Allah marveled at it. "This is amazing. You're amazing."

"I am an unexceptional person."

"The words don't ring true even as they spring from your lips." The pair faced each other, suggestively close, barely a hand's width apart. They stared at each other, taking each other in. The way her headwrap framed her face. The drape of his serpentine locs. He studied her lips; she, his eyes. Ridiculous grins spread across their faces.

Breaking the strangeness of the moment developing, Sleepy stepped between them. "Anything for me?"

"Um." Shaking herself from whatever spell transfixed her, Deaconess Blues scanned the shelf again. "Here."

"What's this?" Sleepy took the odd device which looked remarkably like a hand drill.

"A grappling gun."

"Shit." Sleepy managed to make the word sound like it had three syllables. "I'm no pulp adventurer. If I'm going to be swinging from this, just shoot me now."

"Come on, let's go get us a bop gun," Deaconess Blues said.

VOX DEI *DATA FILES: A marriage of state and local governments and business interests, the Allisonville Correctional Facility models the efficiency of the privatization of government services. By taking a strong stance against criminal elements, local constabularies pursue a "No Broken Windows" community policing policy and local government strengthened laws, governing everything from alcohol and drug possession to those too mixed in debt to be productive in the most troublesome neighborhoods. Sentencing scores of criminals every month to clean up our streets becomes a win-win for law-abiding citizens: the mass incarceration locks away the criminal element and becomes a source of free labor with its rehabilitation programs working for the community. Farming, manufacturing, cleanup crews, the Allisonville Correctional Facility ushers in a new age for our criminal justice system.*

DEACONESS BLUES DROVE. With Knowledge Allah and Sleepy in the back seat, they gambled that her fair skin granted her a measure of freedom from the constabularies who might pull them over or otherwise detain them for not being where they were supposed to be. The trio rode in silence, following the river banks' scenic greenway past the summer homes of the overcity. They weren't too far from the shadows of The Tombs and the undercity's lack of sunlight.

Cutting through Haughville, Knowledge Allah stared out the window with the resigned longing for home. A few minutes later, they approached the colossal stadium of the Indianapolis Aeromotor Speedway, signaling that they entered the excluded city of Speedway. Deaconess Blues turned onto Steambender Alley. The long-winding stretch of road led along the series of garages which housed the airships that competed in the race and aeronautic competitions. The road bled into a private airstrip. An airship loomed in their windshield. Long as a city block, tall as the Madame Walker building.

"It's blimp city," Sleepy said.

"Zeppelin. There's a difference," Deaconess Blues said. "That has a metal skeleton."

Sleepy glared at her as if to ask, "Seriously? You can't give the know-it-all routine a rest even now?" but opted to remain silent.

Soon they reached the outermost gate surrounding the property housing an immense pole barn structure. Barbed wire ringed the top of the gate. A mad grin danced on Deaconess Blues's face. Removing the faceplate of the electro-chirographer pad, she clamped down the servos and adjusted the winding mechanism, deactivating the gate's lock control. Gears winched and the metal frame shuddered before opening.

People scurried about while a siren blared, alerting them to the final approach of an airship, under the assumption that it could possibly be missed. An armed contingent of uniformed men guarded a stack of metal canisters at the far end of the building. With all eyes focused on the landing ship, the trio crept along the shadows of the structure until they were able to reach a wall of crates near the landing area.

From the first day the sight of a bird in flight fired his fancy, man dreamt to one day take to the clouds; to conquer the air as easily as he conquered the land and the sea. Unlike the massive warships of Lockheed or Sir Halliburton, this one did not bristle with armaments. No mighty bombs would drop on unseen enemies or innocent school buildings, nor would the blood-soaked dreams of nation-states be enforced by it. An airship nosed toward them. A ridged watermelon with a hull of black with a red underbelly, gas-filled tubes ran along the outside of the ship and burned to life to ring the ship in a brackish green. Crew workers raised their arms like they were in church awaiting the arrival of the Holy Spirit. Guide ropes dropped into their greedy hands. Turbofans whirred overhead. Gusts of hot winds like a desert breeze whipped them as they anchored the airship. The fat beast lolled to one side like a satisfied cat exposing its belly as the docking crew rushed toward the ship.

The ship hovered quietly, the dull gleam of its matte skin waiting for its mooring lines to be secured. Its mahogany gondola, a canoe-shaped basket with thick glass windows and hand wrought brass details, still smelled of fresh varnish. A pair of large porcelain tanks of gas—labeled "flammable"—were riveted in place like torpedoes stitched underneath. Armed with hoses, the crew took position around the docking bay. One crew member wheeled a loading cart, while another drove a set of portable disembarkation stairs and banister into place. Fitted with brass telescopes and gun boxes, the dirigible bobbed and swayed, bloated by cargo.

"Look how they tricked it out," Sleepy said.

"Those aren't ... tricks," Deaconess Blues said. "They reinforced the frame. Loaded it with armaments. They turned it into a warship."

"Still ... shiny."

"What's the play?" Knowledge Allah asked.

"We become the villains they assume us to be?" She nodded to Knowledge Allah. "One man's villain is another person's Star Child."

"Our very own mothership," Knowledge Allah whispered.

Sleepy knew Knowledge Allah had been waiting for this. An opportunity to take down The Ave. The jutting spire, a symbol of everything Knowledge Allah hated most about the United States of Albion. A wave of nausea swept over Sleepy. He imagined himself squeezing into a small window seat, staring out over the sea of land.

Deaconess Blues's stiff upper lip set to grim resolve, she remained unruffled by the chaos springing up about her. "Aluminum and iron oxide are elements of the fabric doping. This zeppelin ought to be filled with helium or another inert gas. However, as our purposes are of a more combustible nature. I wouldn't advise any more of your chiba indulgences."

"I ain't down with no suicide run," Sleepy said. "This brother don't go out like that."

"I am not one to shrink from such deviltry. Besides, it's not suicide. We are meant to be among the stars, signals from the heavens, showing others the way home." Deaconess Blues stepped from her perch and took his hands. "Nor are we asking you to come."

"What?" Sleepy's sated gaze fixed on her.

"Ancient tribes had truth-tellers, history keepers, and storytellers. You are like one of those ancient griots. We will give you the opportunity to tell our story."

"And we need a distraction," Knowledge Allah echoed.

Sleepy withdrew his hands from her, tasked and dismissed. Though he had no interest in a suicide run, part of him bristled at the idea that he wasn't even considered. The two of them decided without him. They probably planned this in front of him in that strange shorthand of theirs. His lips parted to protest, but no sound escaped. Sleepy nodded to them. "Give me the keys."

Deaconess Blues and Knowledge Allah took positions at the edge of the wall of crates. He backed out toward the rear of the building, ignoring his sense of relief while wanting to feign the injured party. Sleepy strode to the center of the airship bay.

"Citizens of the Universe, do not attempt to adjust your electro-transmitter, there is nothing wrong. We have taken control to bring you this special bulletin," Sleepy shouted. Men stopped working, watching his swaggering waddle. Security froze in bewilderment, not sure what to make of him. "My message is simple. Tonight the Star Child ... all of us will be free. By any means necessary. Freedom or death. I exist between time, outside time. In the between places. I am the voice of truth in these troubled times."

For a heartbeat, everyone stood still. Sleepy stared at them, resolute and defiant. They took in the image of this suited black man standing in the middle of their warehouse. And then everything exploded at once.

The armed men split up, half charging Sleepy, the other half securing the other entrances. Amidst shouts, many of the dock workers grabbed anything within reach which could be used as a weapon. Others took cover. Sleepy turned and ran as a different siren began to wail. It took a few moments for the guards to regroup. They formed a disciplined line and fired carefully. Blasts ricocheted from the nearest walls and a few charges whirred by him. Sleepy ducked as he ran, lowering his head in an attempt to either make himself a smaller target or keep his head from catching a stray shot.

Their commander ran up and down the line, shouting for them to stop. With so many combustibles stockpiled about the warehouse, one errant blast and anything might go up in a pillory of flame. They lowered their weapons and brandished batons and hand blades. The commander deployed them in small teams, hunting packs to surround Sleepy. One pack ran for the nearest exit, blocking it off. Sweat dripped along Sleepy's back, his armpits a scratchy swamp. His suit chafed against him but didn't restrict him much. Calculating that they'd be hesitant to risk damaging their merchandise, he only needed to weave between the stacks of unloaded cargo.

A group of men sealed off his most expedient exit, but he needed to keep moving to draw security away from Deaconess Blues and Knowledge Allah's position. He dipped through a doorway, plunging deeper within the warehouse. A group of men shouted, spying him in the hallways and alerting others. Sleepy scrambled, his lungs huffed and burned. His heart pounded, the muscles across his chest tightened. Despite the harsh gasp of breaths, his body moved on muscle memory.

A squad of men closing in on him, Sleepy rounded a corner, passing a stairwell which connected to another hallway. Another contingent of men bound up the hallway, batons raised and feral snarls on their faces. In a panic, Sleepy whirled around in one fluid movement, doubling back and dashing up the stairs. He barreled up the stairs two at a time. Two men charged down the narrow stairwell. Sleepy raised his arms to shield his face and charged into them. Knocking them off their feet, their baton blows landed ineffectively along his forearms once they realized he refused to slow. He swung his arms back once between them and sent them tumbling down the stairs.

Bursting through the door at the top of the stairs, Sleepy came up along a catwalk. Under normal circumstances, he'd have taken the measure of the slender metal grate that served as the footing. Noting the thin pipe which functioned as a guard rail and the long path, he'd be a wide-open target, he'd have simply surrendered. But he had no time to think. His barreling charge had him committed. His footfalls clanged against the grating with heavy thuds. The guards on the lower level turned to the commotion above them. A commander shouted something Sleepy couldn't understand. Without cargo to risk damaging, the men on the ground dropped their batons and opened fire. Sleepy waved his arms about him wildly as if his arms could deflect rifle blasts. Charges exploded all about him.

Though he hadn't been struck, a new dilemma loomed before him: the walkway was quickly coming to an end. Sleepy swung the door open and slammed it behind him. Stumbling backward, he reached out to steady himself, groping for the door handle. It snapped off as he righted himself. He hoped the destroyed handle would jam the locking mechanism enough to buy him a few moments. A bay window looked over the tarmac of the docking station. This side of the hangar faced the fencing of the airfield. Men banged against the door. Their concerted efforts would bowl it off its hinges with only a couple of shoves. Sleepy withdrew his grappling gun.

With a prayer, Sleepy fired over the fence into the stand of trees behind it. He tethered his line to the thick steam pipe above him. Stepping onto the ledge, he took off his belt and flipped it over the line—the all-too-thin line he grew increasingly convinced would never support his full weight. The guards burst through the door. Sleepy let up a tiny prayer, suddenly feeling superstitious and small. Then leaped from his ledge.

He closed his eyes, waiting for a blast to hit him in the back and send him plunging toward the asphalt. Too many occasions of late had him leaping off perfectly fine structures. His hands burned as he strained to keep his belt in his grasp. The muscles in his arms burned. He focused on simply holding on. The wind whipped him. His pants fluttered. Loosened. Halfway down the line, they puddled at his ankles. He couldn't do anything about the indignity. His backside mooned the entire security staff as he whizzed by.

The stand of trees zipped toward him. He had no contingencies on how to affect his landing. Once he cleared the fence, Sleepy simply let go. He tucked into a ball as best he could, trying to shield his exposed bits from the fall. Crashing through branches, he tumbled through the air, hitting the ground with such force, the landing jarred a *whoof* of air from him. A sudden jolt of pain shot from his feet to his neck. He tumbled to a stop. Eyes closed, he didn't move. His arms outstretched, his legs in a sprawl, his pants bunched at his feet, he didn't want to chance movement for fear of a limb being broken. Or him being paralyzed. Better to remain still and rest in the uncertainty.

After a few moments, he opened his eyes. It hurt to blink. He flexed his toes and fingers. They curled at his command. He breathed a sigh of relief that he didn't suffer paralysis. Pushing up on his elbows, fresh needles of pain stabbed at his neck and along his backside. He rolled over and, leaning against a tree, made his way to his feet. Checking the line, no one pursued him. An emergency air horn blared.

THE AIRSHIP YAWED like a war elephant. A line of guards withdrew from supervising the airship to outflank Sleepy, leaving only a skeletal contingent to defend its access. Deaconess Blues and Knowledge Allah crept behind stacks of cargo. Deaconess Blues noted a package and waved for Knowledge Allah's attention. Gun boxes of military grade ordinance. They intended to fill the ballasts full of it. The entire stock could easily devastate an entire city block. Knowledge Allah shook his head in silent disgust.

They moved across the hangar bay to the mound of munitions nearest the airship. Two guards remained at the station. They looked at one another. Knowledge Allah held up three fingers to count off their desperate charge. Deaconess Blues swallowed hard and nodded.

Three.

Two.

A desperate howl came from above them. Sleepy bellowed as he dashed along the gangplank. The remaining assembly of guards turned their attention upward and took futile aim at his juggernaut bolt. Deaconess Blues and Knowledge Allah glanced at each other and dashed toward the ship. The distracted guards turned in time to catch Knowledge Allah's cane first in the gut and then in the face. He swung it around to crack him in the back of the head for good measure. Deaconess Blues ducked, swinging her leg out to knock the feet out from under the other guard. An elbow smashing into the bridge of his nose and slamming his head against the ground stilled his protests.

They climbed aboard. A guard rounded the corner from within

the airship and drew aim at them. Deaconess Blues threw her portable torch. The man ducked. Before he could regroup, Knowledge Allah leaped at him. After two quick swats with the cane handle, Knowledge Allah tossed the COP out of the doorway and closed the hatch behind them.

The decks of the cabin divided into small rooms, tiny tombs in the greater sarcophagus, connected by tiny ladders Sleepy would have had little hope of navigating. A network of cables, ropes, and pipes ran throughout like capillaries. Pressure hissed from the valves of the Malcolm-Little engines. Mahogany bedecked the main cabin and retained the reek of stale cigar smoke in the luxury box, a sanctum sanctorum for noble breeding. A decanter of pear wine set in the middle of a table spread with finger foods, as a blank-faced automaton whirred out of their way.

Knowledge Allah reclined on a bench, the pose of a gentleman of leisure, while Deaconess Blues stood before an array of membrane discs and tuning forks, lost behind the steady drone and cadence of clicks. She manned the pilot station. The controls warmed the dirigible to a full-throated bluster, pulsing with steam. Baffles and stanchions, ballasts of water, and air ducts pumped furiously.

"Wisdom is water. I'm about solar facts. God is the sun. It's all about the elements," Knowledge Allah said with a brutal curl to his lips. "Jesus died when he was thirty-three. Three and three, Understanding doubled. Three plus three equals Equality. That's all we want, no matter the cost."

"You and your outlandish codes," Deaconess Blues remarked with admirable dispatch. She moved about the cabin, examining the controls with considered elegance. "Your peculiar phraseology never tires."

"The sundial speaks. We prepare to ride as Afronauts."

"You smell that?" Deaconess Blues called out, her skin luminescent in the moonlight shining through the open hangar doors. A static charge hung in the air. The airship lurched free of its moorings. An air horn wailed in protest. "The air smells like freedom."

"Freedom or death," Knowledge Allah said. "We fly into glory."

A GREAT SHADOW filled the sky, the pride of the empire. Clouds blackened into banks of ominous dark swirls by the endless entropy of night. The wind howled. Sleepy raced along the back roads, desperate to beat the landing of the mothership. The gleaming overcity must look so different from up above, Sleepy imagined. Air raid lights filled the sky, spotlights on the stage of the night. The dirigible moved with implacable grace, an airborne whale, strident and regal.

Sleepy hadn't thought of himself as a terrorist, only a victim of relentless circumstance. Even now, his mind wrestled with the cosmic-feeling of dissonance over having stolen COPs munitions and conveyance in an attempt to thwart them bombing the Paul Dunbar Library. And that they now scampered to bring down The Ave. And free the Star Child. And the fact that both the wireless *Vox Dei* and the *Vox Populi*, as well as several posters about town broadcast his image.

His name truly rang out.

Crouching in the driver's seat, he kept an eye on the airship as it veered north, away from the Fourth Ward, The Tombs, or the Martindale neighborhoods. It headed toward the suburbs, towards Allisonville. The Ave.

The bulk of the Allisonville Correctional Facility was a tower just north of Allisonville, like a giant sundial whose shadow marked the time of those incarcerated there. An otherwise respectable complex whose property was surrounded by a wrought iron fence topped with razor wire. The nearby residents could live with the gauche wire, preferring to think of the area as an overprotective office complex. The main tower supported administrative staff and served as a COPs station. Above ground was the exercise compound known as The Farm. Three turrets, guard towers, formed the corners of the walled structure. Most of The Ave remained underground. Layers and layers of labyrinthine hallways and housing units.

The airship drifted toward the tower.

The skies buzzed with activity. Two COPs orthocopter units raced along the horizon. A *Vox Populi* news orthocopter careened toward the scene on an intercept course. News of the hijacked airship preempted all broadcasts. The Cause—at least the faction made up of Deaconess Blues and Knowledge Allah—was on the big stage now. The airship dipped, its trajectory a slow arc toward the main tower. The *Vox Populi* copter hovered, a mechanical dragonfly wanting the best view of the action. The Ave's tower, impregnable and arrogant, saluted them. Slowly, the ovoid silhouette of the airship came into full view. The behemoth canted forward in a sharp downward arc.

Sleepy stared, filled with profound apprehension.

Knowledge Allah stood before the grand bay window. Backlit, his grand gestures were perfectly visible to the spectators as the ship careened earthward.

He raised a clenched fist.

"Vainglorious," Sleepy whispered.

Alarms blared. The administrative offices of The Ave began their evacuation. People streamed from it in near panic, running about not knowing where in the compound might be safe. Spotlights focused on the airship; their intensity drained by the dawning sun. As soon as the COP copters entered weapons range, they fired rounds at the airship. The rest of the vessel ignited into flames. Smoke billowed a dark trail as the ship descended. The breeze blew. The air stank of burnt fuel and potential suicide. Sleepy squinted. The airship seemed to excrete two small packages. Hoping against hope, he swerved the vehicle toward where they might land. The dirigible descended from the black skies. It sank toward The Ave. Slow. Inexorable. Floating low until their collision. Everything happened at once, a series of images broken into shards of memory one tried to forget.

The dirigible exploded. The roar of the crowd. An exhalation of panic. Fire blazed the skin of the ship, peeling it back in blackened sheaths. A flaming skeleton that sank into the building and crashed into shards. A second set of explosions as its cargo went up. A billowy fire cloud, bilious and noxious, almost green against the night sky. A phoenix springing toward the heavens. The smell of India rubber burning. Shrapnel of stone. A body, encircled in flames, stumbled two steps, then collapsed. Fiery scraps blew about in the night breeze. A cascade of rubble. Chunks of concrete. Collapsed steel beams. Shards of glass rained down. The airship collapsed into a fireball, a fiery comet plowing into the side of the main tower. The impact of the flames ignited the munitions on board. A deep rumble, a wave like thunderous applause exploded. Its force rippled through the building. The injured structure suddenly unable to bear its own weight, the tower collapsed. The terrible crash, thunder flattening the eardrums. Smoke and flame, thick and choking, burning the lungs with each inhalation. Shrugging off the building that was the community's shackle. A toxic cloud stalked the Farm.

The streets, which had been so empty a few minutes ago, now streamed with panicked residents. Guards ran along the plaza. They leaped from the turrets out of sheer panic. Neighbors milled in the streets. Storming the sidewalks in fear and confusion, they studied the spreading fires. Huddled like hysterical refugees, curious and afraid of what the destruction might portend. What the violence might mean for them. Some brandished bats or other hastily grabbed weapons. Word would spread quickly: The Ave was down.

Smoke occluded a sea of rubble. Fires flared, damage reaching gas lines. Roiling flames expanded, accompanied by the occasional explosion like mortars landing. Smoke shifted on the stiff breeze, sending people into spasms of coughing fits. COPs scurried about, mostly in rescue operations. Forced to staunch the bleeding operations in priorities: keep more prisoners from escaping while rescuing their fellow officers trapped by debris. Sleepy wandered the periphery, cloaked in the confusion brought about by the bombardment. The rise of acrid smoke stung his eyes.

Air rushed the scene, a wall of concussive force, smelling of desperation and blood. It grew hotter, and he wasn't sure if it was the fiery tumult of wreckage that was The Ave's main tower or his rage. It reminded him of when the city brought down the old Market Square Arena with a series of controlled explosions. The initial blast hit like a thump to the chest, so much so, its echo drowned out the subsequent explosions. A thick cloud billowed down the street like a man on a Sunday morning stroll. The crowd let it overtake them, not knowing or fearing what particles might be a part of the building now coating their lungs, just so that their senses had another way to take in that moment in history.

Watching the skeleton of the airship continue to burn—its tattered shell buckled and collapsed upon itself—Sleepy spied no one immediately fleeing. Praying that the prisoners had been moved, he feared that they remained trapped beneath the ground, like escaping slaves caught in a cave in. Sleepy imagined the panic of those underground. The collapsing ceilings. Cage doors knocked free of their hinges. The shock. The dawning realization of their impending demise.

In the distance, heads dotted the ground, like meerkats checking for predators. Black bodies crawled from tunnels opened by the explosion. Among the wreckage and destruction, figures scrambled from the underground, a stream of ants fleeing their hill. Some of the constabularies fired at the escaping prisoners. Seeing this, something stirred inside Sleepy. The caustic smoke stung his eyes, his vision little more than watery blurs. Soot-tinged spittle dropped to the ground. Sirens sounded. Bodies clambered through barbed wire.

In his mind, many voices rose into a chorus. Knowledge Allah. Deaconess Blues. His father. Lost in the din was his voice. Sleepy felt the anger. The urge to join the fight. To retaliate. Blinking through a haze of pain, he ground his heel into the desiccated earth.

"Your collar up, Melbourne?" Sleepy yelled. "I'm coming for you. I know you can feel the heat on the back of your neck."

TWENTY

FIGHT THE POWER

Vox Populi: This just in. We've just received word of a terrorist attack on the Allisonville Correctional Facilities. Reports are varied. It hasn't been determined if this was part of a plot against the crown or simply an attempt at freeing prisoners. City Ordained Pinkertons have the area cordoned off, as federal level Pinkertons agents have been dispatched to aid in the manhunt.

A THRONG of people slowly gathered. At first, it was just the neighbors, but caravans of vehicles began depositing more citizens to the scene. The crowd became a pantomime of motion and fury and panic. Soon black faces dotted the crowd. Autocarriages deposited carloads of passengers who gathered. They filed in, disciplined and organized. The crowd grumbled, an undulation of agitation. Sleepy waited, carried along by their undertow. A wall of COPs separated them from the crime scene The Ave had been reduced to. In their thick vests, helmets, and shields, the COPs were little more than shadows backlit by the flames, as well as the portable torchlights brought in to illuminate the scene. They kept the gathering throng back a couple of city blocks, but the smoke and dust from the explosion and collapse of the building hadn't dissipated. The constabularies, with their thick nightsticks and steel-riveted riot shields, cordoned off the area as best they could, in desperate need of rein- forcements. Fear glazed their faces. The horde threatened to spill in every direction, blind fury, pent up aggression in search of a target.

Sleepy scoured the skies, not knowing what he searched for. He spied the *Vox Populi* copter overhead. They might record images, but they would never broadcast live. Anything could happen live. Truth might accidentally slip out. They needed time to receive the spin instructions of their masters. Sleepy's mind replayed the image of the massive airship careening overhead, like a grim torpedo targeting the main tower of The Ave. The memory looped as if his mind registered something that he couldn't quite recall. Sleepy retreated to the edge of the crowds. The COPs held their ground. The chants started.

"No justice, no peace."

"Rise up, it's our day!"

"Hey, hey! Ho, ho! These racist COPs have got to go!"

Different shouts went up from different sections of the crowd, gaining traction like they were having a conversation with them- selves, deciding what to do next. COPs swarmed in, continuing to strengthen their thin, black line as well as securing the scene. Several escaping prisoners, like water through a crack in a dam, slipped over the fence. But with reinforcements bolstering their forces, COPs stemmed that flow. The two sides clashed, merging into a mob of chaos. Arms swung blindly, clubs battering sense- lessly. COPs slammed bodies into the ground, zip-tying hands behind backs, and trotted them off to a makeshift detention area.

Smoothing out his suit as best he could, Sleepy ducked back into the crowd. With a slight hunch as he walked, he avoided the steady gaze of any COP. A hand clapped him on the shoulder and spun him around. Sleepy threw his hands up, ready to serve them to whoever sought to manhandle him. It took a few heartbeats for his mind to register the well-dressed figure leaning on a cane. Though for a brief moment, he'd hoped it was someone else. "Desmond?"

"Oi. We heard ..." Desmond craned about, scanning the sides. "These your folks?"

"Most of them. Everyone is heading here to rally. All of our allies. What's the word?"

"I don't know. I keep looking for Deaconess Blues or Knowledge Allah."

"Any ... one else?"

"I haven't seen anyone. Yet."

Sleepy spotted Tigga off to the side, his scarecrow frame difficult to miss, even in the chaos. He cupped his hands to his mouth and shouted, "Ready for what? We're ready for war!" He glanced about to check the mood of the crowd. A few eyes lit up at the notion. Encouraged, he cupped his hands to his mouth again. Before he could begin to shout again, Sleepy snatched him by his collar and dragged him behind the crowd line. Anyone who might have joined in with his sentiment went back to chanting. "Rise up, it's our day!"

"What the fuck are you doing?" Tigga shoved Sleepy away and dusted himself off.

"You Sugar's boy, right? He pay you to come down here and stir the pot? Maybe get folks so riled up, they jump off at anything?" Heated, Sleepy nearly snarled. Bits of spit speckled the man's tie.

"Look around you. They already riled up." Tigga held his arms out, displaying the crowd.

Sleepy wanted to punch him straight in his smug face. Anything to wipe the obnoxious smirk from it. "And you the match that wants to set everything off?"

"I'm just a voice."

"A paid voice. You like the overseer of the plantation who shouts to the boss when one of us was making a break for the wall. Get the fuck out of here."

"Who's going to make me? You?" The man shifted his posture. Sleepy had the element of surprise and the momentum fueled by his girth to yank the man out of position one last time. Prepared and set, Tigga didn't appear as thin as he once looked but rather was dieseled up close, like a man who had spent a year or two in a prison yard strengthening his muscles.

"And me." A familiar voice chimed in from behind him.

Sleepy turned to see Knowledge Allah stepping out of the thick brush. He dragged his damaged orthocopter like a nearly forgotten rag doll, its long blades jutting from the backpack like a spider's broken legs. He strolled with deliberate ease, a hint of threat with each step. Each pat of his jacket released a puff of dust and dirt. Twigs and leaves entangled his hair. His pants would need the services of a tailor or two to mend all the tears. The branches along the trail he emerged from continued to rustle as another figure made its way into the clearing.

"And me," Deaconess Blues offered. Her orthocopter had neatly retracted into what appeared to be a backpack. She picked a stray leaf from her hair.

Sleepy resisted the urge to run or call out to them. Tigga scanned the resolved faces of each of them. He glanced over his shoulder as if measuring the distance between him and the swelling group of residents. His mouth fixed into a grimace. He swished a toothpick from one side of his mouth to the other.

"Jump if you're feeling froggy," Sleepy said. "But we know you dance to Sugar's tune, and he ain't exactly have all of our best interests at heart. *We* know that. But *they* don't know that. All that could change if I see you around us again."

Flinching, the man hesitated, stopping to see if anyone might move to pursue him. Satisfied, he shambled toward the road, not too quickly as to save face. But he did so without a backward glance.

His flash of anger quickly dissipated when Sleepy returned his attention to his friends. He maintained his decorum as best he could. "You're all right!"

"Safe and sound as one could expect," Deaconess Blues said.

"I was afraid that ..."

"Knowledge Allah's orthocopter had some trouble. It took a few charge blasts when the COP copters blasted at the airship. My orthocopter managed to support us both the rest of the way down."

"Good thing it was you two up there rather than me and Knowledge Allah," Sleepy said.

"I suspect at least one or both of us would have objected to how ... intimately ... you would've had to hold me in order for me to pilot us to safety." Knowledge Allah glanced at Deaconess Blues, his eyes huge behind his spectacles, but quickly turned away before the moment became awkward. "One of us would've rather gone down in flames."

Deaconess Blues glanced passed Sleepy. "Desmond, so good to see you again."

"From how Sleepy described it, there was a high probability that we might not reacquaint ourselves with one another." Desmond tipped his hat to her.

Handing his backpack to Deaconess Blues—who managed to get the blades to retract—Knowledge Allah sidled close to him. "Yeah, brother. I'm afraid I lost your cane."

"This life is hard on them," Desmond said, half-distracted. He searched the shadows for any movement. "It is the least pressing of our concerns."

Sleepy started scanning again himself. Keeping an eye on the burgeoning line of COPs and the flight pattern of their orthocopter units. In the distance, dogs brayed as they assembled in tracking patrols. "We need to get to stepping."

"We can't afford to be seen. Sleepy and I are still on the run," Knowledge Allah said in a conspiratorial whisper. "Plus, we're not alone."

"What do you mean?" Desmond said in a grave tone, now on alert.

"Come," Deaconess Blues said.

They brushed back the bushes and tree limbs they had just traipsed through. A hedgerow of sculpted topiary marked the boundary of private property, but on their side of it, weeds and thick tree roots bloomed, shading the creek which ran along it. The growth was so thick the creek could be heard but not seen. They plunged deeper into the greenery. The overhead branches blotted out the morning sun. It was a wonder Deaconess Blues nor Knowledge Allah didn't break their neck when they came crashing through the foliage. Eventually, the underbrush cleared a bit, like they'd entered the mouth of a cave made of sheltering leaves.

"Hold up." Knowledge Allah raised his fist. "It's us. We've brought friends."

A few branches twitched. Sleepy took a sharp breath. On all sides, dead leaves crunched and trodden branches snapped with stirring, tentative movement. Covered with only prison-issued blankets, men stepped into the clearing.

Desmond stopped short. Leaning heavily on his cane, his full weight was supported by it as if he'd lost the strength in his legs. A young man stepped into the clearing. Thin, but muscled, a dancer's frame both lithe and sinewy. With a noble gravitas to him, he carried himself with a proud bearing. One might think the tattered bed linens draped around him were ceremonial robes. His hair locked, the twists dangled past his shoulders. His eyes were like shards of jade, deep and penetrating. His gaze had a way of unwinding a person if they stared at him for too long. Sleepy had never met the Star Child before, much less been in his presence. It was stunning.

Desmond hesitated, not quite believing his eyes. Not wanting his hopes dashed. Fearing that he might not be able to recover if this wasn't real. Sleepy felt something similar when he first heard Knowledge Allah's voice after the airship crashed. Similar, though a pale shadow. Desmond's mouth moved as if trying to form words though nothing came out. His eyes welled with desperate, hopeful tears.

"Hello, Father," Lij said finally. He held his arms out, the blanket draped about him giving him the appearance of the sort of ebony specter Ms. Emma Bennet might summon. Desmond rushed into his embrace. He clutched him tight, breathing him in. A grip so intense, Sleepy thought he'd never let go again.

"Mi deh yah." Desmond held him at arm's length. His words dissolved into barely comprehensible patois, his full Jamaican accent tumbling out in a torrent of emotion. He brushed the hair from the young man's face, touched his cheek, checking to see if he were real, before hugging him again.

"I know. But I'm here now, too," Lij assured him.

Sleepy stepped closer to get a better view of the man. Lij turned to him. Reaching up, he touched the side of Sleepy's face.

"Greetings, Dreamer," he said.

"I'm sorry?" Sleepy asked.

"Stories speak us into existence. Stories of our past inform our present." The Star Child neared him. His hands brushed every person he could. Returning nods, passing peace—issuing respect to those he encountered—yet never breaking his gaze with Sleepy. "Our hopes and dreams inform the stories that shape our tomorrows."

"I ..." words failed Sleepy. The Star Child's green eyes loomed ever larger until they were all he could see. They filled him with desperate hope. As if the young man believed so intently, it was enough for both of them.

"I don't want to break up this reunion, but we still have to figure out a way out of here," Knowledge Allah said. "It's only a matter of time before COPs have this entire area on lockdown."

"I'm not leaving Lij again," Desmond said with a grimace of finality.

"No worries. We'll scout ahead and see about getting some transportation."

Climbing back up the embankment, Knowledge Allah crept to the side of the street. Down the road, the sounds of clanks and the hiss of a steamboiler echoed. A minibus pulled up alongside the burgeoning crowd and deposited men in suits and bow ties. The Lost Nation. The men lined up, somber and stone-faced, their overcoats worn like armor ready to meet their enemy. After shouting a few instructions, Majestic Jamal dismissed them. They marched directly to the thickest part of the crowd to stand between the people and the wall of COPs. Majestic Jamal stepped forward to meet Knowledge Allah.

"Peace, sun," Knowledge Allah said.

"Peace, sun." Majestic Jamal exchanged peace with him. "We were supposed to rendezvous with you at Bird's designated accident site."

Sleepy perked to attention. "That was you?"

"His idea. He was how we knew where you two were in the first place." Majestic Jamal turned back to Knowledge Allah. "He must've had to make the transport tun earlier than we planned. By the time we got there, COPs had the whole scene cordoned off.

Brother Desmond let us know that you were with him and we figured we'd let you be. But when word hit the vine that things had jumped off, we followed everyone else up here to make our stand. Though I suspect some people have showed up just to show out."

"Is Father Justice with you?" Knowledge Allah's voice brimmed with something hopeful.

"We ... he's not ready for so public an appearance. We would need to brace the people. Prepare them for his new incarnation."

"You need to control the story." Knowledge Allah hid the vague disappointment in his voice.

"No matter what you think of his and our ways, you know—you have to know—that we love our people and want to keep them safe."

"We have some ... immorally detained resistors. They're in need of safe transport," Knowledge Allah said. "But you would need to be careful. Sugar's around."

"Sugar is a known quantity. A necessary and sometimes useful evil. But we see him for who he is." Majestic Jamal gestured for the minibus driver to scoot to the back. "We're about to make a return run to Freetown Village. More of our people want to come up and show support. We dare COPs to try to stop us. I'll make the run myself."

"Thank you, sun." Knowledge Allah held onto the outside rail and rode shotgun. He swung the minibus around and veered toward the back road which ran alongside Fall Creek. Knowledge Allah slapped the side of the door to signal to stop. Desmond, Lij, and the men slipped from the bushes and dashed into the bus. They crouched low in the seats. Desmond mouthed the words "Thank you" before taking a window seat near the rear, huddling with Lij.

Sleepy and Deaconess Blues were the last to enter the bus before Knowledge Allah hopped down and joined them. The minibus shifted into gear and took off. They sat in a haze of indecision. They had been through so much and still had much left to do. Only there wasn't a clear starting point. Only the longing to hunker down in silence.

The bus prowled the backroads of the city, careful to avoid any of the main arteries sure to be riddled with COPs checkpoints. The rising swell of anxiety—as if just waiting to be caught—finally pushed Sleepy to speak up.

"What's next?" he asked, giving voice to their dilemma.

"We should best not tarry," Deaconess Blues said. "You two are still wanted terrorists."

"We all are now. We're not traveling with Boy Scouts." Knowledge Allah wrung his hands toward the collection of escapees. "If COPs apprehend us—especially given the magnitude of our sabotage—none of us will make it to a detention cell."

"Once we get to a safe place, we need to procure a new vehicle," Sleepy said.

"And go where?" Knowledge Allah pushed his glasses straight and gestured to the horizon. "Where can any of us call safe?"

"The Colonel's house." Deaconess Blues said.

THEY MEANDERED through Indianapolis on their way back to the Colonel's house. The street lamps still burned with life despite the bright morning. Both the *Vox Dei* and the *Vox Populi* reported wall-to-wall coverage of "the disturbance" at The Ave. Protests ignited across town. Haughville. Old Fourth Ward. The Tombs. Everything moved toward the brink, with the city splintering along racial and class lines. Even with the bomb attempt thwarted—though no one knew the truth about it—events seemed to keep careening in Lord Melbourne's favor.

The front parlor of the Colonel's house was an expansive room hardly ever used, both imposing and cold. Transoms above each door. Vases filled every shelf and topped every cabinet, an ode to whatever aesthetic caught the lady of the house's fancy. Dark wainscoting along the walls gave the room a mournful quality probably meant to deter lingering visits.

They had barely settled into chairs before Deaconess Blues began to pace. Knowledge Allah rubbed his knee before lowering himself into the nearest seat. Ducking out of the room, she came back a few moments later holding a cane. She handed it to him. "It was my father's."

"Thanks." He stabbed the carpet with the cane, taking its measure. "I can't decide if we are lucky chess masters of clever pawns."

"I could sit here and pretend to be some sort of brilliant chess player, but for that, I need to think several moves ahead. Right now, I don't see enough of the board to make my next move." She plopped down into a nearby davenport.

"It's just as important to take advantage of lucky situations. Fortune favors the clever. Or the high." Sleepy tamped chiba leaves into his pipe. "What do you suggest? We go to the Pinkertons?"

"No. Though I doubt anyone got a good look at us at the hangar, you and Knowledge Allah are still wanted as persons of interest at the very least. Escapees at worst."

"That and the fact that we have no proof of what, by any measurement, is a wild story," Knowledge Allah said.

"The closest thing we had to evidence we used to ... effect the largest prison break in Indianapolis history," Deaconess Blues said.

"Wow, we sound doubly screwed when I hear it aloud," Sleepy said. "Assuming Lord Melbourne is alive ..."

"He is. His death would have led the news despite 'the disturbance.' We would need one of his closest conspirators to testify against him to have any chance of a case. But that leaves only Sugar, who is firmly in Lord Melbourne's pocket. Cayt. Dr. Yeager. Tigga. All other operatives working on his behalf on down don't know enough to piece together the big picture for anyone. Even if you put them all together."

"Lucas Pruitt is dead," Sleepy said. The image of Lord Melbourne's bodyguard, Cayt, lodging a bullet neatly in his head replayed in his mind.

"What about his accomplice? Pruitt mentioned having a person on the inside who was his agent to ..." Knowledge Allah's voice trailed off.

"There's no point in dancing along eggshells on my account. You can say it." Deaconess Blues shifted in her seat. With no one forthcoming to say the words, she took a measured breath, dropped her palms to her thighs and said what no one else would aloud. "Kill my father."

A creak came from the doorway.

"Leighton called me an hour or so ago from his hospital bed. Told me what you did to Lucas." Lyonessa stood there. Training a Luger on them, she plopped a suitcase next to her like a faithful canine companion. "Lucas was my friend. So was Lord Melbourne, which was why he had the decency to warn me that I might be exposed as Lucas's accomplice."

"Of course, it was you," Deaconess Blues whispered.

Sleepy waited for the crestfallen face of betrayal on Deaconess Blues. For her attempt to reason with her stepmother. Plead for her life. Bring up fond memories or how much they meant to each other. At the very least, he expected her to cajole her to stay calm, keep a level head, and to not do anything rash. But there were no such negotiations. Deaconess Blues's face hardened in stern calculation like she played back every conversation, every occasion of them being together to see what she missed. There was no shock, no dawning realization, only the exacting inevitability of things. That this was where their pretense of a relationship was always heading. There was no misunderstanding. The woman in front of her was the woman she always sensed she was.

"You couldn't wait to get a hold of The Colonel's fortune, could you?" Deaconess Blues remained terribly still. Her palms rested atop her legs. Her knees pressed together, angled toward her stepmother like she had just sat down for Sunday tea. Her face a demure moue, frozen, betraying no emotion. The perfect eye of a raging storm.

"I could. Patience is my gift. But events tipped my hand. He couldn't see Lord Melbourne's vision. There was a fortune to be made in munitions trade."

"Oh, he caught the vision. He just wanted no part of blood trade. He wasn't going to walk down the same road as his father." Deaconess Blues refused to look at her. Her voice calm and level, still little above a whisper.

Lyonessa grew agitated. She gripped and re-gripped the Luger. Sweeping the room to make sure Sleepy and Knowledge Allah remained where they were, she pointed the gun directly at Deaconess Blues. "Then there was you."

"Me?" Deaconess Blues glanced up at her.

"You had to come back. Couldn't even finish a year at Oxford. As soon as he received word of his precious baby girl's return, he began reallocating funds. He became so secretive, diverting funds, postponing projects. I'm sure it was all about you. His precious Sophine. Last and constant reminder of the long shadow of Lady Trystan. We were on the clock, as it were. Sooner or later, he'd move to block Leighton."

So much jealousy bordering on hate dripped from each syllable. Sleepy couldn't imagine what it must have felt like to be on the receiving end of such disdain, such scorn, especially from someone who was supposed to be a mother. But the wound ran deeper than that. Like faint blood trails from a dozen shallow cuts. It was loss. The way her father was taken from her. The lost connection and longing for her real mother. The betrayal. The abandonment. Being truly alone. Like the light and warmth from being the Colonel's little girl faded for the last time.

"You poisoned my father," Deaconess Blues said, the same way a person chewed on food, still deciding whether or not they liked the taste.

"Yes." Lyonessa turned toward Knowledge Allah and Sleepy, somewhat confused, not knowing what to make of Deaconess Blues's reaction.

"For money."

"Yes."

"And power."

"The ability to affect one's will, that's always more valuable."

"Now you sound like Lord Melbourne." Deaconess Blues's face ever implacable.

"He should be out of surgery by now. You left him in quite a state, but he was prepared for such a contingency. His agent got him to ZeroDyne in time."

"Lord Melbourne played you," Knowledge Allah said. "That monster killed the Chancellor in cold blood."

"Don't try your games with me." Lyonessa's grimace faltered a bit, a flare of doubt taking root. Unsure, she swept the room one more time to hold them in position while she calculated her next move. Deaconess Blues's face hardened, yet was still largely unreadable. "And what of us? Taking a more direct route with us? Gun us down in my father's house?"

"Don't be so dramatic. I'm a pragmatic woman. Enough money has been squirreled away for me to live comfortably ... away from here. For quite a time. Once the dust settles and the law has caught up with you or Lord Melbourne's plan is fully in motion, I can make my return. For now, I'm ... just going to tie you up and leave you for the COPs." Lyonessa waved them to the dining chairs on the other side of the room. She turned to Sleepy. "You, too."

"No," Sleepy said without rancor.

"What?" Lyonessa raised the gun as a reminder in case, somehow, he had missed it.

"Look here, it's been a long night. I've done nothing but run around all night. I've fought COPs. I've rappelled off buildings. Run through woods. I ain't built for all that. My feet hurt. I ain't moving. You either tie me up here or shoot me, cause these dogs are barking and I'm going to let them rest."

"Are ... you serious right now?" Lyonessa waved the gun at him.

Taking advantage of the distraction, Deaconess Blues lunged at her. Lyonessa swung the gun in her direction but was met with a tangle of arms. Deaconess Blues thrust her knee into her stepmother's side, throwing her off balance. She grabbed for the gun, but Lyonessa kept a desperate grip on it. She probably didn't realize that she had begun to bring the weapon up. Deaconess Blues wrestled for a better grip on it. The gun fired a single, muffled shot.

Both Deaconess Blues and Lyonessa froze, their eyes wide with surprise. The gun clattered to the floor. Sleepy raised up out of his seat. Knowledge Allah swooped in, ready to catch Deaconess Blues. The ladies took half of a step away from each other. Each studied the other and then themselves. No patch of blood dampened either of their blouses. At the same time, they turned, tracing the angle of the shot past where Sleepy once sat. A small hole dotted the wall behind him.

"Sophine." Lyonessa held her hands up. "I would never intentionally ..."

Deaconess Blues jabbed her elbow into the side of her stepmother's face, sending her backward. Her arms pinwheeled as she fell. Her head slammed into the side of the coffee table with a heavy thud. She did not move.

"Is she...?" Sleepy asked.

"She's fine." Deaconess Blues checked her pulse before collecting the Luger.

Knowledge Allah studied the way Deaconess Blues held the gun over Lyonessa's still form. His brow knit in concern. "She going to stay that way?"

"Unconscious?" Deaconess Blues tucked the gun into her belt. "I'm not sure, but she'll still remain breathing as normally as one can expect in a corset done up that tightly."

"What do we do now?" Knowledge Allah asked.

"Truss her up for now. We need to end this madness once and for all. Our only recourse is to take this fight to Lord Melbourne."

Knowledge Allah and Deaconess Blues circled to each end of Lyonessa to begin to tie her up. Sleepy lowered himself back into his seat.

"Just so you know," he said, "I was serious about my feet."

———

DEACONESS BLUES MARCHED them through the lobby of ZeroDyne Corporation. A security guard lowered the book his nose was buried in and stood at their approach. Sleepy straightened his cravat and adjusted his smudged suit, which still reeked of smoke and burnt rubber. Deaconess Blues's outfit was slashed as if it had been lashed within an inch of its life by tree branches. Knowledge Allah smelled of sweat, ozone, and piston grease, the cologne of the steam age. She flashed her clearance badge. The guard eyed her warily, glancing at a daguerreotype not especially hidden on his desk. Lowering his head, he double-checked the image and pretended to study the papers on his desk, trying not to meet anyone's gaze.

"Has my clearance been rescinded?" She withdrew the Luger and trained it on the guard.

"No, it's just ..."

"Just what?"

"Y-your guests need to sign in," the guard stammered.

Deaconess Blues nodded. Sleepy picked up the pen to sign in. She pointed to her gun. Knowledge Allah strode around the desk to tie up the guard. Deaconess Blues hit a button behind the desk. Huge gears ground into action to crank open the heavy doors.

"You're sure about this?" Knowledge Allah asked.

"This plan does have a 'let's just march into the lion's den' vibe to it," Sleepy said.

"I don't see where we have a choice." Deaconess Blues led the way. "Lord Melbourne covered his tracks well. Not so much as a fingerprint other than us as witnesses to Pruitt's ravings. Our word against his. Worse, in raising the claim, we'd be positioning ourselves as alternative suspects. We have nothing but circumstantial evidence, nothing that couldn't be dismissed as the intersection of coincidence and shrewd business maneuvers. Our word against his. Very well-monied, well-connected word. If he wanted us dead, we wouldn't have made it out of the governor's mansion."

They walked down the hallway, guards allowing them to pass at every juncture which only heightened Sleepy's feeling of being ground up by the teeth in the jaws of a trap about to spring. But they were too far in to turn back now. The trio neared a second series of double doors, with more sentries on either side. A man stepped out. Thick brown hair with the budding gray of it carefully clipped away. His shirt stretched across his belly, too small and a decade out of fashion, as if he were too cheap to replace it. His white apron was splattered with blood. Not taking particular note of them, he staggered backward and slumped against a wall.

"Dr. Yeager? What happened? Where's Lord Melbourne?" Deaconess Blues demanded.

Dr. Yeager's voice took a while to find itself. His eyes glazed over, in a distant stare, his mind a jumble he struggled to sort. "There are times when you work above what you know you're capable of doing. When something ... outside of you takes over and you're able to create something that you look back on, even a few minutes later, and marvel at what you were able to produce with your hands."

"Dr. Yeager?" Deaconess Blues touched his arm to focus his attention.

"Lord Melbourne is in there." Dr. Yeager raised an arm and gestured vaguely behind him. "I've placed him within a chassis based on your designs. Connecting him to the membrane interface, I don't know if I've ever done finer work."

Pushing himself away from the wall, Dr. Yeager wobbled down the hallway, a man drunk on his own success. No one stopped him.

Sleepy watched him teeter away. "I suspect I may already hate that man."

"Trust your instincts," Deaconess Blues said. "Come on."

They shoved the set of double doors open. Technicians scurried with activity. Machines chirped and beeped. Automata calibrated robotic arms and put away instruments. Doctors and more technicians crowded around a table before parting at the trio's approach. The doctors and technicians scampered out of the room. ZeroDyne Industries guards sealed the room once they left.

The sight of Lord Melbourne froze Sleepy in his tracks.

A brain bobbed, secure in a canister. His body like an autocarriage stripped down and attempting to sit upward, the thing which had once been Lord Melbourne leaned forward. He howled—a sound somewhere between agony and ecstasy—his mouth opening and closing in an arrhythmic fashion, like someone working their jaw after having been punched in the face. In truth, the jaw was strictly cosmetic as a speaker box in the center of his mouth mounting provided the sound to his thoughts. A series of pistons and valves speaking in machine language, interpreting the secret code of steam and power. Mounted within glass facsimiles of eyes were photoelectric lenses, retracting much like a telescopic electrocamera. Steam tendrils snaked from his metal carapace. His arms wagged and flexed in the air. Each movement produced a muffled whir of further pistons and gears, a mechanical creak as if old joints ached and strained to move. When he stood upright, he had the awkward gait of a newborn foal which had been shot.

"It worked." Lord Melbourne's voice crackled with a slight metallic whine, sounding like an intercom with a poor speaker crackling with static. He touched his throat, checking to see if it were him. No nerves ran to his fingertips, but old habits die hard. He held his hands out, inspecting them. "I ... live."

"You're an abomination," Deaconess Blues said.

"Considering your history with abominations, that's quite the stone to hurl." Two fingers reached for Deaconess Blues as if to caress her cheek. She trembled, flinching away. His body, what remained of it, lurched. His mind growing accustomed to its new connections. "Vanity is a small price to pay for continued life."

"I've seen this before," Knowledge Allah said. "On Father Justice."

"His was an earlier design. My body has many refinements. I am still debating whether to have a layer of rubber latex applied to approximate human skin or if I should let them see who it is they deal with. Unvarnished truth." A faint whir came from his chassis whenever he turned. Pistons compressed. Sparks wreathed his head, arcing between the antennae which replaced his ears. He flexed his fingers again, attenuating to finer movements. Lord Melbourne reared, a mechanical thing of functional terror. The gears of his clockwork torso ground with each movement, brass servos bearing the load of gun barrels and impaling instruments. His frame twisted and turned like a pubescent boy getting used to his body. "I am in your debt, Lady Sophine."

"My name is Deaconess Blues." She raised the Luger. "There are debts that cannot be repaid with credits. We will put a stop to you and your maniacal plans. Once and for all."

"While I believe you may have it in you to squeeze that trigger, I don't think she will let it come to that." Lord Melbourne upticked what was supposed to be his chin toward the corner of the room.

Cayt pushed strawberry blonde strands from her face. Hard, green eyes peered from the shadows of her wide-brimmed hat. Half-opening her greatcoat, she displayed her weapons.

"Welcome to the party, boys." Cayt tipped her hat. "And milady."

With a flick of his hand, Lord Melbourne batted Deaconess Blues's gun away. The force of it left Deaconess Blues shaking her hand. Before she could blink, Cayt drew her gun. Already in motion, heedless of any pain in his knee, Knowledge Allah raised a lab chair and swung it like a cricket bat, knocking it from her hand. She stared at her hand like he had chopped off the appendage and left her with a stump. She raised her hands, braced for fisticuffs. Knowledge Allah stepped back, unsure, as if debating how violently physical he wanted to get with a woman. She charged him, grabbed him by the lapels, and head-butted him across the bridge of his nose. Blood exploded from his face as he tumbled backward.

She stripped off her coat and hat. Without them, she seemed a lot smaller. Loosening his collar, Knowledge Allah had her by about six inches and thirty pounds. He moved like a man recalling a former life, his body remembering a hard past used to fighting. Knowledge Allah threw the first few punches wide and tentative, telegraphing each one as if he didn't really want to connect with her. Crouching over to keep herself small, she eluded the punches with ease. Whatever training he had, she had more. She rabbit-punched him in his kidneys. Her footwork matching his while he tried to circle her.

Lord Melbourne turned to Sleepy. "I haven't been trained as a pugilist like Cayt, but let's see what you have."

Without thinking, Sleepy threw a punch. His metal hand swinging up in a blur, Lord Melbourne caught Sleepy's fist. His knuckles burned like he had slammed them into a steel wall. Then it occurred to Sleepy that he would have felt the same had he connected with the cyborg's torso. Lord Melbourne studied the fist in his grasp, a small thing easily crushed with the slightest flex of his grip. An electric arc flashed between his antennae. His voice box crackled with what may have been a laugh. Releasing him, Lord Melbourne grabbed Sleepy about his neck and raised him, leaving his feet dangling a foot from the ground.

Deaconess Blues charged Lord Melbourne and leaped with a scream. Still holding Sleepy, his head swiveled a full 180° to face her. She landed on his back. He spun at the waist, his torso whirled about while his legs remained in place. Not shaken off, she covered his optical receptacles and tore at the tubes that led from the base of his neck into the main chassis. Deaconess Blues could only look on in horror as Lord Melbourne released his grip on Sleepy and ran toward the glass partition separating the other half of the laboratory space. Lowering his head, his antennae gleaming like steel horns, the glass exploded in a storm of glass shards raining down.

With her eyes closed, arms protecting her as best she could, Deaconess Blues fell from his back and skittered across the lab. In a blind scrabble, she hid behind a lab bench.

Lord Melbourne stalked the room. "Your plan is madness."

He had never been stronger. He balled his fist and slammed it into a table, cracking it in two, collapsing in on itself. He howled with glee, his voice box straining to carry the sound. The loudness of it caused the box to click, turning his laughter into a mechanized stutter. "What do you know of madness?"

"I know of its casualties. My father, for one. Lucas Pruitt. Nearly The Tombs," she shouted over the table. "How many must pay the price for your hubris? You are cosigning much of the country to war, both civil and abroad. You get wealthy and perhaps gain power enough to rule but at a terrible cost."

"Your concerns are so … ordinary." Lord Melbourne lumbered about, each footfall booming with each step. He overturned a lab bench with a casual swipe. The contents smashed against the wall. With each assault, Lord Melbourne seemed to grow larger as if a mechanical leech, feeding off the violence. His clockwork body unfurled; his inner workings, a series of nested cloisters. Nearly the size of an elephant, he stomped about the room. The photoelectric lenses serving as eyes tracked Deaconess Blues's movements. "You don't understand. I am resurrected. I have conquered death. If you want to offer up prayers, offer them to me. Even if I have to wipe out a third of the population to inaugurate it, I am the Savior of this age."

The blasphemous statement heated Sleepy more than he would have guessed. Simultaneously, he pictured the pain and the horror that would attend Lord Melbourne's plan. Sleepy swore and focused on Lord Melbourne with snarls of anger. He shook the glass from his clothes as he slowly recovered from Lord Melbourne's choking grip. A terrible feeling struck him. That perhaps Lord Melbourne's condition had rotted away parts of his brain, that he was beyond reason and was a mechanical creature with nothing to lose.

Marshaling his energies, Knowledge Allah launched his leg in a high kick. Cayt wound under it and, without turning, snapped her leg into his back. The force spun him around. Her legs scissored in the air. She delivered another kick, sending him sprawling along the lab bench. He rolled onto his back. Needing space to maneuver, he kicked out with both feet, the action was more to shove her backward than attempt a true kick. He scrambled after her and wrapped his arms around her. He lifted her above his shoulders before dropping her onto her back. He landed on her with his full weight. Cayt seemed unfazed, twisting under him, snaking her limbs around him until she had him half-locked up. She elbowed him in his gut, breaking his struggling hold. Releasing him, she leaped onto the lab bench, reversing the height differential, punching him several times in a flurry, before a roundhouse kick sent him to the floor.

Freeing his blade from his scabbard, Knowledge Allah turned to face her. A smile curled across her face. He slashed at her. Keeping her arms to her side, she side-stepped each feint, not bothering to draw any weapons of her own, ducking and weaving until she found herself next to him. She cuffed him in his jaw before dancing out of range of his next lunging attack. With room to run, she charged at him and leapt. Three kicks in quick succession stomped his chest. His momentum spilled him across a lab bench.

"Switch off," Deaconess Blues cried out.

Lord Melbourne swung a metal claw toward her skull. Dropping to her knees, she slid under its arc as the razored blade sliced past. Knowledge Allah turned his sword on Lord Melbourne. With a hard chop, Knowledge Allah severed a conduit. The hose sputtered about, like an artery unloosed, spraying a blast of steam along the wall. Knowledge Allah rushed toward one of Lord Melbourne's legs, hacking and slashing like he was desperate to cut a path through thickly grown woods. A metal lance dropped from Lord Melbourne's undercarriage. An extending metal arm brought it to bear. The blade began to swivel about, a thrashing scythe casting about in wild thrusts to drive Knowledge Allah back. He deflected the blade as best he could, but a lance thrust slipped past his guard and sliced him along his ribs. Knowledge Allah clutched his side and stumbled. Back-pedaling in a crab-like crawl, his sword still parried the pressing blade.

Sleepy held his breath. Heat blasted him. The steam rose like a fetid cloud, slapping Sleepy into a moment of lucid consideration of his recent life choices. The life of a cog scraping sewage for Commonwealth Waterworks was a distant dream almost fondly recalled.

Beep-beep.

Sleepy began to clamber up the monstrous frame. While Lord Melbourne seemed oblivious, tiny claws along the mechanical monster's spine click-clacked automatically. Sleepy nearly lost several fingers scrambling for purchase along the metal skeleton. He hoped that he would come up with an actual plan soon.

The fight was more desperate and ugly than Deaconess Blues would have imagined. Her father always reminded her that fights were usually brutal and brief, setting within the first minutes. Deaconess Blues threw a tepid punch. Cayt let the punch land, her split lip bloodied her teeth. Though older, Cayt was the more skilled fighter. She had the bored weariness of someone all-too-familiar with this particular dance. To the point where Deaconess Blues realized the woman wasn't simply taking her measure but was toying with her. Allowing her to realize just how outclassed she was.

Deaconess Blues pushed all thoughts out of her head and lashed out.

Cayt cartwheeled out of reach. Deaconess Blues grew exhausted simply watching the older mercenary's athletics. Cayt whirled, locking up Deaconess Blues's limbs while she grappled to gain leverage on her. She pressed her leg into Deaconess Blues's back. Not so skilled in this martial form, Deaconess Blues wound about, throwing elbows and twisting so that Cayt couldn't get a firm grip on her. Deaconess Blues slipped away from her and scrambled to a safe distance. The two stumbled to their feet and circled one another. Deaconess Blues gave up ground by a couple of steps to maintain a couple of arm lengths between them, just out of punch and kicking range, trying to buy herself a few seconds. Cayt tested her resolve, ducking under Deaconess Blues's punch. Her father would be disappointed with her. She was fighting Cayt on her opponent's terms, to her strengths. Cayt smiled before rushing her.

Deaconess Blues ducked low and swung her leg around to trip Cayt, who landed flat on her back, the wind knocked out of her. Deaconess Blues snaked her hand around Cayt's neck. She snapped her head forward, turning it toward the side of her body to break Deaconess Blues's hold. Cayt slammed a series of punches to Deaconess Blues's kidneys. Not knowing what else to do, Deaconess Blues kneed the woman in the stomach and drove her forearm up into the older woman's neck. Reaching over Cayt's shoulder, Deaconess Blues grasped her hand from under Cayt's neck and yanked up. Just like her father taught her. She held Cayt in the chokehold for a few seconds until the woman went limp in her arms. Deaconess Blues released her and Cayt collapsed like a sack of potatoes.

Seeing Cayt fall, Lord Melbourne reared. His mechanical flexing flung Sleepy from him. Sleepy landed with a heavy thud, bouncing off the side of a lab bench. His hand found purchase on the table to draw himself up. When he turned around, Lord Melbourne figured out more of what his new form could do. His hands collapsed on themselves, leaving a hole. From within them came the distant echo of metal snapping into place with chilling clacks. The appendages emerged again like a flower bud blossoming. The meta bulb unfurled into a series of blades. They began to spin like twin errant propellers.

"I'm still getting used to what all I can do. I see the world in an entirely different way," Lord Melbourne intoned. "The ways of the flesh are so ... soft."

Sleepy groped around for anything he could use as a weapon. Two mechanical appendages were sprawled along the table. Earlier prototypes which had been discarded. Sleepy grabbed them and brandished them like short swords. He and Lord Melbourne looked like they danced in a step fashion. The mechanical man waved the buzzing blades, jabbing at the air, forcing Sleepy backward. Sleepy deflected the first feinting blows. Getting more used to his limbs, Lord Melbourne focused his full attention on Sleepy, pressing his attack. Sleepy swatted the whirring blades; the whoosh of air splaying his face. He was running out of room to move, realizing too late that he was being herded into a corner. Treading backward, Sleepy lost his footing and tripped. Lord Melbourne drew back, ready to deliver a finishing blow. Desperate for a handhold to steady himself, Sleepy reached out to grab Lord Melbourne's carapace. Precariously balanced, the machine/man listed. Overcorrecting, he lost his own footing and began to tumble on top of Sleepy. Knowing the end was coming, Sleepy screamed and closed his eyes. The blade whir filled his ears. Lord Melbourne's maniacal laugh of triumph stopped short with a wet thud and a sudden yelp of pain. Mid-fall, Lord Melbourne reacted like anyone would in a fall: his hands reaching out to brace himself and protect his head. The blades buried three-quarters of the way into Lord Melbourne's neck. Boring through the metal casing, his head flopped to the side. The blades kept drilling as if the command had been locked and couldn't be shut off. When his body hit the floor, the rest of his neck snapped free. The canister containing his brain rolled across the parquet floor, stopping at Deaconess Blues's feet.

"No," Lord Melbourne's speakers sputtered and fritzed. "I could have made this country great again. Ours."

"That was the problem: we were invisible to you." Deaconess

Blues crouched and cupped his head casing within her hands. "This country was never great. Or ours."

"It's not fair," Lord Melbourne said. The light from his ocular unit sputtered and faded.

Sleepy and Knowledge Allah sidled next to Deaconess Blues and stared down at the metal pot that served as Lord Melbourne's head.

"What's not fair is that we have a pile of robot remains, the brain of a dead CEO, and an unconscious bodyguard all while we're sealed in this lab," Sleepy said. Everything felt flat and dull, like he was coming down from a ride of chiba leaves. "They're going to rebuild The Ave and bury us under it."

"Are you kidding yourself?" Knowledge Allah asked. "They're going to execute us before we even get back to county lockup. Assuming these COPs security even let us out of this box alive."

"We need a good story," Deaconess Blues said.

"Don't think you light enough to get out of this. You got just enough black in you for you to get lynched right beside us," Sleepy said.

Everything moved fast. Sleepy kept staring at the crumpled form of Lord Melbourne. Some of his clockwork parts still moved, powered by the steam engine on his back. Pincers occasionally click-clacked, startling him. The enormity of his passing, of their actions, numbed him into paralysis. Deaconess Blues picked up a telephone and began to dial. "Alejandra, I need you down in Dr. Yeager's lab. Now!"

A few moments later, a young woman dashed into the room from a rear entrance. A petite woman with black hair dangling to her waist rushed into the room. A gold broach pinned to her lab coat like some sort of badge made her look official. She traced the wreckage in the lab to where they waited. Pausing at the door, she took in the sight of the three of them, an unconscious-and-bound Cayt, a decapitated automaton, and a jar with a floating brain inside.

"I never get invited to the best parties." Alejandra stared at them, then asked, "What happened?"

"We don't have much time to explain. Do you trust me?" Deaconess Blues asked.

"Yes." Alejandra nodded without hesitation.

"We need to get these two out of here."

"What about you?" Knowledge Allah studied the damage and fallen Lord Melbourne. "Your wealth and privilege won't save you. Not from all this. They'll bury you."

"Getting you two out is my first priority." Deaconess Blues nodded to her assistant.

"You two need to come with me if you want out of here," Alejandra said.

Knowledge Allah and Sleepy glanced at each other and back at Deaconess Blues. She nodded, and they followed the young woman through the back exit of the lab. Leaving only Deaconess Blues with the body of Lord Melbourne. Pacing back and forth, her mind raced. She grabbed a few reagents. For once, Yeager's assistants refilled her stock after using them. She might have time to douse the lab and ignite the fluids, possibly destroying enough evidence. The terrorists could have spilled them in the brawl or some other tale that could neither be proved nor disproved.

A commotion erupted on the other side of the lab door. "You will open this door on my authority or, so help me God, I'll have each and every one of your heads on a platter." Soon after, Dr. Yeager pushed through the doors with a phalanx of guards rushing behind him. He stopped short, spying the form of his crowning achievement crumpled on the floor. Stepping over the still form of Cayt Siringo, he dropped to his knees beside Lord Melbourne.

"What have you ... degenerates done?" From the angle and in the light, it almost looked like tears began to pool in his eyes.

Deaconess Blues had the sense "degenerates" was not the word he wanted to use. The beginning of an idea stirred in her mind. "No. Saboteurs." The word tripped from her mouth without the wave of doubt that swelled in her heart. She hoped to project confidence in the story she began to spin.

"You've made quite a mess, Deaconess Blues." Dr. Yeager's face remained inscrutable, assessing the rest of the damage, and probably calculating how to eliminate his competition and advance his career. "It's going to take a fair amount of cleaning up to fix it."

"You're wrong. I didn't make a mess. Lord Melbourne did. Greed does funny things to people. In Lord Melbourne's case, he has stolen, manipulated, and killed to further his ends. And profited immensely in so doing."

"That doesn't explain nor absolve you from responsibility for whatever happened in this lab."

"Hear me out then. Without the audience. They don't have the clearance to hear all of this. And as the Principal Investigator, you have the ranking authority in the facilities."

"Go," Dr. Yeager commanded the guards. Cayt groaned as she stirred. "And take this woman with you. See to her medical needs."

"But, sir ..." The guards stared at each other, unsure whether to follow their orders or their duty.

"This is my lab. The man who pays all of our bills is currently sprawled on the floor, possibly dead. You are to secure the wing and call the constabularies. Until they get here, there's a lot of proprietary information to secure and protect." Dr. Yeager turned to Deaconess Blues. "You have until the authorities arrive to convince me."

"Oh, I have no delusions about my fate. I'm trusting in three things: one, the man who signs the checks is dead and loyalty is hard to find without credits; two, the power of resources to fund an army of barristers on my behalf if need be; and three, the media to muck up any process. Somewhere in all of this mess, there is a story of corruption, of assassination, and crimes against the crown. Intrigue, money, politics, and sex. There is a huge story to uncover, though it lacks a proper hero." She cast a stern eye at Dr. Yeager. "You should do nicely."

"Just so I have things straight," Dr. Yeager spoke slowly to ensure he understood the story and his role in it. "These were saboteurs you let in."

"I was ... unaware of their true intentions." Deaconess Blues tested the next part of the story.

"You certainly have an answer for everything. And Lord Melbourne?"

"He ... malfunctioned." Deaconess Blues paused, knowing that the slightest indictment of Dr. Yeager's work or reputation might unravel their budding detent. An opportunist at heart, he couldn't help but want to frame the story in a way to disparage her. She just needed to wait for the idea to take root. "Perhaps there was an unforeseen problem with my membrane. Something which corrupted his sensibilities. Thus explaining his megalomania."

"Perhaps." It was his turn to mull over his options. "Considering the timeline of events, perhaps his illness took a greater toll on his faculties than anyone suspected. I suppose if my team were to run point on ... the chassis project, we would be able to document each connection, each gear switch, each warped piston. I would write the history of this project. But it would be just that: my project."

"*Your* project?" she asked.

Dr. Yeager folded his arms. "My designs. My authorship. The price of my cooperation in selling this ludicrous tale. Assuming there's enough of a story to convince me, as well as the guards, and later when the City Ordained Pinkertons arrive."

Deaconess Blues considered his terms. Dr. Yeager grinned like he was ready to call checkmate. He would be able to take credit for her work. But she realized she would lose little. All the work she did was the property of the company anyway. They could have all of it. She would control the narrative.

"Ms. Siringo could verify my account. Though all she could *strictly* testify to was that she and one of the saboteurs engaged in fisticuffs." Deaconess Blues turned to Lord Melbourne. "Much more than that and there would have to be a more detailed investigation and accounting of everyone's involvement. No stone left unturned, as it were."

"Fair enough," Dr. Yeager said. The implied threat of everyone's complicity in Lord Melbourne's plan hovered between them. "I also want Lord Melbourne's head. I want the information stored in its robotic ganglia systems. I have theorized that Lord Melbourne might still be operational and may be able to stay dormant for another hundred years."

"He's all yours. I've had enough of that madman for one lifetime." Deaconess Blues tossed him the canister. He could keep all of it. No longer able to stomach his preening leer, she turned her back to leave. While stepping around an overturned lab bench, a familiar binding caught her eye. Her journal peeked out from an open drawer. *Nothing is proprietary around here*, Dr Yeager had taken pains to point out to her. *Everything belongs to the company and Lord Melbourne is the company*. Well, Lord Melbourne was no more. She slipped her journal into her jacket. Let them tinker with her designs, none of it would work without her cybernetic membrane. She glanced around to double check that she was still unobserved. Just in case, however, she bent over to grab his other journal and tucked it into her jacket also. Nothing was proprietary after all.

EPILOGUE: REBEL WITHOUT A PAUSE

"Citizens of the Universe, do not attempt to adjust your electro-transmitter, there is nothing wrong. We have taken control to bring you this special bulletin." The attenuated pulse of Knowledge Allah's voice echoed along the airwaves. *"The forces of Albion, through the machinations of former Chancellor Pruitt, attempted to still our voice. But we are not so easily stilled. The Cause moves forward. The Star Child has been returned to us. Though those same forces hunt him, he walks among us."*

A CLIENTELE strictly down for The Cause crowded the Two-Johns Theater. Rumor had it that the Two-Johns was now on a Pinkerton watchlist. Members of the Lost Nation stationed themselves at every exit, checking people's neighborhood passports. Tigga was turned away at the door.

Unbilled as a security measure, Sleepy stood in the wings, looking over the crowd, preparing to go on stage. These days he moved strictly through the underground, a fugitive in his own city. COPs still searched for him. His home under constant surveillance. Pinkerton Agents probably attempted to stake out the Two-Johns, but they had little reach deep within the community. Sugar saw to that, knowing that his interests rested in Sleepy and Knowledge Allah not falling into a COP interrogation room. Still, with so many luminaries in attendance, the theater was on high alert.

Desmond sat near the front, but off to the side, near an exit. The Star Child hovered nearby, Majestic Jamal led the Lost Nation security team trailing him as he passed peace and listened to people. Knowledge Allah sat between Deaconess Blues and Alejandra.

It was showtime.

"I have a new piece that I've been working on. It's called 'Hole in the Soul—A Work in Progress.' I hope you enjoy it." Sleepy took a step away from the microphone and took a sip from his cup of water. He wanted the silence to press on them like a weight, create a spell to captivate them.

> "You'll always be my daddy
> I'll always be your son.
> Here I am, a grown ass man, and I don't know what
>   that means.
> I look to God and call Him Father,
> But all that I know about fathers comes from you.
> And I never knew you.
> Oh, you were around while growing up.
> You came through, ready to hang out, be my friend.
> You always had jokes or a dirty magazine
> Or a cigarette or a drink to share
> --yeah, you were a Kools and Crown and Coke man.
> My friends thought you were the coolest dad on the
>   block
> But the block had you more than we did.
> And I wasn't looking for a friend.
>
> Daddy, just lift me up.
> All I ever wanted was for you to hold me and claim
>   me as yours.
> Daddy, lift me up.

Bloodshot eyes, liquor on your breath
I swallow his thoughts of me and slowly starve
Fathers and sons full of mystery and history.
How can he love someone like me?
I can hear the disappointment in his voice
Up on the auction block of my childhood.
I'm not that smart, not that funny, certainly not the
    life of the party like he was.
A depressed mess, too dark and left behind.
A hypocrite like me. A sinner like me. A me like me.

What I think when I think of God my Father
Is that He's supposed to be distant
To come around when He feels like it
To make me laugh during the good times
But never around when times got hard.
He might peel me off a twenty
Maybe throw a blessing my way to make up for His
    absence.
But it wasn't like I could count on Him.
Or know Him.
So now I'm not that anxious to get to know that
    Father.
To believe that He loves me for me
To believe that He considers me valuable simply
    because I'm me.

Daddy, just lift me up.
All I ever wanted was for you to get to know me
and show that you actually like having me around
Daddy, lift me up.

The idea of being daddy scares me.
A father's fears consoling a little boy's tears
I don't know if I want that burden
Of revealing God to my own children

To be a reflection of our true Father
I don't know if I have enough love to give
Or if I'm brave enough to let them into my heart
To know what love I have
To know and be known
To risk being a Daddy
I want to go to all of their recitals, knowing that
        they'll suck
And cheer them anyway.
I want to be able to enter their world
Learn who they are and help shape them into the
        best them they can be.
I never want to be too tired to play catch or be there
        to talk
I never want to leave them with a hole where their
        Father should be.

A father's lies. A Father's cries.

Shedding a Father's tears.
Proud.
For who you are. Who you can be.

Father, just lift me up
All I ever wanted is to love and be loved the way I
        knew you would want me to
Perfect love drives out fear.
Father, lift me up.

Sleepy held his breath. The eternal pause between the end of
the performance and the audience's reaction. If they had murmured
"Amens" or "all right now" or "tell 'em" alongside his speaking, he
couldn't hear them. All he heard was his low baritone, his muse
carrying him like an ancient spirit soaring home. But now, now came
the payoff. The moment when he found out if the audience was
with him or against him.

A thunderous roar of applause erupted. The first act of the night usually caught the audience at their highest energy and got them going. But this reception had a special tenor, at least to Sleepy's ear. He stepped off the stage, greeted by hand clasps and back pats.

"Damn, son, that was deep," Knowledge Allah yelled.

"You spoke truth," Desmond whispered as he passed Sleepy to take the stage. Sleepy waited in the wings, the best seat in the house. The lights dimmed.

"Thank you for making it out tonight." Faint strains of his Jamaican accent lifted his voice. "Our gathering is special. What we have here has the makings of a council meeting. We build together, even as COPs increase their stranglehold on us, to occupy our territory and try to get us to turn on one another. In these times, we cling to hope. Of a better way. Of a better future. So I want to introduce you to someone. In the story of our struggle, you called him the Star Child. To me, he's been every bit the son any man would be proud of. His name is Lij Tafari. He has a story to tell you."

With that, the Star Child rose.

ACKNOWLEDGMENTS

It's been a long journey. I often talk about how I started writing steampunk as a joke. Before I knew much about it, I made a joke on Twitter that went: "I'm going to write a steampunk story with an all-black cast and call it 'Pimp My Airship.'" Several editors wrote me to see the final story, which I then had to, you know, actually write.

It started with "Pimp My Airship." The world that was created for it led to (if the stories were to be read in order, the ones in parentheses are unpublished, however): "The Problem of Trystan," "Steppin' Razor," "Buffalo Soldier," ("Babylon Systems"), "All Gods Chillun Got Wings," "I Used to Love HER," "Know the Ledge," ("Axioms of Creamy Spies"), and culminating with this new novel, *Pimp My Airship*.

Jason Sizemore at *Apex Magazine* fell in love with the story. (Little known fact, I subbed the story to him when he was editing an anthology. He "rejected" the story from the anthology because he was restarting the magazine and wanted it for it.) He has been its chief ardent supporter ever since. Co-chief, actually. Rodney Carlstrom, my "Intern Emeritus," has long been after me to do something else with the story. This book wouldn't have happened without the two of them.

I was feeling anxious about this project, especially as it plunged headlong into territories of race, class, and politics. I called up Daniel Jose Older and he gave me inspirational words to live by: "Do that shit." It was a reminder that writers have to be bold and take risks. It can be scary sometimes (which is why it's good to have friends who can nudge you). In the end, taking those risks, accepting those challenges, only makes you a better writer. Well, that's the hope anyway. The readers are the final judge on that.

Lastly, I want to thank my usual suspects: Sally, Reese, and Malcolm for their constant support. Jen Udden. Lesley Conner. Jerry Gordon. J.J. Walker. E Ru Caldwell. The Airship Ashanti Community. And those who've gone unnamed (because that list is LONG) who have loved and supported me so well over the years.

ABOUT THE AUTHOR

A community organizer and teacher, Maurice Broaddus's work has appeared in *Lightspeed Magazine, Weird Tales, Apex Magazine, Asimov's, Cemetery Dance, Black Static,* and many more. Some of his stories have been collected in *The Voices of Martyrs.* He is the author of the urban fantasy trilogy, The Knights of Breton Court, and the (upcoming) middle grade detective novel series, The Usual Suspects. He co-authored the play *Finding Home: Indiana at 200.* His novellas include *Buffalo Soldier, I Can Transform You, Orgy of Souls, Bleed with Me,* and *Devil's Marionette.* He is the co-editor of *Dark Faith, Dark Faith: Invocations, Streets of Shadows,* and *People of Colo(u)r Destroy Horror.* His gaming work includes writing for the Marvel Super-Heroes, *Leverage,* and *Firefly* role-playing games as well as working as a consultant on *Watch Dogs 2.* Learn more about him at MauriceBroaddus.com.

 facebook.com/mauricebroaddus

twitter.com/mauricebroaddus